Ravished by a Highlander

Ravished by a Highlander

PAULA QUINN

FOREVER

NEW YORK   BOSTON

Copyright © 2010 by Paula Quinn
Excerpt from *Seduced by a Highlander* copyright © 2010 by Paula Quinn

Cover design by Diane Luger
Cover art by Franco Accornero
Hand lettering by Ron Zinn
Book design by Giorgetta Bell McRee

Forever
Hachette Book Group
237 Park Avenue
New York, NY 10017

ISBN-13: 978-1-61664-420-8

Forever is an imprint of Grand Central Publishing. The Forever name and logo is a trademark of Hachette Book Group, Inc.

Printed in the United States of America

To my Mom—
Your strength knows no bounds . . .

The Firstborn

Chapter One

❦

*H*igh atop Saint Christopher's Abbey, Davina Montgomery stood alone in the bell tower, cloaked in the silence of a world she did not know. Darkness had fallen hours ago and below her the sisters slept peacefully in their beds, thanks to the men who had been sent here to guard them. But there was little peace for Davina. The vast, indigo sky filling her vision was littered with stars that seemed close enough to touch should she reach out her hand. What would she wish for? Her haunted gaze slipped southward toward England, and then with a longing just as powerful, toward the moonlit mountain peaks of the north. Which life would she choose if the choice were hers to make? A world where she'd been forgotten, or one where no one knew her? She smiled sadly against the wind that whipped her woolen novice robes around her. What good was it to ponder when her future had already been decreed? She knew what was to come. There were no variations. That is, if she lived beyond the next year.

She looked away from the place she could never go and the person she could never be.

She heard the soft fall of footsteps behind her but did not turn. She knew who it was.

"Poor Edward. I imagine your heart must have failed you when you did not find me in my bed."

When he remained quiet she felt sorry for teasing him about the seriousness of his duty. Captain Edward Asher had been sent here to protect her four years ago, after Captain Geoffries had taken ill and was relieved of his command. Edward had become more than her guardian. He was her dearest friend, someone she could confide in here within the thick walls that sheltered her from the schemes of her enemies. Edward knew her fears and accepted her faults.

"I knew where to find you," he finally said, his voice just above a whisper.

He always did know. Not that there were many places to look. Davina was not allowed to venture outside the Abbey gates so she came to the bell tower often to let her thoughts roam free.

"My lady—"

She turned at his soft call, putting away her dreams and desires behind a tender smile. Those she kept to herself and did not share, even with him.

"Please, I..." he began, meeting her gaze and then stumbling through the rest as if the face he looked upon every day still struck him as hard as it had the first time he'd seen her. He was in love with her, and though he'd never spoken his heart openly, he did not conceal how he felt. Everything was there in his eyes, his deeds, his devotion; and a deep regret that Davina suspected had more to do with her than he would ever have the boldness to admit. Her path had been charted for another course and she could never be his. "Lady Montgomery, come away from here, I beg you. It is not good to be alone."

He worried for her so and she wished he wouldn't. "I'm not alone, Edward," she reassured. If her life remained as it was now, she would find a way to be happy. She always did. "I have been given much."

"It's true," he agreed, moving closer to her and then stopping himself, knowing what she knew. "You have been taught to fear the Lord and love your king. The sisters love you, as do my men. It will always be so. We are your family. But it is not enough." He knew she would never admit it, so he said it for her.

It had to be enough. It was safer this way, cloistered away from those who would harm her if ever they discovered her after the appointed time.

That time had come.

Davina knew that Edward would do anything to save her. He told her often, each time he warned her of her peril. Diligently, he taught her to trust no one, not even those who claimed to love her. His lessons often left her feeling a bit hopeless, though she never told him that, either.

"Would that I could slay your enemies," he swore to her now, "and your fears along with them."

He meant to comfort her, but good heavens, she didn't want to discuss the future on such a breathtaking night. "Thanks to you and God," she said, leaving the wall to go to him and tossing him a playful smile, "I can slay them myself."

"I agree," he surrendered, his good mood restored by

the time she reached him. "You've learned your lessons in defense well."

She rested her hand on his arm and gave it a soft pat. "How could I disappoint you when you risked the Abbess's consternation to teach me?"

He laughed with her, both of them comfortable in their familiarity. But too soon he grew serious again.

"James is to be crowned in less than a se'nnight."

"I know." Davina nodded and turned toward England again. She refused to let her fears control her. "Mayhap," she said with a bit of defiance sparking her doleful gaze, "we should attend the coronation, Edward. Who would think to look for me at Westminster?"

"My lady..." He reached for her. "We cannot. You know—"

"I jest, dear friend." She angled her head to speak to him over her shoulder, carefully cloaking the struggle that weighed heaviest upon her heart, a struggle that had nothing to do with fear. "Really, Edward, must we speak of this?"

"Yes, I think we should," he answered earnestly, then went on swiftly, before she could argue, "I've asked the Abbess if we can move you to Courlochcraig Abbey in Ayr. I've already sent word to—"

"Absolutely not," she stopped him. "I will not leave my home. Besides, we have no reason to believe that my enemies know of me at all."

"Just for a year or two. Until we're certain—"

"No," she told him again, this time turning to face him fully. "Edward, would you have us leave the sisters here alone to face our enemies should they come seeking me? What defense would they have without the strong arms of you and your men? They will not leave St. Christopher's, nor will I."

He sighed and shook his head at her. "I cannot argue when you prove yourself more courageous than I. I pray I do not live to regret it. Very well, then." The lines of his handsome face relaxed. "I shall do as you ask. For now though," he added, offering her his arm, "allow me to escort you to your chamber. The hour is late and the Reverend Mother will show you no mercy when the cock crows."

Davina rested one hand in the crook of his arm and waved away his concern with the other. "I don't mind waking with the sun."

"Why would you," he replied, his voice as light now as hers as he led her out of the belfry, "when you can just fall back to sleep in the Study Hall."

"It was only the one time that I actually slept," she defended, slapping his arm softly. "And don't you have more important things to do with your day than follow me around?"

"Three times," he corrected, ignoring the frown he knew was false. "Once, you even snored."

Her eyes, as they descended the stairs, were as wide as her mouth. "I have never snored in my life!"

"Save for that one time, then?"

She looked about to deny his charge again, but bit her curling lip instead. "And once during Sister Bernadette's piano recital. I had penance for a week. Do you remember?"

"How could I forget?" he laughed. "My men did no chores the entire time, preferring to listen at your door while you spoke aloud to God about everything but your transgression."

"God already knew why I fell asleep," she explained, smiling at his grin. "I did not wish to speak poorly of Sister Bernadette's talent, or lack of it, even in my own defense."

His laughter faded, leaving only a smile that looked to be painful as their walk ended and they stood at her door. When he reached out to take her hand, Davina did her best not to let the surprise in her eyes dissuade him from touching her. "Forgive my boldness, but there is something I must tell you. Something I should have told you long ago."

"Of course, Edward," she said softly, keeping her hand in his. "You know you may always speak freely to me."

"First, I would have you know that you have come to mean—"

"Captain!"

Davina leaned over the stairwell to see Harry Barns, Edward's second in command, plunge through the Abbey doors. "Captain!" Harry shouted up at them, his face pale and his breath heavy from running. "They are coming!"

For one paralyzing moment, Davina doubted the good of her ears. She'd been warned of this day for four years, but had always prayed it would not come. "Edward," she asked hollowly, on the verge of sheer panic, "how did they find us so soon after King Charles's death?"

He squeezed his eyes shut and shook his head back and forth as if he too refused to believe what he was hearing. But there was no time for doubt. Spinning on his heel, he gripped her arm and hauled her into her room. "Stay here! Lock your door!"

"What good will that do us?" She sprang for her quiver and bow and headed back to the door, and to Edward blocking it. "Please, dear friend. I do not want to cower alone in my room. I will fire from the bell tower until it is no longer safe to do so."

"Captain!" Barns raced up the stairs, taking three at a time. "We need to prepare. Now!"

"Edward"—Davina's voice pulled him back to her—"you trained me for this. We need every arm available. You will not stop me from fighting for my home."

"Orders, Captain, please!"

Davina looked back once as she raced toward the narrow steps leading back to the tower.

"Harry!" She heard Edward shout behind her. "Prepare the vats and boil the tar. I want every man alert and ready at my command. And Harry..."

"Captain?"

"Wake the sisters and tell them to pray."

In the early morning hours that passed after the massacre at St. Christopher's, Edward's men had managed to kill half of the enemy's army. But the Abbey's losses were greater. Far greater.

Alone in the bell tower, Davina stared down at the bodies strewn across the large courtyard. The stench of burning tar and seared flesh stung her nostrils and burned her eyes as she set them beyond the gates to the meadow where men on horseback still hacked away at each other as if their hatred could never be satisfied. But there was no hatred. They fought because of her, though none of them knew her. But she knew them. Her dreams had been plagued with her faceless assassins since the day Edward had first told her of them.

Tears brought on by the pungent air slipped down her cheeks, falling far below to where her friends...her family lay dead or dying. Dragging her palm across her eyes, she searched the bodies for Edward. He'd returned to her an hour after the fighting had begun and ordered her into the chapel with the sisters. When she'd refused, he'd tossed her over his shoulder like a sack of grain and brought her there himself. But she did not remain hidden. She couldn't, so she'd returned to the tower and her bow and sent more than a dozen of her enemies to meet their Maker. But there were too many—or mayhap God didn't want the rest, for they slew the men she ate with, laughed with, before her eyes.

She had feared this day for so long that it had become a part of her. She thought she had prepared. At least, for her own death. But not for the Abbess's. Not for Edward's. How could anyone prepare to lose those they loved?

Despair ravaged her and for a moment she considered stepping over the wall. If she was dead they would stop. But she had prayed for courage too many times to let God or Edward down now. Reaching into the quiver on her back, she plucked out an arrow, cocked her bow, and closed one eye to aim.

Below her and out of her line of vision, a soldier garbed in military regalia not belonging to England crept along the chapel wall with a torch clutched in one fist and a sword in the other.

Chapter Two

$\mathcal{A}$ cool breeze, moist with the fallen rain, lifted a raven curl from Robert MacGregor's forehead. Looking up, he glared at the pewter clouds as if daring the heavens to open again. 'Twas bad enough he and his kin had to leave Camlochlin during a storm that promised to tear auld Tamas MacKinnon's roof off his bothy. Trekking across Scotland in the mud did not make the journey any easier.

Rob was still unsure if he agreed with his father's reasoning for leaving the clan to attend James of York's coronation. What did laws made by stately nobles, dressed in powdered wigs and ruffled collars, have to do with MacGregors? Only a handful of them knew of the MacGregors of Skye, and none of them would dare venture into the mountains to enforce their laws, even if they did. What fealty did his clan owe to an English king?

"Rebellion is not always necessary," his father's words invaded his troubled thoughts. *"Protectin' the clan must always come first."*

As firstborn and heir apparent to Callum MacGregor's title as Clan Chief of the MacGregors of Skye, Rob had been taught to understand his father's ways of thinking. He knew that civilly showing their support to the new king was the intelligent thing to do. For as much as he cared nothing about politics so far south, there were many in Parliament who believed the Highland ways of life, with a Chief having sole authority over his clan, were outdated and should be abolished. If kissing the king's arse would keep his clan safe and intact, then Rob would do it.

He didn't care if his father was chief or if he was. He'd taken on every responsibility as a leader, and more. He tilled the land, herded and sheared the sheep, repaired falling rooftops and, more times than not, denied his physical pleasure for hard work. He made decisions for his kin's welfare alongside his father and honed his swordplay diligently and by his own choice, knowing that any weakness of body or will could destroy what belonged to him. And it had been in his blood for generations never to allow that to happen.

But it still angered him that he should have to leave his clan to kiss the arses of men who would likely shyt in their breeches on any kind of battlefield.

"Tell me again why ye insisted on takin' this route, Will?" Rob asked his cousin, and yanked on his reins to steer his mount away from a muddy trench in his path. They had left their main troupe on a road just before the English border. The detour was Will's idea, and Rob was beginning to question why he'd listened to him, or why he'd agreed to let anyone else come with them.

"St. Christopher's Abbey," Will called out over his shoulder. "I told ye, Sister Margaret Mary lives there."

"Who the hell is Sister Margaret Mary?" Angus MacGregor growled, rubbing the small of his back. "And why does a daughter o' the Lord interest a black heart like yers?"

"She was m' nursemaid fer six years after m' mother died."

"I think I've heard Tristan speak of her," Colin, Rob's youngest brother, joined in thoughtfully, managing to steer his mount around a mossy incline without incident. Rob was torn between being thankful that his brother Tristan hadn't come with them—mostly for the sisters of St. Christopher's sake—and being angry with himself for letting Colin come along. Clearly, Will had no notion of where the hell the Abbey was. He was leading them deeper into the hills. A band of outlaws could attack them from almost any direction unseen. Not that Rob fretted overmuch about a fight, or Colin's ability to come out of one unharmed. He just preferred that if there was a skirmish of some sort, his youngest brother not be there.

"Do the sisters in England pray as much as the ones in Scotland do?"

"We're no' in England yet," Rob murmured impatiently, glancing at Finlay Grant from over his shoulder. The lad looked stricken for a moment, as if he had just proven himself lacking in the eyes of his leader. Hell, what would he do with Finn if they were attacked? The lad could fight well enough, but he'd always shown more interest in playing the pipes and reciting tales of past heroes than in swordplay. Every laird had a bard, and Finn was determined to become Rob's. As irritating as it sometimes was to have the lad always underfoot, watching what he did and what he said in the event that some heroic deed he performed needed retelling, Rob was fond of Graham and Claire Grant's youngest son. He was a respectful lad with a curious nature, and since he wasn't the source of Rob's frustration, he should not bear the brunt of it. "And nae," Rob told him in a milder tone, "Scottish nuns pray more."

"I dinna care if her knees have worn straight through her robes," Angus grumbled, reaching for a pouch of brew hidden in his plaid. "If she brought Will *and* Tristan into this world, I have nae desire to be meetin' her."

"Hush, Angus." Rob held up his hand to silence the older warrior. "D'ye hear that?"

His companions remained quiet for a moment, listening. "Sounds like the clash o' swords," Angus said, his hand falling immediately to his hilt. "And that odor— That's flesh burnin'."

"The Abbey!" Will's face went pale as he whirled his mount left and dug his heels into the beast's flanks. He disappeared over the crest of a small rise before Rob could stop him.

Swearing an oath that his cousin and closest friend was someday going to get himself and everyone around him killed by rushing headlong into the unknown, Rob raced forward to follow, warning the younger lads to stay behind.

Rob and Angus stopped just beyond the crest, where Will had also halted his horse and stared with both shock and horror at the scene before him. When Colin and Finn reached them, Rob swore violently at his brother for disobeying him, but his gaze was already being pulled back to the small convent nestled within the fold of low hills.

The Abbey was under attack. By the looks of it, the siege had been going on for more than a few hours. Hundreds of dead bodies littered the ground. Only a handful of what looked to have been two separate armies remained while ribbons of black smoke plumed the air, the residue of burning tar. The left wing of the structure was completely engulfed in flames.

"Dear God, who would do this?"

Will did not bother answering Finn's haunted plea, but snatched free his bow and yanked an arrow from his quiver.

"Will, nae!" Rob stopped him. "'Tis no' our fight. I'll no' bring whoever did this doun on our clan! No' for those who have already per—"

The remainder of his words was cut short by a searing jolt of pain in his left shoulder and the whistle of two of Will's arrows slicing the air in the next instant. Stunned, Rob looked down at the thin shaft of wood jutting out of his flesh. He'd been hit! Son of a...Fighting a wave of nausea, he closed his fingers around the arrow and broke off the feathered end sticking out from his plaid. Setting his murderous gaze on the skirmish, he clutched the broken arrow in one fist and dragged his claymore from its sheath with the other.

"Now, 'tis our fight. Colin," he growled before he charged his mount forward. "Ye and Finn take cover or I'll set ye both on yer arses fer a fortnight."

Finn nodded dutifully, but Colin grew angry. "Rob, I can fight. I want to fight."

"No' today," Rob warned, his jaw rigid with fury about to be unleashed. This time Colin obeyed.

Rob had fought in raids before. He'd even killed a few Fergussons, but this was the kind of fighting that flowed through his veins, what he had been trained to do by his father. Protect himself and those in his care at any cost. He didn't care who'd shot him. They were all going to pay for it. Reaching the dwindling melee, he brought his sword down with savage satisfaction, killing swiftly, while Will and Angus fought a few feet away. He was about to strike again when his would-be target screamed out at him.

"Hold, Scot! Hold for the mercy of God!" For the space of a breath, the man withered in his saddle staring into Rob's eyes, and then at the bloody sword above his head. He spoke quickly, gathering what strength of will he had left. "I am Captain Edward Asher of the King's Royal army. We were attacked just before dawn. I am not your enemy."

Rob quickly looked the man over. His dark hair was wet with blood and sweat that dripped over his brow, creating streaks down his dirty face. His garment was also bloodied, but belonging to the king's regiment.

His fury at being shot still unabated, Rob began to turn his mount to cut down someone else.

"Wait." The captain reached for Rob's arm to stop him. "You are a Highlander. Why are you here? Has someone sent you?"

"Ye ask many questions rather than be grateful that here is where I am."

"You have my thanks for your aid."

Rob nodded. "Behind ye."

Captain Asher spun on his horse and barely managed to avoid a blow to his head that would have killed him.

Taking a moment to assure that no other enemy soldiers were in fighting distance, Rob watched with a look of bland interest while the captain felled his attacker to the ground.

"I owe you my life," Asher said, panting.

"Right. Are we done here? There are more comin'."

Asher's shoulders sagged heavily as if he'd had enough

and knew his fate. He didn't bother to look behind him, but wiped his moist brow. "Your name, please."

Hell, the man was half out of his mind. Loss of blood, Rob decided, and taking pity on him, gave him what he asked.

"Robert MacGregor, if I die today you must save the Lady Montgomery." Before Rob could consent or decline, the captain rushed on. "Please, I beg of you, save her. She still lives, I know it." His eyes dipped to the broken arrow in Rob's hand.

Following his gaze, Rob suspected who shot him. His jaw clenched, as did his fingers. "You live. You save her."

"MacGregor!" Captain Asher shouted as Rob rode away. "They burned the chapel. All the sisters—dead. They were all she had. She only did what you or I would have done. Save her before the flames claim her. It is what they want."

Rob set his gaze toward the burning Abbey. Hell. He should find Will and toss him into the flames to find the lady since 'twas his idea to come here. A lady. Bloody hell, he couldn't leave a lass to the flames, even if she'd tried to kill him. With his sword held high, he cut down another rider coming at him and did not look back to see what had become of Asher. He scanned the smoky court-yard for any sign of a female then muttered a string of oaths when he didn't find her. With a look of such dark resentment and determination on his face he frightened two more soldiers out of his path, he rode his snorting beast straight to the fiery entrance. There was only one way to get inside and no time to hesitate. Yanking hard on his reins, he dug his heels into his horse's flanks and heaved the stallion upward onto its hind legs. The charred doors splintered and cracked beneath the weight of his mount's front hooves. Thick smoke stung his lungs and made it almost impossible to see. He called out, "Lady!" His stallion neighed and bucked at the roaring flames all around them, but Rob's hand was strong and the beast was forced to continue. He called out again, and was about to give up and count her among the dead when he saw her. To his astonishment, the lass was trying desperately to put out the flames with a meager blanket.

"'Tis too late, lass. Give me yer hand!"

At the sound of his voice, she whirled around, bringing the blanket to her face to keep the smoke from choking her. "Edward?" She coughed, trying to see through the suffocating haze. "Edward, I—" The blanket slipped from her fingers and her legs gave out beneath her.

Rob charged forward, leaning down in his saddle. Before her body hit the ground, he plucked her from the ashes.

I'm dying. Thank You, Father. Davina had hoped it would be less painful than this. It wasn't the smoke that scorched her lungs, or the pounding of her head, but the memory of the sisters' screams as they burned in the chapel that made her long for Heaven.

"Breathe now, lass." A man's voice, commanding enough to be Edward's, but infinitely deeper, pulled her back.

She coughed, dragging only slightly fresher air into her lungs. Fire lanced through her chest. Fire. She wasn't dying. She opened her eyes to the blur of blackened grass and thick hooves tearing up the earth beneath her. She coughed again and a hand, large enough to span the back of her head, smoothed her hair away from her cheek. She was on a horse—and a man, flung across his lap to be exact. They had come for her just as Edward had feared they would, and now they had her. She wanted to scream, but her throat was raw. She would have leaped from both beasts, but the arm that held her dangling over the horse's flanks was hard as granite. A body passed her vision on the ground, bringing the full horror of what took place this day back to her.

They were dead.

No. "No!" Terror and fury gripped her and she pushed herself up off her captor's thighs. The sight over and beyond his bloodied shoulder stilled her an instant later. St. Christopher's Abbey...her home, was burning to the ground. Everyone. Gone. "No, God, please...not my family," she whimpered. Tears spilled down her face and she feared they might never stop. They didn't, even when she remembered who held her.

"Monster," she screamed, pummeling him with blows to his chest, fighting his strength with the madness of her grief. "Bastard! What have you done?"

"Lady." His voice was so tender that she collapsed against him, needing mercy. "Be still," he said softly against her ear as she clutched his upper arm, staring at the crumbling walls of her home. "Ye're safe now."

"I'm going to kill you," she promised just as softly, leaving behind the bodies of those she loved.

"Ye almost did already, but 'twas no' I who did this loathsome thing."

It wasn't his declaration, but the deep undercurrent of sympathy in it that almost convinced her to believe him. She pushed off his shoulder and stared up at him. He wasn't one of them. His burr was thick and his appearance far more primitive than any man she'd ever seen, English or otherwise. A Highlander. She hadn't been expecting one of those. The Abbess had told her about the men of the North in her lessons and how they wore blankets draped around their bodies, rather than short-coats and breeches. Davina's eyes dipped to the great belted plaid draping one of his shoulders and the bloodstained shirt beneath. This one was big. His dark hair was longer than she'd ever seen on a man and tied away from his face, save for a stray lock, swept free over his eyes by the rushing wind. He smelled of earth and leather... and smoke.

"Who are you then?" she demanded through trembling lips. "What are you doing here?" She waited while he stared at her as if her simple questions muddled his thoughts. Harry Barns had told her that Highlanders were thick skulled, more interested in battle than in books. This one looked like he could take down Edward's entire regiment.

"Edward," she whispered, and a new rush of sorrow flooded through her. "Let me go!" She struggled again. "I must find him. Please," she cried as her captor drew her closer to hold her still. "You don't understand. He will think they have taken me."

"Who will he think has taken ye?" The Highlander withdrew just enough to look into her eyes. "Who did this, lass?"

She was thinking of Edward, not herself or her safety, when she told him. "It was the Duke's men, or the Earl's. I'm not certain. Now please, I beg you, bring me back. I must find Captain Asher."

It was the stranger's eyes that told her what he did not

want to say. Lapis-colored gems that lost their glitter when he finally looked away. Edward was dead. Tears pooled her eyes but she said nothing as she turned in his arms, away from everything she knew, everyone she trusted.

They rode in silence, joined as they raced away by two more mounted Highlanders, and then more waiting at the crest overlooking the Abbey. The man riding with her spoke to the others but Davina did not listen to what he said. When one of them asked her why the Abbey was attacked she told them she did not know, and then said nothing else. She was alone. Whoever this man was behind her, whether he was sent by her enemies or by God to save her, did not matter. She was alone and had nowhere else to go but with him. For now.

Chapter Three

ℛob's shoulder ached. Twice, Angus had insisted on stopping so that he could remove the tip of the arrow still jutting out of Rob's back, but it was too dangerous to make camp so close to the border. Someone had gone to much trouble to try to kill the lass in his arms. 'Twas her they'd come for. Captain Asher's words rang like alarms through his thoughts. *Save her before the flames claim her. It is what they want.* They. The Earl or the Duke. Which ones and why? Why would any man want her dead? Who was she? The captain had called her Lady Montgomery. Was she a nobleman's daughter visiting the Abbey with her family? If so, why the hell was she dressed in novice robes? Whoever had attacked the Abbey wanted her to burn. Was she believed to be a witch? Rob did not doubt she could be, for her beauty near pierced his soul when she first looked at him. She had an almost feline appearance; with large, wide-set elongated eyes as big and as blue as the fathomless heavens behind her. Her pale brows flared upward toward her slightly oversized ears. The perfect hourglass silhouette of her nose ended in a tiny knob stained with soot. Her lips were plump and naturally pouty and as beguiling as all hell.

Rob had heard tales of fairies from their neighbors, the MacLeods. Magical beings so bonnie, one look could fell the heart of the most resolute warrior. As if to add to Lady Montgomery's otherworldly appearance, her hair, though streaked with ash, glimmered beneath the sun in shades of pale gold and shimmering silver. He bent his head to her to inhale her scent. She smelled of smoke and soot, but then, he imagined they all did.

It wasn't difficult to understand why an English captain would beg for her safety. But what were men from the Royal Army doing at St. Christopher's? A dozen questions nagged at Rob's thoughts. The lass offered no answers, though he was certain she could provide them. Save for a gasp now and then at the speed of his horse, she hadn't uttered a single word in over an hour. She barely moved against him, her soft body pressing into his chest, making him more uncomfortable than when she fought him. Shock, he imagined. He could feel the sorrow in her heavy breath and he had to struggle to keep his heart from breaking for her. If he lost everyone he loved, he would go mad with grief. She felt small and vulnerable in the crook of his arm and the need to protect her flared in his veins more powerful than anything he'd ever felt before.

Hell, just what he needed, another responsibility in his life. At least, she would be until he delivered her to England's new king. Already a part of him did not want to give her up, but it was obvious that whoever wanted her dead wanted it badly enough to battle the king's soldiers. The safety of Rob's clan came first. If she belonged to the king, then let the king protect her.

Shifting in his saddle, Rob held back a slight groan through a tightly clenched jaw. His arm was throbbing and growing stiffer with each breath. It would be useless should they be attacked.

"Did ye discover who shot ye through, Rob?" The question was asked by Finlay Grant. Rob should have known the lad was riding close enough to him to see his discomfort.

"Aye," was all he replied.

"Yer faither will have all our heads when he learns o' yer wound," Angus mumbled out loud when they finally slowed their mounts to a more leisurely pace.

Will accepted the small pouch Angus held out to him, and tossed the old warrior a challenging grin. "It gives me great humor to know that ye're as frightened o' the laird as the village women are." Ignoring Angus's fervent protests to the contrary, he took a hearty swig of the potent whisky, shivered in his saddle, and passed the pouch to Rob. "'Tis poison."

Shaking his head, Rob declined the offering. "My faither will understand why I fought. The wound is no' so bad and will be on its way to healin' by the time we reach Westminster—"

The lass whirled around so quickly, she near slipped from his lap. "You're taking me to Westminster?"

Hell, her effect on him was worse than any lethal brew Angus carried in the folds of his plaid. Rob had wanted to look at her again since they left the Abbey, to let his gaze linger over the pale coral of her lips, to take his time studying the perfect symmetry of her countenance, the purity of her milky complexion. But it was the fear and desperation in her eyes as she stared up at him that tugged stronger on his heart. Damnation, what came over him?

"To the Duke of York's coronation, aye," he told her,

severing their gaze. He refused to allow a lass, even one as mesmerizing as she, to make him forget his first duty. "We will meet up with my kin and—"

"No! I cannot go to England. You must not take me there."

The terror in her voice dragged his eyes back to hers. Her bottom lip quivered and Rob resisted the urge to lift his finger to it. "Why? Ye were bein' protected by the Royal army, nae? Ye'll be safe under the king's care."

She shook her head and clutched at his plaid. "I won't be safe there."

Slipping his gaze to the others, Rob caught their troubled expressions. He knew what they were thinking. If they did not return to his father, the Devil MacGregor would suspect the worst. He would leave England with Graham hot on his heels; mayhap even taking the heads of any who tried to stop them and bringing the law down upon the heads of his clan once again. Rob couldn't take that chance. Still...

"Where will ye be safe then?"

"Nae, Rob—"

Rob held up his palm to halt Angus's objection and waited for her to speak. "Where?"

Everything she'd been through seemed to hit her all at once as she looked around, as if searching for something familiar. She trembled against him then let go of his plaid and dipped her eyes to her hands.

"Nowhere."

"She's an outlaw." Angus took another swill from his pouch, then cast a withering look to the heavens. "Had enough o' them to last ten lifetimes."

"English soldiers dinna' give their lives fer outlaws."

Will leaned forward in his saddle and smacked the pouch out of Angus's hand. "That shyt will kill ye. Look how dim-witted 'tis made ye already," he added when Angus gaped at him and then at the brew seeping into the ground.

Rob didn't care if she was an outlaw, a witch, or some magical being who compelled armies to go to war over her. It took him just an instant to decide what to do with her. She had nowhere to go where she could take refuge, even from her grief. He would not deliver her over to her enemies just to be rid of her. "I'll find ye someplace safe," he said, ignoring the more responsible voice in his head and the blasphemies spilling from Angus's lips.

The lass did not appear relieved. In fact, she looked about ready to spring from his arms and take off running. He tightened his arm just a wee bit around her waist.

"Angus, ye'll ride to my faither and tell him what took place here, but tell him in private."

"We need to think aboot—"Angus began, but the authority in Rob's voice stopped him.

"I already have, and this is what ye will do. Assure him that we are well and no' to come after us. 'Twill raise sus-picions if he leaves too soon. The king will learn of this soon enough on his own and until I know what is goin' on, I dinna' want him to know we are involved. If the lady's enemies reside at court, the moment they learn of her escape they will come after us. We need all the time we can get. Tell my faither that I've gone to find her a refuge and I will meet him back at Camlochlin. Go, and take the lads with ye."

"I'm no' going to England."

Rob pivoted around to pin his brother with a murder-ous stare. Colin shrugged off its effect like an unwanted blanket. "If ye send me off with him," he said, his voice pitched low with determination, "I'll break away and follow ye alone."

"I'm staying, as well," Finn announced, pushing back the woolen bonnet from his spray of flaxen hair. "Rob," he added when Rob's eyes darkened on him, "our fathers did not leave us in Angus's care, but in yers, trusting that ye would see us safely returned to them. No offense to ye, Angus." He cut the old Highlander a rueful glance before returning his attention to Rob.

Damn, but the lad was correct. If Colin broke away, and Rob had no doubts his brother would do exactly as he promised, for the lad possessed more courage and arrogance than was good for him, and anything happened to them...

Grazing them with one last scorching look, Rob tightened his jaw and nodded. He'd pound both their arses into the ground later. For now though, they had to keep moving.

"Go, Angus, and tell their faithers that their sons are safe with me." Rob gave his reins a harsh snap and whirled his mount around in the opposite direction. Hell. He didn't need this.

"Let's ride fer another few leagues and then make camp," Will suggested, watching Angus veer off south. "M' arse is killin' me."

Finn cast him a reproachful look before shielding his gaze beneath his lashes. Will caught the subtle rebuke and turned to the lass. "Fergive m' ill manners, m'lady." He offered her a guilty smile shot through with a bit of recklessness and danger that drew lasses to him like bees to honey.

Rob's arm was making him irritable. That had to be the reason he wanted to punch his cousin off his horse.

"What are ye called, lass?" Will trotted his mount closer. He was in good kicking distance.

"Davina," she told him quietly.

"Davina," Will repeated as if it were the most profound sound he'd ever heard escaping his lips.

It was.

When his cousin reached for the pouch of water hanging from his saddle and handed it to her, Rob cursed himself for not thinking of her thirst. He watched her drink, with brief glares at Will, who was watching her as well. Rob never cared that lasses usually preferred Will over him. He didn't blame them. Will's purpose in life was to wreak the same havoc on a maiden's heart as he did on the raiding field, while Rob's was to keep order.

"Thank you."

"Will," the scoundrel offered as if she had asked for his name. Which she hadn't, "son of Brodie Mac—"

"Will," Rob cut him off, not even trying to sound indifferent. "Leave her now." The lass was weary and did not need to be badgered, and to hell with whether or not Will liked it.

"Right, then." His cousin threw him a knowing grin which Rob answered with an even darker scowl. "I'll scout ahead. Come, lads," he called out, taking Colin and Finn with him.

When they were alone, Rob's gaze returned to the back of Davina's head. What had he just dragged them into? He had to question her more about what had happened, but later, after she rested. He felt like hell for not offering her water sooner, but he wasn't a bloody nursemaid. He was a warrior, trained to be compassionate, but always hard. Though he'd grown to manhood in the company of many women, he didn't know anything about soothing them when they wept.

Bending close to her ear, Rob offered her the one thing he knew how to give. His protection.

Chapter Four

I'll keep ye safe, lass. The Highlander's whispered promise echoed through Davina's thoughts while she watched his companion, Will, yank the tip of an arrow out of his shoulder.

Soft golden light from the setting sun filtered through the sparse canopy above their small campsite and fell on the man Davina assumed was the troupe's leader, the man who pulled her from the flames, the one who swore to protect her. His companions had called him Rob. He was taller than the others, or perhaps it was his air of control, even as the wooden shaft tore through his flesh, that made him appear bigger, stronger, and capable of anything.

But could he . . . would he truly protect her? She wanted to believe that he meant it, because every single person she knew in her life was dead, and if Rob was her enemy disguising his purpose, then there was nothing more to hope for.

But she was no fool. Edward and more than a hundred of his men had not been able to protect her, though they had tried. Certainly four Highlanders, two of them barely even men yet, would fall even quicker. Or would they? Saints, but they were savage looking, with their bare knees and huge swords dangling from their hips. What were they doing at St. Christopher's? Were they truly bringing her someplace safe, or to her enemies? Either way, she could not stay with them. If they were innocent, she would likely get them killed. She could ask them boldly if her enemy had sent them but they would not tell her the truth.

Grief clouded her thoughts, but not enough to make her trust the one who might or might not have rescued her. How had her enemies found her even before the coronation? Someone had informed them. But who?

The sisters had never kept the truth from her. Davina knew why she had been taken from her mother's arms as a babe, abandoned by her father, and sent off to St. Christopher's. She understood the value of her existence, for twice now it had cost her everything she loved. When Edward had arrived at the Abbey from King Charles's court, he had told her of the men who sought her demise. And dear God, there were many. Though his warnings birthed a fear in Davina that was almost palpable, she understood his reasons for telling her. Ignorance of one's foe was as dangerous as facing them on a battlefield. And so, she lived in uncertainty and unease, always aware of the danger around her.

In the fading light, she watched Rob walk toward the pebbly brook and bend to the water's edge where she'd washed the soot out of her own hair earlier. He scooped some water up in his hands to wash his face. His wound needed cleaning, but Davina was thankful that he didn't remove his clothing to bathe. She had lived among many men in her life, but not a single one of them emanated such raw strength as this one, nor were any of them as broad of shoulder as he. She was certain it was the primitive belted plaid swinging about his bare knees when he stood to his feet that helped accentuate the comparison—the dusty skins wrapped around his calves—one, with the hilt of a dagger sticking out of it—that bore testimony to his vigor. This man spent his days doing more than sitting idle with his comrades, drinking and waiting for battle to come to him. Following him with her gaze as he turned from the stream and moved around the campsite, she found his gait easy and confident with the kind of pride carried by generations before him. When he angled his head to look at her and found her staring at him, she swung her gaze to a nearby tree.

"Ye know, lass," he said, and she was aware of him moving toward her. "If my sister could be as quiet as ye are fer but a quarter of the time, she'd likely have found a husband by now."

Squatting now before a pile of embers to her right, Will let out a low snicker. He was temptation incarnate, that one, Davina thought when he glanced at her and winked. As darkly intriguing as a wolf, with pale gray eyes and a set of fangs to match.

"Leave Mairi oot of this," said the boy who had defied Rob so boldly when he was told to go to England. He looked to be about nine and ten, lean bodied and quite at ease on his mount on the way here. Dark, silky waves eclipsed eyes that were a dozen different shades of green and golden brown, smoldering eyes that burned with a sense of purpose almost as intense as Rob's. "Ye both know why she hasna' wed."

"Aye, Colin," Will laughed, sprinkling twigs over the building flames. "The men are afraid o' her."

"I believe Colin is referring to my brother Connor."

"I am referrin' to him, as well, Finn. Though I dinna' blame Connor fer fleein' to England." Will's eyes gleamed above the flames, playful and teasing on the young man whose visage alone had made Davina almost forget—for just an instant—the horrors of the day.

When she'd first set eyes on the one called Finn she thought it might be possible that God had sent one of His fairest, undoubtedly Scottish, angels to save her. His hair was pin-straight and almost as pale as hers beneath his bonnet of rich emerald, the same color as his eyes. He sang when he spoke and his eyes twinkled and danced like stars across Ireland's moors. Just looking at him made her feel better. Unlike Colin, who possessed the same dark, dangerous appeal as Rob, Finn was so beautiful Davina felt pity for any young lady who fell in love with him.

"Connor's not afraid of anything," Finn corrected, resting his back against a tree and tossing a handful of berries into his mouth. "Why d'ye think King Charles made him a captain?"

Davina wasn't surprised by this bit of news. The dead king was known to have taken many Scots, even Highlanders, into his army. She wondered if Edward knew Finn's brother. Had known, she corrected, fighting another wave of emotion that threatened to spill from her eyes.

She turned away from the men and found Rob squatting before her. Dear Lord, but he made every other male, including the ones around her, look ordinary. In the dimming light she couldn't see the gold flecks that gave fire to his vivid blue eyes, but she knew they were there. His nose was straight and classically cut, his jaw wide and shadowed just enough to lend to his rugged appearance. Beneath lips crafted, she was certain, for the sole purpose of leading women astray, the hint of a dimple defined the unyielding strength of his chin.

"Are ye hungry?"

"I should help," she said, pushing herself off the ground.

"Ye should sit," Rob corrected, reaching for her robes and gently pulling her back down. "We need to speak," he said, growing more serious, "and as much as it may displease ye, ye'll be doin' most of the talkin'."

Involuntarily, Davina felt her lips press together. It wasn't safe for her to do the talking, for she tended to run on with a topic well beyond its natural end. It was because she hadn't had anyone new to talk with, or hear about the world with in four years, that she was less cautious when she was speaking. She didn't want to converse with this stranger, but she was going to have to find a way to avoid it without piquing his curiosity. If her enemies did not send him, he might just as easily give her up to them if he discovered her secrets.

"Whatever you like, sir," she said, relaxing her mouth. "But before we do, I beg you let me tend to the wound in your arm."

He sized her up with a slow, silent assessment that made her teeth itch. The force of his gaze, the sheer power of will he possessed to refuse her if he decided she was simply putting him off, sent a fissure of panic through her. In that moment, she admired Colin immensely for standing up to his disapproving scrutiny.

"Sir, I wouldn't want you to fall ill with a fever because of me," she added earnestly to encourage his compliance.

"Verra well," he finally conceded, misgivings clearly etched in his features. "But dinna' call me Sir." He sat back, giving her leave to touch him. "I'm no' a knight of the realm, and I've never been considered a gentleman."

Davina didn't know what to make of that declaration, or why the husky timbre of his voice when he said it sent an odd quiver down her spine. "I'll need water," she told him, barely looking at him, her hands folded in her lap. She wasn't about to fall victim to a temptation that was, and always would be, denied her.

"Will." He turned briefly to the others. "She needs water."

"You need to shift a bit," Davina instructed, trying to think of what he might ask her, and what she might or might not answer.

"Aye, that would help." He smiled as he turned, scattering Davina's thoughts like dry leaves in the wind. How could his virility be as tangible as a touch and yet his smile be so guileless and awkward—so much more honest and open than his friend's, who appeared before them on his haunches?

"Ye're gushin' like a peach-faced whelp," Will said, wearing a smirk that boded ill for Rob. "Are ye certain the fever hasna' already come upon ye?"

Davina caught the pouch Will tossed her just before the pad of Rob's boot struck him in the chest. A smaller man would have sailed an inch or two off the ground, but Will only landed hard on his rump and laughed.

"Go easy on him, lass," Will said, springing back to his feet. "He's soft," he added over his shoulder when he was a good enough distance away to safely rest for the night.

Soft? Davina doubted it as she surveyed Rob's back. Even draped in yards of wool he appeared as solid as the mountains in the distance. "After I've cleaned the wound,

I'll need your dagger to cut a few strips of fabric so that I can—"

"Ye'll no' be gettin' my dagger, lass. Though I understand why ye shot me—"

"That arrow was mine?" Her eyes opened wide on him and any hope she had in him helping her faded.

"*She* shot ye?" cried Finn, voicing the disbelief that marked the faces of his companions.

"Aye," Rob answered, drawing out a heavy sigh as if it was the last thing he wanted to admit. "And I dinna' feel at ease with her holdin' a knife to my back."

"That's ridiculous," Davina argued. "I would never stab a man...." Something he'd said suddenly struck her. He'd mentioned earlier how she'd almost killed him, but she'd been too grief-stricken to catch it. "How do you know the arrow came from my quiver?" When he didn't answer right away, another realization hit her like a cannon to her chest, making it difficult to breathe. "How do you know Edward is dead, or who he was? You were not acquainted with him, were you?"

"Nae, I didna' know him," he said quietly, avoiding her searching gaze.

"And you knew I was inside the Abbey." Everything was beginning to make more sense now. Dear God, he was one of them! It didn't matter that he was a Highlander. Her enemies were powerful men with allies in almost every country and fat enough purses to hire mercenaries if their soldiers failed. *Trust no one.* Her fingers balled into fists and her eyes glistened with tears. Here she was concerned about the man who likely took Edward's life. She didn't think about the other three watching her. She didn't care if they killed her.

"Bastard!" She leaned over him and snatched the dagger from his boot.

His reflexes were too quick and he caught her wrist with bone-crushing strength. Before his companions even had time to gain their feet to rush to his aid, he flipped her completely over his shoulder, delivering her flat on the ground so hard it knocked the air from her lungs. Before she could roll away and run, he pinned her with his weight and halted the others with a stroke of his hand.

"Are ye bewitched? Possessed by a demon?" he demanded, his eyes on her as merciless as his fingers still squeezing into her wrist. "Is that why they want ye dead?"

"You know the answer to that," she bit out, then swung at his jaw with her free hand. He blocked her fist with his forearm and grimaced as pain lanced up his arm to his wounded shoulder. "You killed Edward to get to me."

"Who the hell is Edward?" Colin demanded, hovering over them both. He took one look at his brother's dagger clutched in Davina's fingers and bent to pluck it from her grasp.

"Captain Edward Asher," Rob informed him, holding fast against her renewed efforts to free herself. "He was struck doun after he begged me to save her. Aye"—Rob returned his hard gaze to hers when her struggle ceased—"'Twas yer captain who told me about ye."

Was it true? Was that why he saved her? "Edward would not have told you that I shot you."

"His eyes did, when he saw yer arrow in my hand."

Dear God, Edward would have recognized her feathered arrows. "What else did he tell you?" Davina asked, breathless from their fight and still wary of him.

"No' enough, but ye're goin' to remedy that as soon as ye give me yer word that ye're done tryin' to kill me."

"First I would hear all that Edward told you."

He stared down directly into her eyes and hooked one corner of his mouth in a grin that sent her pulse racing. "Ye're no' in a position to bargain."

"Nor are you," she countered, trying to match his confidence. "You're dripping blood all over my robes. When you lose consciousness neither of us will get our answers."

Rob's smug smirk vanished when Will chuckled above them. "She's clever."

Davina waited beneath her captor while he weighed his options. He could kill her so easily now and bring her body to the men who wanted her dead, but if he already knew her secrets and why she'd been hidden at St. Christopher's, why did he insist on questioning her? Did he truly save her because Edward had asked him to? And what if Edward had told him more about her? This Highland warrior might have rescued her with good intentions, but perhaps when and if Edward told him the truth...Oh, she didn't know what to believe, and she certainly couldn't think with him on top of her. Saints, he was heavy, and as stubborn as a bull. Well, she could be just as inflexible. She shifted, trying to pull more air into her lungs, and became uncomfortably aware of every muscle that formed him. Though the Abbess had frowned upon it, Davina often touched the men of Edward's regiment; a tender, light touch to an arm while she spoke, a playful shove when they teased her about her pitiful lack of skill at chess. She'd felt their bodies, but never on top of her. Rob's weight and the heat of his body had quite a dizzying effect on her senses. She would have kneed him in his nether regions if her robes weren't tangled around her legs.

He must have sensed her discomfort because his penetrating gaze on her softened, sending a flutter across her belly. "I'm no' yer enemy," he said thickly, meaningfully.

But everyone was her potential enemy. Edward and even the Abbess had made certain she understood that. She'd never had a friend because there were never any children at St. Christopher's besides her. No villagers to chance sighting her, or hear a rumor of her existence. No one but Davina, the sisters, and a small regiment of the King's Royal army who knew who and where she was. Everyone could be bought with coin...or fear. Anyone was capable of betraying her.

"You're hurting me." She broke their gaze and turned her face away from him, afraid that he might sway her from her caution.

Thankfully, he wasn't a completely uncaring barbarian and rolled off her. The instant she was free, Davina rose to her knees and crawled backward a few inches, her eyes wide on all of them. For the moment, Colin was the only one glaring at her as if he distrusted her as much as she did them. Will was watching her with something akin to admiration curling his lips, while Finn's cherubic expression had gone soft on her.

"Was Asher yer husband?" Rob asked, clutching his shoulder as he sat up. His expression on her was harder to read, for it was neither angry nor forgiving.

"No, he was my friend." She felt a small pang of relief that obviously Edward hadn't told him anything of great importance. But that still didn't explain what Rob and his men were doing at the Abbey on the morning they were attacked. "What were you doing at St. Christopher's?" she demanded of whoever would answer.

"I was acquainted wi' one o' the sisters there."

Davina glanced up and caught the silvery sparkle in Will's eyes behind his mop of straight, minky hair. Acquainted indeed. Did they think her so simpleminded as to believe that one of the sisters would have anything to do with such a devilish rascal?

"Sister Margaret Mary was once m' nursemaid," the handsome wolf told her, seeing the doubt in the quirk of her brow and easing it.

"Now I'll ask ye the same question," Rob said, snatching Davina's attention back to him. "What were ye doin' there?" He pulled on the plaid swathing his shoulders and her eyes followed the wool as it slipped down his chest.

"I lived there."

"But Asher called ye Lady Montgomery."

"My parents were peers. They died when I was a child and the sisters of St. Christopher's raised me."

He said nothing but let his eyes linger over her robes. Then, in a sterner voice, he asked, "Which duke and earl did ye speak of earlier?"

She watched him try to pull his tunic up over his belly using only one arm and failing. "The Earl of Argyll and the Duke of Monmouth." No harm in telling him that much, since he likely knew already.

He stopped moving and looked at her, surprise and a flicker of alarm making his eyes spark like jewels in the twilight. He cut his gaze to Will. "Monmouth? King James's nephew?"

"James is not yet King," Davina reminded him.

Both Highlanders looked at her at the same time, but

it was Rob who spoke. "And ye are no' a novice of the Order."

"But I am. I will take my vows next spring."

Rob's eyes darkened briefly as disappointment skittered across his features. Just as quickly, his resolve hardened, along with his jaw. But the flash of something soft in him was a thousand times more dangerous than his friend's effortless charm.

"Monmouth and Argyll have both been exiled to Holland," Colin said over the crackle of flames.

Davina nodded. "And it was their Dutch army who attacked us."

"Why do they want ye dead?"

She turned to Rob when he asked the question. What if he truly didn't know? She wanted to believe that he didn't, that he'd saved her for no other reason than he was a decent man. She did not know the world or how to stay alive in it on her own and needed someone to help her, just for a little while. That moment of vulnerability she saw in him tempted her to trust him.

"'Tis ye they were after, aye, lass?" he continued when she remained silent. "All the sisters were killed with the hope that ye were among them."

Davina swiped a tear from her cheek at the stark truth of his words. They were all dead because of her.

"Why? Who are ye?"

"I am no one."

Oh, how she wished it were true. She would give anything, anything to have it be true.

Chapter Five

$\mathcal{A}$s breathtakin' as ye are, lass, I canna' believe so many men lost their lives over no one."

It wasn't the way Rob's hard eyes warmed on Davina or the low lilting cadence of his voice when he called her breathtaking that made her look away. Though in truth, she did not know how to react to such boldness, or why it made her palms warm. She dragged her gaze from his because what he said after that was correct, and she could not hide the pain of it.

He moved closer to her, the warmth of his body seeping into her own. "Verra well, then, Davina. Ye are no one. Fer now."

He merely crooked his mouth at her when she looked at him again, but it made her want to tell him everything. She smiled back instead and reached for his shoulder. "Forgive me for shooting you...if you are innocent."

"I am, and I already have." His breath along her jaw as she helped him out of his tunic sent a warm spark down Davina's spine. The firelight bouncing across the golden expanse of his bare back awed her. She didn't have to trust him to appreciate his splendid male physique, something she would surely have to ask forgiveness for later. He looked just as hard as he felt.

"I would not have you think me insolent or unappreciative of what you did for me today." Oh, why couldn't she just shut up? Because she needed something to keep her mind off his silken angles beneath her fingers. She'd never touched a man's bare flesh before and felt her face growing flush. "I do not wish to lie to you, so if we continue to travel together, please consider my silence repayment for saving my life."

"Ye're protectin' me?" His half-smile returned, this time sweet with indulgence.

"All of us."

"Ye must know somethin' o' great consequence aboot these two men that they dinna' want gettin' oot," Will said, stepping around the fire to sit across from her. After giving her one last wary glance, Colin followed him.

Davina shook her head and watched Finn fold his legs beside her. "I know nothing about them save that they have many Protestant supporters here and in Holland who do not favor a Roman Catholic ruler. Monmouth was involved in the Exclusion Bill. . . ."

"The Bill that divided the country into two parties," Colin finished, ignoring the curious look Will aimed at him, and then at Rob. "The Whigs who supported it and the Tories who opposed. James was convinced to withdraw from all decisions made in the government, and was exiled by his brother, King Charles, fer many years."

"That's correct," Davina told him, surprised and intrigued by his knowledge of politics. There were some things she would never tell these men, or anyone else, but what danger was there in finally being able to share her opinions on matters of state and religion? "Unlike the man who is about to be crowned king, Monmouth and Argyll, and many others, staunchly oppose religious liberty."

"Aye, we know," Colin said, watching her over the flames. "'Tis our religion the Protestants want to extinguish. We know where Charles stood on the matter, but we've heard little aboot James of York. What d'ye know of him?"

Davina decided that this young man's full attention was only a little less daunting than the warrior's beside her. Proceeding with caution, she met his gaze. "He is a man who stands for what he believes in."

"Is that so?" he asked, his voice laced with a mixture of curiosity and skepticism.

"Yes, it is," Davina answered, taking up the challenge. "He refused to denounce his faith when the Test Act was introduced several years ago, even relinquishing his post as Lord High Admiral. He faced opposition that would have made other men crumble, and all because of his beliefs."

Colin nodded, and though his features softened in the firelight, his eyes smoldered from within. "I know a man like that, but he wouldna' have wed his daughters to Protestants."

Davina gave him one last, measured look before turning to find the pouch of water Will had tossed to her. She suspected Colin knew more about the Duke of York than he was going to admit. Still, he didn't know everything, and his questions were innocent enough. "That was King Charles's doing in an attempt to convince James's enemies that he had not converted," she said, finding the pouch and turning her attention back to Rob's wound.

"How d'ye know all this?"

She blinked at Finn's softly spoken question. Her hand, in the process of yanking the plug from the pouch, stopped

in mid tug. How *did* she know all this, indeed? A curious question, and the most deadly. She'd been so intent on
boasting her knowledge of the House of Stuart that she
hadn't considered if any one of her listeners would wonder
how she had attained it. Damn her, she had no skills when
it came to deception!

"I read every day," she told Finn, averting her gaze
from his. It wasn't an untruth. "Part of my instruction
at the Abbey included reading over old parchments and
books about England's history."

"Well, I dinna' care who's after ye, lass," Will
announced, thankfully putting an end to the conversation. He pulled part of his plaid off his shoulder, bunched
it up beneath his head, and closed his eyes. "Ye're wi'
MacGregors now."

"And a Grant," Finn added, squaring his shoulders with
just as much pride and offering her a smile that tempted
her to smile back before he too settled in for the night.

They were MacGregors. Little was known about them
at the Abbey. The Reverend Mother had only spoken of
them once while Davina was studying her lessons on Parliament. After centuries of bloody battles with the Campbells and the Colquhouns, the MacGregors had been
proscribed by King James VI back in 1601. They became
outlaws who defied kings and butchered nobles in their
beds. If these Highlanders were true ambassadors of their
clan, Davina doubted the MacGregors followed any laws,
even now. Were they mercenaries then? No, they were
enemies of the Protestant Campbells. Surely they would
not work on Argyll's side. But why should they give their
allegiance to the throne when it was a king who had tried
to abolish them?

"Are you three brothers then?" she asked Rob, hoping to find out more about him while steering their conversation away from herself.

"Colin is my brother. Will might as well be, and Finn is my aunt's nephew by marriage."

Davina nodded and moved a little closer to him to examine his wound. "Why has your father traveled to the king's coronation?" She tore off a length of her robe and saturated it with water.

"Every chief and chieftain north of Edinburgh agreed to attend to show support fer the new Stuart king."

Davina looked at him and found him looking back. "So," she said, a bit breathless by the way he let his cool gaze rove over her face. "You are the son of a chief." She understood now his air of authority and arrogance. "A chief whose name came close to extinction under James VI."

"Aye," he told her quietly, "a chief who suffered under enemies even more hostile than the Duke of York's because of it."

She touched the edges of his wound lightly with her cloth, considering what he said. This man knew what it meant to fight for what one believed in, no matter what the cost. But what were his beliefs? "And yet, your father offers his loyalty to the throne now?"

"The laws against us," he reminded her, "were lifted by King Charles II."

Davina nodded. She'd read that Charles had been a sympathetic sovereign. Too sympathetic, some believed. He had lifted the bans the Puritans had set over England. He had reopened theaters, and brought back the celebration of Christmastide. Under his rule, colorful dress had returned to fashion, and all forms of art were once again allowed to be viewed.

"Do you support the Duke of York's succession to the throne as well?" she asked.

"That will depend on him."

An admirable answer, that. It proved that whatever the reason Rob MacGregor had her in his possession, he at least was not one to be led about by other men's convictions until he formed his own.

"Now I've a question to put to ye, lass."

She closed her eyes, praying that God would forgive her if she was forced to lie to him again.

"Did ye love him?"

Her hands shook, jerking the cloth at his shoulder and making him wince. "How could I love a man I have never met? I've only heard…"

"I speak of Captain Asher," he interrupted.

"Oh." She opened her eyes, then wished she hadn't when she saw curiosity arching his brow. She would have to be more careful with her answers. "Of course I loved him. Edward was like a brother to me." She returned her full attention to his wound, hoping her answer satisfied him.

Apparently it did, for he left her to finish wrapping his wound without another word to her. When she was done, he thanked her, commanded Will to keep first watch, then stretched out beside her and told her to get some sleep. She sat there while he slung his wounded arm over his bare belly and closed his eyes.

What should she do now? She looked around the firelight, catching Will's smile. She didn't smile back, but sank to her elbow, and then her side, and closed her eyes to the sound of Rob's slow, steady breath at her back.

Chapter Six

———⚔———

Captain Edward Asher was going to be ill. Every breath he drew into his lungs was saturated with the smell of charred flesh. Did he dare move? Were they finally gone? Silence clung to the darkness like scum on a pond, somehow even more unnerving than the voices above him earlier. They had arrived sometime after the massacre, as he was rousing from unconsciousness. He'd remained still, knowing he was likely the only one alive whom they could question.

"It is the captain of the regiment," one said, turning him faceup with his boot.

"I can see that," answered another man, the cool slice of his voice warning that his patience was at an end.

Edward knew the voice and the man behind it and willed himself not to breathe. Admiral Peter Gilles, whom the Duke of Monmouth had brought back with him from Utrecht a few years ago, was here to make certain Davina was dead. Edward almost hoped she was, for if Gilles found her with a single breath left in her, he would take pleasure in cutting it out. Known to many as "de Duivel," Gilles was the most ruthless bastard ever to wield a sword. His father, Cornelius Gilles, was a privateer who fought alongside Admiral Piet

Hein, capturing the Spanish silver fleet off Cuba in 1628. The victory was won without bloodshed, and the Spanish prisoners were released. But Peter Gilles was nothing like his father. One had only to look into his pale cold eyes to know he enjoyed killing.

"My lord will be pleased," Gilles drawled. Then, "Check the Abbey."

"But Admiral, there's nothing left of it," the first man pointed out, unaware that his observation shattered Edward's heart.

"Do it, Edgar," Gilles ordered on a low, murderous snarl, "or I'll flay you right here."

Nothing in Edward's life had ever been as difficult as lying there, seemingly lifeless at Gilles's feet. Nothing, save knowing that Davina was dead. He had failed her. Dear God, how would he ever forgive himself? He hadn't yet met Davina when he was told it was she he was being sent to St. Christopher's to protect four years ago. He'd been young and ambitious and he hadn't yet heard her laughter ringing through the somber halls, or her prayers whispered through honeyed lips for mercy for her enemies. He hadn't known how easily she could slay him with her tongue and a soft, teasing smile. He'd wanted to tell her the truth. She deserved that much, but just when he'd finally gathered the courage to tell her, Gilles's men had come. Now it was too late.

"Hendrick," the Admiral called out to another of his men. "Look inside the chapel. I want body counts, regardless of what is left of them. The same for the English soldiers scattered here. I want her found."

He knew he had no right, but Edward prayed to God to keep Davina hidden if she lived.

"Gather our fallen and pile them there. After our search, burn them."

"Admiral?" another voice to Edward's right asked uneasily, as if he doubted what he had just heard.

"Shall we announce to all of England that we were here, Maarten?" Gilles answered, the clip of annoyance in his voice halting any other queries.

Edward had no idea how long he lay there in the dirt and ash dreading a shout that they had found her. He waited with the stillness of death while the fallen soldiers who had attacked the Abbey this morn were dragged somewhere to his left. He had just begun to feel the heat from the fire when he heard a man call out over the crackling flames.

"The Abbey is empty from what we can tell, Admiral. No bodies, charred or otherwise."

"Empty? Twenty-seven women resided here and you found not one?" Silence while something popped in the fire. "They must have all gone to the chapel. Go and aid Hendrick in his search. If he has found even one, alert me."

Edward almost opened his eyes. They would find bodies in the chapel, but none of them were Davina. She had been in the Abbey. He knew it for certain because he had recognized her blue feathered arrow tip clutched in the Highlander's fist just before he . . .

MacGregor.

For the first time since dawn broke, a flicker of hope sparked in Edward's heart when he remembered the giant warrior. Had MacGregor saved her? He had not seemed interested in doing so when Edward beseeched him, but he looked fit enough to finish off what was left of Monmouth's men and canter off with the prize. Was it possible

that his Davina still lived and was safe? Where would
MacGregor have taken her? His belly heaved as the stench
of burning flesh and hair filled his lungs. He gritted his
teeth and imagined her smile to keep from retching. She
had smiled at him often, those huge, glorious eyes going
soft with affection, melting his very bones. He knew she
wasn't in love with him, but that had never stopped him
from loving her with his whole heart.

Sometime later, Hendrick returned to the courtyard
with news of his discovery. There were bodies in the chapel
but all were burned beyond recognition.

"I've no interest in what they looked like, Hendrick,
you fool, since I've never seen the girl. Tell me, how many
bodies did you find?"

"Hard to tell, sir, but Edgar counted six and twenty."

Edward could almost hear Gilles deducing that somehow Davina had escaped. His heart sank even before the
Admiral spoke again.

"Let us finish here. We will search for tracks in the
morning."

How long ago had it been since Edward heard those
last words? Ten sickening breaths or fifty? He'd heard
them taking to their mounts and leaving. He was sure of
it. Or was it just the thumping of his heart? It didn't matter. He had to find Davina before Gilles did. He opened
his eyes slowly. One, and then the other, only to close
them an instant later, burning and tearing from the acrid
smoke. He allowed himself to cough, and then he retched
until every muscle and joint in his body ached. Pushing
himself to his feet, he searched, as best he could, among
his fallen men until he found a sword.

He had failed her, but perhaps God was giving him

another chance to save her life. He turned toward the
gates. He did have a slight advantage. Gilles and his
men would have to wait until morning to find any tracks.
Edward didn't need them—at least not yet. He knew who
had taken her, and Highlanders lived in the north.

Rob woke the next morning to the sound of Will's cheerful account of the time he and Rob raided the MacPherson
holding with Rob's younger brother, Tristan, and Connor
Grant. It wasn't a tale fit for a lady's ears . . . or a soon-to-be
nun's. He'd nearly sighed out loud with regret when she
told him she was an orphan raised in the convent and not
some rich Englishman's daughter. Was she truly a novice?
Had her life been given over to God?

If it had, she gave no indication of it during Will's
interpretation . . . so far. She appeared unfazed while she
sat with Colin and Finn, nibbling on the last remaining
berries they'd picked the night before.

"We were almost away free wi' half a dozen cattle
when Tristan spotted Brigid MacPherson and her six sisters traipsin' across the glen on their way home from their
mornin' bath."

Finn smiled and Colin swore under his breath, both
deducing where the tale was heading and each sharing a
very different opinion on it.

"I suspect," Will continued, "the MacPherson gels recognized their faither's livestock, but hell, ye lads know
that Tristan has a way wi' lasses that makes them ferget,
or no' care aboot anything else."

"Aye," said Finn, his voice tinged with veneration. "I
vow one smile from Tristan could steal the heart of even
the king's mistress."

"'Tis true," Will laughed, "and the MacPherson lasses were nae different. Why, I swear on m' sword, it took less than ten breaths fer Brigid to strip oot o' her..."

Rob cleared his throat as he rose to his feet and cast Will a warning look. He'd been reckless that day, risking injury to himself and to his companions for a few hours of physical pleasure. He took no pride in the retelling of it, despite their victorious raid.

Will answered with a bright grin, bid him good morn, and then turned back to his audience to finish the tale. "We all had..."

"Will, that's enough," Rob said more sternly this time. He didn't want Davina hearing the rest.

He needn't have bothered, for she was no longer listening. Her gaze was fastened on him as he strode toward her. For an instant, she looked frightened—as if her breath was caught somewhere between her throat and her lips. Suspecting that she had seldom seen any half-naked men roaming the Abbey, he tugged on the folds of his plaid draped low on his bare waist and tossed one end over the shoulder she had bandaged the night before.

She blinked and then raised her gaze higher to meet his and blushed. "How does your arm feel?"

"Better."

"I prayed for you last night."

"Ye have my thanks fer that." He was tempted to smile at her. Hell, how many times had he done the like last night? 'Twas unsettling to think how easily he lost control over his own mouth when she looked at him. He'd lain awake deciding what it was about her that attached itself to his heartstrings before he had time to guard against it. She was bonnie, to be sure, but there were plenty of

bonnie lasses at Camlochlin. Mayhap, it was the sweet
vulnerability of her, or the spark of life that, despite the
tragedy that had befallen her, had not been extinguished.
She looked as if a slight wind could carry her off, but she
would stand, legs braced, and face it first. She was braw.
Aye, she was that. Shooting arrows at her enemies instead
of running for her life. Losing everything and everyone
and weeping softly as she rested her head for the night
instead of wailing in her grief. He'd gone to sleep thinking that she was the kind of woman he could lose his heart
to, and that he should bring her home.

But he awoke this morning with a clear head. Tristan
still bore the scar on his thigh from Donald MacPherson's
arrow when the chieftain and his sons had come upon them
that balmy summer morn. Rob's lesson that day had been
hard learned and not forgotten. He would give Davina aid,
but that was all. He would find a refuge quickly and return
to his life. He would never again let a lass rob him of his
good senses and put his kin in jeopardy. Especially a lass
who was responsible for the deaths of over a hundred men.

Which brought him to his other quandary. Why did
Monmouth or Argyll want her dead? Will had been correct
when he called her clever. She had avoided his questions
by telling them all what anyone half interested in James
of York might want to know. But none of it had anything
to do with the massacre at St. Christopher's. Why would
King Charles's army be guarding a novice? What else did
she know that she had not read in a book? Did the attempt
on her life have anything to do with the new king's coronation? She refused to tell him anything, but it didn't matter.
He knew all he needed to know. Davina Montgomery was
danger and risk, and Rob was never careless.

"There is an abbey in Ayrshire," she said, as if reading the deep concern marring his brow. "I will be safe there."

Rob studied her face in silence. She didn't want to go there. It wasn't fear he saw in her eyes that told him, but resignation—as if she had no other choice but to accept her fate. "Ye said ye would no' be safe anywhere."

"I'd forgotten about Courlochcraig. I was not thinking clearly."

'Twas a solution. He could leave her at the new abbey and keep her enemies away from his kin. "Verra well. We shall escort ye to Ayrshire then."

"I would be grateful for that," she said, rising to her feet. She barely reached his chest but gathered her courage around her like a mantle. "My life has already cost too much. I will not have it cost you yours."

"Nor will I." He turned away from her before he was tempted to ponder the extraordinary beauty of her eyes. Was it the filtered sunlight streaming through the canopy of summer green leaves that changed their color to deep cerulean? Damnation, he could find satisfaction gazing into them forever, stripping away all her secrets and...

"Let's clear up and be gone from here." He strode to his horse, pulled a fresh tunic from his saddlebag and tugged it over his head. He disappeared behind a tree to empty his bladder, then thought better of it. He had to assume they might be followed by any soldiers who had survived the attack on the Abbey and mayhap saw him riding off with Davina. A good tracker would spot—or smell—whatever they were careless enough to leave behind.

Peering around the tree, he watched Davina share a word with Finn while they saddled the horses. She possessed no airs of superiority, the way a noble lady might.

She spoke softly and seemed to be even-tempered, save for when she'd tried to kill him with his own dagger. She'd prayed for him.... He studied the heavy robes concealing much of her form and found himself wondering what she looked like underneath. She was thin, that much he could tell. The coarse wool hung off her slender shoulders in folds and bunched at her waist, barely defined by the rope she had belted there. She needed to eat something besides berries, but there was no time to hunt. He prayed they were not being followed. "If we ride hard," he told them all, stepping out from behind the tree, "we can reach Ayrshire in a few hours."

"Ride hard?" The lass turned to him, her eyes round with dread.

"Are ye sore?" he asked her, noting her hand slipping behind her to give her upper thighs a rub.

"I will be fine." She offered him a quick smile then turned away.

Rob stared after her for another moment, cursing the effect her most casual smile had on him.

"We'll need to cover our tracks from here on in," he called out to the others. "We didna' stop here. Will, ye and Colin haul that fallen branch atop the embers. Finn, toss some twigs around the place." His eyes found Davina's again. "Movin' aboot will help ease yer soreness. Scout fer horse waste and cover whatever ye find with leaves."

Her nose crinkled at him before she turned away to her task. This time, he couldn't help smiling.

Chapter Seven

⚔

$\mathcal{I}$t took Davina nearly an hour before she relaxed on Rob's stallion. She hadn't realized her fingernails were embedded into the Highlander's wrist, or that her eyes were squeezed shut as they traveled northwest along pebbly streams and dewy glens scented with heather. She had never been on a horse before. Where was there to go? The size of the beast, the girth, the sudden snorts she was certain were warnings that the behemoth steed was about to fling them off its back . . . were completely new and terrifying to her. She suspected she'd been too numb yesterday to fully appreciate the force of wind that the mount's slim, bony legs produced.

But Davina had learned well how to hold back her fears, lest they consume her, so after an hour, she forced herself to loosen her grip and open her eyes.

What she saw enthralled her. All around her the world burst forth in radiant colors of crimson and green and purple—a world she had never seen before. How many times had she lost herself to her daydreams, imagining a different life? One without gates, with a mother and father who welcomed her into their lives, a husband and children who made her life vital for other, purer reasons. A life without fear of what tomorrow might bring. If only she could abandon herself to the joy of feeling free as easily as she defied her fears. She might take rest against the broad, fit chest behind her and bask in the wind in her hair and the sun on her face. But her whole life was built around warnings and danger. She could not so carelessly cast her lessons away. Not even nestled in the embrace of a man whose body would haunt her dreams for years to come. By all that was holy, she understood now why Eve had given in to temptation in the Garden. Davina knew Rob MacGregor was hard and lean from touching him last eve, but seeing all that male striding toward her in the light of morn sparked a longing of wanting to belong to him. It was what the Abbess called "a base desire," primitive, unholy. Rob MacGregor was unholy for certain, with a sinewy, broad chest feathered with dark hair and a belly carved in small, tight squares. The most sinful of all though was the sensual V curve of muscles below his abdomen, as if they sprang from someplace beneath his low-hanging plaid. It was that image that had invaded her thoughts when he lifted her into his newly padded saddle this morn and then leaped up behind her. His scent had rushed to her head, intensifying the warmth of his muscles, the intimacy of his arms closing around her.

A base desire it might be, but what warm-blooded female would not want a man like that to stand beside her when the world she knew fell apart? And it wasn't simply his strength that tempted her, but his complete command over the situation. The way he'd made certain nothing appeared unnatural at the camp, the careful path he set them on that would leave the least tracks. He was deliberate in his thinking, never second-guessing himself or what the others around him thought of his decisions. It stirred her hope that this Highlander was indeed able to protect her. That he might truly mean to—at least for now. But she didn't trust hope. Not anymore.

"Tell me, lass." The naturally deep baritone of Rob's voice behind her sent unfamiliar, unwanted heat down her spine. "Why does an English lady bear a Scottish name?"

Her back stiffened with the return of caution. "Why do you assume I am English?" she asked, keeping her eyes steady ahead.

"Ye speak like them, and ye're well mannered."

The heavy lilt in his voice played like a melody against her ear, soothing her nerves, but not enough to completely relax her guard. He was clever. He'd already proven that at the camp and the way he'd tricked her with his query about loving Edward.

"I was raised by English nuns. Do you expect me to be troublesome?"

"I didna' know they were English," he said pensively, giving her a moment of true dread that she might have, once again, said too much. "But ye were raised with more men than women and ye still possess all the propriety of a well-bred lady."

Now she did turn to look him in his eyes, misgivings about him clearly showing in hers. "And who informed you that I was raised with men? Those soldiers might have been visiting St. Christopher's, as you claim to have been doing."

"Yer arrow piercin' me from within the Abbey informed me." His voice dipped with the hint of what could have been humor. She wasn't certain, since he hadn't offered her even the barest trace of a smile since he awoke this morning. "A lass doesna' master that kind of skill unless she's been taught fer many years."

Yes, he was clever...and without a doubt, the finest-looking man she'd ever set her eyes on. For a shameful instant, she wondered how he would look with those obsidian curls falling loose around his face instead of being tied back neatly from it. Was he always so serious, so in control? God forgive her, why was she curious about the savage side of his character? She knew that part of him existed somewhere beyond his rigid composure. She'd seen a spark of something purely feral in his eyes when she attacked him last eve. It frightened her and heightened her awareness of his virility at the same time. She really needed to pray.

"Who named ye?"

She blinked, clearing her unchaste thoughts. "My father," she told him and sat forward, away from his body.

"Was yer faither a Scotsmen, then?"

Though her days were often preoccupied with thoughts of her true family, and if they would even know her if they saw her, Davina had never spoken of them with anyone, and she did not want to do so now. "He was."

"And yer mother?" His fingers brushed softly across her belly.

"She..." Davina wiped her brow that suddenly went hot at his touch. She tried to squirm further away from him but there was no place else to go. "She died when I was ten, from what I am told." She tried to relax her breathing, afraid of what questions he would put to her next and how easily she might answer them, begging his protection. But if he was not her enemy, then he was her enemy's foe. If he didn't know who she was then it was best he never discover it. She would not let more people die because of her.

"What were they called?"

His queries were not casual, nor was his touch. She doubted he did anything without purpose—and she was tired of having to be so guarded around him. "They were Lord and Lady Whithorn," she said, hoping that would satisfy him. "I do not wish to think on them."

When she offered nothing more, his muscles tensed behind her and his spine went taut, mayhap with anger or frustration, she did not know, nor did she care. She was only thankful that he did not speak again.

Normally, Davina relished silence. It wasn't because she was used to it. While abbeys tended to be quiet places on the whole, for as long as she could remember, St. Christopher's halls often thundered with the clang of swords and the banging of hammers, rather than whispered prayers. There were always repairs to be done and the sisters used the men they were given to fix just about everything. The soldiers didn't mind. There was naught else for them to do but practice, and bicker, and share stories about their loved ones. Perhaps in another place Davina would have cherished the clamor around her, but most of the time such sounds of normalcy had only served as a reminder of what could never be hers.

How she missed those sounds now. A tear slipped over her lashes at the memory of peering over the tower wall and seeing the men whose faces...voices...had become as familiar to her as her own, lifeless and silent. And the sisters...their screams from the burning chapel would haunt her for ten lifetimes.

Swiping her cheek, Davina fought to push away her

grief, but now her beloved silence only intensified her loneliness.

She noticed that Finn had caught up and was keeping his mount at an even pace beside them. She looked at him through misty eyes. He smiled softly and once again she imagined him to have flown down from Heaven, mayhap on wings he had hidden beneath his plaid.

"Where is your home?" she asked him quietly, desperate for a distraction from her sorrow.

"'Tis on Skye."

She had to smile at that. She'd been right about him all along.

"Is it very far?"

"Far enough," Rob answered from behind.

For what? Davina wondered. Far enough to hide and never be found? What did it matter? If he spoke the truth about everything so far, then he was really bringing her to Ayrshire and he would leave her. She should feel relieved, thankful that God had sent him to help her. But first she had to be certain that it was God who brought this man to her, and not her enemies.

"Tell me how you came to meet Edward."

He shifted behind her, a ripple of honed muscle that sent her troubled thoughts scattering to the four winds, only to be replaced by even darker ones when his hand settled on the curve of her hip. None of the English soldiers in her company had ever touched her with any intimacy. It was forbidden, though Edward had embraced her once. She did not know how to react to this half-dressed Highlander who held her as if she were his.

"Yer Captain Asher was fightin' fer his life. He told me

ye lived after he saw yer arrow in my hand, and asked me to save ye."

Davina smiled and closed her eyes, remembering her dearest friend. Even with his own death at hand, Edward sought to protect her.

"He told me yer enemies wanted ye to burn," Rob went on. In front of him, Davina's smiled faded. So, her captain *had* told him more than Rob had first admitted. What else did he know?

"Did he guard ye under King Charles's orders?"

"No," she told him truthfully.

"Did he guard ye because he was in love with ye, then?"

All of her caution could not have prepared her for Finn's query. Not knowing how to answer, she turned to him and knew by the abashed expression on his face that Rob was staring at him also.

"He did love me," she revealed, desiring to lie as little as possible. He was going to tell her that night by her door, but he never had the chance. Perhaps it was better that he'd gone home to God not knowing that she did not feel the same as he did. "He was a good man and one that I shall never forget."

"A captain has no authority to keep his entire regiment holed up at an abbey to protect a lass whether he loves her or no'," Rob told them both with a bit of a bite in his words. Davina felt him inhale deeply, as if he was trying to rein in whatever it was he was feeling. "I've let ye evade my questions long enough. I would know the truth of all this now, Davina."

He *was* angry. He wanted answers and he wasn't getting them. Still, her name on his lips sounded tender, oddly profound. How long had it been since a man had spoken it? The last was Captain Geoffries when he was leaving her. Before that, mayhap her father...

"If I'm to bring war to my clan fer aidin' ye, I would know why."

At his words, Will, riding slightly ahead of them, turned on his mount and cast his cousin a curious look of his own. Rob ignored it and lowered his voice so that only she, and Finn riding so close, could hear.

"Tell me why ye were cloistered away as if fergotten, but protected like a queen?"

As if forgotten. His words dug deep into the core of Davina's sorrow. Her true family knew she existed, and though a legion of the king's best men had helped raise her, the truth remained that she'd been abandoned. Her childhood was lonely, and her future, if she lived to see it, was crowded with cold smiles and false affection.

But she had also been given so much by God, sisters who loved her and men who had given their lives for her. She had no right to mumble and complain about things not meant to be hers, and she never did. But being in this man's arms, riding with his men across heather-lined hills, as if she were naught but a Highland lass returning home with her husband, stirred her longings more than ever before.

"What have ye to do with the king, Davina? Why does Argyll or Monmouth want ye dead?"

She turned to him, wanting him to see the truth in her eyes, and to look for it in his.

"Do you truly not know, Rob MacGregor?"

"Nae lass, I truly dinna' know."

His answer didn't make her as happy as she'd hoped it would. If he didn't know, then there was still time to keep him out of this—and her selfish longings in check. She could never belong to him, or any man like him. The life she dreamed of was simply that—a dream. She'd known it since she was a child and she wasn't about to awaken that lonely little girl.

"Then please understand," she said, turning forward between his thighs. "I would prefer you know nothing more. I am grateful for your aid and ask no more of you but your release when we reach Courlochcraig."

He didn't move behind her. In fact, Davina was sure he didn't breathe. Then, with a snap of his reins that urged his mount to move faster, he straightened away from her ear and growled. "As ye wish."

Every moment spent between them in silence echoed like a drum in Rob's ears. Whatever secrets Davina knew, she'd made it clear that she was not going to tell them to him. He knew she couldn't be happy about going to another convent, one without an army, but she would rather see him off than tell him the truth. He would have found such courage admirable if he wasn't so offended. At the campsite, he'd found it endearing that she lied to him for his "safety." But the truth was always right there in her eyes—always present when she spoke to him. She didn't trust him, even though he'd risked his life to save her. He was surprised that it should prick his anger so. She had no reason to trust him, but he wanted her to.

Still, how could she when he was delivering her to more nuns instead of taking her to the only place she would be truly safe? Hell, he couldn't bring her to Camlochlin. Doing so would likely lead her enemies there.

He gritted his teeth against the bracing wind and all

the uncertainties roiling within him. He knew what he should do—drop her off and get the hell away from her before there was an army on his arse. But how could he run and still claim the right to be called Chief someday? Fleeing from the unknown was cowardly. But more than that, Rob didn't want to leave her. The thought of it, her suggestion of it, made him want to wrap her in his plaid and head for Camlochlin.

Had Asher loved her? God help the man if he had, for losing one's heart to this lass would cost a man much. Did she love him in return?

Why the hell should he care? The man was dead, after all. Besides that, even if two armies hadn't fought over her—even if she hadn't promised her life to God—which he now believed she had—the last thing Rob needed in his life right now was a lass. He worked all day with his father and practiced his fighting skills at night. He had no time for wooing, and even less inclination to do so. But damn him, the way her expression softened with affection when she spoke of the captain made Rob's jaw clench. Jealousy was a useless emotion and one that Rob had never wasted his time on. He might as well be jealous of God for binding Davina to Him. May the Almighty strike him dead if he ever became *that* pathetic.

Asher was a fool to fall in love with her, and had paid the price for it. Rob would not make the same error.

Chapter Eight

The cross above the bell tower of Courlochcraig Abbey rose high over the old town of Ayr, casting shadows on the five faces looking up at it.

Rob surveyed the perimeter carefully while Colin dismounted and swung open the heavy iron gate that barred their entrance. The Abbey sat perched atop an old motte and bailey foundation, probably built in the days before the Norman invasion. From the vantage point along the tower, one could see in every direction, from the majestic peaks of Arran to the Mull of Kintyre behind. There were few trees to obscure the presence of an enemy, and the Auld Brig, being the main crossing into the port town, was well in sight. He had no army, but at least he could see one coming for leagues.

"Rob?"

He cut his sharp gaze to his brother standing beside the gate, waiting for him to bring Davina through.

"The Abbess approaches." Colin gestured toward a tall, thin woman exiting the convent with four other nuns hurrying to keep up. All were garbed from foot to crown in gray and white habit, arms folded across their waists, hands tucked into their wide sleeves.

Women, Rob reminded himself glumly. Who would protect them if Davina's enemies found her here?

"Good day, Mother," Colin greeted with a reverential bow.

The Abbess stepped past the young Highlander without a glance in his direction. Her gray eyes were as pale and as cool as the stone walls behind her, and they were fixed on Davina while Rob helped her dismount. Encased in stiff white wool, the Abbess's thin face remained impassive while her gaze skimmed Davina's robes, her unveiled head, and her hand clutching the arm of the giant Highlander beside her. Her eyes lingered on their touch long enough for Davina to let him go.

"Lady Montgomery," the Abbess said without even the subtlest shift in her tone to suggest she knew Davina in any way other than that she was already expecting her.

At the mention of her surname, Rob felt Davina go rigid at his side before she nodded her head. He looked down at her in time to catch the cautious glance she cast the Abbess.

"Where is Captain Asher?" the Abbess asked, turning her attention to Rob for the first time and validating his first assumption. "I was under the belief that he would be escorting my guest to Courlochcraig."

"St. Christopher's was attacked, Reverend Mother. Captain Asher has perished."

Only a hint of the pain he had just caused her flashed across her eyes before she lowered them to the ground. "And the sisters?"

"I regret to inform ye that they have also perished." Rob gentled his voice for Davina's sake, as well as the Abbess's.

The Abbess crossed herself, paused, most likely in prayer, and then raised her dried gaze to Rob's. "Who are you?"

"I am Robert MacGregor of the clan MacGregor. These men are—"

He did not get the chance to finish his introduction. The Abbess, holding up her palm, stopped him. "MacGregors. God be with us." If she meant to insult them further, she must have decided to do so later, for her face finally softened when she reached for Davina. "Come inside, child. You will find refuge here." She gathered Davina in her arms then turned to Rob. "There is food and drink inside. You and your men may take your rest before you tell me how she came into your possession."

The Abbess had been expecting Davina, Rob thought as he took up his steps behind the women. Asher or the Abbess at St. Christopher's must have penned her a missive. That would mean they knew her enemies were on the way. But how could they have known, and why hadn't they all fled before it was too late? Who the hell was Davina Montgomery that she should be protected by not only the Royal army, but by the Church as well? Whatever the answers were, she was in great danger. How could he leave her here, defenseless? When she turned to look at him over her shoulder, as if to make certain he was still with her, Rob knew he wasn't going anywhere.

Captain Edward Asher was a resourceful man. If Davina was still alive, he had to find her before Gilles did. And the Admiral *would* find her...eventually. Finally exposed to the world, people were going to take notice of Davina Montgomery. They would question why a woman of such radiance was clothed in nun's robes. Though she would never tell the world her secrets, she was kind and outgoing, and those who met her would remember her, mayhap enough to describe for Gilles, should he question them.

Edward had to find her. He had to warn her—and MacGregor if she was with him—that her enemies did not think her dead and were now, in fact, hunting her.

He couldn't do that on foot, and since the stable as well as the Abbey had been burned to the ground, he had to find a horse and a stream to cleanse himself of the blood of battle before he went searching through towns and villages for her.

It didn't take him long to find both when he came upon a small bothy nestled within a stand of trees. The well provided fresh water, and the steed tethered to the low front gate would provide speed. He washed quickly, filling the well's bucket and dunking his head twice. He leaped upon the horse just as the door of the bothy swung open. The shouting man rushing through it gave Edward pause only long enough to slip the heavy ring from his left index finger and toss it to the tenant.

"Payment for your horse, good man."

He was not worthy to wear the royal signet anyway. Everyone at the Abbey was dead. His men...the sisters. He prayed Davina would forgive him. He prayed for just one more chance to prove his devotion to her.

Chapter Nine

———

ℛob leaned his shoulder against the doorway of the church. It was dark inside save for the soft amber glow of a few dozen tallow wax candles dancing along the polished pews. He didn't need light to tell him Davina was here. Her whispered prayers echoed like harp strings beneath the cherubim-painted ceiling.

It had been three days since they'd arrived at Courlochcraig. Three days longer than Rob had meant to stay. The Reverend Mother had insisted he and his party depart the night they'd arrived, especially after two young novices caught sight of them and giggled all through supper. When Rob refused to go until he was certain they had not been followed, it was Will who'd argued with him first, insisting that if he was forced to stay in a convent for a prolonged amount of time, he could not be held responsible for any of the sisters' broken vows. His warning nearly caused the Abbess to lose her composure, and Rob, the good graces of God.

Arguing with a Reverend Mother was a sin, to be sure, but Rob had made up his mind and only an act of God would change it. In the meantime, he promised to keep his cousin under control. The sisters, he'd told the Abbess, were her responsibility. She wasn't pleased, but she had ceased arguing with him. She'd also refused to enlighten him about Davina, claiming she knew as little as he. When he asked how she recognized Davina when she saw her, the Abbess told him she had seen Davina once when she visited St. Christopher's on retreat many years ago, and that the child was difficult to forget. As was the woman, Rob had thought silently and let the matter drop. He would get no answers, even if the Abbess knew them.

A movement along the church pews caught his eye now and he watched while Davina crossed herself and turned away from the altar.

He was becoming familiar with her habits. She prayed twice a day in the church, once in the morning with the other sisters, and after supper, alone. In between, she mended robes, tended the garden, chopped vegetables, and glanced at him often.

At first, Rob had tried to pretend he wasn't watching her for any other purpose than to keep her in his line of vision should Colin or Finn call from the bell tower that horsemen were approaching. But after the first day, he could no longer deny that there were other, far more perilous reasons why he couldn't keep his eyes off her. The way she drew in one corner of her lower lip, giving her full attention—or seeming to—to her sewing, made him long to feel those lips pressed to his. The way her gaze drifted off to another place, capturing the sunlight in vivid hues of blue and dazzling silver—despite the deep sadness that haunted them—drew him to move nearer, to look closer and find a way to comfort her. Her ethereal beauty mesmerized him, but it was the way she frequently sought him out, as if to convince herself that he had not left her, that tempted him to pull her into his arms and swear his life to her safety. She barely spoke to him in the evenings while she dressed his wound in the company of the other nuns. She did not smile when their eyes met across a table or a bed of geraniums. She had lost much, and soon she would lose him too. They both knew it. He could not remain here with her forever, though the thought was not an unpleasant one, and he would not jeopardize the lives of everyone at Camlochlin by bringing her there. Still, he could not bring himself to leave her yet. Not yet.

When Davina saw him in the doorway, she paused in her footsteps for a moment. Caught between shadows and light, she looked like a vision come to life from a dying man's dreams. Rob swallowed, then pushed off the archway and waited for her to reach him.

"Do you fear for my safety even here?" she asked in that dulcet voice he was growing so accustomed to hearing. It wasn't that she spoke often, but rather that she didn't that made Rob incline his ear whenever she spoke to anyone.

"God has assigned me to the task."

"So it would seem." She tilted her head up and before he could guard himself against it, she smiled at him.

Rob was certain he heard the thrashing of his heart reverberating through the silence. He had the urge to pluck the thin veil that covered her silvery blond tresses from her head—a reminder that she belonged to another. One who knew all her secrets, all her fears, strengths, and desires. One she spoke to each day, and trusted beyond what she was willing to offer anyone else.

Before he could stop himself, he reached out and swept

his fingers along her wrist. A forbidden touch, and more so here in her betrothed's house.

She moved closer as if he had pulled her to him. "What do you pray for, Robert MacGregor?"

"My clan," he told her and then, because he'd never had time to consider the woman he would choose to spend the rest of his days with until he met the one he could never have, he folded his hands behind his back and looked away. "And ye."

"You have my thanks for that." She continued to muddle his good senses when she laid her palm on his arm. "But even God does not expect you to remain here, forgetting your duties to your family."

She was right, of course. He should leave her and return to his kin, where he belonged. "I have no' fergotten my duties." He returned his gaze to hers and marveled at the innocence in her eyes after all she had seen, and the strength in them to send away her only protection. "I am torn by them."

"All the more reason to go," she said, moving away to return to where he had found her.

Rob watched her sit and then followed her, slipping into the pew behind her. "Why did ye no' leave St. Christopher's when ye knew yer enemies were comin'?" He wanted the truth from her on this, at least.

She shrugged her shoulders beneath her robes. "We weren't certain they were coming. The sisters would not have left, and I could not abandon them."

Behind her, Rob moved forward slightly to inhale the sweet fragrance of her hair beneath her veil. "Does a wee lass raised in a convent have more courage than a man raised fer battle, then?"

"Oh, no, I didn't mean to imply that!" She swung around and almost bumped noses with him before he shifted back. "I don't doubt that you are courageous. But I am not your charge. There is no reason to put your life in jeopardy for me."

There were more reasons than Rob cared to admit to her . . . or to himself. He leaned back instead and folded his arms across his chest. "My life is no' in jeopardy, Davina. 'Tis likely that the men who wanted ye dead think ye perished in the fire. They will no' look fer ye here."

"Then why have you ordered both Colin and Finn to keep watch from the bell tower, and why is Will stationed at the gate day and night?"

Rob bit down on his jaw, not liking how quickly she caught the contradiction and called him on it.

"'Tis my nature to be vigilant."

"You're brooding again."

He shot her a dark glance. "Woman, I dinna' brood."

"Sulk?"

"Same thing," he mumbled under his breath.

She shrugged, turning forward in her seat. "Pout, then."

Rob stared at the back of her veiled head. Did she jest with him? If so, 'twas the first time he'd ever seen this side of her. He wasn't certain he liked her teasing him, but it was far better than accusing him in earnest of being sour. When she slanted her gaze over her shoulder and flashed him a smile, he decided that he could live with some teasing.

"Is the Abbess aware that ye're no' as innocent as ye look?"

She turned to face him again with laughter in her eyes

and held her finger to her mouth. "I'll have penance for a se'nnight."

"And 'twill be well deserved."

Against the candlelight, her eyes gleamed with mischief, and her mouth was wide with a smile so bonnie Rob had no trouble understanding why God had chosen her as His own. What had caused this change in her? Had God heard her prayers and lifted her grief? Rob had thought he might never see her smile, never hear her laughter. But here it was, as unexpected as the summer rain and just as refreshing.

"Had I known how sensitive Highlanders were, I would have held my tongue."

He smiled. "As sharp as it is, lass, I fear 'twould have cut through yer lips."

Davina looked pleasantly surprised. Rob realized an instant later that it was part of the sting when she sweetly said, "You're not as thick-skulled as I first thought."

Narrowing his eyes on her, he shook his head. "Och, lass, ye're as ruthless as Mairi."

"Your sister," Davina said, resting her arm on the back of the pew and giving him her full attention. "The one who cannot keep silent else she would have found a husband by now?"

Rob nodded, a bit surprised that she remembered their talk of Mairi so clearly. "She is venomous."

"But you love her."

"Aye, I love her.

Her smile turned wistful. "Tell me about your family," she asked, tucking her hand under her chin and getting more comfortable for the tale.

An hour later Davina knew more about the MacGregors

of Skye than they probably did. She enjoyed hearing about Maggie the most, which pleased Rob, since his aunt held a special place in his heart. When he told her how his father had saved his mother from the MacColls and then carried her home to Camlochlin, she sighed with delight, making Rob want to prove to her that he was as valiant as his sire.

"Those were dangerous times fer my parents. My mother is a Campbell, and—"

"A Campbell?" Davina cut him off, that wary glint returning to her eyes. "Then the Earl of Argyll is your kin. Why did you not tell me this sooner?"

"Because I dinna' consider him kin," Rob explained in a quiet voice. "My Uncle Robert was the eleventh Earl, but he was killed almost a decade ago by the Fergussons. He died childless and the title went to Archibald. I dinna' know the exiled earl, nor do I want to. Ye have nothin' to fear from me, Davina. I swear it."

She nodded, but didn't look entirely convinced. "But your uncle was a Protestant. All Campbells strongly oppose royal authority and legitimate succession—especially when succession to the throne involves a Catholic monarch."

"And what does that have to do with ye?"

"Nothing," she hastened to tell him. "It has nothing to do with me, save that I support my king and his beliefs. Your family does not support the Protestants, do they?"

"Nae," Rob assured her, curious of her keen knowledge of things no other lass he knew would care one whit about. "We are Catholic."

Her taut features relaxed a bit. "That is good to know."

Why, he wanted to ask her? Why was it good to know? And what had driven her to learn so much about the workings of the kingdom—and the beliefs of the men who controlled it? Was it her faith, under the threat of becoming a crime, or her new king that fanned the passion in her eyes when she spoke of either one? But he did not ask. It no longer mattered to Rob *why* men were out to kill her, only that they were. He would make certain they did not succeed.

"You're brooding again."

He blinked, realizing when his brows relaxed that he was. Well, he had his reasons, and looking at her was one of them.

"'Tis God."

She gave him a startled, questioning look, tilting her head to follow him as he rose to his feet. "What do you mean?"

Rob glanced at the huge cross at the altar, then at the veil covering her glorious mantle. "He has chosen a most pathetic man to look after ye."

Chapter Ten

$\mathcal{R}$ob stepped out of the church and into the Abbess. He knew by her rigid posture and cool regard that she was angry. He looked around for Will, suspecting that his cousin was the cause. Rob hadn't missed the way the young novice Elaine had blushed and then granted Will her most radiant smile this morn while he was chopping wood.

"Robert MacGregor, I do not pretend to know or understand the Highland way of life, if your mothers do not bother with teaching their sons to…" Her sermon came to an abrupt halt when she spotted Davina exiting the dark church behind him. Her eyes went from wide with surprise to glacial when she slid them back to Rob. She sized him up from his dusty skins around his calves to his broad, plaid-draped shoulders, then pulled a small cloth from the folds of her sleeve and patted her cheek with it. "You do understand that she is a daughter of the Lord, do you not?"

"I assure ye, I do." Rob couldn't help but glare right back at her, though he knew he should be repentant for the thoughts which plagued him about Davina Montgomery.

"Mother"—Davina rushed forward to deny the

Abbess's obvious unspoken accusation—"we were merely speaking of..."

Colin's shout from the bell tower put an end to the remainder of her words. "Rob, a rider approaches! I'm coming down!"

"Stay there!" Rob roared up at him.

The Abbess's face went deathly pale as Rob drew his heavy claymore from its sheath. "Get inside," he ordered over his shoulder to Davina. When he turned back to the Abbess, his tone warned her not to argue. "Ye, too." From the corner of his eye he saw Will exiting the stable, securing his plaid around his waist. A moment later, Elaine emerged, adjusting her veil.

Thankfully, the Abbess didn't see them. She was preoccupied with gaping at Rob and his sword. "You cannot mean to.... He may need aid."

"Ye'll no' give him entry."

"It is my service to God to do so," she argued, taking a step back when he pulled Davina forward, toward the Abbey doors.

"No' today," Rob said, pushing Davina inside. He nodded to Will, already on his way toward the gate, bow and arrow in hand.

"No!" the Abbess shouted but then fell silent, her hands clutched at the cross dangling from her neck as Will cocked his bow, aimed, and let his arrow fly.

"Dear God, you killed him!" The Abbess sprang forward, searching the road beyond the gate for the dead visitor.

Knowing that Will had aimed at the rider's feet and not his vital organs, Rob yanked her out of potential firing range and pushed her against the stone outer wall with him.

"Hold your fire!"

At the sound of the rider's voice, startled but strong, Rob flashed a smile at the Reverend Mother. "I was taught to question a man before killin' him. Most of the time."

She blinked at him, relief and anger vying for preeminence within.

Rob didn't wait to see which she would offer him. "State yer business here." His voice boomed across the distance that separated them from their possible enemy.

"I come on the king's business," the rider shouted back. "I am Captain Edward Asher of the Sixth Cavalry Royal division."

Impossible. Rob released the Abbess and took a cautious step away from the wall to get a better look at the man. Across the length of the gate, Will plucked another arrow from its quiver. Asher was dead. 'Twas a trap. Some of the Duke's men from St. Christopher's must have followed them here. For a brief moment Rob enjoyed the satisfaction of knowing he'd been correct to stay at the Abbey. But his brother was here, and so was Finn, waiting in the bell tower—at least, they'd better be. How many men were out there? Mayhap, he and Will could kill ten or so before the soldiers reached the gate. But Colin would not stay hidden for long.

Readying his claymore, Rob motioned to his cousin. They had to kill as many as they could before the lads arrived. He watched Will pull his bowstring and take aim. This time, Will would not intentionally miss. They had all been trained well, but no one could shoot as accurately or as quickly as Will.

A woman's shout from behind him just before Will fired his arrow spun Rob on his heels. When he saw

Davina running toward the iron gate, his blood ran cold. Whoever was outside could shoot through the bars and kill her without even getting close. Rob ran toward her, knowing that if the rider had a pistol or an arrow, he would never reach her in time.

"Edward!" she shouted again, ignoring Will to her left when he dropped his bow and lunged for her.

Rob reached her first and closing his arms around her, threw them both to the ground. Davina landed askew atop him. When she tried, unsuccessfully, to break free of his hold, she looked down at him, every misgiving she'd felt from the start clearly etched on her face.

"You lied to me."

Rob opened his mouth to deny her charge, but another voice at the gate reached her ear first.

"Lady Montgomery! Thank God I have found you! MacGregor, is that you?"

It was Asher. He wasn't dead, and Davina's eyes told Rob exactly what she thought of him. He hadn't only lied to her, he'd left her only friend to die alone in the ashes.

"Let me go," she demanded coolly.

Rob did as she asked and gained his feet. Davina and the Abbess had already opened the gate by the time he reached them. He watched in silence as Asher leaped from his horse and seemed about to drop to one knee before her. He might have if Davina hadn't pulled him into her arms.

The captain lived, but how? He'd barely had strength to hold up his sword when Rob had left him. Rob hadn't looked for survivors when he rode out of the courtyard with Davina. His only thought had been to get her away safely. He'd just assumed...

"Asher, I thought ye perished," he said, not really

knowing what else to say. An apology would not be enough.

The captain looked up from Davina's tear-stained face. "I almost did, but not even death can keep me from her." He smiled at Rob before his face disappeared once again in the crook of Davina's neck. Her hero had been returned to her, and Davina clung to him as if he was all she needed to survive.

Rob did not smile back.

The joy of seeing Edward again was so overwhelming that Davina almost forgot about the man behind her. But she couldn't forget. Rob had lied to her. Although her wary heart resisted, she had come to like him. God help her, it was more than that. She was attracted to him, beguiled by the bold confidence in his gaze and in his step, drawn to the passion he had for his family. Not to mention the strange flutters he produced when he looked at her. And he looked at her often. Whether she was pulling weeds in the garden or helping the Abbess prepare supper, his eyes were always on her—on her hair, her face, her waist. She'd even caught him bending around his chair at the supper table to watch the sway of her hips while she served. As decadent as it might be, she liked it.

But he'd let her believe Edward was dead. He had not told her that Archibald Campbell, Earl of Argyll, was his relative. What else had he been untruthful about? And why? Her mind raced with a thousand uncertainties and she clung to the only certain thing she knew. Edward.

"We should get inside the Abbey," Rob said, pulling on her sleeve. "He could have been followed."

"Yes," Edward agreed, looking over his shoulder. "They are but several days away."

Davina looked up at him, her heart crashing in her chest. Rob stepped closer. "Who, and how many?"

"Admiral Gilles and roughly forty of his men from the Dutch fleet," Edward said, turning back to Rob. "He isn't certain the lady is dead, and until he is—"

Rob hauled them both toward the Abbey and shouted up to Colin and Finn to keep their eyes open. Davina heard him barking orders to Will to get his arse indoors as Edward ushered her and the Abbess inside.

The moment the doors were shut and bolted, Rob took command like a general on the battlefield. The Abbess was to collect her most skilled healers and bring them to the Refectory where Captain Asher would be waiting for refreshment and to have his wounds tended. In her happiness to see him, Davina hadn't looked at his blood-stained clothes.

"Thank you for saving her," Edward said, following Davina down the hall.

When Rob didn't give a response, Davina turned to look at him. He was staring at her, and if he'd saved her with the intention of causing her harm, it was nowhere in his steady gaze.

"I only wish that I could have done so myself."

"Oh, Edward." She stopped and clutched his hands in hers. "You're alive," she said, bringing his hands to her cheek. "That is more than I could have ever hoped for. However did you manage to escape?"

"Aye," Rob said, pausing behind them while they embraced yet again. "When I met ye, ye had barely a breath left in yer body."

Was there a challenge in his voice? An accusation? Ridiculous, Davina thought, glaring at him over Edward's shoulder. She should be questioning *him*!

"I was thrown from my horse shortly after you left, MacGregor." If Edward heard the suspicion in Rob's grave tone, he took no offense to it. Of course, he wouldn't. Edward was no fool. Getting a better look at him now, Davina could see clearly that he was in no condition to fight. Especially not with a man who stood at least two heads taller than he, a man who looked fit and ready to face whatever army appeared at the gate with just himself and the skilled, watchful archer at his side.

"Fortunately," Edward continued, resuming the short trek to the Refectory with Davina leading him by the hand, "I fell into a dead sleep and did not awaken until sometime after Admiral Gilles arrived with his men." He told them what had happened after that, everything he'd heard, how he'd lain in the ashes as if dead until they were gone. "I knew when they hadn't found her body that you had to have saved her."

"How did ye find us?" Davina heard Rob ask over her shoulder as they entered the dining hall. "I was careful aboot leavin' tracks."

"No tracks," Edward sighed as he fell into a chair and closed his eyes. "I suspected you would head north and Courlochcraig was on the way." He opened his eyes and moved to stop her when Davina dropped to her knees to remove his boots. She quieted him with a glance in Rob's direction. "I needed to stop for some food and rest and I knew the Abbess would not turn me away." With his gaze still fastened lovingly on Davina, he lifted his fingers toward a tendril of hair that had escaped her veil. "God led me here. He wanted me to find you, my lady."

"Tell me aboot Gilles." The sharp edge in Rob's voice vanquished the tender smile Davina was about to bestow on her dearest friend, and halted the hand reaching for her.

"He is the Duke of Monmouth's Admiral." They all turned toward the Abbess, who had entered the Refectory carrying a cup in one hand and a small tray of food in the other. "A most unpleasant man."

"So, 'tis Monmouth who sent him and no' Argyll," Rob said.

"Mayhap, mayhap not." The Abbess shrugged her shoulders. "Both men have spent the last number of years in Holland. Only God knows who holds Gilles's allegiance."

"Is deception no' frowned upon by yer Husband, Reverend Mother?" Rob's gaze cooled on her. "What more d'ye know aboot this that ye refuse to tell me?"

"Well," the Abbess said evenly while she handed Edward his cup. "Since entering this room, I know that Admiral Gilles is the one guilty of the slaughter of my sisters. But if you mean to question me more than you already have about *why* the Abbey was attacked, my answer will be the same."

There was nothing amiable in Rob's slow smile before he turned his attention back to Edward and waited.

"I met the Admiral only once," Edward told him, "and then prayed I never would again. He is merciless . . . and determined."

"Why do these men want her dead?"

Edward shook his head and averted his gaze when Rob moved around the table toward him. "I don't know."

"Ye think me a fool to believe that, Asher?"

"No," Edward sighed deeply in his seat and set his sorrowful gaze on Davina. "But I risk her life by telling you, and I will not do that. I will tell you this though: we cannot remain here. He *will* find her."

"Edward," Davina told him softly, covering his hand with hers as if he were the one who needed comfort from the truth. "There is nowhere else to go."

The Refectory grew silent, save for the soft footfalls of four young sisters who had come to tend to the captain. Davina thought she heard Rob swear a muttered oath that was surely going to earn him penance under the Reverend Mother's watchful eye later. She turned to him, still on her knees, and found him scowling worse than when he first saw her in her veil.

That is, until he looked at her and his taut, dark features went a bit soft. "Aye, there is."

She knew instantly where he meant to take her, and part of her wanted to go. The Isle of Skye. Mayhap, if its name counted for anything, it existed in the heavens—a place this terrible Admiral Gilles would never dare go. But could Robert MacGregor be trusted with her life? He'd let her believe Edward was dead. Then again, Edward had told them he was down and Davina couldn't really blame Rob for not checking before they raced away from St. Christopher's. No, he was not in league with her enemies, and thinking on all he had done for her so far made her feel foolish for considering it.

"I will not put your home in danger," she said calmly, though refusing the aid of such a man as he was among the most difficult things she had ever had to do. Wishing he could remain with her at Courlochcraig while knowing in her heart that there could never be anything between them was one thing; living with him on his own land, in his care for as long as she needed to be was another. "I refuse to..."

"Will." He turned to his cousin as if she hadn't spoken. "Fetch the lads; we're goin' home."

"Tonight?" Davina sprang to her feet, casting Edward a nervous glance. "Even if I agree to this, Captain Asher cannot travel again so soon."

"Ye have nae say in it," Rob said brusquely, meeting her gaze for just a moment—and a moment was all it took to convince her that arguing would be fruitless. "I've nae intention on makin' Captain Asher travel tonight. When he is able, he can return to England and—"

"Return to England alone?" she cut him off, her eyes wide with disbelief.

"Aye." Rob nodded, already seeking out the Abbess's attention. "We'll need provisions," he began with a pitch in his voice that demanded obedience. "Anything ye can spare will be appreciated. Also, do any of yer sisters have an extra kirtle the lass could wear fer the journey? Gilles is lookin' fer a novice and she'll stand oot less to anyone we encounter on the road withoot her robes." He cut his gaze to Davina next. "That will have to stay here too." He pointed to her veil.

Still reeling at the idea that he intended for Edward to remain behind, Davina missed the satisfaction in the slight curl of his lips when he spoke of her veil.

"I'm not leaving without Captain Asher." She squared her shoulders and tilted her jaw to appear less intimidated when Rob stared at her. She liked that he could make quick decisions and take command over all, even the

Abbess, with the authority of a born leader. Somehow, it made being around him feel safer. But she wasn't about to cower to him, big, brooding Highlander or not. "You cannot expect him to travel all the way to England alone. Look at him! He will be attacked on the road before he reaches the border!"

"Who's going to England alone?"

Davina turned to see Finn entering the hall with Colin at his side, the latter already eyeing Edward caustically. Will hung back, peeling the skin from an apple he'd pilfered somewhere along the way back down to the Refectory.

"No one is, Finn," she replied, returning her unwavering gaze to Rob. "He is my friend."

Rob met the challenge in her eyes with a determined stare of his own. "He's an English soldier, Davina. He willna' be welcome at my home."

"My brother is an English soldier, Rob," Finn pointed out, then grew silent when Rob turned to pin him with an incredulous glare.

"That's different," Colin said, making his way across the room to Edward. "Connor is kin." When he reached the captain, he looked him over the way a cat might size up a mouse before pouncing on it. "Why is he still in possession of his sword?"

"Ease off, cousin," Will called out, leaning his hip against the table and biting into his apple. "He's no' a Covenanter." He paused in his chewing and cut his gray gaze to Asher. "Are ye?"

"No, I am not," Edward told him, looking slightly uneasy around the four north men all staring at him now.

Will was the first to smile at him, or maybe, Davina

corrected herself, it was Sister Elaine standing just behind Edward who was the recipient of his favor, for she blushed a full two shades darker.

"Dinna' mind young Colin, Captain," the rascal Will sang. "He's a wee bit bloodthirsty when it comes to his enemies. Much like his faither—who ye'll be meetin' soon enough if ye come wi' us."

"He's stayin'," Rob ground out and turned to leave. "And we're wastin' time."

Davina looked around at the others for aid, but no one had the boldness to stop him. Not even the Reverend Mother. It blistered Davina's nerves. Who did he think he was, ordering a captain of the king's Royal Army about as if he was nothing but a peasant? Dismissing everything she said as if she wasn't even there! Well, she was tired of being invisible. This meant too much to her. She'd lost everything, everyone who mattered in her life. But God brought Edward back to her, and she wasn't about to lose him again.

"I was wrong about you, MacGregor," she called out, following him out of the Refectory. "I thought you could keep me safe, but I was wrong." When he pivoted around slowly, she gathered her courage and strode right up to him.

"What do you think will happen if Edward is captured by Admiral Gilles? Hmmm? How long can any man hold out if he is tortured? How long do you think it will take Gilles to find out where the MacGregors make their home? His men burned nuns alive. Do you think he will not kill every MacGregor he finds until he finds you?"

She had his ear now and for a moment he looked as though he might give in. She plunged ahead. "And even

if Edward makes it to England, do you expect him to lie
to his king about what happened to me? It will only be a
matter of time before the king's army enters Skye."

"Why? Why will he come fer ye?"

"I cannot tell you. I will not."

"Then Asher stays."

Oh, she fumed, staring at him, *blackmail was quite unat-
tractive.* "Very well, I will tell you! King Charles promised
me to a man who—Where are you going?" she demanded
when he began to turn away from her. "I was not finished.
When he died, he commanded his brother James to—"

"I dinna' believe ye, Davina."

"What do you mean you don't believe me?" She chased
after him as he took up his steps. Damnation, why did she
ever bother to lie when she was so poor at it? "Rob"—she
reached for his sleeve and tugged it—"it doesn't matter
what you believe. Edward cannot go back. He is part of
this now."

He stopped, and when he shook his head, she balled
her fists at her sides. He simply couldn't be this stubborn!

"I'll no' bring an English soldier to Camlochlin. 'Tis
bad enough I'm bringin' *ye.*"

"Well, I'll remedy that for you right now!" she promised through clenched teeth. No man had ever made her
this angry and she needed to get away from him before
she would have to spend a fortnight in confession. "You
have my thanks for bringing me this far," she said, turning on her heel, "but I'm staying with Ed—"

His fingers closing around her wrist and yanking her
back to him put a quick end to her tirade. Pressed against
his hard chest and looking up into his even harder gaze,

she found it difficult to breathe, let alone speak when he plucked her veil from her head and let it drop to the floor.

"Ye're stayin' with me, lass." His mouth descended on hers like a brand, hot and possessive, filling her senses with the taste, the feel, and the scent of him. He molded her to his unyielding muscles, kissing her until she went soft in his arms.

Davina had never been kissed before, and never in her life could she have imagined it to be like this. Her body felt like it was going up in flames, melting away all her defenses, sapping her will to defy him and tempting her to lift her fingers to his face and clutch him to her forever. For a part of her craved the safety of being held in his arms. Protected, not because of who she was, but for another reason entirely. But Robert MacGregor simply wanted her to comply with his decision, and he hoped that kissing her senseless would achieve his goal. As much as she would like to keep kissing him, she wasn't about to give up on Edward. So, with the last trace of strength she could muster, she gripped him by the shoulders and rammed her knee into his groin—just as Edward had taught her.

Stepping back, she watched Rob sink to his knees. "I would ask your forgiveness," she said, staring down at his bent head, her breath falling hard, "but you would likely refuse that as well."

Leaving him alone with his pain, she returned to the Refectory. Instead of going to Edward though, she sank into the nearest chair and prayed forgiveness for putting any part of her trust in a man, and for the strength to face the days ahead without Robert MacGregor at her side.

*   *   *

Rob wasn't aware that Davina had left him, and when he heard the soft chuckle above his head he thought her not only spirited as all hell, but heartless, as well.

"Dinna' get up, I beg ye." Thankfully—or, mayhap not—'twas Will. "This may be the only time in m' life that I get to see ye on yer knees. Let me take pleasure in it a moment longer."

Rob glanced up at him as he straightened, grimacing at his throbbing shoulder and his aching groin. "*May* be?"

"If ye stick around her, aye," Will laughed, offering no aid to his injured cousin. "I'm guessin' ye, bein' the stubborn bastard that ye are, didna' give in to her request to take her captain wi' us."

Rob didn't like the way his faults were being tossed about before him today, but he didn't like how Will called Asher "her captain" even more. But it was true, wasn't it? Hadn't she just chosen her captain over him? "Yer guessin' correct," he said stiffly, rubbing his lower abdomen one last time.

"So we're leavin' him then?" Will asked as Rob turned and headed for the Abbey doors.

"Aye, and she's stayin' with him."

Davina stood alone in the bell tower watching Rob and the others leave Courlochcraig. She did not weep, for tears did not bring people back, or keep them away. Why should Robert MacGregor return to her anyway? He had done so much for her already. She hadn't expected to stay with him. She had even wanted him to go before anyone else came for her. But then he kissed her. She'd nearly shattered to pieces in his arms, and it had nothing to do with force—although the raw strength of his embrace turned her bones to liquid. She didn't want him to leave her, and watching him ride across the bridge carved a lonely, dreadful hole in the pit of her stomach—worse than ever before.

Chapter Eleven

"We should not have left her." Finn, as he usually did, kept his horse close to Rob's while they rode out of Ayrshire.

"'Twas her choice," Rob told him for the third time since they had left the Abbey.

"But would she not have come if we'd taken Captain Asher with us?"

Rob closed his eyes and cursed himself, also for the third time, for not tying Finn to Angus's horse when he sent the old warrior off to England. The last thing he wanted to do right now was think of Davina. 'Twas better this way. He was wrong to offer to bring her home. Just because Asher had found them didn't mean Gilles would. Davina was not his kin. Hell, he had doubts about her even being Scottish. He had no place in her life, not only because her life belonged to God, but because it would likely get him and those he loved killed. Men were out to kill her and both she and her captain were too afraid to tell him why. He certainly wasn't fool enough to believe an entire Dutch fleet had come for her because of whom she was betrothed to—unless they sought to convert their faith. Hell, he'd been mad to even consider bringing her home! He hated leaving her, but she was not his charge, his wife, or his lover. He was quite certain she didn't like him and she sure as hell didn't trust him, especially after Asher showed up from the dead. So what duty did he have to her? None. She and Asher would be quite safe at Courlochcraig. Without an army on the front lawn to trumpet her presence, 'twas easier to hide, and there were dozens of old bolt holes in the Abbey if Gilles did come.

"Tell me again why we could not bring him?"

"He's English," Rob growled.

Finn cleared his throat and looked up from under his emerald cap. "Half of me is English."

"Aye," Rob said, "but that half of ye will never lead an army across the cliffs of Elgol to cause us harm or to change our customs and beliefs."

"And you believe Captain Asher will?"

"He might. I canna' take the chance."

Finn nodded, finally turning fully forward in his saddle, away from Courlochcraig, and hopefully putting an end to his queries.

It wasn't that Rob minded Finn's curious nature. The lad was eager to learn—and that was a good thing. 'Twould help him become a better warrior. But Graham Grant's youngest son wasn't as innocent as he looked. And right now, he knew perfectly well what he was doing. But Rob would not be persuaded to change his mind. The lass had chosen to stay with her captain.

"Rob?"

"What?" He sighed, readying himself for a journey plagued with Finn ever at his side.

"Connor is a captain in the King's Royal Army . . . and my Uncle Connor Stuart is a High Admiral, aye?"

Rob flicked him a lethal look, knowing what was coming. Aye, guileless his arse.

"Well, I was simply wondering... if my brother risked his life to find ye to warn ye of danger, would ye send him back to England knowing this same enemy he warned ye of would shoot him on sight?"

Och, hell, what was he to say to that? He would never have sent his friend away. He would not have left without him either. Rob's stomach churned with the shame that suddenly erupted toward his throat. "What the hell am I doin'?" he asked himself aloud. Instead of admiring Davina's loyalty—which was a virtue he valued above any other—he had let his anger over her affection for Asher control him. Anger he had no right to feel; control he abhorred losing to any emotion—especially jealousy. Damn him to Hades, how could he have let this happen? 'Twas why love was always last on his list of goals. It did horrendous things to men, like make them behave irrationally, recklessly. Not that he loved Davina Montgomery. He certainly was not *that* foolish, and it was high time he began behaving like it.

"Come on," Rob said, wheeling his stallion around.

"Where are we going?" Finn called out, already ten breaths behind. Without waiting for a reply, he kicked his mount's flanks and thundered forward, back toward the Abbey with Will and Colin close behind.

"Ye know perfectly well where we're goin', ye bastard," Rob told him when Finn caught up. "But if ye're so clever, how the hell could ye have let me leave her to the safety of bolt holes?"

"Well, I..." Finn's face went pale looking over Rob's shoulder. "Who in blazes are they?"

Rob turned to see and his blood went cold. A small group of men were riding over the bridge from the west, all wearing the same style of uniform that he'd seen on the men attacking St. Christopher's. They were heading for Courlochcraig. For Davina.

"Ride!" Rob shouted with a flash of his long blade. "We'll cut them off before they enter the town!"

He did not let himself worry if Colin and Finn could stand the battle. He was going to kill every soldier before his lads entered the fray. He drove his mount harder as images of what those soldiers would have done to Davina if he hadn't been there invaded his thoughts. Ignoring the soreness of his wounded shoulder, Rob snapped his reins faster, gaining speed until the outstretched sword in his hand sliced the air with a deadly whistle.

It wasn't long before he came up close behind the last man in the group. The soldier turned, and seeing the enormous claymore above his head, opened his mouth to scream a warning to his comrades. His head flew through the air, forever silenced. In the time it took the next rider to decide to stop and fight or try to outrun the blood-spattered assassin behind them, Rob's blade found its mark cleanly into his skull. A third soldier cried out a foreign word an instant before Rob's sword sank to the hilt in his belly. The others arced now, riding back toward him, their thin swords poised for battle. Yanking his blade free of his last victim's ribs, Rob turned to face the onslaught and gripped his thick hilt in both hands.

The first rider to reach him swung a savage blow to Rob's head, and then looked down in terror at the contents of his own belly spilling onto his horse. The next lost his arm as Rob swung left, then right, splitting yet another down the middle.

Will's sword sliced through bones like butter as he joined the melee, leaving two more dead. Colin's sword proved ten times more brutal in battle than in practice. Sunlight flashed across his blade as it descended upon the lead rider's shoulder, cutting through his neck and killing him instantly. The last soldier alive was locked in battle with Finn, their swords crossed above their heads. Rob took off toward them, his eyes blazing with the unholy flames of rage. But before he reached them, Finn's fist smashed into his opponent's face, throwing the soldier from his saddle. Almost without pause, Finn leaped from his horse and drove his sword deep into his victim's chest.

He looked up as Rob reached him, offered him a valiant smile, and then threw up.

Courlochcraig Abbey was eerily quiet when Rob and the others reached the gates. His hands, steady in battle, shook now. Those men would have killed her and possibly every other woman inside, and it would have been his fault. He'd left her. He'd let his emotions control him and it had almost cost Davina her life. Springing from his mount, he pushed open the heavy gates and sprinted to the doors.

"Davina!" he shouted, needing to see her, and not caring why.

The doors of the Abbey creaked open and he caught a glimpse of a gray veil, then Davina's long silvery blond mane as she pushed her way past the Abbess. For an eternal moment she stood in the doorframe, delicate and terrified as her large eyes widened on his bloodstained plaid. The need to hold her wrenched at his guts, but he'd ponder the danger of it later. He took a step toward her, but she reached him first, running the short distance that separated them and throwing herself into his arms.

Rob lifted her off her feet and held her close, worrying that he would never again find pleasure in anything else but the feel of her.

"I saw you," she breathed against his neck. "I saw what you did to them from the tower."

He wouldn't apologize for it, but she didn't sound like she expected him to. There was no censure in her voice, only gratitude.

He wanted to smile at her, but his eyes caught Asher exiting the Abbey, bandaged but moving swiftly. "We must leave. Now. I must bring her home. 'Tis the only place she will be safe."

"Gilles's men?" the captain asked him, his eyes settling on Davina, still clutched in Rob's arms.

Rob nodded as he set her back on her feet. Almost on reflex he reached out, closing his hand around her much smaller one.

"How many?"

"Ten," Rob answered the captain. "We spotted them ridin' toward Ayrshire and cut them off."

"Rob killed six of them himself," Finn informed them with a measure of pride squaring his shoulders and his clear green eyes set on Davina.

"I would see their bodies."

"That willna' be possible, Asher," Rob told him. "We tossed them into the River Ayr, along with their saddles, and drove their horses off. None wore the trappins' of

Admiral, so I must assume Gilles was no' among them. He will likely look fer them and I didna' want him to find them here."

"Brutal *and* clever." Asher sized him up with a hint of trepidation in his eyes that pricked at Rob's instincts. Why should the captain fear him? Just as quickly as it appeared, though, it was gone and replaced with a genuine smile of gratitude. "I owe you my life once again, MacGregor."

"As do I," Davina said softly, dragging Rob's gaze back to her.

For the first time in his life, the heavy responsibilities of Rob's purpose felt more like a great gift. The endless hours of practicing in the fields with his father and other seasoned warriors like Brodie and Angus MacGregor, Jamie Grant, and his brother Graham, were, at this moment, worth every wound. Rob wanted to protect this lass from anything that would cause her harm, and it was satisfying to know he could. "God has assigned me to the task."

She smiled at him, oblivious to how it smote his heart. "So it would seem."

"This is all verra touchin'," Will drawled from his saddle, "but 'tis time to go. There could be more comin'."

Rob straightened his shoulders abruptly, unaware until his cousin spoke that he was staring at Davina like a lovesick lad.

"Why dinna' we just wait fer the rest and kill them when they get here?" Colin asked with a hint of menace shining his eyes.

"Nae." Rob scowled at his bloodthirsty younger brother. He was going to have to have a talk with him about finding a more productive way to channel his energy.

"She'll be needin' that kirtle now." Rob turned to the Abbess.

Thankfully, the Reverend Mother did not argue, but hurried back into the Abbey to see to the task herself. When she was gone, Rob ushered Davina toward his horse. He stopped and looked over his shoulder when Asher did not follow. "Ye comin'?"

The captain did not try to hide the relief in his expression when he nodded, but his smile faded when Davina fit her foot into Rob's stirrup.

"She's ridin' with me." Rob did his best to take the sting out of his voice at seeing the raw emotion Asher felt for her spilling from his eyes. Rob didn't like it, but he understood it more now after the fear of almost losing her. "'Tis safer."

He regretted his last words the instant he spoke them and the captain lowered his stricken gaze to his boots. *Hell*, Rob cursed himself inwardly. Davina would surely add callous to his list of faults. "What I meant to say is—"

"Her safety means everything to me," Asher said without looking up. The weight of his failure to save her at St. Christopher's was evident in his quiet tone.

"I know it does," Rob said honestly, remembering how bravely the captain had fought at the first abbey. "But she's still ridin' with me."

Wisely, Asher nodded, saying nothing more, and strode toward the stable to retrieve his horse.

The Abbess returned carrying a deep green kirtle and smock tossed over her arm. When Rob reached for them she stopped him, placing her hand over his. Her eyes on him were as hard as the first day he'd met her, her words curt and cautionary.

Without reply, Rob snatched the garments from her and handed them to Davina. He waited while the Abbess gave them her blessing, then gained his saddle behind Davina and rode away from Courlochcraig with his men and Asher close behind.

The clang of the wrought iron gate drove home the gravity of what Rob meant to do, but he had no other choice. It seemed God had indeed assigned him to the task of guarding Davina Montgomery. She would be safe, hidden in the mists of Camlochlin. The peril, he knew as he closed his arms around her, was in what she had already done to him, and continued to do each moment he spent with her.

"She is not yours, Highlander. You would do well to remember that."

He closed his eyes, knowing the Abbess's words would plague him for a long time to come.

Chapter Twelve

Davina looked out over the gold-dappled surface of the great Firth of Clyde. She'd read about its importance during the Battle of Largs, when the Vikings were driven back from their brutal ambitions, but she had never hoped to see it, and never this close. Riding along the coast would be difficult at times, Rob had told her, but the tide, in most places, would wash away their tracks. Davina certainly had no objections. She'd never seen such a grand body of water before, or the sky swathed in ribbons of scarlet and gold as the sun slowly descended. She should have grown sleepy against the cushion of Rob's supple muscles behind her, especially when he tucked her closely to him beneath the wrappings of his plaid, but her heart thrashed wildly in her chest at the sights and sounds around her. Her breath caught at a school of distant harbor porpoises breaking the surface to soar across the horizon. Their freedom touched her with a poignancy that blurred her vision and made her throat burn, for she shared their exhilaration. Thundering along the sandy shore, Davina let the cool wind shed her of the weight of her existence, her past, her future. She was leaving it behind with the aid of a man who had fought his way through flames and six enemy soldiers to rescue her.

For the first time in more years than she could remember, she felt safe. Truly safe. Her mind tried to argue that those who wanted her dead could still find her, but when she voiced her concerns for his family to Rob, he vowed that Gilles would die by his hand should the Admiral ever dare step foot on MacGregor land. He swore to protect her, and even more meaningful than that, he wanted to. It was a wonder she had never dared to hope for.

Of course, she worried that poor Edward believed he'd failed her. She offered him her most tender, thankful smile each time she found him looking at her that day. Her dearest friend had fallen on the battlefield because he'd fought too many alone, and for too long. Yet even wounded and exhausted he'd risen from the ashes to find her. No, Edward had never failed her, but he'd never given her hope before.

Rob did.

She smiled and drew out a soft, cleansing sigh as the sun went down with her eyelids.

She was awakened a short while later, cradled against Rob's chest as he strode on foot toward a small clearing. She couldn't see him but she knew his strong arms held her, his steady heart beat near hers. Only when he set her down—and he did so as gently as his size would allow— did she feel exposed to elements around her.

She sat up, meaning to do her part and help build the camp, but he stopped her with a husky order. "Sleep, lass."

She couldn't, not when the freedom from worry of what tomorrow might bring had been awakened. She even smiled at Will when the first spark from his birch bark became a flame. He winked at her in response and she rolled her eyes.

"You're faring well through all this, my lady." Edward folded his legs at her feet and handed her a small bundle tied at the top with string.

"What do I have to fear when I am in the care of such courageous"—she opened the sack and pulled out a generous hunk of black bread—"and thoughtful men?"

"It's pleasing that you think so of me," he said, then lowered his voice so that only she could hear. "But there is something I feel must be told between us."

He looked ill and Davina suspected what he wanted to say to her. She knew he loved her. She knew how difficult it must be for him to see her riding with Rob. But Edward knew her well, and perhaps he saw even more. She couldn't bear the thought of hurting him and reached her hand out to comfort him.

"Edward, I—"

"Is that black bread?" Finn bent to have a closer look at her lap.

"It is, young sir," Edward answered him. "And there's honey to go with it."

In the firelight, Finn's eyes flickered with a hint of wickedness as he turned them on Edward. "Did ye pilfer it from the nuns, then?"

"No." Edward returned the boy's smile, seeming to forget the grim talk he wanted to have with Davina. "You have a familiar look to you, lad," he said while Davina tore off a chunk of bread and handed it to Finn with the sack.

"My brother is Captain Connor Grant," Finn told him, settling in close to Davina and squeezing the honeycomb over his bread. "Mayhap ye know him."

Edward thought about it then shook his head. "I don't.

But I have not left St. Christopher's in the last four years. I don't know many of the other captains."

Shrugging his shoulders, Finn glanced up at Rob, about to sit at Davina's right. "I don't resemble Connor, do I, Rob?"

Davina glanced at Rob to find him staring at Edward with a scowl so dangerous it would have frightened away the moon had he looked up at it.

"Rob?"

He blinked his gaze to Finn and his jaw twitched before he spoke. "Aye lad, ye do, but ye resemble yer mother more."

"Aye," Finn agreed and gave Colin the sack when his friend joined them. "Connor looks more like our uncle. Him, ye most likely have heard of, Captain Asher."

"Oh? Why is that?"

"Because he was King Charles's High Admiral, and now he is King's James's."

"A word o' caution, Asher." Will slid down the trunk of a thick oak and caught the wedge of cheese Rob tossed him. "Once Finn begins speakin' aboot his kin in the King's Army, he's likely to go on all night."

But Edward wasn't listening to Will. He was staring at Finn, his dark eyes wide with disbelief. "Your uncle is the High Admiral?" He shook his head slightly as if he doubted the good of his ears—or his tongue for seeking confirmation. "But he cannot be."

"Why can't he?" Finn asked, looking a bit insulted.

"Because the king's High Admiral is Connor *Stuart*."

"Aye, I know." Finn bit into his bread and closed his eyes. "'Tis like heaven."

Davina could feel Edward's eyes on her, willing her

to look at him. But she couldn't. Finn was a Stuart. Her gaze traversed his features—his pale, silky hair peeking out from beneath his bonnet; his straight, regal nose. Of course, why had she not seen it earlier? "You are a cousin to the king?" she heard herself asking.

The beautiful boy opened his eyes and set them on her. "Aye, a few generations removed on my mother's side. My father was a close friend of the late King Charles. He helped restore Charles to the throne with the aid of..."

"Och, hell, no' again." Will leaned his head against the tree and closed his eyes.

Finn cast him a wounded look. "She doesn't know the tale. And what's so wrong about telling it? I hope some-day to be as braw as my kin."

"I think you're very braw," Davina told him, stretch-ing her hand to his. She smiled when he looked at her and scooted a little closer to him. "I would like to hear the tale."

"Hell," Will muttered. "I'm goin' to sleep. Colin, ye keep watch tonight."

"But I'm..."

"Colin," Rob cut him off when his brother tried to protest. He said nothing else as he stretched out close to Davina. He didn't have to. Colin tightened his jaw, threw Will a cool glance, and nodded.

An hour later, Edward joined Rob and Will in their slumber. Davina didn't know how any of them could sleep through such a wondrous tale. She could not wait to meet Finn's mother. Oh, what mettle it took for a woman to learn to wield a sword and battle with men! And Connor Stuart, imprisoned in the Tower of London and tortured for months. Yet he too possessed the courage and resolve to withhold the information his enemies had tried to gain from him. It was no wonder Finn took such pride in his family. He had every reason to.

"What became of the man who betrayed your Uncle Connor?" she asked Finn, hanging on his every word and impatient for the next.

"James Buchanan became an outlaw. My uncle searched for him for two years and finally found him living in Suffolk under a false name. He was hanged in London with the blessing of King Charles."

"Chilling, but justified," Davina proclaimed, much to Finn's delight. She studied him a moment longer in the firelight. Oh, how she liked this young man. His large, open smile was like an embrace, inviting one into his warmth. And she wanted to go. She wanted to tell him of *her* family, and how she had yearned for them every day of her life. But finally God had answered her most fervent prayer. How hadn't she known before this?

She blinked, suddenly mortified at how long she'd been smiling at him. When he blushed she turned away—and looked straight into Colin's watchful eyes.

"Ye're an odd lass," he said, crouched on his haunches beyond the crackling embers. Davina wanted to look away, but the power in his gaze held her still. "Why d'ye have such interest in things that dinna' concern ye?"

"But they do concern me," she countered, trying to muster the control she now knew ran through her veins.

She had misjudged this quiet, unassuming lad. First by thinking him any less striking than a dark stallion on the verge of charging. Second, by forgetting that he was there, speaking little and observing more. "They concern us all, do they not?" She forced a smile, aware that she had to be more vigilant with this one.

"Nae, no' all. Most lasses I know concern themselves with cooking and sewing. Most lasses I know"—he looked her over with suspicion searing his green eyes to gold—"save fer my sister—and ye."

"Rob told me of Mairi. She—"

"I know why politics concern her." Colin stopped her before she could sway the conversation. "But why ye?"

She shifted her gaze to Finn and found that he too was waiting for her answer. "What else would you have me care about?" she asked them both quietly and looked down at her lap. "I've lived each day knowing that the people I loved would most likely die because of me. Nothing I ever had was tangible. Everything could change in one horrifying instant. And it did." She looked up at them and now it was Colin's turn to look away. "I read, Colin. I immersed myself in my lessons because what I learned belonged to me and my enemies could not touch it. And I learned about the king because I did not have a father."

Oh, damnation, why was she going to cry now? She narrowed her eyes on Colin, angry with him for making her think on her past. "One more thing," she said before she ended this talk. "I can cook and sew as well as any woman."

Leaving them both staring at her, she flipped around in Rob's direction, shoved her hands under her head, and closed her eyes.

Rob watched her beneath the moonlight. She was so close that his fingers ached to reach out and wipe away the tears escaping from under her lids. He'd heard everything Colin had asked her, and her reply. The emptiness in her life pained him to the marrow. He was fortunate to have had so much growing up, so many who loved him and who he loved in return, without fear of losing them. Gazing at her while her sweet lips moved in prayer and then as she drifted to sleep, Rob wasn't certain which of the two was a greater loss in her life: the absence of her family, or of any sense of permanence.

"I'll remedy it all, Davina," he whispered, finally lifting his fingers to the curve of her cheek. "Fer God has assigned me to it."

Chapter Thirteen

———◆———

*R*ob woke with a start, instinctively reaching for Davina. She wasn't there. He bolted to his feet. His dream of a faceless Admiral snatching her from his arms was still fresh in his mind. He looked around the campsite for Asher, expecting Davina was with him. He wished it didn't, but it boiled his blood to know that the captain had spent the last four years with her—knowing her secrets, knowing what made her laugh, what frightened her. How many times had he comforted her, held her in his arms, mayhap kissed her?

Thankfully, she wasn't with the captain now, but Asher's eyes were fixed on something to his right, just beyond the trees. Rob followed his gaze and soon found Davina standing with Will, his cousin's bow and arrow poised in front of her face.

Rob watched as she widened her stance beneath her skirts. Skirts? Bloody hell! He glared at every man around him, wondering where and when she had discarded her robes for the shift and kirtle the Abbess had given him—and if any of the bastards had dared look at her while she did. None of them looked guilty, but they all had their eyes on her. He couldn't find fault with that, not when she looked so damned bonnie in her new, close-fitting, womanly attire. Leaning his shoulder against a tree, he crossed his arms over his chest and joined the others watching her.

Her fingers were thin and graceful, winding around the shaft of Will's arrow. Her shoulders, straight and relaxed as she pulled back on the bowstring. She closed one eye, aimed, and then fired.

Rob wasn't surprised when the arrow struck Will's makeshift target fifty paces away dead on. His shoulder bore testimony to her skill. The others cheered, and Will, rogue bastard that he was, whispered something in her ear that made her laughter spread across the glade.

Rob was considering the best way to skin his cousin alive when Davina turned, as if sensing him there, his hooded, burning eyes on her, and aimed her smile at him. Suddenly, nothing existed in the world but her.

"You sleep late," she greeted him, curling her weapon under her arm and moving toward him.

Rob had to call upon every last shred of strength he possessed not to push off the tree and drag her into his arms. "I was awake most of the night."

Her smile vanished as she reached him and tilted her face to his, wreaking havoc on his senses. "Not your shoulder, I hope."

He shook his head but said nothing else while his gaze drifted over her features, settling on the full pout of her lips. He'd frightened her the first time he kissed her, and paid the price for it. But he longed to taste her again, not like some possessive, hot-tempered beast, but as a lover, tender and passionate.

When his gaze returned to hers, he found her searching

his eyes as if she caught a glimpse of something kinder, softer, and wanted it as badly as he.

"Well done, my lady." Asher appeared at Davina's side, shattering what had just passed between them. "You are as deadly as you are beautiful." The reverence in his smile faded when he turned it on Rob. "Do you not agree, MacGregor?"

Aye, Rob agreed, but he wasn't about to drop flowery compliments at her feet every time she was in his presence the way Asher did. The man was a captain in the mightiest army in the world. Where was his pride, for hell's sake?

Instead of answering the question—which he'd already surmised was not asked out of friendly curiosity—Rob unfolded his arms and pushed off the tree. "We need to go."

Davina's hand on his wrist stopped him. "Oh, but don't you want to give it a try?"

"What?" Rob asked, taken aback for a moment that she would so boldly seek a compliment from him.

"The bow." She held hers up to him. "I'd like to see if you are as good with it as you are with a blade." Her smile widened into a grin. "It will be fun."

Rob shook his head, thinking of a thousand different things he'd rather do with her for fun. "We have nae time fer pleasure. We have to keep movin'." He looked over her shoulder rather than at the disappointment on her face. "Will, get rid of that target and let's get this place cleaned up."

He didn't look back at Davina again as he strode away. 'Twas best not to, else he might end up like her captain, languishing after something that was forbidden. Hell, he'd had a hard enough time remembering that she was a novice of the Order when she was draped in His robes. Her soft curves, so delicately defined now in her kirtle... He stopped and turned back to where she was still standing with the captain.

"Where did ye change yer garment?"

She pointed to a thick stand of trees in the distance then looked down at herself. "It's a bit snug. It must have belonged to one of the younger novices."

He knew he was scowling but he couldn't help himself, just as he couldn't stop himself from thinking no lass in all the world ever looked so fine in something so plain.

"It looks...ye look bonnie in it." He tightened his jaw to keep himself from smiling at her like some besotted, dimwitted fool. But he knew 'twas already too late.

The next few days were hell for Rob. More difficult than any raid or training time with his father had ever been. He ate little and slept less, battling with himself night and day against feelings that threatened to control him. He was happy that Davina had put aside her grief and was enjoying herself on their journey. Though she sometimes fell into a silence so deep he thought he could almost hear her thoughts, 'twas her laughter that filled the air, and his heart, while she practiced archery each morning with Will or tried to learn how to ride a horse on her own under Colin's careful instruction. But despite his best efforts to prove to Davina that he too was good-natured, Rob found himself snapping at the others for minor offenses. The fact that he was trying to prove anything to her at all goaded his temper, but riding with her was the true cause of his foul mood. It wasn't the feel of her pressed to his chest and clutched in his arms that did it, although he was certain that having her so near, as if she were his, helped to fan the flames.

It was Asher. The captain rode at their side constantly, usurping Finn's place. At first, he pretended interest in the MacGregors, but soon his true purpose for rubbing stirrups with Rob became clear. He talked to Davina ceaselessly, preventing her from speaking overmuch to Rob, or him to her. At first, Rob told himself he didn't mind. Davina and her captain were friends. They shared a past together. It meant nothing. He certainly wasn't going to let some childish emotion cloud his reasoning. But Asher did nothing to hide the fact that he was in love with her. Davina knew it and cast all her smiles Asher's way. She even laughed when he reminded her of a day two summers ago, when he had tried to shear one of St. Christopher's sheep and the woolly beast bit him on the arse.

Rob wanted to punch him in the mouth. What kind of man couldn't shear a damned sheep? It wasn't any better when they stopped to eat or sleep. In fact, 'twas worse. Every step she took found Asher right behind her. Twice Rob had to block his path when she left to relieve herself. *That* had almost cost Rob his temper, but his resolve held firm...and he was damned proud of it.

When Asher didn't have her ear, Finn usually did, and if the lad wasn't so young, Rob would have worried most about the effect that particular male had on Davina. Twice Rob was sure he'd seen her wipe tears from her eyes while she stared at the lad, thinking she went unobserved.

Not so. Rob's eyes were ever on her, taking in every gesture, every smile, every flawless curve that shaped her. He knew how she breathed because he lay awake at night watching her sleep, aching to hold her, kiss her, make her his own. She was crafted of stardust and secrets and he was lost. He knew it, and he didn't like it.

Unfortunately, his brother Colin knew it, too, and did his best to reassure him not to fret about it, they all were a wee bit lost to her—a truth that only made Rob more irritable. Still, he hadn't cracked any heads yet. He worked harder than he ever had in his life at harnessing his emotions. When he didn't, bad things usually happened; like breaking Donald MacPherson's arm after he shot Tristan with his arrow, or when he left Davina at Courlochcraig and then had to kill six men to get her out.

There was one bright light in his gloom, though. He was pleased to discover that Davina had indeed taken notice of his balanced temperament when they stopped for the night outside of Dumbarton.

He was sharing a word with Will after they made camp when she came up behind him. "You've been very patient with Edward."

Rob wasn't entirely happy to hear her bring up the captain—since it was the first time in days her guardian wasn't stationed at her side—but he refused to behave like a sulking boy. "Why should I no' be patient with him?"

She shrugged her shoulders and offered her usual smile to Finn when he sat across the fire. She hadn't smiled at Rob in days. "I just thought that his not including you in our talks might have angered you."

"Why should it?" Rob asked her, sparing her a brief, uninterested glance before he turned back to Will. He wasn't completely certain that if he continued looking at her above the firelight he wouldn't crack and confess to already having thought of a solution to Captain Asher.

"You might," she said with a marked sting in her voice,

"because it can seem a bit rude and you *have* been snarling about like a bear with a thorn in his paw."

Rob turned to her, a smile of detached amusement narrowing his eyes. "Ye just told me how patient I've been."

"I was being pleasant"—she smiled back at him to prove it—"with the hopes that it might rub off on you."

Hell, the last thing he wanted to do was grin at her like some heart-struck lackwit, but he enjoyed her flashes of temper, even at the cost of Will chuckling at him. She had strength in her she wasn't even aware of, passion he wanted to feed.

"I simply wanted you to know," she said, trying to look as uninterested as he, "that Edward means no offense. He has been at my side for a long time and it's difficult for him to just hand over my well-being to you—especially when you hold me as if..."

"As if what?" he prodded when she grew silent.

"As if I belonged to you." She didn't look anywhere near as angry as she tried to sound. "I don't, in case you had forgotten."

He hadn't, and that was part of the trouble. He wanted her—God forgive him, and he was growing tired of fighting it.

With an oath on her lips she was sure would cost her a month of confession, Davina returned to the fire and took a seat across from Finn. She tried to keep her eyes on the hare roasting over the spit, but they kept flicking back to Rob. Saints, but the man was as rigid as an arrow. She knew how close Edward had come on several different occasions to getting swiped by the snarling bear. She'd felt the tightness of Rob's muscles behind her whenever

Edward commanded all her attention. Why was he trying to convince her that he was unfazed by it? On the other hand, what if she was wrong? What if he truly didn't care one whit if Edward tossed her over his arm and kissed her senseless—the way Rob had at Courlochcraig? And, dear God, why couldn't she get *that* out of her mind? Every blasted time she looked at his mouth, she wanted him to kiss her again. He didn't. What if he didn't like her and was just following some sense of duty? It would explain why he scowled at her whenever she caught his eye. She really shouldn't have been cheeky with him. Whether he admitted it or not, he didn't like Edward. If he didn't like her either, there would be nothing to stop him from leaving both of them where they sat while he returned home. "Please God, don't let him do it."

"Don't let who do what?" Edward appeared over her, holding a handful of red berries and wearing a tender smile that should have been soothing. It wasn't. How could she tell him how just being near Rob made her feel safe and cared for without wounding Edward to his heart?

Rather than lie to him, she took the berries he offered and patted the ground beside her, inviting him to sit. When he did, she moved a bit closer so that the others could not hear her. "I would like you to try and get along better with Rob. He isn't trying to take your place."

Unlike Rob, who was as difficult to read as the Latin scrolls burnt to ashes, along with everything else at St. Christopher's, Edward's emotions played openly across his face.

"Can he take my place?"

"Of course he can't, but he isn't trying to, Edward." She took his hand, trying to convince him. "I don't think he even likes me." He certainly didn't look at her the way Edward did, with his whole heart exposed at her feet.

"He has gone out of his way for someone he doesn't like. Wouldn't you say?" Edward chuckled mirthlessly.

"Not really," Davina told him with a soft sigh that she didn't know she expelled. "He's a noble man with a deep sense of duty to those around him. That's all. Will told me that Rob is firstborn and will someday lead his clan. The task of protecting them will fall on his shoulders. He is merely doing what he has been taught to do—the same as I."

"You sound disappointed that it is not more than that," Edward said softly, looking away from her gaze.

"Edward, please don't be a fool." She hushed her voice when Colin and Finn glanced at her over the sizzling hare. "You know that my life is not my own."

"Yes, I know it," Edward whispered and glanced across the flames at Rob. "But does he?"

"He doesn't know who I am, Edward," she said following her friend's gaze. "For whatever reason, I don't think he cares." She smiled, dipping her gaze to the flames. "It is odd, but it makes me feel as if I don't care either." And oh, how could she ever explain to Edward how wonderful it felt not to care? "I should tell him," she said, looking up into her dearest friend's eyes again. "He deserves to be told. I want to tell Finn that he is my cousin."

"You cannot tell them the truth," Edward warned her, shifting his gaze to Rob once again when the Highlander began to walk toward them. "Do you think he will still bring you to Skye knowing he might bring the entire realm down on his family's name once again?"

There it was, her fear spoken aloud. She shook her head.

"He is right. Skye is most likely the only place safe for you, my lady," Edward said quickly. "Remember who you are."

Davina stared at him until the sting behind her eyes began to ache. Then she dipped her gaze to her lap. She didn't want to remember. For once, she just wanted to be Davina, and not James of York's true firstborn daughter and heir to the throne of the three kingdoms.

Chapter Fourteen

John Henry Frasier grinned when his wife bent to kiss his cheek, and then continued counting the coins stacked in his palm. "Thirty-three…" His thick, gray brows drew together in a moment of forgetfulness. "Or was that thirty-four?"

"Twenty-nine," his wife called over her shoulder, untying her apron behind her back as she left him.

"Twenty-nine?" He shook his head and drew out a long sigh. "'Twas another slow day in the tavern."

"I know, but soon the festivities in England will be over and our patrons will return."

He glanced up from his small bundle and smiled at his wife's generous rump swaying beneath her skirts while she climbed the stairs to their rooms above the small tavern. What would he do without his Millie, always reminding him of brighter things?

"Come to bed now, John. 'Tis late."

"In a moment, my love. Let me wallow in my poverty."

She laughed from the second landing, setting his poor memory to ruin once again. "You never wallow, John. Don't forget to lock up," she added, disappearing around a corner.

"Aye. Now where was I?" He plucked a coin up in his beefy fingers and gave it a thoughtful look. "Thirty-four, thirty..." He stopped counting when a gust of cool night air swept his silver hair over his forehead.

"My apologies," he said, turning in his chair toward the door. "We are closed."

The figure framing the doorway sent an even icier chill down his spine. The patron made no motion to suggest he heard John's words, but slowly stepped aside to allow four men behind him to enter.

John stood up and shoved his coins into the pocket of his apron. "I've only a few coin if you mean to rob me."

A low chuckle came from the doorway as the figure stepped into the soft light of the tavern. John narrowed his eyes, getting a better look at the man. He wore breeches and a coat that hung well past his knees. A wide-brimmed hat shadowed half his face, but his eyes flickered a pale gray in the firelight.

"Do I look like a thief, old man?" The voice rumbled from someplace deep within his wide chest. "My comrades and I have been on the road for many days and we could use some strong ale to heat our blood."

John eyed the other four cautiously, hoping the man spoke true, for they were all too big to fight off, even with the heavy stick he kept propped in the corner.

The jingle of coins coming from the doorway drew his attention. The man held up a small pouch and shook it again before he tossed it to John. "Five cups of your best ale. Or better yet, make it whisky. I've always wanted to taste what is claimed to be the finest brew in the three kingdoms." He sauntered into the tavern, his coattails swaying around his boots. When he reached John, his lips curled into a thin smile. "That is, unless you refuse to take my gold?"

"Gold?" John's eyes widened, as did his grin. "Why, I wouldn't dream of sending thirsty men away. Have a seat. Have a seat." He gestured to all of them, even pulling out a chair himself. "I have just the thing for good gentlemen such as yourselves, brewed it myself." He swept his fingers through his thinning hair and smoothed the wrinkles from his apron. "Make yourselves at home while I fetch your drinks."

What good fortune! Oh, wait until Millie heard of this. He kissed the pouch and shoved it into his pocket with the rest of his coins. Gold! He stopped suddenly on his way to the cellar, plucked the pouch back out, untied it and looked inside, then closed his eyes and kissed the thin leather again.

He returned to his generous patrons a short time later and set down a tray carrying five cups and a dark brown bottle of his very best whisky on the table before them. "Prepare to have your palates enchanted, gentlemen," he said, pouring their drinks.

He watched, smiling from one ear to the other while the man who paid him removed his hat and raised his cup to his friends.

"To the Prince."

"You mean the King, aye?" John asked, still grinning.

"No, I mean the Prince." The man brought the cup to his lips. He took a sip, then looked up at John. "You speak the truth, Tavernier, I've never tasted anything so fine."

John couldn't be happier and bowed his thanks, listening to the soft jingle coming from his pocket. "There is plenty more."

"This will suffice."

John cast his eyes around the table at the others. They remained silent and stoic and none of them looked at him. Tucking the tray under his arm, he scratched his temple. "You're not from here."

Those cool gray eyes slid to him. "Why do you say that?"

"Your speech, it has a peculiar sound to it. Like nothing I've heard before."

"Tell me, old man." The patron set down his cup and turned to look directly at him. "Has a lady stopped here seeking food or shelter? She is my master's wife and has fled without a trace. She might have been alone. Perhaps donned in a nun's robes?"

"A nun? Traveling alone?" John chuckled softly and rested his hand on his belly, then stopped and quirked his brow. "I saw no nun, but I did see horsemen. I didn't think anything about it at the time, men have been riding toward England for the past fortnight, but now that you mention a nun..."

"Yes?" The patron set down his drink slowly and narrowed his eyes on John.

"Well, the horsemen were riding the other way, toward the Abbey."

The stranger rose to his feet and swooped toward him like a hawk that had just spotted its prey. "Abbey? Where?"

John mopped his forehead with his sweaty palm. Something about the stranger had gone so terribly cold and threatening. Even the air seemed to pulse with foreboding around him. "Old Courlochcraig in Ayrshire," John said and darted his eyes toward the stairs. No need to fear, he reassured himself. He'd dealt with mercenaries before. He would serve them, tell them what they wanted, if he could, and then see them out the door.

The patron moved closer; his genial smile returned.

"You've been most helpful," he said and turned to one of his men. "Maarten, ride south and collect the rest of my men who left us at our last stop. Tell them their search is over and bring them with you to Ayrshire. I will meet you there."

John was about to let himself breathe again when the patron stopped and set his gaze upward.

"Are there rooms above stairs?"

"Only mine, and I'm afraid I'm quite weary. If you wouldn't mind finishing your..."

"You would not be untruthful to me, would you, my friend?" The patron slipped his arm around John's shoulder. His breath sluiced warm down John's neck. "Not after I paid you so handsomely."

"Of course not."

"Who is in the room?"

"Only... only my wife, Millie, good sir."

"I believe you," the patron said gently against his ear.

John did not see the flash of the dagger that sank into his belly, but he felt it. His mouth opened when he looked down at the blood soaking through his apron and his gold spilling to the freshly swept floor. He wanted to scream. He thought he did. The patron was still close, watching him as John's last gurgled breath left his body.

Admiral Gilles yanked his dagger from the Tavernier's stomach and set his eyes on the stairs as the old man crumpled in a heap at his feet. Pushing the body away with his boot, he ordered Hendrick to collect his gold and wait for him with the others outside while he searched the room above.

"Millie?" he called, turning the hilt of his dagger around in his fingers. "Are you alone?"

"I don't think she understands the propensity for evil running through Gilles's veins."

Asher stood with Rob and Colin by the banks of Loch Awe just south of Kildun Castle. Despite the laughter coming from the water's edge, or, it would seem, because of it, the captain raked his fingers through his hair.

Rob couldn't keep himself from smiling when Davina, crouched beside Finn while they washed their hands, splashed the lad in the face instead. She had changed much since he'd plucked her from the flames. In fact, it seemed the farther away they rode from England, the better her moods became, and his, as well. Her prayers were filled with thanks and every day her laughter rang out like music filling the meadows and glens as they rode through them. Rob loved the sound of it and the way it made her eyes dance. He would have liked to be the cause of her joy, but he had trouble giving himself over to meaningless pleasures like chasing grouse or hiding behind trees while she tried to find him. He wondered if her heart had been this light at St. Christopher's and if she had enchanted Asher's men with her graceful movements and the tinkling melody of her mirth the way she did with his. She seemed most alive, though, when she talked about the new king and his determination to stand for what he believed in—a topic Colin, at least, never grew weary of discussing with her late every night when they thought everyone else was asleep. Still, there were times when she spoke to no one, withdrawing into herself to a place that still haunted her eyes. "She understands evil well enough, Asher," Rob told the captain without severing his gaze from Davina. "I think she still dreams of the massacre at St. Christopher's."

"No, she is forgetting. She doesn't know him."

"And ye do?" Rob asked, turning to him. He almost wished Asher had remained uninterested in him. The man fretted like a woman with a dozen bairns and no way to feed them. And for some reason, which Rob suspected had to do with Asher making Davina happy, he was trying his hardest to make friends with Rob.

"I know enough," Edward said. "The man is called 'de Duivel,' for mercy's sake."

"My faither was called the same thing fer many years. Now there's a man ye should fear."

"Bloody right," Colin agreed, then shouted to Davina. "Look out behind ye!"

She screamed with laughter when Will, sneaking up behind her, snatched her up in his arms and held her over the water.

"I swear on my sword I'm goin' to beat him senseless one of these days," Rob growled, halfheartedly.

"A single strike ought to do it." Colin smirked and winked at him before he too was lured away by the laughter coming from the loch.

"By the way"—Edward cast his anxious gaze around the sparse tree line behind them—"you are aware that we're on Campbell land, are you not? They don't take kindly to Highlanders."

Rob ground his jaw and prayed for patience. "My

mother is a Campbell, dinna' fear. We will be safe here tonight."

But the captain wasn't listening. "God protect us," he muttered, looking suitably horrified at Colin tackling Finn. "I fear this noise will alert the dead."

Rob was about to turn and ask him how in bloody hell he had attained the rank of captain when he feared a man so much that the sound of laughter could make him tremble in his boots, but Davina broke away from her captor and came rushing toward him, capturing his attention instead.

Instinctively, Rob opened his arms to her, pleased that she sought protection from him rather than Asher. He caught her up in one arm and with the other stretched out before him, palm open, stopped Will, who had been in hot pursuit, dead in his tracks. His cousin went down like a felled tree, clutching his nose, blood already seeping through his fingers.

Immediately, Rob bent to help him. He hadn't meant to hit him in the face, but Will ran straight into his hand. "Och, hell, is it broken?" he asked as he hauled his cousin to his feet.

Still clamped in his other arm, Davina wriggled to be free then gave his chest a firm slap. "How could you do that to him?"

Rob angled his head at her, surprised by the flash of anger in her blue eyes.

"He was only having some sport with me!"

If she was trying to make him feel worse than he already did, she should have said anything but that.

She shoved his arm off her and went directly to Will. "Oh, you poor thing," she cooed like a wife whose husband had just returned from battle. "Sit back down and keep your head tilted forward."

Rob rolled his eyes heavenward. Hell, 'twas just a bloody nose. Will had received worse than that training with him. When he looked at Davina again, she was glaring at him. Her cheeks were flushed, her nostrils flared, and her damp hair fell in wild disarray around her shoulders. Hell, she was bonnie.

"What is the matter with you?" she charged. "All you do is frown at everyone. You never just enjoy yourself. Why, you're no fun at all!"

Before he could reply, she whirled on her heel, fanning her long tresses in a wide arc around her, and stormed off to the water's edge.

He followed her, determined to set her straight. There were many things he enjoyed, like working up a good sweat on the practice field, and raiding, and playing chess. He liked playing chess.

"Davina, I—"

"What happened to Will?" Finn disengaged himself from Colin and stared at the man milking his wound like a lass.

"Robert punched him in the face for chasing the lady," Edward informed him.

Rob glowered at him over his shoulder. "I didna' punch him, and why the hell are ye right behind me?"

"Of course, now he's going to bite off Edward's head," Davina practically hissed while she soaked some reeds in the water.

"Mayhap our rogue cousin will have more sense now, aye, brother?"

Rob met Colin's knowing gaze and then closed his

eyes. He knew how it looked. He didn't like Will or Asher giving Davina so much attention, but it didn't mean he wished his best friend harm. Or did he? What the hell was happening to him? Davina was to blame, of course; his wee fairy goddess who enchanted all the men around her. He moved aside when she shoved past him on her way back to Will.

"I think ye should—"

"Shut up, Finn," Rob said, and set off after her again. When he reached her, he waited while she wiped Will's face with the wet reeds, patient even when his cousin slipped him a furtive smile from the corner of his mouth. Rob wouldn't be baited.

"Poor Will," Davina soothed, giving Will's nose a thorough looking over. "I do not think it's broken."

"'Twouldn't be the first time if it was." Rob only meant to ease her worry. He realized too late that it was a mistake.

"By your hand?" Davina straightened, wiping her hands on her gown, and gaped at him.

"Nae, not by me. I . . . I only meant . . ." Rob clenched his jaw. Why in blazes was he stumbling over his words? He could admit when he was wrong—though such occasions rarely arose. Mostly because he never acted rashly. He was usually patient, deliberate, never truly letting anything disturb his calm. But that had all changed since he'd met Davina. He could blame his brooding disposition of late on a dozen things, but he knew she was the cause. He wanted her. Despite the danger she might or might not bring to his clan, despite her promises to God, he wanted her, and not being able to have her was winding him up tighter than a bowstring. He barely recognized himself and he didn't like it. He looked down at his cousin. "I didna' mean to strike ye," he said, trying to make amends.

Still clutching his nose, Will—who'd faced his share of sword-swinging Highlanders bent on cutting off a limb, expelled a withering sigh. "'Tis understandable, cousin. I know how ye frown upon games." He finally let go of his nose and rose, as good as new, to his feet. "But mayhap with her, 'tis more than that, aye?" He winked and strolled off with a victorious grin on his face.

Rob fought the urge to fling his cousin into Loch Awe.

"You frown upon games?" Davina looked more stricken than when Will's face crunched under his hand. "And why would it be more than that with me? Is it my happiness that makes you angry, Rob?"

Och, hell, he didn't want her to think that. He reached for her hand to stop her when she moved to walk away from him. "Davina, I . . ." He looked up and scowled at finding Asher and Finn standing close by, watching and listening to what he had to say. "I wish to speak to ye. *Alone.*" He held out his arm to stop the captain when he moved toward them. Asher skidded to a halt, careful not to make contact with Rob's palm.

"Stay here." Rob softened the edge in his voice, sympathetic, though he hated to admit it, to what drove the captain to follow her, for he was just as pitiful. "She'll be safe with me."

Edward cut Davina a hesitant look, and then nodded and watched in silence while Rob lifted her to his saddle, leaped up behind her, then trotted off toward the woods beyond the campsite.

Chapter Fifteen

❦

*W*hat could he say to her? What *should* he say? Rob had no idea. The one thing he never spent much time training with was lasses. He'd never had time for them. At least, not for anything more meaningful than a few hours of pleasure. After that, he threw himself back into what was most important. His duties to his clan. Duties he had tossed to the wayside since holding Davina Montgomery in his arms. Each day while he battled his feelings toward her, he also battled his logic for bringing her home, for not questioning her more about why an earl and a duke wanted her dead. 'Twas enough to drive his rational heart mad. But the more he rode with her, the more he came to know her, the less he cared. They had covered a good distance of leagues with her perched sideways on his lap, and not once had she complained. She had lost almost everyone she loved, yet she found joy in things as simple as a sunset or—he smiled rather hopefully at the stand of short hawthorn trees up ahead—a canopy of tiny pink blossoms.

Aye, he thought, bringing them to the trees. What chance did his sensible heart have against the sweet thrills she found in the mundane?

Clearing his throat, he dropped his gaze to the top of

her head. He was glad she wasn't facing him. Looking at her had a way of muddling his thoughts. Then again, so did wee flowers in her hair. He plucked one from her silvery blond tresses—a harmless act that left him aching to touch more of her.

"Davina, I want to..."

"Yes?"

Damnation. She turned. "I..." he began, but when she smiled up at the blossoms falling around their heads, he forgot everything else in the world and let his eyes bask in the sheer rapture of her. And here was another difference still—she was beguiling to the point of distraction, and utterly and delightfully unaware of it. "Davina, I have been a fool and though I canna' promise it, I will do my best to avoid bein' one in the future."

Her gaze fell to his and her smile remained, emboldening him to continue. Her forgiveness, like her joy, came easily. "I may no' participate in the things ye like to do with the others, but I'll never stop ye from doin' them. I know ye need to."

Aye, he knew she needed more in her life than protection. She needed joy and freedom to be who she was— whoever that might be.

"Thank you." Her voice was whisper-soft while she looked at him, a mixture of surprise and hope stirring something within her that made his heart clench. "My life has changed so much since...since you came into it." She did not pull away when he lifted his fingers to the curve of her jaw but tilted her head to his touch. "I feel like I have just been born. I've always wanted to see what was beyond the Abbey walls, but I was afraid. I am not afraid when I'm with you."

Rob swallowed once, twice. He didn't think she could have made him any happier in that moment. But he was wrong.

"Your friends have become my friends, my family."

"Aye, that pleases me," he said, wiping a tear from beneath her lashes, and fearing the drum of his own heart that told him he would battle any army for her; a duke's, an earl's, or even a king's.

Nae, he couldn't. He was already sworn to another duty. He wanted her to understand. "While my brothers and sister were chasin' sheep in the meadows, I was bein' molded into a man who would someday wear my faither's tartan. When ye come to know Callum MacGregor and what he has done fer his clan—what he is doin' fer them now—ye'll understand how hard I must work at makin' certain his tartan will fit."

She studied him quietly, carefully, searching deep within his eyes. "It sounds like you had a childhood very much like mine," she finally said. "Your path was set for you and you had no choice in changing it."

"I've never wanted to change it."

She smiled at him rather sadly, seeming to understand the battle being fought inside him—the choice he had been "molded" to make. "Truly, Rob, the last thing I want to do is bring danger to you or your clan."

He said nothing, feeling worse than before.

"You've never wanted to chase sheep in the meadows then?" Her eyes shimmered with playfulness, tempting him to forget the battle.

"Nae," he smiled.

Her mirth faded watching him. She blinked, looking

unnerved by something that just crossed her thoughts. "Did you chase many women?"

"Nae," he replied, dipping his gaze to her lips.

"Not even one of those MacPherson girls that Will told about?"

He would have preferred her not knowing about that day, but the dreadful anticipation widening her eyes as she waited for his reply had the strangest, most satisfying effect on him. He'd been beating himself up every day telling himself that he wasn't jealous of her captain, and here she was a tad bit jealous of the MacPherson sisters. His smile deepened, his blue eyes teasing. "She chased me."

When she drew in a shocked breath, parting her lips beneath his curious touch, Rob bent his head to hers. He knew he shouldn't kiss her, but he was tired of fighting what he felt for her. God help him. God help them all.

Davina sat motionless, save for the heart thumping wildly in her chest. She had time to realize what he was going to do, but she didn't move away. She didn't want to. After days of riding perched in his lap, acutely aware of the powerful length of his fingers before her, his breath behind her, his arms around her, she wanted something more. Sinful or not, she could not stop her dreams at night, dreams that Rob had invaded, taking the place of everything else. She awoke most mornings breathless from his ghostly, sensual touch and a bit ashamed of the pleasure she took in touching him back. She knew she should stop him now as his fingers slipped behind her nape, drawing her closer, angling her head higher to receive him, but she wanted this too much. Having never been kissed before, she was frightened by the forceful need in his first kiss, but this time his lips grazed hers, a tender, beguiling caress so intimate she was glad she sat nestled in his lap else she would have melted into a pool of liquid at his feet. The smooth stroke of his tongue coaxing her lips apart sent fire through her veins. So much better than her dreams. He took her mouth with exquisite thoroughness, molding her lips to his, tasting her with a hunger he did all he could to control. When he curled his arm around her, drawing her closer and deepening their kiss, she had the feeling of falling deep into a chasm where only he existed, ready and waiting to catch her.

Then he let her go.

His release was so sudden that it left Davina reaching for him with one hand and holding her heart with the other. As if letting her go pained him as much as it did her, he clutched her fingers grasping at his plaid and held them to his mouth.

"Fergive me," his voice broke on a ragged, remorseful breath. "I fear I canna' resist ye, even knowin' ye belong to God."

She watched his lips while he spoke, enraptured by their sensuous contours, remembering how they felt pressed so tenderly against hers, how he tasted of berries and checked desire. Always so in control. She had begun to fear that he didn't like her, but it was God he was worried about. She wanted to tell him the whole truth of it, but not now. She might tell him later and pray he would not turn her away. Now though, she wanted him to kiss her again.

She pulled him down slowly, knowing by his own words that he couldn't resist her. He was the first man in her life who couldn't. Even her father had stayed away.

Shyly at first, she tested the supple surrender of his mouth, dragging her lips over his, inhaling the hot sweetness of his breath. He groaned as if she'd caused him pain, and then closed his arms around her, pressing her to all his hard angles. She opened her mouth to his, clutching his plaid in both hands as he crushed her in his arms. She felt his tongue against her teeth, soft, thrilling, probing while the scent of him, the size of him enveloped her like smoke. She wanted to take refuge in it, to hide away in the shelter of his embrace, to feel wanted as she did right now for the rest of her life. But her life was not her own and too many warnings were going off in her head, though now they had nothing to do with her enemies.

"No." She fisted her hands at his chest and pushed off him. "We mustn't."

This time, he did not ask her forgiveness but stared at her, his breath short and heavy and his eyes burning into her like gleaming steel.

She looked away, closing her arms around herself in a futile attempt to drive out the cold longing she let invade her. "It will be dark soon. We should be getting back to the others."

"Aye." His voice was low and rough as he flicked his reins and turned his mount around.

They rode back in silence. Davina tried to concentrate on the sounds of life teeming around her, rather than on the truth that her life had not changed at all. Edward was correct, she was still James VII's daughter. There was no place for love in her future. If her enemies didn't find her, a marriage would be arranged for her, either to God, or one that best served the kingdom. She would never have a true family and while her heart longed for one, she had prepared herself for the lonely years ahead. She wished Rob had left her at Courlochcraig, when her heart was still guarded, her expectations, realistic. Now, after days of being held in the indomitable power of his embrace, after knowing the passion of his kiss, the thought of him leaving her left her trembling with a fear far greater than for her safety... or for his.

Peter Gilles tugged at the tips of his gloved fingers before pulling his hands free. The bitch was a wildcat, he thought, striding across the courtyard of Courlochcraig Abbey. He lifted his fingers to his face and winced at the stinging marks the Abbess had left there while he was strangling her. She'd fought hard and clung to her silence, even at the threat of death. Not that he would have left her or any of her novices alive after they'd seen him. They all had to die, but the rest he left to his men. Killing the Abbess was satisfying enough.

He would have liked to have taken a little more time with her. He enjoyed breaking courageous, spitfire women, but he'd grown impatient—one of his many faults to which he freely admitted. In the end though, her death served his purpose—as death usually did. Upon seeing her holy mother gasp her last breath, a rather striking young novice screamed what he wanted to know. A traveling novice called Davina had arrived at Courlochcraig, but she hadn't arrived alone.

Reaching the front gate, Gilles mounted his horse and scowled at the quiet Abbey. He hated Highlanders, and according to the fair Sister Elaine, their guest was escorted by four of them—and an English captain who had arrived later and needed healers. The captain couldn't be Asher, as Gilles had seen him dead. If he wasn't dead, he soon would be. The Highlanders could prove to be a more taxing nuisance, though. What Gilles knew of them from his years at Dutch court was that they fought with purpose and passion, mainly for their religious beliefs. Zealots. The Admiral spat onto the ground. There was nothing worse.

He tapped his boot against his mount's flank. How long did it take to kill a few women? They were losing precious time. If all went as planned, the exiled Earl of Argyll should have landed his ships in the west of Scotland by now to secure support. Monmouth would be arriving in England soon after that to pronounce himself king. Gilles didn't think the duke would make a satisfactory leader, but really, what concern was it of his? He only had to make certain there was no one else left to claim the throne after he killed Monmouth and Argyll and made the way for the true king.

Elaine had said the Highlanders were from the clan MacGregor, but she knew nothing more about them or where they were heading when they left. Their tracks were probably gone by now, but at least he knew which direction to take, that is, if they could get the hell out of Ayr.

"Maarten!" he shouted toward the Abbey. Clicking his tongue, his glare grew blacker at the silence around him. He was about to ride through the Abbey doors and finish the nuns himself when his captain exited, followed by the rest of his men.

"What was the holdup?" he asked when Maarten reached him.

The captain looked up, but only for a moment, then

pulled his sickened gaze away and dropped his blood-stained dagger to the ground. "Nothing. It is done."

"Good. Now let us be off. With any luck, Edgar and his party are on the lady's trail and have left us markers. We—"

"Not unless the lady has drowned in the river we crossed getting here," Hendrick informed him, reaching for his reins. "One of the sisters took great pleasure in telling me that the Highlanders killed our men and dumped them in the river. The leader, she said, slew six on his own."

Gilles's face contorted with rage and beneath him, his mount pranced backward at the viselike grip of its rider's thighs. "So, James's daughter has a champion. I'll make certain to kill her while he watches."

Maarten watched his Admiral wheel his horse around and thunder away from the front gate. "De Duivel," he whispered to himself, horrified by what he and the others had just done...again. "Perhaps God has finally sent a warrior to deliver us all to hell, where we belong."

Chapter Sixteen

Davina knew something was amiss just before they reached the tree line. It was too quiet. The sun was not yet down, so the men could not be asleep. She turned nervously to Rob and found him studying the campsite and slowing his mount to a silent halt.

He held his finger to his lips to quiet her while he peered through the thin tree trunks.

A moment later Davina heard the roar of hooves pounding the bank from the north. An army! Her heart nearly fainted in her chest. Where was Finn...Colin? She clutched at Rob's plaid to keep herself from calling out to them. Somewhere to her left a bird whistled softly, seemingly unfazed by the oncoming intruders. When Rob whistled back, her heart slowed, knowing who the bird was. She was still afraid to look at who was coming though. What if it was Gilles's men, or Argyll's? They'd found her before.

"Forgive me," she whispered, looking at Rob instead of over her shoulder at the approaching riders.

"Fer what, lass?" he asked just as quietly.

"For putting your life and the lives of the others in danger. I fear it will not stop."

Her name, falling so softly from his lips, set her pulse racing all over again. He brought his fingers to her face and traced the contour of her cheek. "Nae matter who comes, I'm no' goin' anywhere."

"But if you're hurt . . . or killed—"

He smiled directly at her and dipped his face closer to hers. "Trust me." His breath fell softly on her lips. "Ye have nothin' to fear."

Confidence, forged generations ago, lit his eyes like fiery kilns, igniting her faith in him. Allowing herself to give in to it, she exhaled the breath trapped in her lungs and nodded.

"Connor!"

She and Rob turned at the same time to see Finn charge through the trees on foot. "'Tis Connor! Connor!" he called out again, waving his arms at the riders.

"Dinna' move from here," Rob warned her and slipped from his saddle. His pulled his claymore from its sheath and held it at his side while he strode into the clearing.

Davina wanted to call out to him but covered her mouth with her hand instead. He knew what he was doing. He wouldn't die. With that thought firmly in her mind, she finally turned her eyes on the army. It was not as large as she feared, and the men were donned in the same deep red and white military attire as Edward.

Finn reached the soldiers first, tearing off his cap and waving it over his head. "Brother, 'tis me, Finn!"

The lead rider slowed his mount and leaped off before it came to a complete halt. He held up his hand to stop his men as he charged toward Finn, his smile wide and his sun-streaked hair peeking out from beneath a wide-brimmed hat cocked up on one side.

"Connor, what the hell are ye doin' here?" Rob threw down his sword and embraced the tall captain next.

"My men and I were sent to Glencoe last month to quell a small uprising between the MacDonalds and the Campbells. We are on our way back to England fer the coronation."

"Ye're a bit late," Rob pointed out.

"Aye," the other admitted with a dimpled smile as languid as his voice. "When I heard that most of the Highland chiefs were attending, I delayed my departure." He angled his head around Rob's shoulder and looked directly to where Davina was still hiding. "Is yer family with ye?"

Rob laughed and shook his head. "Nae, Mairi is in England."

"Then I am not late enough."

Everyone on Rob's side was smiling, save for Colin, whose scowl had grown blacker than Rob's on his angriest day. Still, it looked safe enough to Davina to dismount and join them.

Captain Connor Grant's wry grin deepened into something so nakedly male, so innately seductive, it near stopped her in her tracks.

"Yers?" he asked Rob without taking his eyes off her.

"Nae, she—"

"Davina," Finn plucked his cap from the ground, fit it back over his tousled hair, and raced to her side. "'Tis my brother, Captain Connor Grant."

Connor stepped around Rob and sauntered toward her. He moved with absolute power and the lithe, leisurely grace of a lion, confident in his prowess to catch his prey if it fled. Davina resisted the urge to step back and sized him up as boldly as he did her.

He wore the same military style short coat as Edward, but Connor's was crisper, silver buttons polished against scarlet, and fitting more snugly over a trim waist and shoulders almost as wide as Rob's. Like Finn's, his hair, when he removed his hat to greet her, was absent of any curl, cut slightly shorter and streaked in bold shades of flaxen and honey. But that was where the resemblance ended. His nose was sharper, his startling blue eyes shaded by more experience, and his smile, accented with a deep, roguish dimple on each side, banished any trace of innocence.

He reached for her hand and then flicked his gaze to Edward when the other captain stepped forward and introduced himself.

"May I also present Davina Montgomery, who is in my care," Edward added and dropped his gaze to Connor's fingers wrapped around hers.

"In *yer* care?" Connor asked skeptically, swinging his glance to Rob.

"We found her at St. Christopher's Abbey just ootside Dumfries," Rob said, shoving Edward out of his way.

"They were burning it down," Finn added, getting in on the conversation. "When we arrived, there was little left, and then Rob got sh—"

"Who was burning it down?" Connor dropped Davina's hand and gave his full attention to Rob.

"The Dutch," Rob told him soberly, "We are no' certain whose orders they were followin', the Duke of Monmouth or the Earl of Argyll. They killed the sisters, and Asher's regime of men."

Connor's jaw went taut and when he looked at Edward

again, sorrow and rage vied for dominance over his features. "What were yer men doing at the Abbey?"

When Edward didn't answer him right away, he settled his gaze back on Davina, but she looked away. She wasn't about to tell him anything. Captain Grant might be her cousin, but she knew firsthand that in noble courts, family sometimes meant very little.

"Connor." Rob pulled the captain's attention back to him. "'Tis gettin' dark. Make camp here tonight and I will tell ye what we know."

"Aye, my men could use the rest," Connor agreed, "We'll leave at first light. If the Dutch have arrived in England and have killed our soldiers, I must inform the king."

Davina bit her lip, worried what Rob might tell him, and then remembered that he didn't know much.

"So, ye are certain that the men who attacked the Abbey were Dutch?" Connor walked along the moonlit bank with Rob at his side. They did not venture far from the camp, but stayed well enough away so that the others could not hear them. "Did ye see them?"

"Aye, I saw what was left of them. I didna' know who they were until the lass told me."

"Could she have been mistaken?"

Rob shrugged his shoulders. He hadn't considered that she had. "Could Asher?"

Connor looked back at the camp and at the dark-haired captain watching them from his place by the fire.

"Accordin' to him," Rob continued, "the men were led by Admiral Peter Gilles."

"Gilles?" Connor's attention snapped back to Rob.

"Aye. D'ye know him?"

"I know of him. Satan's bloody arse, Rob," Connor said, raking his hand though his hair. "This does not bode well for the king. Though Gilles is the Duke of Monmouth's man, 'tis rumored that he has affiliations with William of Orange."

Rob thought about the implications while they walked. "So," he said after a moment, "the king may have enemies more powerful than he suspects."

"Aye, he may," Connor said thickly. "After Monmouth was exiled, Prince William staunchly denied any affiliation with him, or with Argyll, Gilles, or any of the Exclusionists who opposed a Catholic succession. Though my uncle did swear to having seen the Prince with Monmouth and Gilles when he was in Holland, William is James's son-in-law and with no other proof against him, remains in good standing with the new king."

"I understand why William would plan a rebellion against the king," Rob said, knowing firsthand now why England's politics were important to his clan. "With James gone, the prince's wife, Mary Stuart, is next in line fer the throne. But what will Monmouth benefit from such treason?"

"The Duke of Monmouth is Charles II's illegitimate son."

Rob stopped and looked at him. It made nae sense. If Monmouth deposed the king, Mary Stuart would claim the throne as James's firstborn legitimate daughter. Why would William give his support to a man who vied for his wife's succession? And why, after all Davina had told them about the new king and his policies, hadn't she told him that Monmouth claimed titleship to the throne?

"Supporters of a Protestant succession, including the Prince of Orange, rallied fer Monmouth to be named Charles's heir before the Exclusion Bill," Connor told him. "King Charles came very close to legitimizing Monmouth on a number of different occasions, but he never did."

What did any of this have to do with Davina?

"'Twas James who was formally acknowledged and Monmouth spoke severely against him in the House of Lords," Connor continued. "When Charles began hanging some of the duke's supporters, Monmouth fled to Holland with the already exiled Argyll. 'Tis been rumored that he returned a few months ago, but we did not know with any certainty."

"So Monmouth hates James fer religious—and more personal—reasons. Why no' strike James?" Rob asked. He hadn't tried to figure any of it out before. He hadn't cared, but now, feeling as if he was on the threshold of learning Davina's secrets, he did.

"Aye," Connor agreed. "And why an abbey full of nuns?"

"'Twas Davina they had come fer," Rob told him truthfully. Connor may have given his allegiance to his king, but he would die before betraying the MacGregors.

Connor looked at him, then over his shoulder again at the campsite. "Why her?"

"She will no' tell me why. No' the truth anyway." Rob's eyes found Davina when she laughed at something Finn said. "Nor will Asher." His eyes hardened when they settled on Davina's captain among the men. "He is in love with her."

"Are ye?"

Rob flicked his gaze to his friend. "She is a novice of the Order."

"Come now, Rob. She is obviously more than that," Connor pointed out dryly. "What has she told ye?"

"No' much, save that she is an orphan. Her parents were nobles from Whithorn. She refuses to tell me any more."

Connor smiled and shook his head at him. "Mayhap she hasn't given ye answers because it's obvious ye don't really want them."

"Ye're right. I dinna' care," Rob said in a low, warning tone. "I'm no' goin' to let her die."

"Well, I don't believe her family is from Whithorn," Connor said, watching her loop her arm through Finn's. "'Twould seem she is more than a baron's daughter."

Rob sighed, giving in to his own curiosity. He didn't believe it either. He knew in his heart that she was someone very important to the kingdom, but he didn't want to know any more than that. He didn't want a sound reason why he shouldn't ... couldn't bring her home.

"She could be Monmouth's sister," Connor ventured out loud. "King Charles was known to have fathered many bastards. She is beautiful enough to be a Stuart." Connor's voice went soft as the firelight made Davina's hair shimmer like misty clouds around a full moon. "Of course, then," he added uneasily, "that would make her my cousin."

His cousin. *Your friends have become my friends, my family.* Nae, she couldn't be. Rob looked at her, and then at Finn. They could be siblings. Och, hell, she couldn't be a Stuart. But even as his mind rejected that appalling notion, everything seemed to make more sense now. He fought back the sickening wave that washed over him. He didn't want to believe it. Hiding a novice from a duke was one thing; kidnapping the king's daughter was another thing entirely.

"It still does no' explain why Monmouth or anyone would try to have her killed," Rob said, hoping they were wrong. "Even if she is one of Charles's illegitimate bairns, she is no' a threat. A son always precedes a daughter. Unless..." Unless she was not illegitimate—and Charles was not her faither. Rob stopped and closed his eyes as everything suddenly became clear. Hell, if he was correct he was about to bring the entire Royal Army down on Camlochlin, and mayhap the entire Dutch army with it. "Connor, could she be James's daughter?"

For a moment, Connor simply stared at him, as if he could not comprehend such a possibility. "James is an ogler of women, to be sure, but I've heard of no children born to him save fer Mary and Anne from his marriage to Anne Hyde. He has no children from his second marriage to Mary of Modena. And why the hell would the king's daughter be living in a convent?"

For protection, Rob thought. Protection James was able to provide for his other two daughters who were forced to wed Protestants. His eldest daughter, Mary, was William of Orange's wife and next in line for the throne. Rob had another thought that drained the color from his face. What if Mary was not the king's firstborn?

Rob didn't realize he'd groaned out loud until Connor gripped his shoulder. "What is it?"

Davina hadn't just been living in an abbey. James had hidden his true heir away to ensure a Catholic succession should he perish—which birthed a new question. If

Connor didn't know of her, no one else likely did, either. How had her enemies found her? She had been guarded by over a hundred men. Any one of them could have betrayed her to her enemies. They were no longer a concern. But something else was. Monmouth, Argyll, or William of Orange was trying to kill the king's heir...and the only reason to do so was if they were planning to take out the king, as well.

"Rob, what is it that brings such terror to yer face? Ye must tell me."

"Aye, I will," Rob said setting his fiery blue eyes on his friend. "And then ye must swear to do somethin' fer me."

It didn't take Davina long to decide she liked Connor Grant almost as much as she liked Finn. After his talk with Rob, he seemed more somber, even barking out to his men to be awake at the crack of dawn. But after an hour of sharing his rations and his memories of Camlochlin, the merriment that he shared with his younger brother returned to his eyes and his inescapably contagious laughter warmed her insides more than the flames crackling before her. She did catch him staring at her from across the fire. It made her uncomfortable because he was looking at her the way she often looked at Finn, as if trying to recognize similarities between them. But when their eyes met, he winked and flashed her a lighthearted smile before he turned his laughter back to the men around him.

She found Rob staring at her as well, and something in his quiet regard stirred her blood, her emotions. His smile was not frivolous when he graced her with it, but tender, somewhat pained, and utterly beautiful.

Davina knew, nestled in a circle of family and friends,

tucked beneath a blanket of stars, that nothing in her future would ever be as difficult as resisting Robert MacGregor. If she lived to be forty she would never forget how his mouth felt against hers, or the shudders that weakened her when he pressed her to his body. Oh, he made her feel so alive. Even now, sitting close to him, close enough for his arm to brush hers, his musky male scent to invade her senses, her mettle dwindled, her breath stalled, and her nerve endings burned for something she did not fully understand. She closed her eyes to pray but the sound of his laughter lured her to look at him. When she did she forgot what she was asking of God. To change her path? To let her stay with Rob forever? What was a se'nnight of brooding compared to a smile so captivating it sucked the breath right out of her, or a kiss so beguiling that just the memory of it enraptured her? She wanted to be the one who brought joy to his life and fire to his eyes; the only one privy to his intimate expressions, his most private thoughts and desires.

And she wanted to trust him with hers.

"How does Tristan fare?" Connor asked Rob, bringing Davina's thoughts back to the present.

"He's still a careless rogue bastard," Colin answered for his brother, his voice dripping with the anger he'd been holding back since Connor arrived. "Much like yerself."

The blithe flicker in Connor's eyes sharpened like frost-tipped daggers on Rob's brother. "Ye wish to accuse me of something?"

"Aye, of tearing oot my sister's heart," Colin growled right back at him. "Talk of yer casual dips into the English loch of promiscuity has reached even our remote part of the world, Captain Grant."

Connor's features went hard. When he spoke, the deep, drawling pitch of his voice set a tremor to the air. "Ye speak with the boldness of a man. Use caution, else I'll be forced to remind ye that ye're still a lad."

Colin met the warning with a slow, challenging snarl. "Heed yer own words, Captain, else I'll be forced to make ye eat them."

Instead of putting an end to what, Davina was sure, was about to become a fight, Rob merely exchanged a knowing smirk with Will. Connor Grant smiled as well, and looking at him, Davina could imagine him moments before a battle he knew he was going to win.

When they both rose to their feet, she shot a concerned look at Rob, and received a reassuring wink in return.

"Lads," Will called out to Connor's men, then took a bite from an apple he'd pilfered from one of their saddle-bags, "ye're aboot to see yer captain on his knees."

"Never," one of the English soldiers called back as Connor and Colin moved a safe distance away. "The boy is about to be taught to respect his better."

"The MacGregors have nae betters." Eyeing the soldier with amusement, Will spit a seed from his lips. "Aye, Rob?"

"Aye," Rob agreed, still smiling, much to Davina's vast delight. "Colin, show these *English* how a Highlander fights."

His youngest brother's thick claymore came down upon Connor's sword with a clash that made half the men, including Will, cringe on impact. Connor met the blow with an upward thrust just as forceful. Davina shivered beside Rob, then froze altogether when he slipped his plaid off his shoulder and covered her with it. She did her best to ignore the warmth of his closeness, and the memory of all that hard muscle closing around her when he'd kissed her, by watching Colin parry and jab with brutal precision. The boy's lean physique lent to his agility, but the force in his blows erupted from someplace stronger than sinew. In the end however, it was Connor's experience and perhaps his own Highland upbringing that proved victorious. He took no joy in it though and even quieted his men when they began to cheer him.

"Hell, MacGregor," he said, out of breath when he placed his hands on Colin's shoulders, "my words are bitter indeed. Come to England with me. The new king needs men like ye."

"The lad would rather be flayed skinless and thrown into a vat o' hot oil," Will laughed, tossing his apple core over his shoulder.

"I'll only fight fer Scotland, Connor," Colin told him, returning his sword to its sheath. Will nodded and leaned his head against the tree he was sitting under. "But I will go to England with ye."

"What?" Will sat up and cast him a stunned look.

"I want to meet him, this new king." Colin didn't take his eyes off Connor, save for when he glanced at Davina. "What I have heard of him has piqued my interest."

"Just dinna' come back in an English uniform," Will warned him, then closed his eyes again.

"Finn will come as well," Connor told his brother as he returned to his place at the fire opposite Davina.

"Nae!" Finn protested. "I don't want to go to England." He turned to Rob, his eyes wide with pleading. "I want to go home."

Davina didn't want him to go with Connor either.

She didn't know how long she would be in Skye or if she would ever see him again. She didn't realize her shoulders had stiffened until Rob rubbed his hand over them.

"Ye're a Stuart, lad," Rob said gently, his affection for Finn evident in his voice. "England will likely be yer home one day, as 'tis yer brother's."

"I'm a Grant, as well. And my home is Camlochlin."

Rob smiled, as did Davina, but both for different reasons.

"He's stayin'," Rob told Connor in a tone that put an end to the topic.

Davina didn't know if Mairi MacGregor had anything to do with Connor leaving Skye, or if he left out of loyalty to the royal side of his family, but it was clear that the conversation between Rob and Finn pained him. "Captain Grant?" she said, hoping to return him to his pleasant mood. "Finn has told me wondrous stories about your mother. Is she truly as brave as he says?"

Connor looked up, his easy smile returning. "Probably more so."

"I cannot wait to meet her," Davina told him, sincerely eager for the day. "Tell me more about your family, won't you?"

Connor looked at Rob and something secretive and cautious passed between them. Then he told her all she wanted to know, and their laughter lasted long into the night, coiling the threads of happiness and hope around Davina's wary heart.

Chapter Seventeen

ℛob walked along the bank alone, unmindful of the spectacular sunrise splashing the loch with glittering hues of gold and burnt orange. It was only the second time he'd left Davina since Courlochcraig, but there were enough men with her this morn. She would be safe without him for as long as it took him to bathe. But soon he found his need to think clearly prevailing over his need to be clean. So he walked slowly, barefoot over the reeds and mossy rocks, his boots dangling from his hand at his side. He had enough good sense to know that being plagued by thoughts of Davina Montgomery—or Stuart—would lead to no good. But what good was good sense when all his other senses were consumed with her? How would he be able to make wise decisions for his clan if he had to see Davina, talk to her every day at Camlochlin, without being able to touch her again? More importantly, when had his duties to his clan ceased to matter compared to her safety? How could he be so reckless and still consider taking her home knowing who she was? God have mercy on them all, she was the king's daughter! Aye, he was certain of it now. He'd watched her last eve and the way she stared at Connor and Finn as if they were the brothers she'd been searching for all her life and finally found. Now, the emotion he saw in her eyes when she spoke of the king made sense. She was his daughter....Hell, he was falling in love with the king's daughter! 'Twas bad enough that he'd decided to risk God's wrath by kissing her, by wanting her so badly nothing else mattered. But the bloody king...

When he came to a sandy inlet he dropped his boots and looked out over the loch. She was heir to the throne! She could never be his and the danger she posed to the people of Camlochlin had increased tenfold. Still, now more than ever he knew he had to protect her. He had already decided to continue on with her when he told Will and the others last eve who he believed her to be. Camlochlin was their home and they had a right to know what decisions he was making that could affect their future. As he suspected, the lads agreed to bring her home despite the danger. Aye, they had all gone mad.

How the hell had Gilles's men found her? How did her enemies know she even existed when it seemed no one else did? Of course, Asher knew who she was, and the Abbess at Courlochcraig knew, as well. Rob understood now why both of them had refused to tell him anything. But what about Davina? When was she going to trust him enough to share the truth with him? Mayhap William of Orange knew of her through his wife, Davina's sister. Were Monmouth and Argyll planning a rebellion with the Prince of Orange? Which one of them had ordered Davina's death?

None of those questions mattered when weighed against the fact that she was the king's daughter. Even if her enemies never found her, her father would surely come for her. What would Rob do then? Would he lead his clan into war over a lass? And what if she wanted to go? What if she knew her duty, and like him, was determined to see it done?

He should send her away now, before he lost his heart, and everything else, to her completely. He should, but he wasn't going to. Not after he'd kissed her and felt her heart beating frantically against her round breasts. Especially not after she'd kissed him back—her plump, warm lips curious at first, and then as hungry as his own. She was innocent, but her mouth was so sweetly wanton that he was tempted to give up everything in his life just to taste her again.

He tugged his shirt over his shoulders, tossed it to the ground, and stepped into the water. The frigid sting numbing his calves was just what he needed to quell the raging fire Davina incited in him. Squatting, he used a length of his plaid to scrub himself clean. He cupped his hands to gather the water and splashed it onto his face then loosened his hair and ran his wet fingers through it. He would bring her to Skye, keep her safe, and be content with just that for now. Aye, he could do it. As long as no one ever tried to hurt her, he could be content. He would worry about the king—and his own father—later.

He straightened, feeling better, and shook the water from his hair.

"I was looking for you."

He snapped his head up and knew he was a fool for thinking anything could douse what Davina stirred in him. Just looking at her made his muscles tighten with a need to have her, hold her, protect her. She stood alone, her fingers entwined in front of her, resting on the soft green wool of her skirts. She'd tied her hair up at her temples, exposing her slightly oversized ears, the sweet contours of her face. She was as slight as a veil, utterly defenseless against the storm that lurked in the distance. How could anyone want to hurt her?

She was looking for him. *"I am not afraid when I'm with you."* Aye, 'twas worth every tormenting hour spent in front of his father's sword to hear her say that.

He cleared his throat to keep himself from smiling at her like some watered down, doddering excuse for an English captain. "I was just aboot to start back."

"Why?" She blocked his path to stop him from going. "Rob, I don't want you to think you have to . . ."

"But I do." He moved closer toward her, drawn by the strength she cloaked around herself, and seduced by the vulnerability she tried to conceal beneath it. Then he remembered who she was and stopped. "I must."

"No." She took a step forward. A soft blush stole across her cheeks as her gaze traversed his bare chest and belly, his wet hair streaked across his face giving more depth to the startling need in his eyes. "No, Rob. I won't let you. You have done so much for me without even knowing why I am hunted. One day, you will understand why I have not told you."

He already did. She did not trust him.

"I will not risk your life until then."

When he opened his mouth to speak, she held up her palm, stopping him. "I've already asked Connor to take me away."

Rob wasn't sure whether to laugh or go find Connor and punch out a few of his teeth. "He isna' takin' ye any-where," he told her instead, not caring how hard he was scowling at her.

"No, he isn't," she agreed, moving dangerously closer to him. "He is suddenly very eager to return to England. But he has assured me that he is as gallant a man as you and has agreed to have his men escort me to Ireland without question. No one will find me there."

Was she mad? Ah, God help him, was he? "I will find ye," he vowed. He did not expect her eyes to go all soft and liquid on him, or the effect her tears would have on the last shred of his good sense.

"No, Rob, please." Slowly, she lifted her fingers to the wound in his shoulder. The wound she'd given him. It was almost completely healed now. She touched it and his muscles twitched beneath her fingertips. "You don't understand—"

"Then help me understand, Davina." He could have told her then that he knew the truth—that Connor knew it as well. But he wanted her to tell him—to trust him with her life.

"It is too dangerous," she said softly. "I won't have you hurt...or worse because of me. I'll be safe in Ireland."

His hands clenched into fists at his sides. 'Twas all he could do to keep them there and not drag her into his arms. He couldn't have her, but he was going to keep her alive. "Ye'll be safe with me."

When she looked at him her eyes were full of regret. "But no one else will be."

Rob knew she understood what protecting her meant and once again, she was trying to protect him, finding some inner strength to turn him away. It made him ache even more to protect her. And he would. Her enemies would not find her in Skye, and if they did, Rob would slash open their throats before they reached Kylerhea.

"My clan will stand behind my decisions. They are MacGregors and if they need to fight, they will. And we will win."

"You sound so certain," she told him, drifting closer still until he could feel her breath on his chin when she looked up at him. "So sure that all will be well. You make me believe it too. But I..." She closed her eyes and moved now to step away. "I cannot..."

He snatched her back, hauling her to his chest with a force that knocked the breath out of her. He didn't care who the hell she was. He'd never cared about England or her kings before, and he wasn't going to start now. "Trust me, Davina." He bent to her and brushed his mouth over hers. "Trust me," he found himself pleading, wanting it from her more than he'd realized, more than desire, more than possession.

Her smile was all the answer he needed, but when she flung her arms around his neck, he smiled back and covered her mouth with his.

"Very well then," she whispered..., breaking their kiss. "There is something I would like to tell you. But later." She smiled again, blushed, and then met the passion in his kiss when he lifted her off her feet.

"Rob." Connor's voice wrenched Davina's mouth away as she turned, scarlet to her roots. Her mortification was made complete by the sight of Edward standing at Connor's side and wearing a look of crushed disbelief on his face.

Connor, on the other hand, didn't look surprised at all by the couple's passionate embrace, but he did spare Rob a measured glance before he spoke. "We grew alarmed when ye didn't return, Miss Montgomery, but I see ye are in good hands."

When Davina slipped down his body and out of his arms, Rob's initial instinct was to grab for her hand and pull her back, but she was already halfway to Asher. Clenching his jaw to keep himself from calling her back, Rob watched her captain lead her away.

"We'll be leaving shortly."

Rob turned his glacial gaze on his old friend. "Then be on yer way, Connor." He pushed past him and bent to retrieve his boots. "But she's stayin' with me."

"Ye're still taking her to Camlochlin then?"

"Aye."

"Ye've thought this through, Rob?"

"Aye, I have." When Rob straightened, his eyes, eclipsed by his damp, dark locks, were level with Connor's. "And I willna' be moved on it."

"I understand ye have formed an attachment to the girl," Connor said, hurrying to catch up when Rob strode off. "But nothing can come of it. If we are correct about who she is, the king will never agree to a union between the two of ye."

Pausing, Rob turned on him, his voice rigid with control. "Hell, d'ye think I dinna' know that?"

"Judging from what I just saw, I don't think ye care."

Rob rarely lost his temper. He'd found, thanks to his constant training, that when he did, 'twas very difficult for him to get it back and noses usually got broken. He did his best not to lose it now with a friend. "If I didna' care, I would have…" He ground his jaw around crass words that were not in his character to utter. "I'm no' Tristan."

"I know," Connor told him sincerely, seeing the storm pass. "And that's what concerns me. Ye are not reckless."

Rob turned away, knowing where the conversation was

heading and preferring not to hear any more of it. Davina and Asher were just up ahead and he kept his eyes on them as he walked.

"I will do as ye asked me last eve," Connor said, catching up again. "I'll warn the king of Monmouth's, and possibly William of Orange's plans, but keep from him the truth about his daughter's rescue until we know more, but ye cannot bring her to Camlochlin, Rob. 'Tis too dangerous."

"I have nae choice in the matter, Connor," Rob told him. "And as long as ye dinna' tell the king where she is, she will be safe. Whoever wants her dead willna' find her there."

"Mayhap ye're correct, but what if ye're not? The Admiral found her once already."

"Aye, and I am curious to know how he did," Rob said. Something pricked at the edge of his memory, but when he reached for it, it eluded him. "There must be someone at court who knows of her existence. That is why I ask ye no' to tell the king that she lives."

"Rob," Connor stopped him just before they reached the campsite. "Though I spent my years at Camlochlin with Mairi and Tristan, I consider ye my brother. I don't agree with what ye're doing, but I'll stand by ye on it. I'm leaving six of my men with ye to escort ye to Oban. I have a small ship docked there and my men will take ye to Sleat. 'Tis faster than traveling on horseback, and the men can be trusted to deliver ye without revealing yer whereabouts should anyone question them."

Rob nodded and smiled for the first time that morning. "Ye have my gratitude, Connor. I know I ask much of ye by keepin' the truth from the king—" Connor drew in a deep breath, proving the task would be a difficult one. "—When ye get to England, try no' to get into trouble with Tristan, and remember how many daggers Mairi keeps under her skirts."

Connor laughed, then looked over Rob's shoulder at Davina. "Keep my cousin safe, and yer heart in yer chest, old friend."

"I will," Rob promised, knowing he could accomplish at least one of the two tasks.

Chapter Eighteen

I don't know which of the two disappoints me more, my lady." Edward did not look at Davina the entire way back to the camp. She was thankful he didn't, for his words and the tone in which he spoke them stung enough. "That you've surrendered your virtue to a man like him, or that you are foolish enough to trust him with your secrets."

"How dare you speak of my virtue, Edward?" She didn't realize the snap of her voice until he blinked as if she'd struck him. In the past she would have felt terrible for speaking so harshly to him, but not now. Not after such an insult not only to her, but to Rob, as well. She knew she'd been wrong to kiss the Highlander, but God have mercy on her, the sight of his hard body dripping wet and half naked was impossible to ignore. Still, she could have found the strength to do so if he hadn't looked at her with such longing in his eyes . . . if he hadn't vowed to find her if she left him . . . if he hadn't asked her to trust him yet again. She had no idea what kind of man her father had planned for her if she lived, but she had known enough men to convince her that none could ever compare to Rob MacGregor. She wanted to toss her title to the four winds and live a normal, quiet life with a man who held her as if his very life depended on her. She wanted to be his. Just his and nothing more.

"It disappoints *me,* Edward, that rather than be thankful for all that *a man like him* has done for us, you look down on him as if you were that much better."

Edward's eyes finally met hers as they entered the camp. He looked far less repentant than she expected. In fact, the spark of anger in his eyes made her want to step back.

"Though my faults will no doubt become clearer to you throughout this journey, I will still be at your side, even after he abandons you."

Davina blinked up at him, then looked the other way when Finn called her. Out of all the men there, she didn't want a Stuart to see her mettle crumble to pieces. She wondered how it was only just now that she realized the full weight of the fear she had lived with for so long—fear Edward constantly perpetrated. Whatever his motives were all these years, it had stripped her of so much. With all her heart she wanted to give Rob what he asked of her, her trust. But the truth was too immense. She had learned well the value of her life as the successor's heir to the throne. Rob, too, had seen the cost of it on St. Christopher's front lawns. Would he be so willing to fight for her if he had to battle more than the Duke of Monmouth's men?

When he stepped into the camp with Connor, she couldn't help but look at him. His presence made her nerves tingle with life. The sight of his sculpted chest, glistening arms, and tight belly reminded her of how capably he'd fought Gilles's men by the bridge in Ayrshire. He walked like nothing could stand in his way. He held her, both on his horse and off, like she was his woman. His kiss made her forget her past and her future.

As he passed her, his eyes, like two fiery jewels, slid to Edward's and darkened at what he saw looking back at him. Davina turned in time to catch the challenge in Edward's gaze and scowled at him. Was he mad? A fight between the two men would surely end in Rob's favor. Thankfully, Edward's confidence of a victory could not hold up against Rob's and he dropped his eyes to his boots.

Soon, Davina's attention was pulled to the men's cheerful farewells. She was swallowed up in Connor's surprisingly warm embrace first. When she faced Colin, she smiled awkwardly. She had shared many late-night talks with Rob's younger brother, but he concealed well his impressions of her and her views behind his harshly chiseled features and watchful wolf-colored eyes. As she expected, he didn't smile back.

"I'm going to speak to him," he promised, striding toward her. "And I'm going to discover if he is deserving of yer esteem."

Davina knew who he meant and nodded. "I pray that he is."

Miracle of miracles, his mouth curled into a smile that Davina was certain would fell more lasses than Finn's.

"So do I, fair lady."

Davina let Finn take hold of her hand when the men finally left, and then she listened to him when he took his place at Rob's horse's flanks and proudly told her everything there was to know about the courageous Captain Connor Grant.

Edward rode at a distance behind them, but Davina

could feel his eyes on her, hear his warning in her ear as clearly as if he was speaking into it.

Say nothing, else he will leave you.

And so, despite the desire to confide her most terrible secret to Rob, she told him nothing as they journeyed to Oban—and hated herself for it. Oh, when had she become such a self-serving, cowardly wretch? She was afraid he would leave her, but her fear no longer had anything to do with her safety. She was falling in love with him—hopelessly, maddeningly in love with him, and the thought of never seeing his face again, never feeling his arms around her, never kissing him again made her ill with despair. She didn't want Rob, or anyone else to die because of her, but thanks to her champion's skill and confidence she didn't believe anyone would. It was a weak excuse, that, but convincing herself of it made it easier to remain silent as they boarded the English ship that would bring them to Sleat.

Normally, Rob didn't enjoy traveling over water. He much preferred his feet firmly planted on solid ground. He couldn't deny that the English ship was the finest, if not the largest vessel he'd ever been on, but it still pitched too much for his liking. To keep himself steady, he leaned his back against the foremast and braced his legs beneath him. His eyes settled, as they always did whenever she was away from him, on Davina. Against a backdrop of a vast azure sky, she stood like Calypso at the bow, her shoulders thrust back against the gale, her pale tresses whipping behind her like a pennant.

Rob's eyes softened on her, as did his heart each time he beheld her. And the closer they came to Camlochlin, the more of her he saw. 'Twas like watching a butterfly breaking free of its cocoon and slowly unfolding its wings to fly. Hell, he wanted her to fly. He wanted to fly with her. He hadn't pressed her about what she wanted to tell him the morning Connor left. He could not force her to trust him with such a secret. He could only hope that with time she would.

When she turned and waved at him, her cheeks pink and her smile wide, his knees nearly gave out. Of course, it could have been from the ten-foot swell crashing against the hull. She laughed, mindless of the fathoms below. She might have spent many of her years afraid of an unseen enemy, but being tossed about on heaving waves gave her pleasure.

"Is that Skye?" she called out, pointing to a small isle to his left.

"Nae, 'tis Eig," he shouted back, then clutched the mast above his head when the ship dipped to the left. Her laughter was snatched up by the churning wind as she bid him come to her. He shook his head, not really caring if she thought him foolish or afraid for staying so close to the foremast. He wasn't about to go overboard for any lass—unless he absolutely had to.

She appeared as insubstantial as a feather when she let go of the railing and moved toward him. At that instant, the stem of the ship pitched upward, lifting the bowsprit toward the heavens. Instinctively, Rob reached for her with his free arm and pulled her against his chest. She landed with a thud that stole her breath—and his—for a different reason entirely. He stared down into her eyes, lost in their silvery blue depths, slain by a carefree smile as radiant as the sun peeking over the Cuillin hills.

"Careful, lass," he said softly, deeply while her long hair coiled around him. "I dinna' want to lose ye."

"Nor I you," she told him just as meaningfully and then drew her bottom lip between her teeth as if she'd said too much.

Damn his will to resist her. He'd given up that fight when she'd flung her arms around his neck the morning Connor and Asher found them together. He smiled, dipping his mouth to hers and his hand down her back. At the alluring indent just above her buttocks, he spread his palm wide and pushed her deeper against the crook of his thighs. He held her close while he took her mouth and the seas bucked and rocked beneath them. Softly at first, his tongue stole around her mouth, tasting, stroking her until she quivered in his arms. No man had kissed her before him, and none would ever kiss her after him. Each day that he held her in his arms was another test of his will not to caress her, claim her, and kill anyone who tried to harm her. But he was lost and would fight it no longer.

The sweet wantonness of her response made every inch of him grow tight and as he moved his lips over hers, devouring her now with need, he brushed his stiffness against the warmth of her niche.

She pulled back, eyes wide, cheeks flushed. Rob ground his jaw, for the apology he would have offered her felt trite and insincere. He was not sorry. Even now, he wanted more of her.

"My lady?"

Rob and Davina turned together to Asher standing just a few feet away, his hands rolling into fists at his sides.

"Are you all right?"

Glaring at him, Rob pulled Davina closer in a possessive

gesture, and to help conceal her effect on him. He had been patient and as understanding as any man could be about Asher's feelings toward Davina, but he was tired of her captain constantly wedging himself between them, and he refused to be insulted by an Englishman.

"She has no', nor will she come to any harm in my care, Captain."

The rigid pitch of Rob's tone alerted Will that someone's head was about to roll. Asher slanted his gaze in his direction when Will began to move forward. "You've no idea," he said, turning back to Rob, "the force that will come against you."

A force most likely led by ye, Rob thought, pushing off the mast and moving toward him. How easily he could toss Asher over the side of the ship and be done with him once and for all. Davina would hate him for it if he did. Rob knew Asher was jealous, but something about him had changed when he'd come upon them with Connor, locked in each other's arms. Before, there had been caution and constant worry in the captain's eyes, but since that morn, there was only black anger, and for the first time, Rob saw him as a threat. Would he alert the king to Davina's whereabouts to keep her from him? "Let them come," Rob told him, his jaw taut, and his gaze hard as granite, "and let them fear me."

Asher offered him a pitying smile. "You may be skilled with a sword, MacGregor, but a few dozen Highlanders against an army is no match."

Rob returned his smile with one riddled in arrogance. "Nae army will ever reach us alive."

"Sentries?" the captain asked.

Rob shook his head and flashed him a cool grin. "Cannons."

Finn's shout from the fore top pierced the stunned silence that had descended on deck. "Land! 'Tis bonnie Skye ahead!"

Asher and Davina turned to look north at the Sleat peninsula rising from the waves. But Rob's gaze cut longingly westward, beyond Loch Slapin, toward the misty peaks of Sgurr Na Stri and the Cuillin mountains. Home. The place of his heart. The thing he loved above all else—His eyes drifted to Davina rushing back to the railing—save for her.

Chapter Nineteen

⟨T⟩hey docked in Tarskavaig Bay on the western shore of the peninsula and traveled north along the rugged coastline. Tarskavaig, Finn was happy to relate to Davina (riding at her flank, of course), was one of the largest crafting settlements on Skye and had a long history steeped in Norse origins.

But instead of relishing the quaint beauty of the dozens of small houses scattered across the shallow valley before her, Davina's thoughts clung to the man sitting behind her on his horse. She'd dreamed of seeing the world outside St. Christopher's gates, had wasted away her days lost in other places where mothers and fathers didn't have to give up their babes. But now, when one such place lay spread out around her, none of it mattered. Edward had been right when he said Rob had no idea what would come against him, but she knew, and it gnawed at her until she felt ill. If the MacGregors shot their cannons at the King's army, there would be war. She couldn't let it come to that. She'd had plenty of time to think on the ship and she knew that Edward had been wrong about one thing. Rob would not abandon her even if he knew it was the king's army he might be facing. Her heart was certain of it now, for she'd tasted it in his kiss, felt it in the strength of his embrace, and the tantalizing proof of how he wanted to possess her.

The memory of his readied manhood between her thighs heated her insides and made her acutely aware of every hard curve pressed against her back now. She might have been raised in a convent, but she wasn't completely ignorant of what took place between men and women. The Abbess at St. Christopher's had told her, preparing her for the day of her marriage, if it ever came. Besides that, she'd seen enough sheep and cattle, and even horses to know what the mating ritual was about. As basely primitive as it might be, the thought of her and Rob locked in nature's ancient dance made her tingle to the soles of her feet. She wondered what it would be like to lie with him, to hold all that strong male body in her arms, to hear him whisper words of love while he made her his. *Never, Davina,* she forced herself to think logically. *It will never be. You were not born for this life.* Someone would find her, either the Duke's men, or God forbid it, her father's.

She should never have let Rob bring her to Skye. It wasn't too late. She had to tell him the truth and gather her strength to request that he bring her back to the ship before Connor's men left Sleat. They could still take her to Ireland. It had to be this way. She couldn't bear the thought of anyone dying because of her.

Edward looked as miserable as she felt while they trotted over carpeted bluebells, past hillocks lined with grazing sheep that took no notice of them whatsoever. Davina pushed her friend from her thoughts. She knew why he was angry. He'd been honorable to her and to his king, putting his love for her aside only to see her surrender hers to a Highlander. She would speak to him about it later. But for now, Edward would have to wait.

Determined to her purpose, she turned in Rob's lap and looked up at him. The moment she did, she felt her fortitude wilt. A smile lurked at the edges of his mouth, and, as if he knew her concerns before she spoke them, that unconquerable confidence he possessed shone like embers in the smoky blue of his eyes, wilting her anxious heart, as well.

God and all His saints help her, she loved this man. And because she did, she had to tell him the truth. "Rob?"

"Aye, lass?"

"There is something I must tell you."

"What is it?" he asked rather nonchalantly and lifted his gaze to the hills above her head.

"I'm afraid you're going to be angry with me for keeping it from you, even lying to you."

He dipped his eyes briefly to hers. "I willna' be angry, but I will expect ye to be truthful from now on."

"I will. I'm going to," she promised, girding up her loins to finally tell him. He wouldn't leave her, so she had to leave him. "Rob?" She tugged on his sleeve for his full attention. When she had it, she forged on straight ahead before her nerve left her. "I'm King James's daughter." There, she said it. It wasn't really so difficult. She'd never spoken those words aloud to anyone before and it was quite freeing, finally sharing this weight with someone other than Edward. She realized with her next breath that Rob hadn't said a word. Oddly enough, he was back to smiling.

"Perhaps you did not understand me," she tried again. "I am the King's..." The remainder of her declaration

came to an abrupt halt when he slowed his mount and slid
out of his saddle.

"Off yer mounts, men," he called over his shoulder to
Will and Finn without taking his eyes from hers. "And
pay yer princess the homage she is due."

Davina watched, stupefied, as the three Highlanders
dropped to one knee. They weren't angry, nor did even a
crease of concern mar any of their brows. They must think
her jesting, or mad. Yes, she thought she saw Finn's bright
grin beneath his bent head. She had no idea what to say to
them, or how to react. She'd worried over many possible
different reactions, but disbelief was not one of them.

Slipping from the saddle, she turned to them—to Rob.
"You don't believe me again but I am being truthful with
you. Edward will attest to my claim. Won't you, Edward?"
She didn't wait for his support, but continued on, twisting
her skirts in her fingers. "I'm James Stuart's firstborn—
which most unfortunately—makes me next in line for the
throne. I don't think you—"

"I know what it makes ye, Davina," Rob said, still on
one knee and looking up at her with lapis eyes. The sound
of her name on his lips almost made her smile. She shook
her head to clear it.

"But I . . . Oh please, do get up—all of you." The three
men obeyed, and upon straightening, Finn winked at her.

Davina's eyes opened wide as it dawned on her why
none of them were surprised. She blinked back to Rob.
"You already knew?"

"It doesna' matter."

"It certainly does!" She pulled away from his touch
when he reached for her. "Are you mad? You knew who I
was and you still brought me to Skye?"

"Aye." That, and his deepening smile were all the reply he gave her.

"I cannot let you! I will not! You saw what Gilles's men did at St. Christopher's."

"The Admiral is nae longer yer concern, Davina, nor is Monmouth or Argyll."

She wasn't certain if it was Rob's stubborn conviction or her own foolish hope that tempted her to believe him. Oh, if it were only true. "And my father? If he comes for me, and you—"

"Yer faither thinks ye dead and will continue with that belief fer as long as I can help it."

It was true. The Abbey and all the inhabitants of St. Christopher's were naught but ash. Gilles might believe her alive but he would never go to the king with his suspicions. Was she really free? Could she truly walk away from everything she'd prepared for her entire life? "Do you think you can keep me hidden from the world, then?"

His eyes swept over the vast landscape, toward the jagged cliffs and high frosty mountain peaks well beyond the bay, and he nodded. "Aye," he said, returning his gaze to hers. "I do. What will it take fer ye to trust what I say, lass?"

Before she could stop it, hope sprang up in Davina's heart like a wellspring. Hope offered to her by no one else in her life but by this one man. She did trust Rob, more even than Edward. Could she finally enjoy a life where she was simply Davina and not heir to the throne—even for a little while? Oh, God, please. Just for a little while. She smiled as she allowed that hope to spill forth. "Then let us be away."

As if he'd been standing on the edge of the earth

waiting for her and this moment when she surrendered all her fears to him, he closed the gap between them in two strides and gathered her into his arms. "Before nightfall, we will be lost, Davina. Ferget yer past and dinna' look back."

She clung to him while his lilting burr against her ear sent sparks down her spine. Lost. Lost in his arms, his kiss, his sometimes brooding, always breathtaking eyes. But what of her duty to England and to her Catholic faith? It might someday be up to her to uphold everything her father believed. Here it was again, the question she had pondered so many times alone in St. Christopher's bell tower. Which life would she choose if the choice were hers to make? "I won't look back," she whispered as their lips met.

"As enticing as your chivalry is, MacGregor—" Breaking the spell between them, Edward cantered his horse forward and cast Rob an apologetic look. "You must know that the king will never cease searching for her the moment he knows she's alive."

"Who is there to tell him, Asher?" Rob put to him curiously, menacingly. "No' Captain Grant, fer he gave me his word no' to speak of her."

Edward's horse bucked and neighed beneath him. "If the men who sailed us to Sleat are questioned—"

"They dinna' know who she is," Rob reminded him and lifted Davina back into his saddle. "And even if they did, they dinna' know where we're goin'."

"They brought us here!" Edward laughed.

"But we are no' stayin' here," Rob informed him, leaping into the saddle next. "Many know that the MacGregors live on Skye, but most dinna' know where. We prefer to keep it that way."

"Well," Edward asked, a bit impatiently. "How do we get there?"

Passing them, Will's devilishly handsome smirk belied the tremor of anxiety marking his voice. "A short ferry ride across Loch Eishort and a careful trek through the chasm o' hell, and there we will be."

Riding up behind Will, Finn laughed and shook his head with bewilderment. "How is it that ye can face a horde of MacPhersons bent on killing ye, but ye're afraid of heights?"

Will's only reply was a quick smack to the back of Finn's head as the lad passed him.

Davina wasn't worried about Will's "chasm of hell." She'd been there before when Gilles's men attacked her home, and she lived through it, thanks to the man behind her who feared nothing—save of course, for a few waves churning beneath his boots. Smiling at the memory of her brave champion fastened to the ship's mast, Davina nestled closer against him.

"Is Camlochlin as beautiful as this?" she asked softly, finally taking in the splendor of the waterfall-laden shore coming into view as they traveled northward.

"No' yet," Rob answered close to the ear. "But soon 'twill be."

Chapter Twenty

After crossing Loch Eishort, Will became increasingly agitated, even snapping at Finn when the lad chatted on endlessly to Davina about the Vikings who perished there long ago while trying to cross the cliffs of Elgol. Davina found it rather amusing to watch the self-confident warrior come undone by the landscape. He didn't bother to conceal his fear, but assured Davina, while mopping his sweaty brow with his sleeve, that soon she would be clinging to Rob the way a terrified child clings to its mother.

When they rounded the end of Loch Slapin, following its edge south, Davina understood the cause of Will MacGregor's anxiety, for the cliffs, dotted with caves and moss, rose up as high as the heavens and vanished into a hovering mantle of pure white mist.

"You don't expect us to cross that on horseback, do you?" Edward groaned, teetering in his saddle as he craned his neck at the view. "There must be another way."

"There is; through the hills," Rob told him with a gentle snap of his reins. "But 'tis the longer way 'round and trust me, this way is safer if ye dinna' want an arrow in yer chest. Keep yer horse under yer control. Stay behind me and ye'll be fine."

Angling her head around Rob's shoulder, Davina offered Edward a soothing smile as he reluctantly trotted forward with a pale-faced Will behind him and Finn at the rear.

"Ye're no' afraid, then?"

Aiming her generous smile at Rob, Davina shook her head and then turned to glory in the view. She hadn't been entirely truthful with him, for her heart beat madly in her chest. Who wouldn't be afraid perched at the edge of the world? No dream, nor idle fancy could ever have prepared her for this place. Breath held, she spread her gaze over the chiseled behemoth of the Cuillins looming from the clouds across the loch. But she had no more time for fear and with Rob at her side, no more cause for it.

"How high are we going?"

"To the top."

The urge to clutch his hands to her chest passed as they climbed the narrow precipice above Loch Scavaig, its whitecaps crashing into the rock face below. She looked down, bending far enough over Rob's horse to make Will swear at her.

Tossing him a hasty apology, she settled into Rob's chest and slanted her curious smile at him. "Are you not afraid of falling into the water?"

"I've crossed these ledges too many times to fear fallin' off them. And I'm no' afraid of the water. I just prefer my feet on solid ground."

"To be certain, you're a steady, unshakable man, Robert MacGregor."

He thanked her, and then bent his mouth to her ear when she giggled. "D'ye find fault with those qualities, then, Princess?"

Over the course of their journey together, Rob's deep, melodic voice had begun to feel as if it were coming from inside her, rather than from close behind. The touch of his body against her back, the caress of his arms coiled loosely about her waist had become familiar to her, comforting, and more profoundly intimate than even kissing him felt. She had no idea what kind of life awaited her beyond this ancient threshold that even Vikings could not penetrate, and though she was excited to begin living, she did not want the journey to end.

"Of course, I don't find fault with you, save for if you're going to call me Princess from now on. But I do believe you could use a little more pleasure in your life."

"D'ye now?"

"Yes." She turned to look up at him fully and was surprised that she could find anything more beautiful than the scenery. "I would like to help you..." His eyes were the color of the landscape, but infinitely more tender. "...find pleasure."

"I canna' wait." His slow, salacious grin made her burn below her navel and she blushed, realizing too late how shameless her offer sounded.

Oh, to Hades with pretenses! She could not wait either. She wanted him to kiss her. No, she wanted more than that. She wanted to surrender all to him and trust him with the outcome. She wanted to get lost in this dream and never ever return. She closed her eyes and parted her lips, but only his warm breath touched her mouth. "Later, Davina," he promised huskily. "I must keep my wits aboot me, else we *will* fall. But later..."

She opened her eyes to his and smiled. "Do I make you lose your wits, then?"

"Och, aye, lass." He nodded, the truth of his enchantment warm in his eyes. "Ye do."

It was a haven nestled cozily within purple hills that danced in the spring breeze and jagged mountain ranges swathed in gossamer. Davina had plenty of time to bask in the awe of Camlochlin as they raced down the ridge from the cliffs and across the heather-lined glens toward the castle carved from the black mountain behind it. Camlochlin castle was a daunting sight, with its jagged turrets and armed Highlanders patrolling the walls, but Rob lived there, so Davina knew there must be warmth inside.

Toward the north, all the way to the braes of Bla Bheinn, small cottages and woolly white sheep scampered over the rolling hills. Frothy whitecaps from Loch Scavaig rolled gently toward the bay of Camas Fhionnairigh from the west, adding soothing music to the air.

"Rob?" she said as the wind, sweet with the fragrance of heather and peat, whipped back her hair. "If Gilles tries to take me away from this place, I will kill him myself."

"Save yer tender sentiments until ye've met my aunt."

She turned and quirked her brow at him. "I thought you said she was very kind and loving...and whatever is tender about me threatening to kill Gilles?"

"Maggie MacGregor is verra kind and lovin'—to me," Rob corrected with a grin that made her dizzy enough to swoon a little. "...and 'tis tender because ye'd kill him fer Camlochlin."

He made her head spin, but he still didn't make any sense. She shrugged her shoulders, giving up, and turned back toward the approaching castle. The doors were opened now and people were stepping out, tilting their heads to the guardsmen above and then back to the riders. One woman pushed her way through the thickening crowd, shielded her eyes from the sun for a moment to see if the guardsmen were correct, and then took off at a brisk pace toward them.

"Robbie?" she shouted in a commanding voice that didn't match her small stature. When she reached them, Davina was first struck by her beauty, and then by the panic in her vivid blue eyes. "What are ye doing back here? Where is yer father, and why in blazes are ye traveling with an English soldier?"

Springing from his saddle, Rob stepped into her waiting—though impatient—embrace. "My faither is in England, safe and unharmed."

The woman visibly relaxed. Apparently, Rob knew what answer she needed to hear first.

"I will explain everything to ye after I've—"

"And who might ye be?"

The smile Davina wore faded from her face under the woman's palpable scrutiny. She could only be Rob's Aunt Maggie, the spitfire sister of the Devil MacGregor. Davina didn't need to take notice of the woman's petite, slightly hunched frame, for she herself was not much taller. It was her blunt candor, and the timing of it that, according to Rob when he'd told her of his family that day in Courlochcraig's church, sometimes caught folks off guard.

"She is Davina," Finn answered cheerfully for her as he strode toward them. "And she is a princess," he added, kissing his aunt by marriage on her cheek, "so be pleasant to her."

Davina went pale, but when Finn caught her eye, he

flashed his boyish grin. Rob did not look pleased, but he said nothing to refute Finn's introduction while he helped Davina dismount. Was he going to tell them all who she was? Why would he? The probability was more than a little unsettling. It was downright terrifying. The importance of keeping her identity secret had always been vital to her existence. She wasn't sure she was ready for it to become common knowledge.

"Where is Jamie?" Rob asked his aunt while she followed Finn with a skeptical scowl over her shoulder.

Maggie cut her caustic gaze to Edward next. "He went to Torrin with Brodie fer..." She snapped her mouth shut and her guilty gaze crept back to Rob, who was waiting patiently for her to go on. "All right, fer flowers!" she practically snapped at him.

Unfazed by her slight outburst, Rob shook his head in disbelief and uttered a muffled blasphemy. "Will, show the captain inside and put him in Colin's room fer now." When he turned back to his aunt, he seemed to have soothed his temper. "Aunt Maggie," he managed to say rather calmly, "yer husband shouldna' leave the clan unprotected fer flowers."

"But look around ye, Robbie," she appealed, stretching out her arms at her sides. "Do ye see any orchids? Ye know they're my favorite and when Aileen stopped through here a se'nnight ago with the MacLeods she said the orchids were blooming a deep shade of purple this year in Torrin."

"Well, now I understand," Rob conceded benignly. Davina couldn't help but smile at him. "Ye'll tell me aboot the MacLeods bein' here after I've seen to the clan," he said, back to being the formidable leader he'd trained his whole life to be. "Fer now, will ye take Davina to a room and have whatever she wants brought to her?"

"Whatever she wants?" Maggie MacGregor arched a curious black brow at him and folded her arms across her chest. This time, though, she wouldn't argue with her brother's son. She turned instead to Davina, appraising her once again from foot to crown. She studied Davina's face with lingering intensity before arriving at some conclusion Davina wasn't sure fell in her favor.

"Well, come on then, Princess." Maggie waved her hand at her and turned for the castle.

"Go on, lass," Rob urged when Davina paused and gave him an anxious look. "I'll see ye shortly."

Davina didn't want to go inside without him. It wasn't the foreboding castle that made her uncomfortable, but the diminutive woman in front of her who'd looked over her shoulder in time to see Rob reach for her hand and scowled darker than Rob and Colin put together.

"Are ye the reason my nephew is not in England with his father?" Maggie asked her when they were out of earshot from the others.

Davina inhaled deeply before she answered. What were they going to think of her when they found out who she was? When they realized how much danger Rob had put them all in, and how she'd gone along with it. She realized at that moment just how like a princess she had behaved thus far. Rob's family would see her as nothing more than as a spoiled, selfish bratling. "I'm afraid so," she answered truthfully.

"Well, ye're lovely enough to turn a few heads," Maggie said, glancing up at her from the corner of her eye.

"But a bonnie face isn't enough to keep Robert from his duties."

"It was never my intention to..."

"Are ye a Stuart?"

Davina nearly tripped over her feet at the unexpected question. Maggie's arms caught her, though just barely.

"Aye, I thought as much," the smaller woman said, reading Davina's eyes as easily as if she were reading a Gaelic scroll. "My Jamie's brother is married to a Stuart. I thought ye were her when I first set eyes on ye on Rob's horse."

Davina looked over her shoulder for Rob, but he was gone. What should she say? How much should she tell this stranger who tore away her secrets with less effort than it took to peel an onion? She did the only thing she could without having to admit who she was to anyone else but Rob. She evaded the question. "Robert and Finn told me of Lady Claire. I am curious to meet her."

"Aye, sweeting," Maggie spared her a glance that was both kind and shrewd together as they entered the castle. "I'm sure ye are."

Davina had never been inside a castle before. She'd seen many drawings of their glorious grand halls and stone stairways in her books, but walking into Camlochlin felt like stepping back through time and into a dream. She looked around, turning a full circle in order to take in the full size of everything around her, from the two-foot-thick doors riveted in wrought iron, to the cavernous corridors lit by candelabras and carved iron wall sconces. There were many people hurrying about, each one looking at her, many of them smiling.

While Maggie led her toward the stairs, issuing

requests to this person or that about their guests' needs, Davina's eyes were fastened on the great tapestries lending warmth to the halls. She'd never seen such workmanship and felt ashamed of her own needlework skills.

"I'll put ye in Mairi's chambers fer now, until we get another cleaned."

Davina barely heard Maggie, but nodded. She would sleep on the floor without complaint if there were no other chambers available. She inhaled, trying to place the oddly pleasant scent lacing the air. It smelled like the hills, only richer, smokier. Whatever it was, she loved it and everything else about Camlochlin. It was Rob, menacing and formidable, until one gained entrance into its warm, sheltering core.

She didn't think anything could affect her more than Rob's home, until she stepped into Mairi's room. It wasn't the painted walls or the rich dark furnishings that made her emotions spring up hot and heavy, but the lesser comforts, like the delicate brass comb set beside other feminine trinkets on a small table by Mairi's bed, the dried sprigs of heather arranged in a painted clay vase on another table by the window. Even the twin swords crossed above an alcoved hearth bore testimony to something Davina never had. A father who loved and indulged her.

She swiped a tear from her eye when Maggie touched her hand. The smaller woman did not question her, but simply took her hand and patted it.

"Do ye like rabbit? To eat?" Maggie clarified when Davina blinked at her.

The question was so out of the blue that Davina blurted out the truth before she could stop herself. "N . . . no." She cringed, hoping she hadn't just insulted her host on a meal she was preparing. "What I mean is...I prefer not eating meat...but I would be happy to share anything...." Her words trailed off and she couldn't help but smile at the woman grinning back at her.

Chapter Twenty-one

$\mathcal{D}$avina didn't see Rob again until several hours later that evening. In the meantime, she enjoyed a hot bath, a host of female visitors who brought her food, handfuls of colorful kirtles, and information about the MacGregor men of Camlochlin, and a short nap on a heavenly soft mattress.

Their laird, she learned from two of the women who prepared her bath, was fair and patient, and according to Agnes, who spilled more water onto the floor than into the basin when she spoke of him, as striking as the Cuillin ridge in winter.

When Caitlin MacKinnon brought her a tray of warm leek soup and sops, Davina giggled and gasped when the dark-haired beauty told her of the rogue, Tristan, and how he enjoyed inciting his younger siblings' fury as much as he enjoyed ridding lasses of their virtue.

"He is cunnin', and sometimes thoughtless," Caitlin confided. "But ye willna' care aboot those things once he smiles at ye. Ye'd do well to steer clear of him," she added, looking over Davina's long, flaxen tresses with a glint of envy in her eyes. "Will is just as handsome, and no' half as wicked."

Davina found that a little hard to believe after spending so much time with Will. But she liked Caitlin and suspected that the girl cared for Tristan and was trying to keep her out of his bed.

"What about Rob?" Davina asked, sipping her mead and trying to sound as indifferent as possible. She believed she already knew much about him, but she was curious to know what the women of the castle thought of him.

Caitlin followed her to the bed and sat with her as easily as if they were close friends sharing kitchen gossip. "Och, dinna' waste yer time on that one. He has little use fer anything that willna' benefit the clan. Besides, I think his faither wants him to wed Mary MacDonald. Mary's faither is one of the four main chiefs on Skye and..."

Mary MacDonald? Davina's heart sank to her feet. Rob hadn't mentioned her—or his plans to take her as his wife. But how could she fault him for keeping secrets? How could she be angry with him for kissing her while being bound to someone else, when she had done the same thing? Still, her heart felt as if it had just been torn in two.

Thankfully, Maggie pushed through the door before Caitlin could tell her anything else she couldn't bear to hear.

When Rob's aunt saw Caitlin, she gave her the kind of look one might aim at a cellar rat that had wandered into the kitchen. Seeing her, Caitlin swept off the bed and hurried out of the room without another word or look in Maggie's direction.

"What has that trollop been telling ye that brings such gloom to yer face?" Maggie asked, shuffling toward the bed to primp Davina's pillows. "Hell, ye look worse than when ye got here."

Davina sighed quietly and handed Maggie the cup of mead when she held her hand out for it. She didn't bother lying, since she was so poor at it and Maggie had already proven that she could see right through her anyway. And so far, the woman hadn't regarded her like she had the plague. Davina wanted to keep it that way.

"She told me of Rob's betrothal."

"His what?" Maggie gave the pillow a soft punch and motioned for Davina to lie down. "To who?"

"Mary MacDonald."

"What nonsense," Maggie huffed. "Mary is a mouse who hides behind her father's rather large arse every time my Robbie looks at her. He does not even like her."

Davina looked up into Maggie's huge blue eyes and had the urge to throw her arms around her neck. She might have done it too if Maggie wasn't tucking her in like a mother.

"Do ye like flowers?"

Smiling, Davina nodded, already growing accustomed to the way Maggie veered from one topic to another.

"Good, because my Jamie has returned from Torrin with a cartload of orchids. I'll have Agnes bring ye some after yer nap. They are lovely. I swear the man has a gift fer picking out the bonniest ones. Not a one of them is wilted."

When Rob's aunt asked her next question, Davina suspected the purpose behind her quirky diversions was to catch folks completely off guard.

"So then, ye have tender feelings fer Robert?"

"Yes," Davina admitted, unable to conceal the answer already softening her features. "I think he is one of the best men I've ever known."

"Do ye, now?" Maggie asked curiously and sat on the bed beside her. "He can be quite intimidating when he wants to be. Ye're not afraid of him then?"

"Oh, heavens, no," Davina smiled and closed her eyes. She hadn't realized how exhausted she was, or how badly she missed lying in a bed until her head hit the pillow. "He saved me, you know. He rode straight through the Abbey doors and saved me from the flames."

She barely heard Maggie leaving the room a short time later. She was asleep in minutes and already dreaming of her champion.

Rob entered the Great Hall with Will and Asher, and Finn close behind. He looked around for Davina and spotted his aunt instead. She crooked her finger at him when he reached her chair and kissed him on the cheek when he bent to her.

"What was that fer?"

"'Twas fer being so much like yer father."

As was often the case, Rob had no idea why Maggie would bring that up now at supper. He hadn't seen her all day, having returned just a few moments ago from see-ing to the villagers. Rather than ask her to enlighten him, he chuckled softly, pulling out his chair to sit. There was only one person his aunt loved as much as him and his uncle—and it was his father. If Maggie saw similarities between them and wished to blurt it out when the notion struck her, 'twas fine with Rob.

"She'll be along anytime now," Maggie said know-ingly when he lifted his gaze to the entrance of the Great Hall. "She woke from her nap a wee bit ago. I sent Alice and Agnes to help her prepare fer supper. Did ye know that she doesn't like to eat meat?"

Rob glanced once again at the entrance and smiled. So, it wasn't just men who fell helpless to Davina's natural enchantment. "I did notice that she ate a good amount of nuts and berries on our way here," he said, knowing how much his aunt despised the practice of eating flesh. Davina had won her over easily. "Ye have my thanks fer seein' to her comfort." When Maggie's gaze softened on him as if she could see his heart right there in his eyes, he looked away, turning his attention to her husband.

"What were the MacLeods doin' here?"

Jamie Grant looked up and smiled at the server placing his trencher on the table. "Padraig MacLeod is actin' as chieftain while his faither is in England. He stopped through here on his way back from meetin' with Alisdair MacKinnon's son in Torrin to bolster their alliance wi' us all in these uncertain times. I had a missive penned to the MacDonalds in Portree, vowin' the MacGregors' support, should they need it."

"Good," Rob said, bringing his cup to his mouth. He felt a wee bit guilty about thinking Jamie had left Camlochlin to pick flowers. He should have known there was another reason for his going to Torrin. Though many Highland clans fought against each other, if the new king thought to bring his English laws down on them, they would stand together.

"The MacKinnons are with us then?"

"Of course. Skye will always stand secure against outside influences. Our hope is that King James will... Rob?" Jamie paused until Rob looked away from the entrance and back at him. "She must be an extraordinary lass to be able to distract ye from yer passions."

She was his passion, and he was past caring who knew it. Hell, what in blazes was taking her so long? He hadn't seen her since this afternoon and he missed her face so much he was tempted to go get her himself.

"I've grown accustomed to havin' her near," Rob said, his gaze already being pulled back to the stairs.

"I've been informed that she is a princess, mayhap even a goddess." Jamie winked at Finn, sitting across from him, and then dipped his bread into his stew. "But I doubt yer faither will accept divinity as a good enough reason no' to return to his side."

"I made my choice, Uncle."

"And ye couldna' have chosen to take her to England with ye?" Normally, at this point in any conversation with this particular nephew, Jamie would never have pressed on. Rob was someday going to lead this clan and he'd learned well not to be rash in his thinking. He weighed and measured each decision he made before acting upon it, and once he set his course there was no changing his mind. But he'd never set his course in a different path than his father's, and never for a lass—who came attached to an English soldier.

Rob ground his jaw, deciding how best to begin. He had intended on telling his kin the truth about Davina, but exactly how could he do so without sounding like an impetuous whelp ruled by his emotions? "Her life is in grave danger," he said, knowing in his own heart that that was the emotion that ruled him first. "I pledged myself to protecting her, and this is the safest place I know."

"Why is she in danger?" Jamie asked him evenly.

"Because she is ..." They had a right to know, to choose whether or not to stand with him, should anyone come to Camlochlin to remove her. "She is King James's firstborn daughter and heir to the throne."

Everyone at the table sat motionless and mute, save for Finn, Will, and Asher. Rob expected shock and dismay and was about to close his eyes to wait out the silence.

"I thought James's daughter Mary was the Princess Royal," his aunt said, also seemingly unfazed by the news.

"So does everyone else in England."

"How did she come to be in yer possession?" Jamie asked him calmly, though he'd dropped his bread into his food and left it there.

Rob told them about the attack on St. Christopher's, and who was behind it and why. "There is likely a rebellion brewin' involvin' the Duke of Monmouth, the Earl of Argyll, and possibly William of Orange. Connor has agreed no' to tell the king anything aboot her—"

"She is his daughter," Jamie interrupted.

"A daughter he cloistered away in a convent and has never seen," Rob bit out.

"If ye don't plan on telling her father that ye have her," Maggie asked, "what do ye intend to do with her?"

Here was the part of the tale that would prove all the other emotions that had subsequently directed him. "I intend to keep her."

"Fer how long?" Jamie stared at him so still that Rob wondered if he was breathing.

"Fer as long as she'll have me."

His uncle leapt to his feet, startling Maggie, who then glared at him to show her disapproval. "Ye'll bring the entire realm doun on our heads!"

"That is what I've been trying to tell him," Asher interjected smugly, but then looked away when Rob's eyes sliced through him like hot irons through butter.

"Robert," Jamie continued as if the captain had not spoken at all. "Tell me ye dinna' mean to claim the king's daughter. Tell me ye are no' willin' to throw away everything ye've worked at protectin' fer this lass?"

"I dinna' know if I can tell ye that, Uncle," Rob said, staring at the entrance where Davina stood, her small hands twisting the scarlet and green earasaid draped over her skirts. Her hair was swept away from her temples with two small pearl pins while the rest fell like liquid sunshine down her back. When their eyes met, she smiled slightly, as if the very sight of him reassured her. Rob rose to his feet as the need to go to her overwhelmed him. Behind him, he heard the others push out their chairs as well.

"Good evenin', yer Royal Highness."

Rob turned his smile on Jamie, understanding all too well the reverence replacing the anger in his uncle's voice. He knew every man in the hall was overcome by Davina's unearthly beauty. He didn't like it, but he would learn to live with it.

When he looked at her again, her smile had vanished.

Chapter Twenty-two

𝒟ear God, he'd told them. He'd told them all. For a sickening moment, despite Alice's gentle nudge behind her, Davina stood motionless in her spot. Her anxious gaze passed over the man who had addressed her as no one had before him. What should she do—besides resist the instinct to turn and flee back to her room? She wouldn't do that. The time for hiding was over. This was Rob's family. If he trusted them enough to tell them who she was, then she too would trust that they would not betray her. She realized, as that moment passed into another, that it was not fear that paralyzed her when the people at Rob's table stood at her entrance, but harsh, stinging reality.

She was Lady Davina Stuart, Royal Princess, heir to the three kingdoms. No matter how far she ran, how well she hid, or how right she felt in her new Highland garb, she would never escape it. Whether here on Skye, or in an English castle, no smile would ever be sincere.

But Rob's was. Her weary heartbeat faltered when he moved toward her, his smile intimate and reassuring. He didn't care who she was. He'd kissed her, touched her as if she were his to possess. He watched her with eyes that burned to touch more of her, that warmed at the sight of her, and danced at the sound of her laughter. She wanted him to kiss her, touch her, possess her. She wanted to stay with him here in this busy fortress, surrounded by common folks while she grew heavy with his babe and became the mother she had missed having.

When he reached her, he fit her hand into his broad one. "Come," he said on a breath as ragged as her own. "Meet my kin before the sight of ye fells them to their knees next."

She went with him, walking at his side until they reached the table and the men still on their feet. He introduced her to his uncle and the others who were meeting her for the first time, simply as Davina.

She liked Jamie Grant twenty breaths after she sat down. It wasn't the guileless charm of his smile or the worried look in his eyes that he tried so hard to conceal when he spoke to her that warmed her heart to him so quickly, but the way his smile broadened with love when he looked at his wife.

"How does Connor fare?" he asked Rob while Maggie cast Davina's cabbage soup and crisp oat cakes an approving look.

"He fares well," Rob said, and washed down his mouthful of bread with a swig of ale. "But I fear he's no' as brave as ye or Graham had hoped."

"And why might that be?"

"Mairi," Rob told him, bringing a heaping spoonful of rabbit stew to his mouth. "He near wet his breeches when I told him she was still in England."

Will agreed with a hearty laugh, ignoring Finn's insulted glare.

"That's no' fear, lad," Jamie corrected, taking less offense. "'Tis wisdom."

Rob nodded, conceding the point, and went back to eating. Davina watched him beneath the shadow of her lashes. Compared to Edward and the men who had lived with her at St. Christopher's, Rob ate like a starving bear. She liked his lack of table etiquette and the passion of his appetite, and then remembered that he hadn't eaten a hot meal in weeks.

"Captain Asher." Jamie turned to Edward next, doing his best at keeping the conversation light. "D'ye know that Connor Grant and young Finlay here are the High Admiral's nephews?"

"I wasn't aware of it until recently," Edward answered, bringing his cup to his lips. He took a sip and shivered in his seat. "That's quite potent," he said hoarsely.

Brodie, Will's father, cast him a contemptuous look. "English."

"D'ye know him then?" Jamie continued.

"Who?" Edward cleared his throat behind his fist.

"Connor Stuart?"

"I saw him only once, briefly. I hope to have the pleasure of meeting him someday."

"Ye'll find him less amiable than his nephew o' the same name," Will said, reaching for the bread. "Admiral Stuart is a wee bit less concerned aboot guttin' a man based mainly on suspicions."

"I didn't know ye'd seen him," Finn said to Edward while the men around the table agreed that Stuart was a wary bastard.

Davina had gone back to watching Rob when he cast a curious look at Finn. He appeared to be about to say something, but Maggie's soft voice stopped him.

"Robbie"—she offered him a slightly less contented

look than the one Davina was giving him—"is the rabbit tender enough?"

Rob's spoon paused on the way to his mouth. He slanted a guilty glance in Maggie's direction and murmured, "Aye, 'tis fine."

"That's good, dear. I'm sure yer approval would be a great consolation to its mother—if she wasn't roasting over the pit with the rest of her offspring."

Will snickered behind his cup. Brodie delivered a sharp elbow to his ribs, and Rob, looking at his spoon with a measure of distaste, dropped it into his trencher and pushed his supper away. Maggie smiled at him, then shot her husband a critical frown.

"Ye would do well to show as much wisdom as my nephew one of these days."

"That's no' wisdom, my love," Jamie defended. "'Tis fear."

Soon, the conversation flowed to other, less passionate topics. Davina basked in the joy around her, especially Rob's. His laughter was rich and robust when Jamie told him about the pig that escaped the pens and bit Brodie on the arse hard enough to keep him asleep on his feet for two nights. They shared toasts to the demise of the hated Fergussons and to the MacPhersons' defeat in the next raid, but it wasn't until supper was over and a small group of them retired to the private solar that they discussed the king and Davina's relationship to him.

They asked her questions over warm wine, pillowed chairs, and the crackle of a toasty hearth fire. Why had she been hidden away since her birth? Did she know of anyone outside of St. Christopher's who knew of her? Did she have contact with the king? What were her father's ultimate plans for her? Each query stripped Davina of another layer of her guard. And as she answered each one with the truth, she understood how it must feel for a soldier to finally shed his heavy armor after a battle.

When they were done, Rob lifted his cup to her and claimed her heart once and for all with a slant of his mouth and a soft nod of his head.

"So." Maggie, sitting closest to her, leaned in so that only Davina could hear her. "Ye were imprisoned and set free from yer bars. I understand better now how ye feel about my nephew."

Davina looked down at her and thought that Maggie MacGregor was the most beautiful woman she had ever seen, and at that moment, the saddest.

"Rob"—Jamie's voice stopped Davina from pondering the reason for Maggie's regret—"I dinna' have to tell ye how concerned I am about all this. But we will discuss that later, in private." He turned to Edward without waiting for Rob's reply. "Tell us what ye know aboot this Admiral Gilles. How many men are at his disposal?"

Edward shook his head. "I don't know much. He is a close ally to Prince William and commands a fleet of over a thousand men."

"Dinna' ye mean that he is a close ally of the Duke of Monmouth?" Rob's eyes glittered like a snowy, starlit night as he set down his cup.

"What?" Edward looked as visibly shaken as he had on the morn of Monmouth's attack. "That is what I said."

"Edward, dear, you said Prince William." Davina offered him her tenderest smile, sympathizing with his tenuous place here among men who considered the English as detestable as the plague.

"Did I?" His breath broke on a strained chuckle. "I fear your strong whisky has muddled my thoughts."

"'Tis Angus's whisky, blame him," Brodie drawled from his seat. "And ye'll no' be tellin' him that I wasted any on ye when he returns."

Jamie asked other questions and Brodie threw in some of his own, but Rob remained quiet—like the night air just before a storm. Davina looked at Edward. The storm was heading for him.

By the time the wine was finished and the fire died down, Davina was a wreck. What had Edward said to produce such a murderous gleam in Rob's eyes? When she tried to ask Rob, he pushed her gently aside and followed up the stairs after Edward.

"Something is troubling him," Finn said, appearing at her side and following her gaze. "And me, as well."

"What is it?" Davina turned to him, hoping he could shed some light on Rob's foul mood.

"Well, Captain Asher told us tonight that he had seen my uncle once. But the night after we left Ayrshire, he told me that he hadn't left St. Christopher's Abbey in four years."

"That's true. He hadn't."

"But then when did he see my uncle?" Finn's green eyes widened on her, as if she should know the answer. She didn't. "Admiral Stuart has been in France for the past four years. Before that, he was in Holland."

"Holland?" Davina repeated softly, her gaze rising up the stairs. Was Edward in Holland before he came to her? It would explain how he'd known that an exiled duke and a banished earl were her enemies. But why would he not have told her he was there among them? And why hadn't

he told her that he'd seen Connor Stuart? He knew the
High Admiral was her cousin. Why had he kept so much
from her? She could feel the blood leaving her face and
growing cold in her veins as her trust in Edward fell to
pieces at her feet. She realized with heart-stopping clarity
why Rob had gone after him. No. No! There had to be an
explanation—one that did not involve treachery. Edward
would never have betrayed her. He couldn't have. Not
Edward. Never.

Chapter Twenty-three

———✦———

$\mathcal{R}$ob prayed to God he was wrong. If he wasn't, England's new king was about to lose one of his captains. He found that once Davina had stopped following him from the solar, his steps lost their fervor. He wanted to reach Asher before she could stop him, but he wished he didn't have to. His hands curled into fists as he climbed the stairs. He prayed he was wrong. So what if Asher was the only other man in the king's garrison, including the king himself, who knew of Gilles's ties with the Dutch prince? It meant nothing. Surely, it didn't mean that Davina's closest friend had betrayed her. But something else, that suddenly made sense when Asher spoke of William of Orange, did.

When Rob reached the captain's door, he fought to harness his fury and pushed it open without knocking. "I have some questions of my own to put ye, Asher," he announced from the doorway.

"I suspected as much," the captain said, turning from the narrow window with weariness marking his features. "If this is about Prince William, I assure you I—"

"'Tis aboot the Abbess at Courlochcraig."

"The Abbess?" Asher asked, perplexed. "I don't—"

"She was expectin' Davina," Rob told him, stepping inside and closing the door behind him.

"That's right." The captain smiled, relief clearly etched in his features. "I sent her a missive asking her if I could bring the Lady Montgomery to her."

"Aye, I thought so." Rob didn't smile back as he stalked across the room. "The thing that nagged at my thoughts at the time was how ye knew Gilles's men were comin'."

Asher almost swayed on his feet at the unexpected turn the conversation had taken. At this, Rob would have smiled if he didn't want to kill the man directly in front of him now so badly.

"But now I believe I have figured oot the great mystery. Ye knew Gilles was comin' because ye had told him where to find her when ye met with him and William in Holland. 'Tis where ye saw Admiral Stuart, aye?"

Asher opened his mouth, likely to deny the charge, but Rob's palm in front of his face stopped him.

"I could hold ye here in the cellars until Stuart visits Camlochlin again, but that might be years from now and I doubt he will recognize what's left of ye by then."

"I had not yet met her," Asher admitted, surprisingly composed, as if he'd carried his own secret for too long and was relieved to finally be released from it. "I was young and you do not know Admiral Gilles. He is ruthless and cruel."

Rob felt sickened by the sight of him. He had to call upon every shred of control he possessed not to draw his sword and run the traitorous bastard through. "So, ye didna' tell them where to find her fer a purse, but because ye're a coward."

"I was a fool. I did not—"

"Ye would defend yerself in this?" Rob snapped his hand outward, closing his fingers around Asher's neck. "Nothin' ye say can justify what ye did to her. Ye led those who would kill her straight to her door!"

Asher gagged and turned a deep shade of crimson when Rob used the wall to anchor him off the ground. The captain kicked his feet and clutched at the steely fingers crushing his pipes. "Yes, I . . . did it, and I have had to live . . . with . . . MacGregor, please I beg you, let me . . . let me seek her forgiveness first."

"Ye dinna' deserve it!" Rob roared in his face, now level with his own.

"Rob! Let him go!"

The order came from Davina, standing at the now open door, both arms stiff at her sides, a pool of unshed tears shimmering against the firelight. Finn was behind her and stepped around her to enter the chambers first, his eyes fixed on the man losing consciousness in Rob's hand.

"Let him go, Rob," she demanded again, but still she did not move from the entrance.

Rob didn't know how much she'd heard, but seeing her, seeing the anguish in her innocent face, tempted him to snatch the last breath from Asher's body. Nae, he would not have her see him do it. As much as he wanted to, he knew she would never forget such a sight.

Releasing the captain, he turned to her. Hell, he didn't want her to find out this way. "Davina, listen to me—"

But when she finally moved away from the door, she went directly to Asher. "Seek my forgiveness for what, Edward?"

Though he'd just faced death at the hands of an enraged warrior, 'twas a slight, trembling lass who caused the captain to come undone. "It was my fault," he confessed, holding one hand around his throat and the other over his face. "I told them where to find you." He sobbed, unable to look at her.

Rob couldn't tear his eyes away from her. He wanted to go to her, to pull her away from the truth he knew was rending her heart in two. The only man ever to win her trust had betrayed her.

"You told them where to find me?" she echoed on a broken breath and sank to her knees in front of her closest friend. "Why?"

"It was before I knew you." Asher's hand fell away from his face and his rueful gaze met hers. "I hadn't fallen in love with you yet. I—"

Her palm cracked across his face with enough force to split his lip. "Everyone died because of you!" she screamed, her voice so ridden with sorrow that Finn almost reached her before Rob did.

"Come away with ye, now, my love," Rob whispered against her temple as he scooped her up in his arms. She did not weep against him, but continued to stare at Asher with disbelieving eyes as Rob carried her to the door. Somehow, her silence tore at his heart more than her tears. He wondered how she would ever trust anyone again.

"He's no' to be let oot of this room," Rob told Finn before he left the chambers. "I will return in the mornin'."

"You can put me down," Davina said quietly when they stepped into the hall and Finn shut the door after them.

"Nae, lass, I want to hold ye." Rob pulled her closer and closed his eyes when her tears began.

They did not end when, alerted by Davina's scream a

few moments earlier, Will, Jamie, and Maggie came running up the stairs.

"What happened?" Maggie rushed forward when she saw Davina cradled in her nephew's arms.

"Finn will tell ye. He's in Asher's chambers." Rob's jaw grew tight while Davina did her best to muffle her heartrending sobs in his plaid.

"Poor gel," his aunt cooed, stretching her arm to stroke Davina's head. "Whatever 'tis cannot be that terrible." When Davina did not look up, Maggie gave Rob a concerned look. "Ye'll tell me later what happened. Bring her to her room now. I'll follow ye and stay with her tonight."

"Nae, she's stayin' with me." The flat pitch of Rob's voice left no room for argument. He didn't wait for one either way, but turned his smoldering gaze to Will. "Asher is yers fer the evenin'. Do what ye will. I'll finish it on the morrow."

Will's eyes lingered on Davina's face buried in Rob's shoulder. His features hardened and he nodded before he left them, furious with the man who made her weep and fixing to punish him for it.

Maggie's small hand on Rob's arm stopped him when he moved to leave. "Robbie, she is the king's daughter."

'Twas easy to ignore the warning plea in her soft gaze. Rob had decided before he'd brought Davina here what he thought of her father. His mind was set, and now more than ever, he knew he would never let the king take her from him.

"The king gave up his claim on her long ago. She is mine now."

He didn't care what his aunt said next. He didn't care what his father would say when he returned home or how many armies came against him. He would fight for her. He would die for her.

He carried her to his room, his bed, where he wanted her to sleep each night and wake up safely in his arms.

"Don't leave me," she wept, clinging to his neck when he bent to lay her on the mattress.

"I never will," he promised, lying down beside her and pulling her into his embrace.

Her tears came hard and long into the night, tugging at the deepest fibers of Rob's heart. He didn't know what to say to comfort her, so he remained silent, stroking her hair and keeping her close. She'd lost everything in the massacre at St. Christopher's, but she'd kept her pain within, along with her secrets. Tonight though, the arrow of grief finally punctured her armor and all he could do was hold her as the river spilled forth.

"They were my family," she whispered, finally pausing, her voice barely audible against his neck. She shook her head at the memories that were too painful to remember, but were always there nonetheless. "I could hear the sisters' screams coming from the chapel and I could not get outside to save them."

Rob kissed the top of her head and felt his own eyes sting from the torment brought upon her by a man who claimed to love her.

"I prayed for Edward to live. I prayed so hard. I loved him and his men as if they were my brothers. How could he have done this terrible thing?"

"I dinna' know, my love."

Her body relaxed in his arms and she nuzzled her face deeper into his neck. His muscles reacted, tightening with the need to taste her mouth, her tears, her pain, and take it upon himself. God help him, he had never loved anyone or anything as much as he loved her. The realization did not shock him, for he'd known for some time that she had claimed his heart. But it frightened him to think what he was willing to give up for her. And how could he tell her now that Asher had proven that love could not be trusted?

She shifted slightly, molding her soft curves to his hard ones and muddling his thoughts until only desire remained. He kissed her temple, murmuring soothing promises he prayed she could believe. When she angled her face, he traced kisses along her brow, her wet eyelids, her cheeks. Her lips parted and her warm breath fell upon his chin.

"Rob," she whispered, her voice aching with a longing as strong as his own. He dipped his mouth to hers and met the sweet ardor of her waiting lips.

He did not crush her to him to satisfy the physical need raging within him, though it cost him every ounce of self-control he possessed, but spread his fingers over her face, then behind her nape, softly, slowly, drawing her to him as his tongue stole inside her mouth. She tasted like fine wine and warm tears, and he kissed her like a parched wanderer who had discovered his oasis.

He wanted to taste every inch of her, to quench his hunger on the firm tips of her breasts, the quivering velvet of her belly, and beyond. He wanted to look down at her beautiful face while he claimed her body, and more, her heart.

But he could not do it this way, not when her heart was so broken. Not when the trust she had guarded so diligently had just been tossed at her feet, used and forsaken. He would do whatever it took to bring it back to life, and prove, however he had to, that he would treasure it. So he withdrew from the sweet, hungry lips that thirsted for him, as well.

"D'ye know how much ye mean to me, Davina?" he asked her, and looking deeply into her eyes, he couldn't help smiling.

Their arms entangled, touching each other's faces, she smiled back at him. "Yes, I do."

How could she not doubt him after the man she'd believed in for four years proved false? But this was who she was, a forgiving, guileless angel spun from the harp strings of heaven.

"Ye have the kind of courage men pray fer on the battlefield. Yer cousin Claire is goin' to love ye."

"Tell me what kind of man is he who loves her?" she asked him, her tears finally ceasing.

"Graham Grant is a patient man," he told her, washed in her warm breath, completely lost in the glimmering blue of her eyes. "He's clever and convincin', and has nae trouble at all bendin' his wife's strong will to his."

"And him?" Her smile softened while she traced her fingertips over his lips. "Is he stubborn, as well?"

"No' with her. With her, he bends like the heather on the hills."

"I think I'm going to like him."

"Ye will no' be alone. Most of the lasses here do. But he is loyal to his wife and loves her alone."

"It is what I have always wanted," she said on a wistful, hollow sigh. "Claire's life...Maggie's...and, if your father is anything at all like you, your mother's."

Rob wanted it too. He hadn't before, not with any of the lasses at Camlochlin. "'Tis a good life. A complete one." he said, thinking of his father. "But ye could be queen."

"I think I would rather be a servant."

Rob thought of the veil that had covered her glorious mantle at Courlochcraig. Rather than enter a battle he was doomed to lose, he'd let himself forget God's claim on her. But now, knowing who she really was, he questioned if there was any true claim at all.

"Would ye have defied yer faither fer God?"

"I would defy the world for God," she told him. "But I would not have had to defy my father. I've always known who I was and what was to become of me. My father left documents with the Reverend Mother at the time of my delivery, decreeing that should he produce a son after me, I was to be given to God. What no one else in the world knows, save for myself, the Abbess who raised me, and now you, is that if he ever became king with no male heirs, he would openly appoint that title to me. He would wait a full year after his coronation, and if after that time, he still had no sons, I was to be returned to him and prepared for marriage to a man of his choosing." She looked up into Rob's solemn gaze and laid bare her heart for his eyes alone. "I don't want to be surrounded by people who smile at me while they plan my demise. I don't even know my true sisters, Mary and Anne, but I know we will have nothing in common, save for loveless marriages." Fresh tears spilled over her lashes and she swiped them away. "Now that my father is king, my destiny looms before my eyes, Rob. If only I had known him…if, for even one day, I had felt his love for me I don't think my duty to him would feel so bleak."

Rob's heart twisted in his chest. Her duty. How could he of all people blame her for doing what she was born to do? How would he ever let her go if she chose her duty over him?

"There is still time to pray that his young wife bears him a son." She smiled, seeing the anguish in his eyes. He could not bring himself to smile back at her.

And what of her duty to God? 'Twas her faith that molded her, not some stately English court. 'Twas God she knew and trusted. He didn't want to ask her. He didn't want to hear her answer, but he had to know. "And if the king does have a son, would ye defy God fer me, Davina?"

"I would not have to," she answered softly, tilting her mouth to his. "Remember, it was God who assigned you to me."

Chapter Twenty-four

No man in the three kingdoms or beyond would ever compare to the one in Davina's arms. If she was married and widowed a hundred different times, and each of her husbands loved her, it would always remain that her heart belonged to Rob alone.

Ah, God, You sent him to me knowing that I would love him beyond reason.

Her heart beat at a frantic pace as she closed her eyes to kiss him, praying that God would not have sent him only to ask her to give him up.

Molding her lips to Rob's fine ones, she knew her heart never would. She knew what she meant to him— not because of land or her name, but simply because of her. He told her every time their eyes met. Rob was an intimidating man even when he wasn't brooding, but not with her. Never with her. She couldn't recall a single time when he didn't seem to melt at the sight of her. He made her feel cherished, adored, and alive. Oh yes, she knew what she meant to him. He proved it when he brought her to Camlochlin.

As she ran her palms down his sculpted arms, she marveled that a waif dressed in loose robes had won the affection of such a magnificent man. When she dragged her fingertips over the belt at his hips, his body went rigid, his kiss, more passionate.

Only he could have picked the pieces of her heart off the floor and handed them back to her whole again. Only he could make her forget everything and everyone in her life, becoming the most vital thing in it. She was his, and she wanted to give him everything; her love, her trust, her body.

She lost her breath when his shaky fingers slipped beneath her earasaid and slid it off her shoulder. She did not think about what they were doing, or would be doing shortly. She reacted to his hungry mouth, to the silky demand of his tongue, and the raw need in his touch purely on instinct. She loved him and she wanted to share this deeper, sacred intimacy with him. Consumed in his heathery scent, she let him intoxicate her further when he rolled her on her back—her bottom lip captured between his teeth—and cupped his hand around her breast. Her nipple tightened between his thumb and forefinger and sent a fiery charge to the crux between her thighs.

"Rob, I—" She squirmed beneath him as strange, titil-lating heat coursed through her blood.

"I want ye to be mine, Davina."

She wanted it too. She wanted to watch his restraint fall away, the discipline he'd practiced every day at her side come undone. She wasn't afraid of what lay beneath Rob's iron control. She wasn't afraid of anything with him.

With a groan that snapped his muscles taut, she pulled his belt free and dropped it to the floor. He broke their kiss only long enough to curl his mouth into a sinuous, sensual snarl that made her insides ache and her face grow warm.

But clearly, he liked her boldness.

The remainder of their clothes came off in a tangle of arms and legs that left them both panting, but when Rob took her nipple into his mouth and sucked, she realized she had gone beyond the point of returning. He was going to take her. His hot, heavy arousal pressed against her belly attested to it. A part of her that she did not understand quivered for it, even as her mind began to protest. She didn't care about laws—being with him felt too right, as if she was born to love him. She was frightened, though, of his size and suddenly ashamed of her inadequacies.

"I don't know what to do."

His voice was a tight moan along her breast. "I will teach ye."

"What if I don't like it?" she queried with a bit more panic in her voice.

"Ye will," he promised and he spread his tongue over her nipple, a slow, languid caress that made her spread her legs wider before she could stop them. He didn't mount her, though the sight of him, dark and wild for her, riddled her thoughts with stallions ready for mating.

His eyes gleamed on her like blue-gold flames, basking in what he saw. Rising over her, his shaft hard and long poised over her moist flesh, he lowered only his face to her mouth, her throat, kissing and licking down between the swell of her breasts until he reached her belly.

Her body jerked at the intimacy of his kiss. She gasped at the forbidden touch of his fingers and then of his tongue as he spread her and stroked her until she writhed beneath him. Fleetingly, she wondered if what he was doing was sinful, or if winding her fingers through his hair and pulling his dark curls free was an acceptable part of nature's dance. But even Solomon from the Good Book delighted in his beloved. With each salacious lick of Rob's tongue, he drove all conscious thought from her head and left her trembling with a need that burned her to her very core. The gentle scrape of his teeth over her bud sent waves of scalding spasms through her muscles, and when he sucked her into his mouth, flicking his tongue over her engorged passion, she cried out on the brink of pleasure's pinnacle.

They could both be killed for what they were doing, but Davina didn't let herself think about that now, just as she didn't think about falling off the ship or over the jagged cliffs of Elgol. She was done with being a coward. She loved Rob and she wanted more of him, all of him. Her heart would be forever bound to his and if she had but one night, this night only, to give herself to him freely, fully, she was going to take it.

"Come here to me," she whispered, her voice ragged and unfamiliar to her ears.

He went, lowering himself onto her and enfolding her in his arms. "I dinna' want to hurt ye, my love."

"I would forgive you a thousand times if you did."

"Och, lass, but ye slay my soul with yer smile. I will become a pitiful blossom-wieldin' slave to yer happiness."

"But you will be happy too." She smiled and opened her mouth to his.

He made love to her slowly, taking his time to ready her untried body to receive him. When she flicked her tongue over her lips and arched her back, just slightly enough to rub herself over his swollen shaft, his patience left him. Snaking his arm beneath her waist, he hefted her hips upward with a grunt of pure male demand. Spreading her wide beneath him, he surged against her, from the tip of his glistening head to the thick, throbbing base, harder than steel.

She shuddered, afraid of what he was about to do, but she reached for him as anticipation blended with trepidation and searing, shameless desire. She clung to him while he broke through her barrier with slow, tender persistence. Pain speared through her like a burst of flame and she cried out, certain that he'd torn her open.

"Davina." He was there, above her, his breath hot against her mouth. She opened her eyes to him, ashamed of her tears, and then astounded to see them in his eyes as well. "I love ye, lass," he whispered deeply, running his fingers over her cheek. "Ye will always be first and foremost to me."

She believed him. Oh God, thank You, thank You, thank You. "And you to me," she vowed as he kissed her mouth, her chin, the swell of her breast, sinking a little deeper into her with each tender surge.

The pain increased as Rob stretched her, but still he pushed, plunging inside her with slow, salacious strokes that began to feel deliciously good. How could she ever be afraid of anything with this man? She trusted him fully, wholly, with her life, her happiness, and with her heart. She loved being in his arms, the feel of his hard body atop hers, covering her, cherishing her. He was more than she ever could have dreamed of.

Her muscles clenched around him and he groaned with pleasure and buried his length into her.

"I hope ye want this life with me, Davina." His voice was thick and heavy with need.

Yes, yes, she did.

He pulled his length almost free of her tight sheath and

rose up above her. "Because tonight ..." He slipped his hand behind her nape and dragged her toward his hungry mouth while he thrust deep inside her, impaling her to him again, and then again. "I want to get ye heavy with my bairn, and tomorrow"—he drove into her harder, faster, staring into her eyes as he shot the full bounty of his seed inside her—"I want to marry ye."

Rob awoke from a dream and ran his palm over the soft indentation where Davina had fallen asleep in his arms. His dream faded and left the terrifying sense of losing her in its wake. He sat up in his bed, ready to take her back.

Darkness replaced the honeyed glow of the dying hearth fire. Silence clung to the thick stone walls and seeped deep into Rob's marrow, drawing his gaze toward the only source of light in the room.

She stood at the window. Her face, tilted toward Heaven, was bathed in the pearly caress of moonlight. His heart accelerated at the sight of her lost in his large tunic. Her arms were crossed over her chest, her hands unseen beneath his long sleeves, as the wind whistling over the hills lifted her pale tresses softly off her shoulders. Dear God, she looked so vulnerable, so alone, and so utterly beautiful standing there that he nearly leapt from the bed.

The need to go to her was maddening, but her silence was the comfort she gave to herself—the comfort no one else was able to give her. Rob was loath to disrupt it, though he wanted to be the one to offer it to her.

He whispered her name, unable to control his own mouth, or the need to follow her wherever she went.

Hearing him, she turned her head, granting him full

view of her face as she smiled. "I love when you say my name."

"Aye?" Rob's voice pulsed along with his heart as he tossed his legs over the side of the bed. Standing, he drew his blanket around his shoulders and went to her. "Callin' ye 'wife' is oot of the question, then?"

"Not if I have anything to say about it." Her smile grew as wide as his when he reached her.

"Nor I," he promised, stepping behind her and closing his arms around her beneath the blanket. He wanted to carry her back to bed and make love to her until the morning, but she returned her pensive gaze to the world outside his window. Where was she going? What was it that sometimes drew her away, leaving her so serious and withdrawn?

"I willna' let any harm come to ye," he breathed across her ear.

"I know that." She covered his hand on her chest with her own. "I was just thinking about my father," she said after a moment. "I have done the like many times throughout my life. Wondering if he would know me, if he had ever felt the void at his feet where Mary and Anne played. It is foolish to dwell on such things, I know..."

"'Tis no' foolish." He pressed his lips to the back of her head and closed his eyes, following her to a place where no one had trod before him, and loving her all the more for allowing him to come.

"Do you know how difficult it is to know your family exists, living their lives every day without you, without wanting you in it? I used to pray for him to come for me—him and my mother. But he never did. Later, I understood why, but it did not lessen the isolation. I filled my days with dreams of being someone else. Someone not vital to the kingdom. Just me—out there, living, loving, with no fear of tomorrow. I languished over how different my life would have been if I wasn't the daughter of the Catholic heir to the throne, until I finally hated that I was, and accepted my fate without a fight." She turned in his arms, the shadows gone from her eyes as she looked up at him. "And then you snatched me from the ashes and stirred my dreams back to life."

Rob smiled, pulling her closer. "Ye've nae need to dream anymore, my love," he said, kissing her mouth. "I will give ye everything ye need, everything ye want, and more."

He swept her up and carried her back to bed. This time, they made love slowly, curiously, as if they had their entire lifetimes to squander away on nothing more pressing than what made the other groan with delight, or smile in ecstasy.

But they didn't have a lifetime. Rob knew her father would come for her eventually, and now, knowing how badly Davina had always wanted him in her life, his fear that she would go with him to England to fulfill her destiny nearly overwhelmed him. Nae, he would take her as his wife and help her forget all she lost, give her everything as he had promised, and pray that the king never found them. Even if he did, James did not know her. He'd never visited St. Christopher's. There was no one left alive from the Abbey to identify her as the king's daughter. No one but Asher...and that would be remedied in the morning.

Chapter Twenty-five

$\mathcal{R}$ob wasn't in bed when Davina opened her eyes the next morning, but Maggie MacGregor was. She sat at the edge of the mattress, her bright blue eyes riveted on her groggy subject with a mixture of dread and intense interest.

Davina bolted upright, grasping for the blanket to cover herself. She felt her cheeks go up in flames as Maggie's gaze flicked over her bare shoulders.

"I...I..." Oh, dear God, what could she say? Sickeningly, she remembered what Maggie had called Caitlin MacKinnon. A trollop. Davina was worse than that. She was a lusty, wanton wench who fell into a man's bed the day he brought her home. She wanted to weep—or pull the blanket over her head and pray Maggie would be gone when she peeked out again. What was she doing here, and why wasn't she saying anything?

"Where is Rob?" Davina finally managed, dragging the blanket up to her chin.

Maggie stared at her a moment longer before she sighed and shook her head as if she was having trouble of her own getting the words to come out of her mouth. "He rode to Portree a few hours ago to fetch a priest."

Relief flooded through Davina. Then he truly was

going to wed her. She hadn't really doubted it. So far, Rob had kept his word on everything he'd told her, but she'd been afraid to hope that this was all real. That he was real. By tonight she would belong to a clan. She would have a husband, a sister, brothers, cousins, uncles, and...aunts.

"I know what you must be thinking of me," she said softly, looking away from Maggie's penetrating eyes. "But I vow to you that Rob is the first..." Her voice trailed off. Betrothed or not, she was still too ashamed to speak of her maidenhood aloud.

Maggie made a little sound, like a dull blade had just scraped across her heart. She pushed herself off the bed and began to pace in front of it.

"It does not matter what I think. Robert made that clear before he left." She met Davina's shameful gaze and sighed again. "I do not think poorly of ye. Robert is not careless with his affection as Tristan is. I know there is deep emotion involved here, and *that* is what distresses me."

"Why?" Davina asked on a whispered plea.

Maggie cast her an incredulous look. "Because ye are the king's daughter! Have ye fergotten that, gel?"

In truth, she had. For once.

"And if bedding and wedding ye were not bad enough," Maggie continued, pacing faster, "he thinks to deceive the king about yer identity. He is going to tell him that ye are a novice named Elaine, and that ye claimed to be the king's daughter because ye thought Robert was the Princess Royal's enemy and ye had hoped to give her time to escape. But of course, she didn't."

Davina quirked her brow at her, confused, but Maggie barely took notice enough to clarify further. "Och, but my brother is going to skin him alive, if yer father does not do so first."

Davina sat still on the bed as her world crumbled around her. Maggie was right. She couldn't wed Rob without it costing him his life if her father ever came here. Oh, how could they have been so foolish, so reckless? Even last eve she knew in her heart that she could never escape who she was. But crushed against his strong heart, she could pretend.... Tears streamed down her face and she swiped them away, not wanting Maggie to see her weakness. But still they came, until finally she covered her face with her blanket and wept.

"There now, sweeting." Maggie hurried to her and pulled her into her arms. "There's no need fer that."

"I must leave here before it's too late," Davina cried. "Will can bring me to—"

"Will knows Robbie's heart and will never go against it. Nae, ye cannot go."

"But I must. I won't let Rob die for me. I didn't want him to bring me here, but he would not be swayed."

"Aye, that is my Robert, as stubborn as his father."

"And then when I saw Camlochlin and met all of you, I was happy he hadn't listened. Oh, Maggie, what am I to do? I love him."

"I know, child, I know," Maggie soothed, wiping Davina's eyes, and her own, as well. "Mayhap, all is not lost. King Charles gave Claire to a Highlander, after all."

"His cousin," Davina pointed out, wiping her nose. "I am the king's daughter."

"Nae." Maggie cupped her face and smiled at her, concealing well the misgivings that plagued her heart. "Ye are Elaine, a young novice who deceived my nephew out of love fer the king's daughter. I will make certain that everyone at Camlochlin remembers it well."

Davina shook her head. "It will not work."

"It will if I say it will. Remember, I am the Devil MacGregor's sister and I can be just as fearsome as he."

Through her tears, Davina couldn't help smiling at the tiny woman in front of her. "I don't doubt that."

"Ye would do well not to. Besides, Robert's scheme could be successful. According to him, no one knows what ye look like. Even if the king does find ye, he cannot prove ye are his child, and will never set a possible commoner on the throne." Maggie patted her hand. "So ye see, ye've nothing to fret over. Now dry yer tears. Ye have already won part of the battle. I like ye, lass. God willing, I believe ye can make Robert verra happy. But ye best brace yerself. Being the wife of a MacGregor is no easy task, as Kate will surely attest when ye meet her."

"Tell me about her," Davina said, needing something to take her mind off the perilous position she had put Rob in. "I've heard much about Rob's father, but only a little about Kate."

Maggie's face went soft, proving that Rob's mother held a special place in her heart. "She loved my brother at a time when 'twas a crime, punishable by death, to do so. Ye will have an ally in her."

God help her, Davina thought, as the possibility of a life here sank in once again. How would she ever measure up to the women of Camlochlin? She had to decide what to do once and for all and stick to it, no matter what the outcome.

Her decision came easily when the door burst open and Rob plunged inside the room. Windblown and slightly out of breath, as if he'd raced the entire way home to be with her again, he ravished her soul and vanquished her fears. Unbidden memories of his naked body invaded her thoughts and she felt her cheeks grow hot. Lord, he was handsome, hard and lean, and so very . . . big.

She almost laughed out loud when he scowled at Maggie and she scowled right back.

"What are ye doin' in here?" he demanded, clearly worried about what his aunt might have said to Davina. "I told ye this morn what I decided. I willna' change—"

"What are *ye* doing in here?" Maggie countered just as menacingly.

"'Tis my room."

"Good, then ye're familiar with the way out."

When he stubbornly stood his ground, Maggie rose off the bed wagging her finger at him. "Ye're not wed yet, and until ye are, ye'll not be seeing any more of her! Now out with ye so I can help her dress."

Rob looked over her head at Davina clinging to his blanket. Everything he wanted to tell her was there in his eyes, his tender expression. She smiled at him, feeling the same way, and he fumbled for the door. "The priest is here."

"Dragged him from his bed, did ye?" Maggie teased, laying a hand on his back to help him out. Before her nephew had a chance to answer, she closed the door in his face.

"He loves you very much," Davina told her when they were alone again.

"Aye, and ye, as well." Maggie grinned at her, then lifted her nose to the air and sniffed. "Is it just me, or does he smell like flowers?"

*   *   *

The castle was abuzz with activity by the time Davina descended the stairs with Maggie a few hours later. People bustling this way and that, set to chores that hurried them on their way. Women smiled when they passed her and the men looked her over approvingly while they hefted baskets of various foodstuffs to and from the kitchen.

There was to be a celebration at Camlochlin today. Her wedding. Davina breathed deeply, but her hands still shook. She was going to do it. She was going to defy the king, deny her kingdom, and risk the consequences. She had no other choice. She would wither and vanish without Rob in her life. For the first time in her life she prayed that if her father ever set foot in Camlochlin he would not know her. Her days of pining over him, of yearning for a normal life, were over. Everything she had ever wanted, and more, were about to be hers.

She smiled at Alice across the hall and lifted a self-conscious hand to her pinned-up hair.

"Do I look acceptable?" she asked Maggie, trying to quell the thunder of her heart.

"Ye look more ravishin' than the Cuillins in winter."

Davina turned and gave Will her happiest smile. She missed him and his playful flirtations that made Rob brood and growl.

"I chose the silver gown." Maggie stepped back and surveyed her work with pride curling her lips. "It complements her coloring nicely. Look there, she has silver in her hair."

Will raised his gaze to the soft curls tumbling around her face and smiled. "Aye, I've noticed."

Davina blushed and looked around, expecting to see

Rob behind her looking like he could crack Will in two with his bare hands.

"You taunt him," she accused with humor lifting her voice.

"I enjoy watchin' him lose his head. It reminds me that he's just a man, like the rest of us."

Yes, Davina thought—not finding Rob in the crowd—that could be difficult to remember. "Is he in the church?"

"He'll be there when the time comes."

Davina nodded. That was the one thing she was certain of.

"He's…" Will's eyes reflected the glimmer of her gown when he spotted a buxom girl hurrying toward the Great Hall. "…preparin' some things."

"He's a wolf," Davina smiled, shaking her head after him when he took off in pursuit of the poor girl.

"He's a tame pup compared to Tristan," Maggie huffed, then took her hand and pulled her down the hall. They were stopped by a lovely woman with a mane of golden curls and deep blue eyes. Her smile was warm, as was her hand when she clasped Davina's.

"So, this is Elaine, the lass who won Robert's staunch heart! I am Aileen, Graham and Jamie's sister."

"Saints, help us, he brought the MacLeods." Maggie looked heavenward and slapped her hip.

"Of course he did," Aileen said, still smiling at Davina. "We are practically kin."

Davina saw the slight resemblance to Jamie and shared a word with her until Maggie interrupted them.

"Where is Jamie?"

"He is with Faither Matheson in the cellars, prayin'

over someone, I think. I heard Brodie talkin' aboot Last Rites."

The color drained from Davina's face. Dear God, she'd forgotten about Edward! Was he locked in the cellars? Was he going to die on her wedding day? He had betrayed her trust and broken her heart, but she didn't want him to die for it.

"Maggie, I must find Rob!"

"We'll find him, sweeting. Don't ye worry about it."

"No!" Davina clutched her arm. "I mean now. This moment. Before it's too late!"

"Before what's too late?" Maggie grimaced and tugged her arm free of Davina's taloned grasp. "What's come over ye, gel?"

"There he is now."

Davina followed Aileen's finger and took off toward her future husband. They met halfway across the hall and Rob's breath seemed to catch in his throat as he reached for her hands.

"I didna' think ye could ever be more bonnie than the day I took ye from St. Christopher's, but I was wrong."

"Rob, where is Edward?"

The warmth in his eyes vanished along with his smile. "Dinna' concern yerself with him any longer, Davina. I've taken care of it."

"By killing him?"

"He isna' dead yet, but 'tis what he deserves." He raised his voice an octave, then ground his jaw. "We will discuss it later."

"We will discuss it now!" She pulled her hands away from his and narrowly escaped him when he reached for her again. He was scowling in full force now. "Release him," she said nonetheless.

"Are ye mad? D'ye think I am?"

"Please, Rob."

"Nae."

"I beg you, please."

She saw his resolve falter behind his dark expression. But just as quickly he snatched it back. "Davina, ye canna' ask this of me. He will leave Camlochlin and go directly to yer faither."

"He won't. I know he won't. He did what he did a long time ago. Much has changed since then."

"Aye, he loves ye," Rob growled at her.

"Yes, he does, and that is why he will not betray me again. Spare him, please. I cannot bear the thought of him dying because of me. So many have already."

"I canna'—"

She stepped into his arms and reached for his face, cutting off his refusal. "I have asked you for nothing until now. Grant me this, Rob. I cannot stand before God with a merciless man."

He stared into her eyes while her heart beat furiously against him, until she thought he would deny her.

"Verra well," he said finally and caught her in the crook of his arm when she flung her arms around his neck and thanked him profusely with kiss after kiss.

"He's never to leave Skye, though," he told her in the midst of her kisses. "I'll have him shot if he tries."

"Yes, yes, anything you want."

He withdrew from her slowly, and with eyes that smoldered like brands, he said, "I want ye to be mine, and then I want ye in my bed."

*   *   *

The ceremony went smoothly, despite the tapping of Jamie's boot against the cold church floor and his constant turning to look over his shoulder, as if he expected the king's entire garrison to come crashing through the doors.

Davina barely remembered the priest's soft benediction. Her gaze was fastened on Rob's throughout. Her vision filled with his handsome face and loving smile, while her thoughts overflowed with brand new hopes for her future. She would make him happy, this strong, determined man who gave her his heart, his home, and all that she'd ever wished for.

In the Great Hall, they feasted on roasted lamb (from which Davina and Maggie abstained), fresh breads and fruit pastries, a variety of soups and broths, and Camlochlin's finest ale and whisky. Rob moved about the guests with an ease that was bred into him as the clan's future Chief. But no matter who he spoke to, or what topic they engaged, his gaze found hers across the room. His smile was intimate and eager.

Davina knew he wanted her, and though her body still ached, she wanted him just as much. She wanted to be alone with him, to touch him, explore him, breathe him, taste him, and tell him how desperately she loved him.

She wasn't prepared though when, setting down his last drink, he reached for her and traced her lips with the pad of his thumb.

"Bid good eve to our guests." His command was low, throaty, and riddled with desire.

She blushed and averted her eyes from the dozens watching as he kissed her. When he bent to scoop her up in his arms, Will's cheer rang through her veins and made her cover her face in Rob's fresh plaid.

Her mortification was soon replaced with awe and the sting of joyful tears when Rob carried her into his chambers—their chambers. Hundreds of candles lit the room like stars on a summer night. Lush bouquets of purple heather filled every corner and permeated the air with the soft, sweet scent of the Highlands.

"You picked all this yourself," she said, remembering how good he smelled this morn.

"Finn and Will aided me." He dipped his mouth to hers and carried her to the bed. "Does it please ye, Davina?"

She nodded, unable to form the words without weeping. Yes, yes, it pleased her. Oh, God, yes! Everything he did pleased her. Every button in her gown that he loosened, every tender kiss he pressed to her exposed flesh, pleased her. He saved her life and sheltered her in the safety of his capable arms. She didn't think anything could make her love him more—until he picked flowers for her!

"I love you," she whispered as his body covered hers and he sank deep within her. "Only you until I die."

Chapter Twenty-six

$\mathcal{K}$ing James sat alone in the royal solar staring blankly into the hearth fire, a silver cup of wine dangling from his fingers. He paid no heed to the music or merriment wafting upward from the Banqueting House below. His coronation had drawn every nobleman in England and Scotland to Whitehall Palace, as well as many Highland chiefs, all eager to pay their new king homage and kiss his royal arse. But none of them could be trusted. Indeed, it was more than likely that one or more of them were responsible for the tragedy that left him in his present condition, drunk and heartsick.

She was dead.

Soon after the ceremony proclaiming him king, word had come with Lord Dumfries that St. Christopher's Abbey had been burned to the ground. No one was left alive.

Davina.

With no witnesses, it was impossible to know who had committed the terrible crime.

For over a se'nnight after the celebration had moved from Westminster to his new home at Whitehall, James had pretended good humor during the day. He'd greeted his guests, ate, drank, and smiled when the moment demanded it, but his thoughts were always on her. At night, like this one, he sat in his solar alone, too filled with grief and anger to feign anything else. Who was responsible for killing her? He racked his brain while he doused all his regrets with the finest wine in England. He had too many enemies to count, but none of them knew that Mary was not his firstborn.

Charles had known, of course. James had told his brother soon after Davina was born. At first, the previous king reviled the notion that his niece was being raised as a Catholic. But eventually, Charles stood by him, as he had done on so many other occasions, knowing his younger brother to be a rebel of sorts and a man of secrets. Indeed, James had wed Anne Hyde, a commoner, in secret. He had denounced Anglicanism and kept his conversion hidden for many years—a task he had hated, but one serving the throne. When Davina was born, he knew she would be raised in the Protestant faith, even against his wishes, so he removed her from court. An act of rebellion it might have been at first, but after years passed with Charles producing no legitimate children, and with opposition to the Catholic faith growing steadily, it became imperative to keep his firstborn hidden from the world.

The nuns of St. Christopher's Abbey knew who she was, as did Captain Geoffries, and after him, Captain Asher and his men. His dear wife Anne had cried out for her daughter before she expelled her last breath. How many were in attendance at her deathbed? Mary and his youngest, Anne, had been there, along with the Bishop and Lords Covington and Allen of Parliament. Besides them, James had no idea who suspected that the child his wife wept for had not died at birth.

He took another swig from his cup, then let it drop to the floor. Little Davina. He had seen her only twice in her life after her birth, once when she was but two years of age, and then again when she was one and ten, a year after her mother left the earth. It was too dangerous to visit the Abbey, but he'd arranged for the Abbess to have his daughter brought out of doors while he and his troupe passed St. Christopher's on their way to Edinburgh. James had wanted to bring her to Spain, or even France, where he'd spent many years before the Restoration, and where he had first been introduced to the Catholic faith. But Anne wanted to keep her close, so they kept her in Scotland, and left her in the care of nuns. Anne had never seen her daughter again.

Davina became another secret amid the many he had been forced to keep during his life. Now she was dead, and he grieved, not as a king whose hope in an heir to carry on his beliefs was lost, but as a father who never had the chance to know or love his daughter.

There came a knock at his door. He allowed entry and looked up as his young wife Mary entered the solar with three guards stationed around her.

"My lord." She curtsied and bowed her head dutifully, the dark ringlets around her ears bobbing. "One of your captains has returned from Scotland and requests an audience with you."

He couldn't tell her. He couldn't tell anyone why he was here in his solar drinking his way into unconsciousness instead of enjoying the festivities in the Banqueting House.

Davina might as well have died at birth like the four other babes after her. Anne had wept that her stillborns were God's punishment for what they had done. But his true firstborn hadn't perished in the womb. He had seen her, so small, so innocent, smiling up at Captain Geoffries as if he was her father instead of the man trotting outside the gates of the Abbey with a boulder on his heart. Surely, God had not forgiven him, and never would.

"I don't wish to see anyone. Send him away." James waved his wife away with a heavy hand.

"Your daughters Mary and Anne inquire after you, as do their husbands." She broke away from her guards and rushed forward, falling on her knees when she reached him. "I pray you come to the Banqueting House, lest they see your absence as a sign of fear of your enemies."

Ah, yes, William of Orange, his son-in-law, who had done everything in his power to stop him from succeeding to the throne. Now there was a man capable of murder. Unlike James's other nephew and archenemy, James Scott, Duke of Monmouth, who opposed James's ascension openly, William smiled while he plunged his dagger, denying, even as one bled, that the weapon was his.

"Husband." Mary squeezed his hand when he closed his eyes, too weary to think on the rest of his enemies. "Whatever is troubling you, you must put it aside. You are the king and you have many supporters. I am one of them."

James looked into her dark, imploring eyes. He never thought he could care for a woman the way he had for his beloved Anne, but Mary of Modena had proved him wrong. It had taken her some years to adapt to her significantly older husband, but he believed she cared for him. She was dutiful and quiet in audience, but at night she shared with him, not only her body, but her thoughts and opinions. What would she think of him if she knew he had abandoned his daughter?

"There are things I would tell you, wife."

"Later." She patted his hand and then kissed it. "First, speak to this captain. He says the matter is an urgent one. After that, come sit by my side and still the tongues that flap against you."

He smiled at her faith in him, her strength. Anne would have liked her. "Very well, show him in and then inform my guests that I will join them shortly."

He watched her leave, the three guards following close behind. When the door closed again, he shut his eyes and saw his daughter's face. She'd been cherubic at two, with plump, pink cheeks, hair the palest shade of yellow, and eyes as big and as blue as the heavens. When he saw her again nine years later, it was from a distance; but his gaze soaked in every detail of her form, the way she moved across the courtyard on her way to the church, and how she paused ever so briefly and looked out beyond the gates as if she could sense him there.

He'd taken every precaution. He thought no one knew of her and still he'd sent an army to protect her should his enemies ever discover his secret. But it hadn't been enough.

A knock at the door shattered the image of her face. James allowed entry and briefly looked up as two men entered the solar. One of them he recognized as Captain Connor Grant, the High Admiral Stuart's nephew. Grant's companion, a younger man garbed in Highland fashion, set his bold gaze on him, and then on the cup discarded close by.

"Yer Majesty," said Grant, dropping to one knee. His companion remained standing.

"What are you called, young man?" James asked,

genuinely amused for the first time in a fortnight. Now here was something out of the ordinary. He didn't know whether to scowl at his audacious guest, or smile at him.

"I am Colin MacGregor, Yer Majesty."

"MacGregor..." Yes, he should have guessed it, the king thought to himself, sizing the lad up from the tips of his muddy boots, to his eyes, lit from within with quiet confidence. "Are you from Rannoch?"

The lad shook his head. "Skye," he said, glancing around the solar. He didn't look overly impressed with the finery surrounding him, but rather surprised to find the king alone.

"Ah, your Chief is among my guests."

"Aye, he is my faither."

The pride in his voice pleased James. He had met the infamous Devil MacGregor and his family after the ceremony and had invited them to Whitehall. The chief was a man James wanted on his side. A bit secretive himself, MacGregor disclosed to no one exactly where on Skye he lived. Oh, it would have been simple enough to find out, for James's cousin Claire lived among them, wed—by Charles's approval when he was alive—to Connor Grant's father. But James did not ask. As long as the MacGregors never came against the realm again, he would let them have their secrets. Some men needed them. "Why did you not arrive with him?"

"That is what I've come to speak with ye about, sire," Captain Grant said, rising from his knee. He gave the Highlander a hard look for his lack of submission before he turned his attention to the king.

"Yes, yes, sit." James offered. "What is this urgent news you have for me?"

"'Tis about the attack on St. Christopher's Abbey."

James's heart halted in his chest. It took every ounce of will he possessed to remain in his chair and to keep his voice steady when he asked the captain what he knew about it.

"I know who is responsible fer it."

"Who?" James asked hollowly. His beringed fingers clutched the armrests until his knuckles grew white. At last...at last, a name...

"Admiral Peter Gilles, sire. The Duke of Monmouth's right-hand man."

Now the king sprang to his feet. The murderous rage that had been eating away at him night after night had finally found direction. "If what you say is true, they will both die beneath the Wheel. What proof do you have of your accusation?"

Grant looked down at his hands. When he spoke, his voice was low and strained with reluctance. "Colin was there when it happened."

James turned to the young Highlander, unable to keep the question or the familiar sorrow from his eyes. Had he seen her? Had he seen his child die? "Tell me everything, MacGregor. Leave nothing out."

He listened while Colin told him why he and his brother had gone to St. Christopher's and what they saw when they arrived: The Abbey engulfed in flames, a scant number of his English soldiers engaged in battle with the Dutch. Colin's eldest brother and two of his companions had charged forward on the side of the English but were fortunate to escape with their lives. His brother was wounded by an arrow and decided to return home rather than proceed on to England. "We met up with Captain

Grant in Inverary and told him what had happened at the Abbey."

"And Gilles? Was he killed?"

"He was no' there," MacGregor told him, his gaze sharp, his voice steady. "Before he died, one of yer men told my brother who commanded the slaughter."

"Sire"—Captain Grant dragged the king's attention away from the messenger's—"the Duke of Monmouth is guilty of killing yer men, my brothers at arms. I don't know if the Earl of Argyll is also involved, but I would remind ye that my uncle has misgivings about William of Orange, and did share them with the late King Charles."

"Yes, I know. Connor Stuart was my brother's closest ally, and has since become mine. He is loyal to his family to a fault. He will be pleased when I tell him of your great service to the throne. As for William, I am well aware of his position in regard to a Catholic monarchy, but I cannot move against him until I have proof of his treason."

The captain nodded and James moved toward the door. "Now, if there is nothing else, I would like a few moments alone to think on what you have told me before I return to my guests." He waited while Grant bowed to him again and left the solar with his young companion following behind.

"MacGregor." The king stopped him at the entrance. "A word before you go." He ushered the young man back inside and closed the door behind him. "Tell me, did you see...a woman...a novice..." Ah God, he hadn't spoken of her to anyone since Anne died. But what did it matter now who knew? If Colin MacGregor had seen Davina before she died, James had to know. He had to know for certain that his daughter was truly dead. "She would have had..." He paused again, fighting to keep his emotions in check. "...hair like the sun and eyes like the sky."

Something...something registered in the boy's eyes, pity, perhaps, or melancholic curiosity. Whatever it was disappeared an instant later. "There were nae survivors."

"A body then?" the king pressed, blocking the door when his guest reached for it. "One matching her description perhaps? I must know."

"Why?

James stepped back, unaccustomed to such boldness... and to being studied so intently. The boy had a stoic face and nerves of steel, but the flare of fire in his eyes belied his calm outward appearance.

"'Tis no' with disrespect that I speak," the young Highlander said. "Fer I dinna' know ye yet, but why do ye care so much aboot a novice ye never knew?"

James squared his shoulders, ready to remind this whelp who he was speaking to and what could befall him if the king so ordered it. But he found that when he opened his mouth he had no stomach for self-aggrandizement.

"Because she was my daughter," he finally admitted, though it didn't make him feel any better, "and I sacrificed her for my faith." He laughed at himself but there was no mirth in the sound. "I don't know why I'm telling you." He shrugged his heavy shoulders and stepped away from the door. "It does not matter anymore." He went back to his chair and dropped into it.

"Is she the reason ye are in here alone, so drunk that ye canna' hold yer own cup?"

James looked up from beneath his hand. He could not help but like this boy's candor when so many around him offered him false reverence. "You are either very courageous, or extremely foolish."

"Both, sire," Colin said and flashed him a confident grin. "I am extremely courageous." Without invitation, he took the chair Connor had been sitting in a few moments ago. "I have been told that ye possess the same quality."

"And who has told you this? Your father?"

"Nae, someone who has come to mean a great deal to me. This person told me that ye've sacrificed much fer yer Catholic faith, even denouncing yer position as Lord High Admiral. D'ye regret it all then because ye lost yer daughter fer it? Would ye give up yer faith now, or ask others to do so?"

"No, never. My faith is all I have left."

The boy smiled, looking more like his father than James first realized. He rose from his seat and crossed the room to the door. When he reached it, he paused and turned to look at James one more time.

"Abraham sacrificed his child fer his faith."

James nodded and turned his somber gaze to the hearth fire. "But God let Isaac live."

"Aye, He did," the boy said and left the solar.

Chapter Twenty-seven

—◆—————

$\mathcal{D}$avina stared at the ceiling, watching the waning light of the candle flames flicker within the shadows. She and Rob hadn't left their chambers since the priest had married them three days ago, save to visit the garderobe. Their baths were prepared in-room by male servants and Alice brought them their meals—much to Davina's mortification every time the woman knocked and stepped into the room. The handmaiden didn't look at them, save for the one time when Davina caught her glancing appreciatively at Rob lying in bed with the blanket riding over his hips.

Thankfully, when Alice's eyes skitted over him, it was one of the rare times in three days that Rob wasn't as hard as a battering ram. Davina blushed at how many times they had made love during the day, and during the night. For the first pair of days, her body had been sore and he took her slowly, tenderly. But this morn, and lord, her boldness still shocked her, she'd woken up to his stiff erection jutting upward while he slept, and climbed on top of him.

He hadn't minded her disturbing his slumber, but smiled at her, wilting her muscles altogether. His kisses were hot, his tongue demanding as he cupped her rump in his hands and set her atop his unyielding passion. Oh, but it felt good riding him, looking down at the sensual pleasure in his face, pleasure she gave him as she ground her hips down his length, then up again, panting with her own release until she felt him spurt his precious nectar into her over and over.

Later, he took her from behind, bent over the bed with far less tenderness than he'd used previously. They slept in each other's arms after that, woke, ate, made love again, and then fell back to sleep.

How many hours ago had that been? Davina had lost track of time. She was hungry, and though she loved spending her days with Rob, she suddenly felt tired of the same four walls.

"Rob." She poked him gently in his side to wake him. "I'm hungry. Rob?" This time she gave him a little shake.

"Alice will be here soon," he said sleepily, without opening his eyes.

"She won't. I think it's the middle of the night. I'm just going to go to the kitchen..."

"Nae." His heavy arm fell over her waist and he hauled her to him with barely any effort. "Stay here."

She waited until he began to snore again, and then she carefully lifted his arm and slipped out of the bed. The floor was cold. She looked around for her slippers, but couldn't find them in the fading light. Her belly growled, coercing her toward the door in nothing but Rob's heavy tunic.

She peeked out. The halls were dark and silent. She waited a few moments, hoping that Alice would appear at the stairs carrying a tray of something scrumptious.

Was everyone asleep? She hoped so as she moved away from the door. She'd have to go through the Great Hall to get to the kitchen, but she'd often pilfered the larder at St. Christopher's in the middle of the night and had much experience with stepping over sleeping bodies.

Her belly grumbled again, echoing down the empty halls. She padded down the stairs, peering left and right. Thankfully, there was enough light from the tall candle stands on the first floor to see which direction she was going.

She stepped out of the shadows and stopped in her tracks at the two men rounding the corridor, coming right toward her. They were laughing and hadn't seen her yet. Davina turned to flee back up the stairs but came to an obedient halt when one of the men called her name.

It was Will. She breathed a sigh of relief and turned to give him an explanation of what she was doing in the halls at this hour, barefooted. But when she looked at him, his silvery gaze drifted over her long, loose hair, down Rob's tunic, to her bare calves. She heard his breath catch, and when he finally met her gaze, he wore a pained expression that made him appear more vulnerable than she'd ever seen him. Somehow, it made her feel more self-conscious than when he raked his scandalous smiles over her.

The man beside him took a step forward then stopped at the dagger at his throat. "John," Will said without taking his eyes off her, "go find a plaid fer Rob's wife. Now."

Sheathing his dagger, Will studied her in the candlelight while John took off toward the Great Hall without a look back. "Greetin's, fair lass. I was beginnin' to grow concerned fer ye." His mouth hooked into one of his familiar slight half-smiles when her cheeks grew flushed. "I'm thankful to see ye lookin' yer best. Where's Rob that he should let ye wander around the castle alone at this hour?"

"He's asleep," Davina told him, awkwardly crossing her arms over her chest. "I was hungry and just on my way to visit the kitchen. I didn't see any danger in it."

"Lookin' like that?" His eyes roved over her one last time before he dragged his gaze away, avoiding her altogether. "This might be yer home now, lass, and we, yer kin. But no' every man is yer brother."

John returned with a long, tattered plaid, handed it over to Will, and was promptly sent on his way.

"Put it on," Will said, tossing her the garment. "Then go back to yer room and make yer husband fetch ye some food."

"Aye, sound advice."

They both turned to see Rob descending the stairs, clutching his plaid around his waist. "Ye should have awakened me," he told Davina when he reached her.

"I tried," she said, wrapping the plaid around her shoulders.

He offered her a repentant smile then glowered at Will when his cousin gave him a pitying look. "Off with ye now." Rob kissed the top of her head. "I'll fetch ye somethin' to eat."

"Some fruit and perhaps some bread and honey," Davina suggested gratefully as Rob urged her along. "Good night, Will," she called over her shoulder, smiling at Rob's best friend when he tossed her a lecherous wink. He might be a wolf, but he was as safe as a puppy with her. "And thank you for the plaid."

"Are ye done lookin' at her, then?"

Will blinked the reverence from his eyes and turned

his usual reckless grin back to Rob. "Aye, until tomorrow, or whenever the hell ye let her leave yer bed again."

Rob gave him a foul look then smiled when Will clapped him on the shoulder. They were more than cousins. They'd been friends since birth and there was no one Rob trusted more than William MacGregor.

"Come, have drink wi' me," Will offered, leading him down the corridor. "Yer wife willna mind if ye're a wee bit late. I discovered where m' faither is hidin' Angus's brew." In the dim light, his eyes gleamed with trouble. "There's no' much left, and if we finish it off, there's bound to be some good fightin' when Angus returns."

Rob looked back toward the stairs and draped the bulk of his plaid over his shoulder, but the sudden chill that coursed through him remained. His father was due home within the fortnight.

"In here," Will whispered, leading him into a small storage chamber adjacent to the buttery.

Rob waited while Will rummaged through dusty crates and shelves stocked with everything from used candles and rusty shearing blades to empty wooden buckets too old and cracked to be of any use.

"Ah, here we are." Will turned with a fistful of candles in one hand and two cups in the other. "Make room on that table fer me, would ye?"

Rob swept his forearm across the surface, clearing the table of debris. "Have ye been keepin' an eye on Asher?" he asked while his friend lit the candles and blew dust from the cups.

"Aye." Will bent to a small curtained alcove behind one of the crates, stuck his hand inside, and smiled. "He roams the castle by day wi' his eyes fixed to the floor."

Straightening, he held up a large bottle, corked at the neck, and offered Rob a victorious grin. "I dinna' think the captain will try to leave, but his door remains locked at night."

"Good," Rob said, still undecided if he'd done the right thing by letting Asher live. "Put him to work tomorrow. He needs to earn his keep if he is to stay here."

"Aye, I'll have him clean the stalls in the stable house. He should feel right at home with the rest of the shyt."

"Will?"

"Aye?" his friend glanced up from tugging on the cork.

"How will I explain him to my faither?"

Will smiled and tossed the cork over his shoulder. "Right then, what's a traitorous English soldier in yer castle compared to the king's daughter in yer son's bed?"

Rob groaned and ran his hand over his jaw while Will poured their drinks. "I've made an enemy of the man my faither traveled all the way to England to support."

Taking pity on him, Will handed him his drink and patted his shoulder. "He's yer faither. At least ye know he willna' kill ye. Now." He held up his cup. "Let us drink to yer happiness—as short-lived as it may be."

He grinned at Rob's hard look before they both downed their whisky.

"Och, hell!" Rob's entire body quaked at the liquid fire scorching his innards. "How do they drink this shyt?"

Will clutched the edge of the table and squeezed his eyes shut. "Damned if I know." He lifted the bottle and poured the remaining liquid onto the floor. "What?" he asked at Rob's incredulous stare. "'Tis poison. 'Twill end up killin' someone one o' these days."

"Aye," Rob laughed. "Most likely yer faither when Angus finds his brew gone."

"Nae," Will said, replacing the empty bottle. "M' faither can handle that cantankerous auld bastard." He blew out the candles and followed Rob out of the room.

Rob pushed open his door and settled his gaze on Davina asleep in his bed. The king's daughter. He risked much for her and he doubted his father would understand. But Rob didn't care. He crossed the room silently and set the tray at the bottom of the mattress. How could he have taken her anywhere but here? In Camlochlin, England's laws did not matter. Isn't that what he believed? He climbed into bed beside her and watched her while she slept. How could he have kept himself from falling in love with her? 'Twas like asking a starving man to resist a banqueting table heavy with the most delectable dishes. He kissed her temple and smiled when she stirred. Her hair, like silver and gold spun together, fell over her creamy cheek. Tenderly, he swept it away. Her lips, like soft petals from the rarest rose, curled into a languorous smile. He would battle a king for her, defy his father and lay aside his birthright if he had to. He bent his head and tasted the glorious bouquet of her breath. She opened her eyes and Rob felt himself falling, helpless to stop, unwilling to save himself. He loved her. God, he loved her.

"I was dreaming of you," she whispered, reaching for his face above hers. "You were holding our babe."

"Aye?" He could barely speak, barely breathe looking at her, seeing what she had seen. "Did she look like ye?"

Her eyes opened wider. "How did you know it was a girl?"

"'Tis what I want. A daughter as bonnie and as brave as her mother."

She coiled her arms around his neck and kissed the smile from his mouth. When her belly rumbled in response, they both laughed.

Withdrawing from her, Rob sat up, pulling her with him. "I brought yer food. Come here, lass, and let me feed it to ye."

He stretched his long legs out beneath her as she straddled him, looping her legs around his waist. She watched him while he dipped a piece of oat bread into some honey and held it up to her mouth. She took a bite, closing her eyes and sighing with delight.

"'Tis how ye taste to me." His voice was deep with desire, rough with the restraint it took not to push her back down and hear her sigh that way as he entered her. He fed her sliced apples next and clenched his jaw when she laved her tongue over his fingers. He'd pilfered some berries as well, and offered each from his own lips, kissing her as she accepted. His heart stalled, enraptured by her laughter when he spilled some honey down her chin. He licked it away, growing hard beneath her. Soon, he no longer cared about the food, nor did she as they tugged and tore at their garments, hungry for something else.

He lifted her over his heavy arousal, groaning as he bent his knees and plunged deep. She was moist, tight, and willing. So willing. She tossed her head back, covering his hands in the thick folds of her hair. He tunneled his fingers through her tresses and pulled gently, arching her back and taking her firm nipple into his mouth. He sucked, pulling soft, sweet moans from her parted lips as he guided her over his stiff erection.

She was heaven, hot, wet, and scintillatingly snug as she rose up over his engorged head, then back down to his base. He closed his hands around her full rump, gliding her up and down, gyrating her hips until his breath grew heavy and labored. He wanted to saturate her, fill her with his passion, but not yet. Not yet.

Drawing her close, he sucked the pulse at her throat, blending his tight moans with hers as her breasts rubbed his chest, her heart taking up the rhythm of his.

When she buried her face in his glistening neck, he clutched her to him, never wanting to let her go. Her sheath grew tighter, wetter around him, driving him wild. He thrust harder, faster, lifting her off his thighs until she tossed back her head and cried out his name. He watched the beauty of her rapture as she shuddered and convulsed in his arms, over his shaft, riding him, milking him of his seed in wave after torrential wave of fevered ecstasy.

Ah, he was hers, and the satisfied smile on her face as he fell back on the bed proved that she knew it.

Chapter Twenty-eight

$\mathcal{D}$avina stood ankle-deep in the freezing water of Camas Fhionnairigh, her hands covering her mouth as she doubled over with laughter.

"Which one of ye lads did that?" Finn did his best to appear menacing—which would have been a difficult task to achieve, even without a mouthful of water—but the horde of children jumping up and down around him were too busy laughing to notice.

Finn mopped his dripping hair out of his eyes and narrowed them on little Hamish MacGregor.

"Run, Hamish!" Davina screamed as Finn bolted after him. "Come children, we must help our comrade!" Hiking up her skirts and kicking water at her heels, Davina led her exuberant army toward their enemy.

She clapped her hands and cheered when young Marybeth MacDonnell plucked a small rock from the bank and flung it at Finn's back, giving him pause long enough for her older brother to catch up and swing his foot around Finn's ankle.

With their enemy down, the mighty army wasted no time surrounding him and splashing him with water.

"Finn, what have I told ye aboot losin' a fight?"

Davina looked up from Finn's drenched face to find Will standing over him shaking his head with mock disappointment.

"Must ye leave all the victories to me?" He drew in a suffering sigh then skimmed his shimmering gaze over Davina and her cohorts.

"Madam, children, prepare to be sorely defeated."

Davina knew Will loved her as he tackled her into the next swell then took off after poor Hamish. Finn also loved her, evidenced by the way he'd fastened himself to her side when she left Rob's chambers a se'nnight ago and had barely left it since. She loved them too. She loved Maggie, and Jamie, and even Brodie—who grumbled at her the same way he did everyone else. She loved Camlochlin and the magic of its laughing children and swirling misty mountaintops.

Wringing out her braid, she waded through the shallow surf, laughing and shivering with the cold when Finn sped past her on his way to either aiding Will, or sabotaging him. She set her eyes over the vast hills and smiled when she spotted the one she loved the most bringing a herd of woolly sheep back to the pasture with Jamie and Brodie circling the herd's flanks. Rob worked hard every day, seeing to the good of his clan, his land, and his livestock. Jamie was often at his side, as was Will—that is, when something more interesting didn't distract him.

But Will was not the firstborn son of the clan chief of Camlochlin. The duty of seeing his clan continually fed, comfortably sheltered, and kept warm on frigid Highland nights was Rob's alone...or would be, and his dedication to it earned him Davina's full faith and trust. She wished he would spend a few hours enjoying the fruits of his labor, rather than always sweating over them. It would take a bit of convincing, but Davina was patient. She didn't even mind seeing so little of him during the day, for his stamina lasted long after he returned to her each night, honed and hard from his labor and as hungry for her as he had been on their first night together.

She almost waved, but Rob wouldn't see her from where he was. Looking around, she felt a wave of contentment wash over her. She belonged here, surrounded by nothing but beauty and freedom. Everything before Camlochlin felt like a distant dream, and each day she forgot more of it.

"You look happy."

She stopped and looked up at Edward, less concerned with Finn or Will's proximity than he was.

"Please let me speak." When she nodded, he continued. "I wanted a chance to tell you that I've hated myself for four years. I hated what I did to you and more for never having the courage to tell you."

The truth of his words was in his eyes. Davina believed him. She understood now why he had spent almost every day with her afraid of the day after that. He did not deliver her when the enemy he knew was coming finally did, but fought an army and begged a stranger to save her. "I forgive you, Edward."

His guilt-ridden expression faltered and he allowed himself to smile at her. "He's right. I don't deserve your forgiveness. I hated him for the way you both looked at each other. But seeing you truly happy these last several days has helped me see things less selfishly."

"She gained mercy fer ye once, Asher," Will said, coming to stand at Davina's side. "Dinna' expect her husband to grant it again."

"Ye're not supposed to speak to her, Captain," Finn reminded him, appearing at her left.

"He may speak to me if he wishes," Davina corrected, then followed Finn's skittish glance over Edward's shoulder. She gave them all a reassuring smile through her chattering teeth. Rob was still too far away to see them clearly. She would speak to him later about Edward and tell him she had forgiven him. "If we don't show others mercy, none will be shown to us. We all do things we regret. None of us are perfect." She turned her playful smile on Will. "Despite what you tell yourself each night when you lay your head on your pillow."

Finn laughed, as did Caitlin MacKinnon swaying toward them, her dark hair bouncing around her flushed cheeks.

"There ye are, Captain Asher. I was lookin' fer ye."

Edward cracked a tiny smile, then looked away from Davina's widening grin.

"Ye were such a help yesterday carrying all those heavy bags of oats fer me," Caitlin practically cooed and looped her arm effortlessly through his. "I was hopin' ye might lend me yer strong arms yet again."

"Of course," Edward promised with a bit of a flush in his own cheeks.

Poor man, Davina thought watching him and Caitlin leave. He hadn't had a woman smile at him with such brazen intentions in four years.

"I think she fancies him," she said, completely missing the smirks that passed between Will and Finn. "Will Tristan be angry?"

This time, she didn't miss their laughter.

*   *   *

Rob tapped the lagging sheep's rump with his stick and went back to squinting. Was that Will chasing his wife at the water's edge? Were those her bare knees she exposed while she ran from him? Hell, he was going to do some serious damage to Will's pretty face later. And Finn… what the hell was he doing splashing around in the waves like a lad of five summers when there were sheep to be sheared?

"She has settled in verra quickly."

"Hmm?" Rob turned to Jamie. "What?"

"Yer wife." His uncle pointed toward the banks with his staff. "She seems quite happy here."

Rob nodded and peered down into the vale. Aye, she was. She told him so every night. What right had he to complain when his wife loved his land and his kin as much as he did? It was what he had wanted, what he had hoped for. He just wished she didn't enjoy herself so much without him.

"It took Claire almost half a year to get used to livin' at Camlochlin after Graham brought her here. She only truly settled in after Connor was born."

"Claire led a verra different life than Davina," Rob pointed out and tapped another sheep. "The only adventure Davina found while growin' up was in her books." He narrowed his eyes while two fat ewes wandered off back up the hill. "Who is that she's talkin' to?" He almost didn't recognize Asher out of uniform and draped in a Highland plaid. The traitorous bastard's back was to him as well, but Rob knew every body in Camlochlin… and that one did not belong. His jaw tightened on a muffled oath and he took a step forward.

258   PAULA QUINN

"Will and Finn are with her, lad," Jamie pointed out when Rob reached for his claymore. "She's in nae danger from the captain here."

"I told ye, ye shoulda' killed him when ye had the chance." Brodie drawled, a bare heather stem clamped between his teeth. "'Tis no' too late."

Aye, a slow death would suit well, Rob thought, pushing his way through the herd. That he'd allowed Asher to live at all still galled him, but the bastard's boldness in speaking to Davina was too much.

"Look there, Robert," Jamie called out to him. "He's leavin' with Caitlin, and yer wife is safe and sound on her way back to the castle. Dinna' go chasin' after her. We need three of us to bring the sheep in."

To hell with the sheep. Rob had a fox to deal with. He was halfway to the castle when a fiery arrow pierced the sky followed by a cry from the battlement walls.

Rob was still too far away to hear it clearly, but he didn't need to. The arrow meant there were riders approaching. Quickening his pace to a run, he spared a look toward the hills leading out of Camlochlin. Gilles could not have found them. Not so soon, anyway. When he saw no one in the distance, his heart thudded in his chest. The cliffs. Och, hell, 'twas worse than Gilles.

"'Tis the laird!"

He heard the call plainly now and came to a dead stop. His father was home. And he was early.

Chapter Twenty-nine

$\mathcal{R}$ob watched his father top the crest of Camlochlin just as the sky turned dark with rain, and for the first time, mayhap in his life, he felt like a child. 'Twas discomforting to know that even as a man of seven and twenty years, he was a wee bit afraid of his father—not of his anger, but of his disappointment.

"Why is he early?" Jamie puffed out, reaching him.

"What the bluidy hell does it matter why?" Brodie caught up and spit out his stem. "He's here."

Hell. Hell.

"Look at him," Maggie said, appearing at Rob's side. "Must have frightened the shyt out of them English noblemen when they saw him coming."

Rob summoned his courage to the task ahead. Here was the true guardian of Camlochlin, father over everyone in this vale. Protecting his children from harm was the Chief's duty, but for Callum MacGregor, 'twas his passion, a passion that burned from someplace in his father that Rob could never understand. How was Rob going to tell him that he had put his entire clan in dire risk in his father's absence? And as if that wasn't enough, that he'd wed the king's daughter?

But even hating what he had to tell his father, Rob did not regret his decisions, nor would he change a single one.

His mother waved at him, easing his troubled thoughts. Rob was glad she was home. Camlochlin was not complete without her.

"Welcome home, Callum." Maggie was the first to greet her brother, thankfully giving Rob a short reprieve. "How was yer journey?"

"Much more uneventful than some others, I'm told." Callum slipped from his saddle, kissed his sister's head, and pulled off his gloves. "How is it here?" He deliberately turned to Rob, waiting.

"I'm certain Rob has much to tell you, my love." Kate MacGregor looped her arm through Rob's and aimed her smile at her husband. "But it can wait until after we've enjoyed our homecoming, can it not?"

Without waiting for his answer, she spun her son around and pulled him toward the castle.

"Angus told him some of what happened at the beginning of your journey," Kate leaned in close and told him. "Your father wanted to leave right then, but Angus said it would alert the girl's enemies."

"I hear we have a most interestin' guest," said Tristan, smiling at him when Rob turned to find him keeping pace at his side. "Where might she be?"

"Did ye have to bring *him* home?" Rob asked his mother tightly, then cut his brother a dark look when Tristan quickened his pace and entered the castle before him.

"Is she truly King James's daughter, Robert?"

"Aye, mother, she is. Did Colin tell ye then?" he looked

over his shoulder, but saw only Angus and his father. "By the way, where is he?"

"Colin stayed in England with Graham and Claire, as did Mairi. And it was Connor who told us."

"Where is our guest, son?" his father asked behind him when they entered the castle.

"She must be dryin' off."

"Drying off?" His mother raised a curious brow at him.

"Aye, she was runnin' in the loch with Will and Finn."

His father stared at him for a moment, as if waiting for something more. When no more came, he gave his wife a quick sigh when she shook her head at him. "Ye'll explain that later, as well." He squeezed Rob's shoulder. "Come, we'll wait fer her in the Great Hall. I'm hungry fer somethin' hot." He rubbed his flat belly and looked longingly down the corridor. "At least tell me if there's beef in the kitchen."

Rob smiled. Mayhap, his father wouldn't kill him after all. Then again, he didn't know that the king's daughter was now his daughter as well.

Trying desperately to dry her thick locks before the hearth, Davina rubbed her hands through her hair until her palms itched. She'd heard the guard call out that the laird had returned. Without wasting a moment to look out the window, she'd dashed around the room, pulling off her wet clothes for something dry, warm, and presentable.

She was already taking too long. What a horrible impression she was making as each moment passed, but her blasted hair wouldn't dry!

Settling for damp, she finally scrambled to her feet,

pulled back the handful of hair that was falling over her eyes, pinned it in place above her forehead, and raced out of the room.

She and Rob should have known his parents would return earlier than expected. Colin probably had told them who she was. She should have been better prepared. Now, she looked like...

She walked straight into someone's chest. Instinctively, hands came up and closed around her arms to keep her from falling.

"Oh, pardon me!" She looked up and smiled at a man she hadn't seen in Camlochlin before. "I was not watching where I was walk..." Her words trailed off as his broad, breathtaking smile washed over her like a cool, refreshing rain shower. For a moment, she forgot where she was rushing off to.

"Ye must be Lady Davina," he said, slipping his palm down her arm and taking her hand in his. "Now I understand that daft smile on Colin's face when he spoke of ye."

Tristan. It wasn't his strong resemblance to Colin that convinced Davina who he was, though one had only to examine the chiseled angles of his face with a clear head to see the similarities, even down to the dimple in his chin, a feature he shared with both of his brothers. It was the effortless magnetism he exuded, the hint of something dangerous and unattainable beneath the warm veneer of his rich hazel eyes, the promise of a swift defeat in the sensual curl of his lips, that made Davina pity Caitlin MacKinnon and even Brigid MacPherson... and every other woman in Camlochlin.

"You must be Tristan."

"Ah, ye've heard of me, then?" He flashed her a grin

that was neither vain nor modest—the absence of both somehow lending to his appeal. His lashes were long and lush, as was his hair, but he was saved from perfection by a slight bend in his otherwise strong nose. He leaned in a little closer and bent to her conspiratorially. "Dinna' believe everything ye've been told. 'Tis only half true."

"It is that half that I was warned about." Davina smiled right back at him, appreciating his stark, male appeal, but less affected by it as the seconds passed. No one could compare to Rob.

Rob! His father! She suddenly remembered where she was heading and pulled her hand free of his.

"Oh, dear, I must go. I should have been outdoors to greet your parents long ago."

"I'm sure they'll agree the wait was worth it. Come, we'll find them together." He offered her his arm and a softer, reassuring smile when she paused. "I assure ye there is nae half of me that wishes to incur my brother's wrath should I lay one of my treacherous hands upon ye."

"Nonsense," she said, accepting his arm. "Rob would never hurt you overmuch."

"I was speaking of Colin." He quaked a little beneath his plaid for emphasis. "That one might seem unassuming, but when it comes to me, he is a merciless despot. I have nae idea why."

She laughed, tugging him along. She liked Tristan and his cavalier manner, so different from Rob's or Colin's. She hoped his father shared his easy nature.

"Ye should no' worry yerself so over making a good impression on my faither," Tristan said while she practically pulled him down the stairs. "Ye're the Princess Royal. What does it matter what anyone thinks of ye?"

She stopped so quickly, he almost continued down the next step without her. "Then, you know? They all know?"

"Of course. Why d'ye think we hastened our return?"

"Is your father terribly angry with Rob for bringing me here?" she asked, chewing her bottom lip.

Tristan smiled, tracing his gaze over her features. "He'll understand when he sees ye."

She didn't believe him for a moment. Taking a deep breath, she continued her hurried pace. "I do look forward to meeting Graham's wife, Claire. Tell me, is she easy to get along with? She is my cousin, after all, and I—"

"She isna' here. She remained in England with my sister and Colin."

Davina paused again. "Colin remained in England?"

"Aye."

"With the king?" She turned to look at him.

"Aye."

"That is most interesting," she said, thinking about what it meant. Did Colin find the king worthy of her praise? Or had he remained in order to scrutinize him further? Suddenly, she had to know. She had always wondered what kind of man her father truly was beyond what she'd been told by the sisters. If Colin liked him, it boded well.

"Colin likes him then?"

"I dinna' know. But yer faither seems fond enough of him. He invited us to sit with him at the dais the night Colin arrived."

Hmmm, whatever did that mean? Colin wasn't the friendliest soul in Scotland; that much was certain.

"And what did *you* think of him?"

"The king?"

Davina nodded as they approached the Great Hall. Tristan shrugged his shoulders. "I found him to be a wee bit quiet and reserved. No' what I expected actually."

Davina was about to ask him what he'd expected when he pushed open the doors to the Great Hall.

Her eyes settled immediately on the family table, to Rob first, her rock, her anchor, and she drew strength from the love in his tender gaze.

She looked to the man sitting across from him next and felt her legs shake a little beneath her skirts. He looked more dangerous than any man at the table— bigger, rougher, like he'd been born to wield a sword and rain terror down on his enemies. His eyes were a startling shade of blue, even from where she stood, and they held the power to immobilize.

"Faither," Tristan called out, confirming her presumption of who the man was and moving her toward the table where the laird was now rising to his feet. "'Tis my profound pleasure to present Lady Davina Stuart."

Callum MacGregor's gaze seared on the crook of Tristan's arm where her hand rested lightly. When he raised his eyes to his son, he did not have to speak a word. The warning in them was complete. She was a princess, and no one was permitted to touch her—especially not his rogue son.

Unfazed by his father's rapier-sharp glare, Tristan offered her an unrepentant smile before he released her. "Now 'tis clear to see why Rob brought her here. Aye, Faither?" he murmured, giving her one last look before going to his chair.

Davina caught Callum's uneasy gaze shifting to Rob as Tristan's implication settled in. She could almost hear him praying that Rob hadn't touched her...or worse. Before Davina had time to worry about what they needed to tell him, the tall, broad-shouldered chief returned his attention to her. "My lady." He dropped to one knee, and the others around the table whom she did not know did the same. "We are honored by—"

"Oh, no, I beg you, don't do that." Davina reached for the laird with one hand, waving him up with the other. "Stand to your feet. Please, my laird." He looked up at her and Davina cursed herself for the emotion in her eyes. "Please, don't bow to me."

He straightened and Davina saw Rob in his softening smile.

"Oh, aren't you just the loveliest young lady to grace Camlochlin's halls." The compliment came from a breathtaking woman standing to the right of Callum. Her eyes were the color of onyx, large and round and ringed by lush black lashes. Her hair was just as dark and fell in glossy waves down her back. "I am Kate, Robert's mother." Her smile was as wide and inviting as Tristan's as she pushed past her husband and took Davina's hands in her own. "Heavens, you look more like Claire's daughter than the king's. I trust our son has made your stay here comfortable?"

"Oh, yes, my lady, thank you. Everyone here has been wonderful."

Kate patted her hand and offered Rob a pleased smile. "We're delighted to have you here, are we not, darling?"

"Aye," her husband said with just a little less enthusiasm. "Rob told us aboot the men who came fer ye at Courlochcraig."

"But it can wait until after you've eaten," Kate insisted, offering her a chair.

Perhaps this would not be so terrible, Davina thought, walking around the table to Rob. The laird didn't seem half as fearsome as Will and the others had led her to believe. Kate MacGregor was certainly one of the warmest people she'd ever met and as likable as Tristan. Perhaps they would take the news of their son's marriage easier than she thought. She waved at Finn and Jamie when she passed them and bent to kiss Maggie's cheek when she reached her next. She caught the surprised look the chief tossed his wife when Maggie reached up from her chair and touched Davina's cheek lovingly. But her hopes dashed to the floor as she took her usual seat beside Rob. She wasn't sure if it was Rob's sweetly intimate smile or her own breathless gush in response to it that made Callum MacGregor's handsome smile fade. For a terrifying instant, Davina feared that everything she loved was about to be taken from her again, and this time, she would not survive it.

Chapter Thirty

$\mathcal{M}$y lady—"

"Davina, please, my laird."

"Davina," Rob's father corrected with a slight nod. "I was just done tellin' Robert that ye have one less enemy to fret aboot."

"Oh?" She raised her brows, thankful for something to take her mind off the inevitable. They were foolish to believe that either of their fathers would allow love between them, let alone marriage. But it was too late. It was done, and by God, she wasn't going to let anyone take from her again.

"Once the king discovered the names behind the tragedy at St. Christopher's," Rob's father went on, all stoic and serious, much like his eldest son, "it didna' take him long to discover what Argyll has been up to. Confident that the Campbells will stand with him in an uprisin', the earl has returned to Scotland to build his army. When I left the king, he was already makin' plans to stop him. Argyll will never make it to England alive."

Davina didn't know how she should feel. It was wrong to take joy in someone's death, but she was happy that the king would soon have one less enemy. And so would she, thanks to Rob. If he had gone to the coronation with his father, she would be dead and her father would never have found out about Argyll until it was too late.

"Monmouth and Gilles will no' be difficult to find with an army on their heels," Rob told her, leaning in closer.

She looked up at him and relished the hope he always stirred in her. "The king owes you much," she said, staring into his eyes, aching to stroke his jaw, to run her fingers along his lips.

"The king"—Callum's voice was cold enough to cool the soup Agnes had just set in front of Davina—"so I am told by my son Colin, is inconsolable over the presumed death of his daughter."

Davina went still, unaware and uninterested in her food or anything else, save for what Rob's father had just told her. Why would he say such a thing? Her father... inconsolable... over her? It couldn't be true. He had to be lying, perhaps hoping to touch some part of her heart that ached for a man she did not know so that she would want to go to him.

"The king has nae right to grieve over the daughter he abandoned at her birth," Rob said, the anger in his voice pulling his father's hard gaze to him.

"Ye presume to know the rights of a king now... or a faither?"

"A faither?" Rob laughed hollowly. "He doesna' even know her. Mayhap he grieves because he sat passively by while his second daughter was wed to a Protestant who schemes fer his title."

Davina angled her face toward Rob, but refrained at the last moment from defending the king's reasons for allowing Mary to wed William of Orange.

"Robert." The clip of annoyance in his father's voice was emphasized by the clap of thunder that suddenly shook the walls, and Tristan, who until that moment had looked utterly bored with the topic, sat forward with a curious smirk slanting his mouth. "I dinna' know what ye had in mind fer—"

"Callum." Kate touched his husband's arm. "You are upsetting our guest. Look, she has yet to take a sip from her cup."

"Aye," Maggie chimed in. "Let us speak of more pleasant things at the table. Tell me, Kate, did Mairi's staying in England have anything to do with Connor?"

"We hope so," Kate told her. "It is why we let her stay on with Claire when she asked."

"Ye did no' tell the king that his daughter lived, did ye, faither?"

Kate gave Rob an exasperated sigh and went back to eating.

"D'ye think I want an army ridin' over those hills?" his father replied dryly.

"I had nae choice but to bring her here."

"Of course you didn't, Robert," his mother agreed. "Your father knows that."

Callum turned to grant her the full force of his scowl, which she ignored—much to Davina's admiration.

"I'm no' questionin' yer valiant efforts to keep her safe," the laird said, returning his attention to his son. "But now we must decide what to do with her."

"I have already decided," Rob said boldly, piquing Tristan's interest yet again. "And my decision will no' please ye."

Callum's jaw jumped with the effort it took to refrain

from speaking words Davina suspected he might regret later. He drew in a deep breath before he spoke again, conceding only slightly to what was clear before his eyes. "Ye care fer her. But despite what ye believe, Robert, there are laws even we must abide."

"And if we canna' abide them?" Rob asked, matching the intensity of the gaze staring back at him. "What then, faither? Did ye obey the law when 'twas a crime to speak yer own name? Or when ye took a Campbell fer yer wife?"

"Nae, son, but—"

"No, he didn't." Kate set down her spoon and picked up her serviette to dab the corners of her mouth. "And we are not asking you to do something you cannot abide. We understand the Princess is in great danger and that the safest place for her right now is in Camlochlin. Isn't that correct, husband."

Judging by the flash of fire in his eyes when he set them on his wife, Callum MacGregor was losing his battle for control fast. Fortunately, before he could reply, Rob did.

"She will always be in danger anywhere but here."

Callum opened his mouth to say something, but once again, his wife beat him to it.

"But the king will never let her—"

"Katie." With one word the chief stilled the entire table, including his wife. "If ye continue to interrupt me every time I open my mouth, I will take our son to the solar and speak to him alone."

"Forgive me," Kate amended, albeit a bit stiffly, and severed her injured gaze from his.

It was clear to Davina in that moment how much the Devil MacGregor loved his wife. For his eyes lingered on her too long, as if willing her to look at him. When she didn't, he muttered an oath under his breath even as he reached for her hand and covered it with his own.

The tender gesture was enough to earn him the forgiveness he sought when Kate rotated her wrist and entwined her fingers through his.

Here was what Davina wanted. She wanted to be sitting here twenty years from now with a husband who loved her more than his pride, a man who scowled at the rest of the world but melted at her slightest touch. She wanted Rob and she was tired of others dictating her life.

With a clear head and a determined heart, Davina slipped her hand to Rob's and closed her fingers around his, just as his mother had done to his father. She did not pull away when Callum's eyes lifted from their forbidden touch to meet her gaze.

"My laird, I want to stay here. I love your son and never wish to be parted from him. I will not abide any law—from king or father—that tries to take me from him."

Callum said nothing as one eternal moment stretched into another. Davina was certain Kate had stopped breathing. Indeed, everyone at the table had.

"Faither"—Rob broke the silence and gave her hand a reassuring squeeze—"she is my wife."

Kate closed her eyes as her husband sprang from his chair and raked his disbelieving gaze over Maggie and her husband first. "Is this true?" When his sister nodded, he brought his fist down on the table hard enough to rattle their cups. "He will be hanged fer this!"

"Nae, Callum," Maggie defended quickly. "Not if the king does not know where she is or who she is." She carefully told him about Rob's plan to claim Davina was a novice called Elaine, but as she spoke, and her brother's expression grew blacker, Davina had to admit to herself how ridiculous the scheme sounded.

The laird agreed, and settling his scorching gaze on his son, he spoke through clenched teeth. "Ye dinna' realize what ye've done, or mayhap ye do and ye're both too blinded by yer hearts to care. Either way, I will tell ye. Yer marriage will mean nothin' to the king. 'Twill be annulled before she is dragged back to England. Ye, my son, will be hanged fer violatin' her. Or mayhap, if her faither is merciful, tossed into a dark dungeon somewhere. I—" His words trailed off as Davina covered her face in her hands and began to weep. "Fergive me, lass, if my words cut yer heart," he said, softening his tone slightly, "but ye need to hear them. Ye both do." He stared at his son as if he didn't know him. "Rob, how could ye no' have thought this through? What the hell did ye think ye were doin'? Weddin' her willna' keep her with ye. He'll come fer her, and when he does ye must no' tell him that ye took her as yer wife. D'ye understand?" He looked at Davina. "And ye, d'ye understand that 'twill cost my son his life?"

Davina nodded her head, knowing he was right. They'd both known it all along, but they chose to live as if they were asleep, safe from the world, lost in a dream. She turned to look at the man who had rescued her and taken her to a place where love meant more than her name. The man who had become her dream in the flesh.

But now it was time to wake up.

Beside her, Rob stood slowly to his feet. When he spoke, his voice was as hard and as sharp as steel. His words cut straight through to her heart. "And if she carries my bairn, faither? What should we tell him then? Ye've had yer say and now I shall have mine. I will do whatever needs to be done when the time comes. But I willna' deny her. And whether or no' ye or anyone else in this clan stands by me, I willna' let him take her from Camlochlin."

Rob took her hand and began to turn away from his father, but the chief's strong hand stopped him. "I know ye well enough to know when ye willna' be moved." Callum's smile looked pained as he turned to look at his wife, and then back to his son. "We'll figure somethin' oot and when the times comes, yer clan will stand at yer side."

"Your father loves his family very much," Davina said softly at Rob's side as they climbed the stairs. "You are like him in many ways."

She wasn't going to tell him what she had decided. He would only try to convince her not to fear. A task she had already achieved, because of him. But this was different. This time, it wasn't her life that was in danger. It was his. This time, she had the power to stop it.

"We mustn't sleep together again."

He laughed, but there was no trace of mirth in the sound. "The hell we won't. Yer my wife and nothin' will change that . . . or us."

"But what if—"

"Everything will be well, Davina," Rob interrupted her. "Yer faither may never come here. He may never need to. Angus tells me that the queen seems very much in love with him. Mayhap he will have his son."

"He is inconsolable over me, Rob." Saying it felt even more foreign to her ears than when she heard Callum speak it. "I wonder why he would be saddened by my death."

She didn't realize they'd reached the top of the stairs until Rob took her hand to walk with her down the hall.

"Mayhap he deserves what he feels...fer whatever reason he is feelin' it."

"He left me to protect me for a duty that might some-day be mine to inherit."

Rob stopped, dragging her to an abrupt halt with him. "An inheritance ye dinna' want."

"A duty, just like yours," she reminded him.

"Nae, Davina," he argued. "'Tis nothin' like mine. I've trained my entire life fer mine. What d'ye know aboot leadin' a kingdom?"

"Why are you shouting at me?"

"Why are ye considerin' this fate?" he countered. Then, trying to regain his ever-composed temper, he clasped his hands behind his head and turned away from her. But not before Davina saw the flash of alarm in his eyes. He was afraid of losing her. She understood and she wanted to comfort him the same way he'd done for her so many times.

"Rob," she whispered, coming up close to him. "There is no other life for me but you."

He turned, gathering her in his arms, sweeping her away with a kiss that brought tears to her eyes, and then to their chamber, kicking the door closed and locking the rest of the world outside.

Chapter Thirty-one

*B*loated, agitated clouds darkened what was left of the meager sun and the warmth she provided. The sky rumbled like a thousand horses charging across the heavens with Thor in the lead. Crackling bolts of lightning pierced the twilight, hurled by the angry god at the arrogant mountains. But they stood, impervious and unyielding against the onslaught. Nothing on earth or in heaven moved in the waiting stillness before the sky tore open and the clouds spewed forth sheets of icy rain in a violent flash for which the body had no time to prepare.

Admiral Peter Gilles hated the Highlands.

He cursed the Stuarts and all their descendants one more time as he hunkered low beneath the sparse branches he'd ripped from the trees earlier. But there was no relief to be found from the pelting rain.

He was used to cold weather, but this was the kind of frigid chill that seeped into the marrow of your bones and made you utterly miserable. The kind of cold that made you want to curl up in something warm and go to sleep. Forever.

"Is it close to morning?" Hendrick queried through clicking teeth when the rain finally stopped.

"How the hell should I know?" Maarten replied, sounding equally despondent from his makeshift shelter.

Gilles looked up at the heavens. Through the shadowy haze, he could make out the stars for the second time in the last four hours. Dead of night had passed quickly and the morning would be coming soon. It was the one thing, the only thing agreeable about this wretched place. Daylight was getting longer, giving him more time to hunt.

But he was going to have to find his prize soon or risk losing his men in a mutiny. He'd have to kill them, of course. Either way, he would be one man against the MacGregors. Not favorable odds.

The days were getting longer and his time was running out.

They were making progress, even though everything was wet here. All the time. It made maneuvering over the mossy hillsides difficult and dangerous. But there was at least one Tavernier in every village he and his men had traveled who knew of the MacGregors, leading them ever northward. Gilles did not find her with the MacGregors of Stronachlacher, but a most helpful fellow in Breadalbane was good enough to tell him of a clan of MacGregors living on one of the isles northwest. Exiled from the rest, they lived in the mists, rarely seen or heard of.

She was with them. Gilles knew it in his guts, but where? Which isle? No one knew, and if they did, they would not say.

He hated Highlanders too.

Something caught his attention and he looked around, realizing what it was. Birds chirping. The dawn had finally come. "Hendrick," he ordered, leaving his shelter and slapping his soaked hat across his thigh, "find us something to eat. Nuts, berries, I don't care.

"Maarten, gather the rest of the men and—" He stopped suddenly and tilted his head south. "What is that sound?"

"More thunder."

"No." He listened for another moment then beckoned Hendrick back to him. "Horses. Tell the men to take cover."

A little while later, they watched the narrow road from the other side of a muddy hill.

"Sounds like a small army," Hendrick murmured, waiting for the riders to appear.

"Twenty, perhaps thirty, no more."

"Covenanters, perhaps," Maarten offered.

The sound grew louder until it shook the ground and silenced the birds above. Gilles held his breath as the riders came into view. They wore no military regalia, but their tight formation, and their size, suggested otherwise. They could belong to any one of the Lowland barons, but what were they doing in the Highlands? Their pace was not urgent, but not leisurely either. As they passed him, Gilles spotted a younger man, too young to belong to an army, dressed in the unsightly garb of a Highlander. But it was the rider beside him, his face partially hidden behind his hooded cloak, that held Gilles's cool gaze.

"Men," he said with a smile, keeping his eyes on James of York. "We have found her."

"Where?" Hendrick peered at the riders through narrowed lids.

"There." Gilles tugged his earlobe, directing Hendrick's line of vision in the right direction. "That man is her father."

"The king?"

"Yes, the king." Gilles sneered at the troupe as they rode away. Clever of James not to travel with his entire army lest he draw more attention to himself, but risky, as well.

"Why don't we just kill him now then?"

"Because, imbecile, James still has many supporters. If we kill him first and then kill two of the men who have outwardly claimed his title, suspicion will fall to the prince and his succession will be difficult, if not impossible. My lord has a grander plan, one that will bring more support to his side, not less."

"A Dutch king," Hendrick grinned.

"Yes, if we do this right." Gilles smiled back at him and patted his cheek. The man could not match wits with a cricket, but he could fire a pistol with almost perfect accuracy—and he didn't mind killing women or children when the need arose.

"James's Highland companion has obviously told him that his daughter lives, and is leading him to where she is hiding. All we have to do is follow them."

"And then what?" Maarten asked as Gilles straightened and strode to his horse. "How do we kill her with not only MacGregors guarding her, but the king's men, as well?"

"Let's find her first, Maarten." Gilles grinned at him as he placed his hat on his head and brought the rim down low over his brow. "We can discuss ways to kill her after that."

Was it possible that he was finally going to see her? Meet her? Perhaps even kiss her blessed cheeks? James tried to remember how many times he had prayed for mercy from God in the last several days. God, the only One who could understand how a king could grieve so over the loss of his child. But no, Colin MacGregor had understood also. How could a mere boy show so much compassion when men twice his age and a hundred times more cultured than he would think a king odd for his sorrow?

"I have something to tell ye," the young MacGregor had told him four days after his father had gone home. "But ye must swear first on yer kingdom and on yer faith that after I tell ye, my kin will always find mercy with ye. Ye must swear never to bring them harm, nor any shame."

James had grown fond of Colin since he'd arrived at Whitehall. He was quiet and agreeable while the king answered his many questions about everything from his battles in France and Spain to his views on the Covenanters. Their conversations had helped James through the worst days of his grief. The king had even found himself smiling while he watched Colin practice in the list with Connor Grant and some of his finest men. He was not only quick with his mind, but with his arm as well. The boy would make a fine soldier, if only James could convince him to remain in his garrison.

"You have my solemn oath," the king had promised him easily, already trusting the stranger more than any man in his Great Hall.

What MacGregor told him next proved that he trusted his king, as well.

"Yer daughter is alive."

They were words James would never forget hearing, though he could not remember what he said in response.

How? Where was she? Who was she with? Was it possible that she had been given back to him as Isaac had been returned to Abraham?

Colin told him everything while James laughed with joy and then wept, then laughed again. She had been rescued... rescued at the very last moment by Colin's brother, Robert MacGregor. She had spoken of the king often and not with anger or resentment, but with admiration. Admiration! Oh, what had he done to deserve such mercy? The sisters had been kind to her but—and this made the king weep all the more—Colin told him there was an emptiness in her eyes, haunting and so very quiet that it had nearly broken all their hearts.

"Where? Where has your brother taken her?" James had asked, and this was when the boy looked like he might change his mind and tell him nothing more.

"We didna' know who she was at first, but my brother knew that whoever wanted her dead could be here with ye. He wanted to keep her safe. We all did."

"Where, son?"

"Robert took her home."

And that was where they were headed now. To a remote part of Skye hidden in the mists—a place called Camlochlin—a place the boy asked the king to forget the moment he left it. Colin had assured him that the only way to reach his home alive was if he accompanied the king and his men. Even if James found Camlochlin on his own, the MacGregors were not expecting them, and since the king did not carry his banner—lest his enemies find him on the road with only a scant number of his men in his company—the MacGregors might attack before they realized who he was. So James had taken Colin with him when he and his men left England in the cover of night. He told no one where he was going, not even his wife, lest someone question her. At Colin's request, he did not tell Captain Grant, either. He thought about it now and turned to his young companion.

"I must confess I am disappointed in my captain for not telling me about Davina."

"Captain Grant left everything he loves to serve ye," Colin told him and cast the dark heavens an even blacker look. "He even broke my sister's heart, fer which I will never fergive him."

The king smiled. Such a serious lad, he was.

"My brother asked him no' to tell ye until he was certain there were no traitors in yer midst. If word got oot that she lived and she was traveling with MacGregors, 'twould only be a matter of time before they found her."

"And yet you told me."

Colin nodded but said nothing more. It was clear to James that the boy had misgivings about what he'd done. Was he worried that his father would be angry with him for bringing the king to his misty home? Or was it something else? Someone else?

"Your brother went to much trouble to see to my daughter's safety," James said vaguely, looking around at the landscape. "Since he didn't know who she was at first, I must assume that he did not do so for me." He slipped his gaze to Colin when the boy remained silent. "Does he care for her then?"

"We all do," Colin muttered through his teeth, averting his gaze from the king's.

"I see," James said with a heart almost as heavy as when he believed Davina was dead. The promises Colin had asked him to make made more sense to James now. This Robert MacGregor cared for her. Perhaps, he'd even fallen in love with her, and every king before him knew firsthand how possessive Highlanders were.

Dear God, he should have taken more men.

Chapter Thirty-two

𝒟espite the fact that Callum MacGregor's smiles were often laden with worry when he set them on her, Davina was happy the laird was home. It gave Rob a reprieve from seeing to everything himself, giving her more time to help teach him how to have fun and less time for her to think about her father ever coming for her.

Unfortunately, her husband was a terrible student.

He knew how to swim, but flatly refused to follow her into the water. He didn't even shiver when she scooped some of the freezing water into her hands and splashed him thoroughly. He didn't crack a smile either. When one of Maggie's beloved piglets escaped from its pen, Rob simply watched, arms crossed over his chest, while she, Finn, and little Hamish chased it around in circles until they collided with one another and sank to the ground laughing. He gave dancing a valiant effort during the celebration of the birth of little Alasdair MacDonnell, but after stepping on Davina's foot and sending her reeling into Tristan, he decided it was safer for all involved if he watched from his seat. He did try to teach her how to play chess, but after she yawned a dozen times, he gave up.

When Davina tried to watch what *he* did for sport, she

ended up missing half of it with her eyes squeezed shut. She'd seen men practice swordplay before, but none of the men at St. Christopher's had ever wielded a blade with such raw power that she could feel the sting of clashing metal from a hundred paces away. Rob was brutal on the field, merciless against his opponents, including Will. He parried with impressive speed and dexterity for a man his size, and swung his giant claymore with a single purpose—to devastate. It was only when his father brandished his blade against him that Rob grew winded. The rest she could not watch and sneaked off, without Finn's notice, to pick some flowers.

Thanks to the frequent spring rains, the hills were bursting with color. Above her, the sun vied with the clouds for supremacy, casting the tall grass in lush golden-green hues.

She almost stepped on Tristan, lying on his back within the purple heather and wild daffodils. His eyes were closed, his hands canted behind his head, buried beneath his silken mane of tousled waves, boots crossed at the ankles. He looked like a handsome prince who'd stumbled into a faerie patch and fallen under a sleep spell so some mischievous queen could have her way with him. In fact, he appeared to be waiting for it. Davina quirked her brow at him and rested her blossom wielding fist on her hip. She'd barely seen him doing any work in the few days since he had returned home. Now that she thought of it, she'd hardly seen him at all. He wasn't spending his days—or his nights—with Caitlin. That privilege had fallen to Edward, and Davina couldn't be happier. The wicked scoundrel—as so many of the young women of Camlochlin were wont to call Tristan—had not chased one skirt, as far as Davina could tell.

"Tristan, are you ill?"

His smile flashed, but he did not move or open his eyes. "Would ye think better of me if I was?"

What an odd thing to ask. "Of course not. Why would I?"

He shrugged his shoulders. "'Twould provide me with a suitable reason fer no' doing something else."

"Well, now that you bring it up, I did hear your father mention the wood needed chopping."

"Rob'll see to it."

"As he sees to everything else?" she asked, with a bit of a sting in her voice.

Tristan yawned. "'Tis his duty as firstborn."

She thought of giving him a good slap with her flowers. It might not jar his sense of responsibility, but at least he would open his eyes and give her the courtesy of his attention. "I see," she said softly, deciding on decorum rather than violence. "And your duty as second born is to bed..." Her gentle admonishment came to an abrupt halt when he opened his eyes and finally looked up at her. There was a challenge in his gaze as he pushed himself up on his elbows that she wasn't sure she wanted to engage. But as he waited for her to continue, something in his daring smirk changed. He knew what she was about to say. He'd heard it a million times before and knew exactly how to reply; only today...today the accusation pierced a bit deeper.

"Forgive me," she said contritely, looking down at her flowers. "It isn't my place to speak to you so."

He stared at her in silence until she turned away, ready to head back down the hill.

"Consider yerself fortunate that ye dinna' know yer faither, lass."

She stopped and pivoted on her heels to find him sitting up and staring now at the fortress his father had built. "How can you say such a thing? Your father is . . ."

"Stubborn and unfergiving and verra hard to please if ye're no' exactly like him." Tristan tore his troubled gaze away from the castle and the thoughts that provoked him. He offered her a thin smile and shooed her away. "Off with ye now. I've a dream to finish."

He began to lie back down but Davina dropped to her knees in front of him, spilling her flowers at his feet. Dear God, she couldn't deny how beautiful he was when he smiled. She suspected it was almost too easy for him to have any lass he desired, but the misery he cloaked so well wrenched at her heartstrings. He was correct. He was nothing like his father, nothing like Rob or even Colin. He was the rogue, the prodigal son who wasted away his days sleeping in the heather or bedding other lairds' daughters.

"You can change."

"Aye, and fit into the MacGregor mold of pride, arrogance, and vengeance. Nae, lass," his smile was pure seduction. "I'd much rather make love."

"That's not true! I can see it in your eyes."

"Aye, believe me, 'tis." He laughed, and then grew serious again as his gaze swept over her features. "And it pleases me to know that 'tis true fer Rob, as well."

Davina glared at him and his smile deepened. "It is terrible of you to take pleasure in the fact that Rob has disappointed your father by taking me as his wife."

"Lass," he said more gently, "my faither may have been angry, but he was no' disappointed in Rob. He is no' blind, and he doesna' hate yer kin the way he hates . . ." He stopped, catching himself and veering off from what he was about to say. "Ye've been welcomed here by all, and 'tis easy to see why."

"Who does your father hate?" Davina asked, not letting him change direction. "Is it Caitlin? I know Maggie doesn't like her, but—"

He laughed again, this time tossing his head back as the clouds passed and sweeping his sun-drenched hair off his shoulders. "Caitlin is a bonnie lass to be sure, but she wants what I canna' give her. Mayhap yer Captain Asher can. I hope he can."

"He is not my captain."

"Aye, so I've heard. Fergive me," he repented sincerely.

"Then who?" she pressed.

He plucked a daffodil from the ground and studied it for a moment. "I prefer wild flowers to the delicate ones."

Davina watched him, not knowing what he meant. Finally, he met her gaze. "Her name is Isobel. Isobel Fergusson. I saw her again at the coronation. Her brother did this when I was a lad." He pointed to the small curve in his nose where it had been broken many years before.

Fergusson. Where had Davina heard the name before?

"Davina!" Finn's cheerful voice coming up the hill interrupted her. "Ye should have seen it! Rob nearly cut off the chief's finger!"

Lord, she was glad she missed it, she thought, turning to greet her cousin. Before she did, Tristan caught her eye and puckered his lips, motioning silently for her to keep their conversation secret.

"I almost maimed my faither to impress ye, and ye were no' even there."

She returned Rob's smile as he hiked up the last few

feet behind Finn to reach her. All the beauty around her paled compared to him, and when he finally reached her and folded his long legs to sit close to her, she let her hungry gaze drink in every inch of him. The single black curl that always escaped his queue was damp from the exertion he'd expended in the practice field. His face was a bit flush, giving even more vivid color to his eyes. His smile faded, but not altogether when he looked at his brother.

"What are ye doin' up here alone with my wife?"

"Tryin' to convince her to leave Camlochlin with me, but she's fallen in love with Will and willna' go."

"She knows who is the better man between ye then?"

Davina was about to tell her husband not to be cruel, especially now that she was aware how inadequate Tristan felt, but Rob's eyes sparked with humor and his brother answered swiftly and with equal measure.

"Aye, she does, and after sharin' *yer* bed."

Rob was about to reply but thought better of it and turned to Davina instead. "Now ye see why Colin hates him."

"Speaking of Colin," Finn said, closing his eyes and getting comfortable on his back on the other side of Tristan. "Why did he wish to stay in England?"

"I dinna' know," Tristan said, plucking petals off a daffodil and dropping them into Finn's hair without his notice. "The lure of the king's garrison, mayhap? The idea of his hated Covenanters lurking within the shadowy corridors of Whitehall? One never knows what chillin' notions go on in that lad's head."

Finn moved as it he was going to sit up and Tristan snapped his hand back. But the boy only shifted, settling into the heather more deeply. Tristan smiled at Rob and Davina and set another yellow petal on Finn's flaxen crown.

"What's it like?" Finn asked in a groggy voice.

"What's what like?" Tristan asked, slipping a sprig of heather into Finn's locks next.

"England."

"'Tis gloomy and no' verra clean. But Whitehall Palace is grand, indeed."

"Tell us about it," Finn urged.

Davina listened intently to Tristan's description of her father's home. Was it truly possible that a structure could be built so big as to hold a thousand rooms? When Rob slipped his fingers through hers, she offered him a brief smile, happy that he was with her, content to do nothing more than sit here in the blossoms. But Tristan's words held her in awe and too soon she returned her smile to him. A statue-lined garden almost as big as Camlochlin? A private theatre? Tennis courts? What in the world was tennis?

"The ladies there are just as splendid," Tristan told them, his golden-brown eyes warming on her. "But ye, bonnie lady, would outshine every one."

When her smile deepened into a blush Rob tightened his hand around hers and vaulted to his feet, dragging her with him. "We'll see ye lads later."

Davina barely had the chance to bid them farewell before Rob pulled her by the hand down the hill. She nearly lost her footing trying to keep his pace and finally dug her heels into the ground to stop him.

"What is the matter with you?"

"Nothin'," he said, giving her another tug.

She tugged him back and then slapped his hand when

he did not stop. "Are you bothered by Tristan's comfort with me? Because if you are, then you are being a silly fool."

He finally stopped and turned to look at his hand first, and then her. "Woman, ye know I dinna' suffer such boyish flaws."

She did her best not to smile, remembering his constant brooding scowl from their days of traveling with Edward. "Of course. Forgive me," she indulged. "But you will tell me why we left in such haste. I was enjoying hearing about...Oh, I see." She looked away, realizing finally the cause of his displeasure. "I was curious, that is all."

His jaw danced around the right words to say. "Davina, I doubt any garden could be more bonnie than what lies before ye here. And hell, if 'tis a tennis court ye want, I will build ye one."

Now she did smile looking up at him. "Have you ever seen one?"

"Nae, but I—"

She moved closer to him and held her finger to his mouth, halting the remainder of his words. "I don't desire such things. You are my heaven on earth, Robert MacGregor."

His sexy mouth hooked into a smile that ravished her senseless. When he cupped her face in his hands and drew her in to gently lick his way into her mouth, she responded with a dreamy sigh. God have mercy, but the man knew what to do with his mouth, and his tongue. The taste of his hunger seared her nerves and weakened her kneecaps. She wanted him and for an instant she forgot where she was. Tristan's voice, calling out to them that the rain was about to come, jarred her memory.

"Come, hurry," she whispered against Rob's mouth as he slowly withdrew. When he moved to kiss her yet again, unconcerned with the blackening clouds, she giggled and sprang from his arms. "Catch me"—she smiled at him, taking a step backward down the hill—"and I am yours until the rain ends."

She squeaked with surprise when her ever-pragmatic husband took off after her. Whirling on her toes, she ran, picking up speed and laughing as she went. She was about to swing open the castle doors when they opened on their own. She stopped herself just before she collided into Callum MacGregor's chest. Rob was close behind. She knew it because his father's eyes settled on her first and then on the tall man behind her.

No one spoke a word for an eternal moment, then the chief stepped aside, sweeping his bandaged hand over the threshold.

"'Tis goin' to rain," Rob explained, stepping past his father after Davina did.

"Aye, I can see that," his father replied, but Davina and Rob barely heard him as they took their chase up the stairs, leaving laughter in their wake and an unbidden smile on the mighty chief's face.

Chapter Thirty-three

$\mathcal{R}$ob caught her before Davina reached their chamber door. His arms closed around her, and spinning her to face him, he gave her a short, victorious laugh that set her blood to burning.

"The clouds are heavy, my love. 'Tis goin' to rain long and hard."

"I hope it never stops," she vowed, smiling breathlessly into his face.

His mouth came down hard on hers, devouring her softness, tasting her with his lips, his tongue, and his teeth. Pushing the door open with his boot, he carried her to the bed and fell, locked in her embrace, onto the soft mattress. Labored by their run, and by the passion that came upon them as relentlessly as the rain outside their window, they tore at each other's clothes, feasting on the flesh they exposed. Naked and wild for each other, Davina traced the muscles in his chest with her fingertips, her lush, wet lips. He caught her nipple between his lips and she arched her back as a knot of sheer arousal erupted between her legs.

He lifted his face from her heaving breasts, his eyes both dark and gleaming together. "I have wanted ye since we left our bed this mornin'."

She giggled, not knowing this wicked seductress who possessed her when she was alone with Rob, but liking her. "Is that why you would not play with me today?"

"This is how I want to play with ye, wife." His voice was like the low rumble of thunder outside as he moved up her body and raked his mouth over the thrashing pulse at her throat.

Curling her legs around him, she writhed very deliberately beneath him, delighting in the effect she had on his body. She loved what she did to him, this man of steel and seriousness. She tore away his control, his restraint, until the passion that ran through his blood for her could no longer be contained.

"You are so strong and hard," she drawled like a languid siren against his ear. The tormented groan she pulled from him as his open mouth found hers made her want to weep with joy. Let every lady in Camlochlin swoon over a charming smile. She had won the love of a man who shared his most intimate smiles for her alone. "I love you," she whispered over and over, sliding her hands up his face while he kissed her.

He broke away from their kiss and looked down into her eyes as he impaled her deeply. She responded by arching her spine to meet his slow, moist thrust. He closed his eyes as ecstasy rocked him, a sinfully decadent smile pursing his lips and making her wetter. She loved his weight on her and pushed up against him. He withdrew and thrust hard, his mouth descending hungrily on her throat. His breath was hot on her skin as he ground his hips against her own, wedging himself as deep in her tight sheath as she could take him.

Spasms of ecstasy wracked her body and she slid her

hands over the firm mounds of his buttocks to drive him deeper still.

"Ye are wicked." He ran his lips over her smile. "And ye're goin' to bring this to a quicker end."

"You mean your defeat," she smiled into his mouth.

"Aye, my defeat."

She opened to his plunging tongue as her climax tightened her body around his stiff, scalding erection. He withdrew, then sank deeper into her again, torturing, teasing, satisfying her with every slow, grinding thrust until she cried out, clinging to him.

Driving into her harder, he swallowed up the sounds of her pleasure with tight, thick groans of his own as his seed spilled hot and wet inside her.

Spent, he collapsed beside her and drew her into his embrace. She closed her eyes, spooned against his rigid angles, and thanked God for the millionth time for bringing Rob into her life.

"Rob?"

"Um?"

"You are turning me into a wanton wench."

"Good." His warm breath against her ear stirred her blood, proving her point to herself.

She smiled and nestled closer. "Do you think your parents like me?"

"Aye, love," he whispered groggily, his smile visible in his voice.

"I'm glad," she sighed, entwining her fingers in his. "I want them to like me."

She thought they did too, despite the danger she might someday pose to their clan. Kate was kind to her and had done everything in her power to make Davina feel at home in the castle. Callum was careful not to discuss the king in her presence and she was thankful for it. Each day she spent at Camlochlin drove her thoughts further away from her father and what might happen if he found her. The king would not come for her, just as he never came for her when she was a child.

"Rob, who are the Fergussons?"

He shifted slightly behind her. "Why d'ye ask aboot them now?"

She stiffened, trying to come up with a reason that would not involve his brother. "I heard someone mention them today and I recalled the name but could not—"

"Davina, ye'll no' bring up that name around my kin, especially my mother."

"But why? Who are they?"

"They killed my uncle. My mother's brother. Remember, I told ye in the church at Courlochcraig."

Oh, dear God, yes, she did remember now. What was Tristan thinking? She would have to find him and speak to him later.

"Who mentioned them?"

"What?" Davina squeezed her eyes shut and prayed forgiveness for the lie she was about to tell her husband. When she did not answer right away, he asked her again.

"Oh, I don't recall," she said and turned in his arms. "It's still raining."

He caught her meaning right away and smiled so seductively she nearly forgot why she was trying to distract him.

Pulling her on top of him, he swept her hair off her cheek. "Ye're good at keepin' secrets, my bonnie love." His smile deepened, along with the blue of his eyes. "But I know what will make ye talk."

He glided his fingertips down along her sides then tickled her until she doubled over him. He rolled over her and captured her laughter in his mouth before he made love to her again.

Davina sat on the deep, alcoved window early the next morning and watched Rob while he slept. His queue had come loose and black curls spilled around his face, softening his chiseled features. He snored softly with one arm tossed above his head and the other resting low on his bare hip. The blanket covered just enough of him to tempt her to climb atop him and wake the slumbering beast beneath.

She blushed at herself and smiled, turning toward the rainbow arching the sky outside. She wasn't ashamed of her desire for her beloved, but thankful for it, knowing the God she trusted, the Father she loved wanted the best for His child, and so He sent her Rob. She still had much to teach him about enjoying recreation out of doors, but they had plenty of time for that.

"Has the rain stopped?"

"Yes." She turned to Rob, leaving the window. "And there is a most magnificent rainbow spearing the heavens." She climbed into bed with him and kissed his smiling mouth. "Let us ride beneath it on your horse. I miss riding with you."

"I can take ye to Torrin this afternoon," he said, sweeping his hands over her back.

"No. The rainbow." She pushed off him and crossed the room looking for her kirtle and earasaid. "If you don't come," she said when he didn't move from the bed, "I will ask Will or perhaps . . . Tristan."

Bending for her shift, she smiled when he snapped back his blanket and swore something she would not repeat.

They returned to the castle soon after the morning meal was finished. A few dozen inhabitants still loitered at the tables in the Great Hall when Rob and Davina stepped into it. Finn was the first to greet them.

"Ye missed breaking fast and 'twas venison and bannocks!" He caught his error quickly and cast Davina a sheepish look beneath his long lashes. "And a verra tasty flower and herb salad with toasted oat cakes."

"Oh dear." Davina pouted and looked longingly toward the kitchen. "I am famished. I'll go see if there are two servings left for me and Rob."

Finn followed her like an eager puppy while Rob joined the others.

"Enjoy yer ride?" Will asked from the other side of the table with a mischievous arch of his brow.

"Aye," Rob growled at him.

"Where'd ye go then?" Tristan took a sip from his cup and grinned at his brother's snarl.

"Nowhere. We just rode."

"Just rode?" Angus intoned, then belched.

Brodie cast his burly cousin a disgusted look and then swung his gaze to Rob. "Nowhere, eh? I told ye lads he's gone daft."

"And as soft as a babe's arse." Angus rose like a mountain, pushing back his chair and shaking his head with pity as he crossed Rob's path to leave the hall. "Yesterday 'twas Finn wi' flowers in his hair, and today ye're ridin' under rainbows. What the hell is next, Robbie, chasin' butterflies in the meadow?"

"She told ye," Rob said, glaring at Will first and then at Tristan. He knew when he was defeated, but he didn't appreciate being called soft as a babe's arse.

"She told Finn before ye left," Will informed him, doing his best to control the smirk creeping along his mouth. "Finn told us."

"So?" Rob snatched the cup of mead his brother offered him out of his hand and swigged it down. "It made my wife happy, and in truth, I enjoyed it too. If any one of ye thinks that makes me soft I'll remedy that assumption right now in the field."

They all shook their heads and went back to drinking. Rob gave them all one last lethal look before he spotted Davina exiting the kitchen with Finn and their food.

Her cheeks were still flushed from the wind snapping against her face. Hell, he was glad he'd done as she asked. He didn't care what the others thought of him. They hadn't heard her breathless joy as she chased a bow of colors across Camlochlin's vast green vale. They couldn't know how good she felt in his arms, pressed to his chest, nestled in his lap while his horse thundered over his land. She enjoyed life and he wanted to enjoy it with her. So, she liked chasing piglets and splashing around in the loch. What the hell was wrong with taking a little pleasure in the day?

He smiled at her when she reached him, and then cast a murderous look over her shoulder when Tristan snickered.

"Cook was kind enough to let me choose the best portions of meat for you, and the bannocks are still warm, my love." Davina happily handed him his trencher and Rob flung his brother a smug grin. He might have gone a wee bit soft, but he was eating well.

"Where's my faither?" he asked, cutting his meat.

"Solar," Will answered. "He retired with yer mother, Jamie and Maggie. I think they—"

A thunderous roar reverberated through the hall, silencing every conversation in mid-sentence and sobering some of the men. "Where the bluidy hell is m' brew?"

Immediately, Brodie sprang to his feet, his eyes wide on the entrance, waiting for Angus to appear. They all heard his heavy footsteps pounding closer.

Davina watched with the rest of them, afraid to swallow lest the sound attract the giant Highlander and bring him to them.

"Brodie, ye bastard scoundrel son of a whore! What have ye done with it?"

Davina caught the hint of a furtive smile curling Rob's lips when he looked across the table at Will. What had they done?

Angus stormed through the doorway, set his furious gaze on Brodie, and balled his beefy hands into fists. "Ye drank all m' brew and now I'm goin' to beat ye senseless."

"I didna' touch yer fokin' brew, ye—"

He was silenced rather brutally by a cracking punch to the jaw. Everything happened so quickly after that Davina had no time to register it all until later. Brodie went sprawling into Will's lap then bounced back up an instant before Angus's even bigger son, Patrick, took a swing at him. Will wasn't about to sit quietly by while two brutes beat up his father, and sent Patrick flying into the wall with two sharp, clean punches to the face. Rob pulled Davina to her feet, picked up their trenchers, and calmly led her to a table on the far side of the hall. She turned in time to see a chair sail across the table. It would have hit

Finn if Tristan had not plucked him from his seat at the very last instant.

"Rob, do something!" she pleaded, beckoning Finn and Tristan to her table.

"And spoil their enjoyment?"

She turned, swallowed hard, and gave her husband an incredulous stare. "Enjoyment?"

"Aye," he said, chewing his food as if nothing was going on around him. "They like to fight. 'Tis especially good fer Brodie. He'll be more pleasant fer the next few days."

"It is madness!"

"'Tis the MacGregor way," Tristan corrected her, slipping into a chair to her right. "Ye'll get accustomed to it soon enough."

"But they could have killed Finn!" she argued, smoothing the smiling lad's plaid over his shoulders before he took a seat.

"No' with a chair, love," Rob assured her, then scowled when he realized he'd forgotten his mead.

"Will is bleeding," she pointed out regrettably and sank into her chair. "Oh, Rob!" She tugged on his plaid without taking her eyes off the melee. "Seamus MacDonnell just hit Will from behind. Look out!" She bolted back to her feet and screamed in Will's direction and then turned on her husband. "Robert MacGregor, do something! He is your closest friend!"

Davina had no idea that Rob would have shamed Will if he moved to protect him against men who were too drunk to do any real harm. As it turned out though, Rob didn't need to do a thing. A cry from the battlements stilled them all.

Chapter Thirty-four

$Callum$ was the first to reach the castle doors, with Rob close behind him. It wasn't every day that the MacGregors had visitors, and while most who came here were usually from neighboring clans, no one had forgotten Davina's father...or Admiral Gilles.

"Finn," Rob ordered as the lad caught up with him, "bring Davina to my mother!"

"She went to the chapel."

Before Rob could reply, his father pulled on the doors, stepped outside, and shouted up to his patrolling guards. "Which way?"

"From the hills, m' laird. Aboot thirty riders. Too far yet to see who they are."

Rob felt his heart crash and splinter at his feet. Unless Gilles had recruited more men on his journey, it had to be the king.

"Banners?" he pushed past his father and called to the guards.

"Dinna' see any."

"Load the cannons!" Callum roared and spun around to the men watching him from the doors. "Alert everyone. Prepare fer the worst."

Rob turned to Will and without a word spoken between them, his bloodied and bruised friend nodded and set off toward the chapel.

"Uncle," he said to Jamie next. "Find Asher and bring him to us. If Admiral Gilles is among those men, the captain will know his face."

"And if 'tis the king," Brodie reminded Rob somberly, "Asher could identify yer wife."

"And 'twill be the last thing he ever does," Rob growled and caught the heavy claymore Angus tossed him.

"Laird," a guard shouted from above. "A Highlander leads them. M' thinks 'tis Colin!"

Rob felt as if someone had just shot him through the heart. Colin. Nae, it couldn't be. And if it was, then whoever was with him had likely forced him to bring them here. But even as Rob told himself that his brother would never betray him to the king, he knew that Colin could not be controlled by royalty, sword, or pistol. If Colin did not want to be here, he would have died at the hands of their enemies rather than lead them to Camlochlin.

The lethal scowl on his father's face as he searched the hills told Rob that Callum knew it too.

"If he brought the king's men here—"

"We dinna' know who travels with him yet, Robert, or if 'tis even him," was all his father had to say on the matter.

They waited, armed and ready while the castle came alive with shouts behind them. Rob could hear the heavy cannon wheels grinding across the battlements above, where more of his kin waited with arrows cocked and ready to fly.

"'Tis Colin," Rob's father said and raised his hand to halt the archers.

A wave of panic washed over Rob such as he had never felt before. Why was his brother here? What had he done? If he'd told the king that his daughter was here, would he point her out as well? Sick to his stomach, Rob looked toward the chapel's outside entrance. They weren't going to take her from him.

"It's the king."

Everyone's eyes turned to Asher exiting the castle with Jamie. "He travels without his banner, but his regal bearing is difficult to conceal."

"He's correct," Callum told them, his sharp eyes fastened on the large troupe coming over the hills only a few hundred feet away now. The lead rider was in fact his son. The man beside him pushed back his hood to reveal a somewhat pale, yet familiar face as his eyes scanned the battlements, and then the men beneath them.

"Stand doun!" Callum roared to the guards and then waited while the riders grew closer. "Shyt," he groaned and then turned to his son. "Remember, I beg ye, what we spoke of. Dinna' tell him ye wed her, Robert."

Asher was the first to fall to his knee when the king reached them. Callum followed, keeping his stormy gaze on his youngest son as he leaped from his saddle.

"Faither, I—"

But Callum raised his palm to quiet him as the rest of his men knelt behind him, following his example.

When Rob was the only one still standing, the king glanced at Colin. "Your brother, I presume?"

Colin nodded and met Rob's murderous gaze. "I told only him, Rob. No one else knows."

Rob's fingers tightened around the hilt of his sword. If

Colin was not his brother, he would have run him through then and there and to hell with the king.

"Where is she?"

Rob cut his dark gaze to the king when he spoke. Rob hated him, hated him for leaving her, for sentencing her to a life without her family, for never bothering to see her.

A thread of hope emerged from the gloom. Elaine. Davina was Elaine.

"She isna' here," Rob said, giving Colin a warning look that said if he contradicted him, he would regret it. "It has all been a—"

But the king was not listening to him. His eyes had settled on someone behind Rob, and his face...his face told Rob who it was without having to look.

"Daughter." The king barely breathed the word, as if what he was seeing could not be real. His eyes gleamed with tears as he slowly dismounted. "You have changed little since last I saw you."

God, nae.

Now Rob did turn to her and found tears streaming down her face. Instinctively, he reached his hand to hers to comfort her, but she dropped to her knees and dipped her head.

"Arise, Davina." The king reached for her, paused as if she might flee, and then gently pulled her up by the shoulders.

Everyone around Rob ceased to exist—everyone but Davina. He could not move. He could not breathe as he watched her set her shimmering eyes on her father for the first time. Everything in him wanted to snatch her away from the man reaching his fingers to her face. But she closed her eyes, as if the moment she had dreamed about for so long had finally come, and only his touch would prove it real.

Losing Davina suddenly became more real for Rob than ever before. This was what she wanted. What she had always wanted. Her father. He took a step toward her, but Callum's hand on his arm stopped him.

"You will never know how sorry I am for not being in your life."

The king's softly spoken words were like daggers to Rob's heart. If any other father had uttered them to his wife, Rob would have rejoiced for her, knowing how desperately she needed to hear them. But this father had the power to take her away—and as Davina covered her face in her hands and wept, Rob doubted she would resist.

That is, until she lowered her hands and looked at him with her whole heart in her eyes.

Following her sorrowful gaze, King James turned to Rob and sized him up with a worried crease marring his regal brow. "You are Robert MacGregor," he said, revealing that Colin had told him much. "You are the man who saved my daughter's life."

Looking at her, Rob recalled that wondrous day, and every day after that. It hadn't taken him long to fall in love with her modest smile, her playful laughter, her glorious eyes always on him, always expecting him to leave her. He never would. But her heart was soft, so very soft. 'Twas yet another reason he loved her. She'd forgiven Asher for betraying her. She would forgive her father too.

"I owe you much more than I can ever repay," the king went on, grasping Davina's hand in his. "You gave me back my life."

And you mean to take away mine. Rob did not speak

the words aloud. He couldn't. He couldn't think of his life without her.

"MacGregor"—the king turned to Rob's father—"might you invite us in from the chill? There is much you and I must discuss."

Callum ground his jaw and spared his eldest son a sober look before he nodded and gave the command to see to the king and his men's comforts.

"Captain Asher," the king greeted, patting Asher on the shoulder before following Callum inside. "Young MacGregor has told me of your courage, as well. You too will be rewarded."

Rob watched them enter Camlochlin with rage clouding his vision. It was not directed at Asher for the praise he'd received. The captain was a coward. Rob knew it, and so did Asher. It didn't matter what the king believed. Nae, his wrath was directed at his brother, and as Colin tried to step into the entryway, Rob stepped forward and blocked his path.

They waited in silence until they were alone, and when they were, Colin spoke first. "Brother, I—"

"Colin," Rob's sharp voice cut him off, "from this day on, I am nae longer yer brother."

Colin backed up a pace as if Rob had struck him. His eyes rounded with stunned disbelief. "How the hell can ye say that to me? I brought him here through the hills as we have been taught. I—"

"What did he offer ye?" Rob asked calmly. Too calmly. Anyone else would have backed further away, knowing Rob's slow temper was about to snap.

"What?" Colin nearly spat the word at him.

Rob came at him like a bull, grabbing Colin's tunic at the throat and hauling him against the wall with one hand and tearing Colin's sword from its scabbard with the other before his brother could reach for it.

"Ye told him! Ye told him, Colin! Now, I'll ask ye again. What did he offer ye?"

Colin stared at him with his own brand of rage making his eyes blaze like molten gold. "I should run ye through fer what ye accuse me of, *brother.*"

He did not blink or cringe when Rob's fist came at his face. But the blow did not come.

"Let him speak, Rob," Tristan said, holding back his brother's wrist.

Rob yanked his arm free and turned away, not wanting to hear what Colin had to say.

"Why did ye bring him here?" he heard Tristan ask.

"I brought him here because if our faither—or any one of us—believed Mairi was dead and she wasn't, we would want to know. I heard Davina's pain of never knowin' her faither. He heard it too." He pointed to Rob's back. "She spoke of him often, did she no', Rob?" he challenged, but did not wait for an answer. "When I met the king, I had nae intention of tellin' him anything—"

"Then why did ye!" Rob shouted, turning to him once again.

"Because his pain of never knowin' her was just as great!" Colin shouted back. "She's his bairn, Rob. He loves her."

Rob moved toward him, but now his rage had passed and he stared quietly into his brother's eyes. "So do I, Colin." He said nothing else and entered the castle alone.

"I knew he loved her," Colin said thoughtfully, looking after him. "We all did, but—"

"He took her as his wife," Tristan told him quietly as they headed inside.

"Och, nae," Colin stopped and raked his hand through his hair. "He knew who she was. He couldna' have."

"He did, nonetheless."

"Damn fool!" Colin swore.

Tristan tossed him a quelling look over his shoulder and shook his head. "I should have let him hit ye."

Davina sat in Callum's private solar with Rob's parents, two of the king's guardsmen standing behind her, and her father. Was he real? Was any of this real? She pinched her thigh twice to convince herself that she was awake. The second time she pinched too hard and jumped a little in her chair. Beside her, the king patted her hand and gave her a tender smile before turning his attention back to Callum.

"You have a most impressive home, MacGregor. It was clever of you to build here. The landscape makes it virtually impossible to arrive unseen."

"Aye, there was need fer such when I built it." Callum poured four cups of warm mead and handed the first to his wife.

"Ah yes, during the proscription," the king said, accepting his drink next. "You were an outlaw and a rebel then."

Was this truly her father's voice she was hearing, his warmth seeping into her skin, his scarred, calloused hand atop hers? Davina wanted to turn and look at him, take in every angle. She'd dreamed of his face and now here it was, just a few inches from her own.

"Aye," Rob's father said, standing over her with her cup. "There was need fer that as well."

Davina took her cup with a shaky hand, wishing it was something stronger. Her father had come for her and she doubted he would leave without her. Dear God, help them all. Why did he come now? What was she to do? There was only one thing. But how could she leave Rob, or Camlochlin? Everyone at St. Christopher's had died because of her. She couldn't...she wouldn't let everyone at Camlochlin die for her, as well. She looked toward the door. Where was Rob? He would never let her go if she was forced. Would he let her go if she went willingly?

"You are trembling, my dearest." Her father leaned in closer to her, washing her in his scent. "I understand my arrival was unexpected—"

"I am fine, really," she said, quickly wiping a tear from her eye. "Just...overwhelmed."

He smiled at her and Davina took in every crease, every crinkle that lined his comely face. How long had she wondered what he looked like? She thought his hair would be pale like hers, but it was completely gray now. His dark blue eyes were somber, shadowed by years of battle, on the field and off. His nose was long and straight, and his lips were thin, probably not prone to smiling. Until today.

"I am overwhelmed, as well."

Was he? She wanted to believe him. Did kings become overwhelmed by their children? He'd said he had seen her. When? Had he visited St. Christopher's when she was a child? Why hadn't she been allowed to see him if he had been there? She wanted to ask him, but smiled instead. He hadn't forgotten her.

And it was when she was smiling, as if her life had

just become complete, that Rob opened the solar door and stepped inside. The flames in the large hearth trembled at his presence, for he brought the cold with him, spreading it to each of them until his mother bounded from her chair and went to him. She spoke in a hushed voice against his chest, but whatever she said did not comfort him. His anguished, angry gaze remained fixed on Davina.

He said nothing, nor did he take a seat or pour himself a drink. He simply stood at the door, a barricade of raw brawn and single determination.

Davina felt faint with the need to go to him, to tell him she loved him and nothing would ever change that, but she would not let him die for her. But it was Rob's father and not her own who stopped her from moving. With one look Callum spoke to her, reminded her of Rob's fate should her father learn of her Highland marriage. She was the king's daughter, whether she liked it or not, and the ruler of the three kingdoms had not cloistered his firstborn in a nunnery to save her for a life as a commoner.

"Yer Majesty," Callum said, shifting his powerful gaze to the king, "ye have met my son, Robert."

"Briefly, yes," James said, studying Rob's scowl with a wary smile. "Tell me, MacGregor, do all your sons share a common mistrust of nobility?"

"Sadly, nae." The chief looked genuinely disappointed. "Ye met my son Tristan in England, if ye recall."

The king chuckled softly at what could have been construed as an insult. "Knowing most of the nobility in England and Scotland, I'd say you taught *most* of your sons well."

"Aye," Callum agreed. "'Tis difficult when yer own nephew plots against ye."

The king nodded, raising his cup to his lips. "It is only a matter of time before Monmouth is caught, and Argyll as well."

Rob made an impatient sound, pulling Davina's cautious gaze to him. He stood alone, so tall and strong, folding and then unfolding his arms over his chest, the lines of his jaw rigid. The solar suddenly seemed too small with him in it. She was surrounded on all sides by men of great power and skill, but none of them made her heart accelerate, her mouth go dry by the sheer force of Rob's indomitable strength. Like the mountains that rose up around his home, he was unbendable, unbeaten by the storms that raged around him. He'd protected her when he could have chosen not to, he'd promised to keep her safe, and he had. She felt treasured in his arms, untouchable by his side. If she lost him, she would cast her heart into the sea and never love another.

Rob ignored his father's warning glance with a black look of his own and asked boldly, "And Admiral Gilles? What are yer men doin' aboot him?"

The king looked up at him without censure, but with refreshed curiosity. "We will find him."

"Before he finds her?" The flagrant challenge in Rob's voice was undeniable.

"He will never find her here, sire," Callum interjected before his son spoke again. "And if he does, as ye know now fer yerself, we will see him comin' long before he arrives."

"Leave her here?" the king asked. For a moment he seemed to be considering it, but then his gaze shifted back to Rob. "You have my deepest gratitude for saving my daughter, but I am afraid I must decline."

Instantly, Rob rushed forward. Just as quickly the two soldiers standing behind Davina drew their swords.

"Nae!" Callum shouted together with Davina and Kate, and flung himself in front of his son, shielding his arms around him. "Stand doun, Robert, or would ye have yer mother see our blood spilled before her eyes?" He spoke quickly, quietly, his voice thick with emotion and restraint. "M' lord," he turned to look at the king. "Let us discuss this further. Yer daughter's safety means much to my son. He—"

"And so does my daughter, obviously." The king stood to his feet and tilted his head to stare hard into both their eyes. "I suspected this. But she is my heir. Her future has already been decided."

"But not by me." All eyes turned to Davina rising slowly to her feet to face her father. She would not tremble. She would not falter, and she would not cry. Not now. If there was any way to stop this, to stop her father from taking her, or Rob from starting a war he would lose, she had to take it. "Being your daughter has taken everything from me. I love it here, father. I love these people. I beg you, do not take them from me, as well."

Her father's eyes softened on her. "Davina, I give you my solemn oath that you will never want for anything again. I should not have left you to nuns. I have regretted it since the day I handed you over, but God spared you for a purpose, and someday you will fill it."

"I know that I must, but it is not what I want," Davina argued through her tears. "I do not want anything your courts have to offer. Perhaps if I had been raised in them as my sisters were, I would feel differently."

"You will come to feel differently," he said tenderly,

but when she shook her head, his voice took on a harsher tone. "And him," he said, turning to Rob. "Do you love him also?"

Her eyes darted to Rob, remembering his words to his father. He would never deny her. She looked to Callum next, recalling all too clearly his warning, as well. "I . . . I know my duty."

Over the king's shoulder, Rob stared at her with a look of such replete sorrow she was certain it would haunt her until her dying day. She would have fallen into his arms had both their fathers not been standing between them.

"Gather our men," King James commanded his guards over her head and snatched her hand. "We are leaving."

Chapter Thirty-five

———————

*R*age seared through Rob's blood and was finally unleashed with a groan that nearly brought him to his knees. As if in a dream from which he could not awaken, he watched the king pull Davina toward the door he'd been blocking only a few moments ago. She turned, tugging on the fingers that held her, and looked at him for the last time.

Rob woke, and with a roar that brought a dozen English soldiers and Highlanders alike to the solar, he leaped for the king.

His father tried to stop him and both men nearly careened to the floor. Rob met Colin's horrified gaze as he bounded back to his feet, then followed it downward to the two gleaming swords pointed at his throat.

"Tell yer men to lower their weapons against my brother," Colin shouted. "Ye gave me yer word."

Rob barely heard him and lifted his arm to swipe the swords out of his way. His wife's cry stopped him.

"Please, please, Rob. You cannot die."

"I am dead if he takes ye from me," Rob told her across the length of the blades, desperation hardening his face and softening his voice.

"MacGregor," the king warned Rob on a low snarl. "I could take your head right now for this."

"Oh, Father, please, don't let this happen." Davina closed her tearstained eyes and prayed from the depths of her soul.

"Daughter," the king answered, thinking she was speaking to him. "I understand that you feel indebted to this man for—"

"No, no," she argued through her tears. "It is more than that. Please, do not harm him. I forgave you for leaving me, but I will never forgive you if you kill him."

Her father's stern expression collapsed at her vow and he looked, for a moment, like he might be ill. He raised his hand to her cheek and a small, sorrowful sound escaped him when she moved her face away. "Give me a year. One year to know the daughter I've not known for over four and twenty. Let me give you all that I have never been able to give you before, and if after that time you are still unhappy, we will discuss a different path for you."

When she nodded her agreement, Rob moved against the tips of the blades until two trickles of blood broke the surface. "Davina, dinna' agree to this, ye are my—"

"Rob!" Davina held up her trembling hand to silence him before he sealed both their fates. "I have decided. You will let me go."

"Nae!" Rob's eyes darkened on the guards keeping him still. He was going to crack their skulls in half and then step over their dead bodies and kill anyone else who stood in his way. But the instant he moved, Jamie and his brothers threw their bodies into his and held him with the aid of his father.

"I let you live today, Robert MacGregor," King James

said, motioning for his guards to lower their weapons. "My debt to you is paid. If you come after her, I will have no choice but to have you shot."

"Please, don't," Davina mouthed silently to her husband as the king hastened her away.

"Son, she does this fer ye," Callum hushed, grasping Rob from behind. "She wants ye to live."

"Rob, fergive me," Colin implored. "I will make this—" His apology was cut short by Rob flinging them all off him.

They all rushed for the door to stop him from going after her. Angus slammed it shut and whirled on his heel to further block the exit, should Rob try to kick the wooden one down. But Rob did not bother. She left. Nae, she chose to leave, just as he had feared. In an instant he had been changed, defeated, broken in two. He turned his back on the men watching him, went to a chair, and fell into it without another word.

He didn't hear the door open again. He didn't care who came in or went out. She was gone. That was all he knew.

It wasn't until sometime later, when Maggie pushed open the door and told them that Colin had gone after the king, vowing to make things right, that Rob left the solar with his father, and a whole new fear descended on him.

"Ye lied to me." Colin reined his frothing mount to a halt after stopping the king's troupe just beyond the braes of Bla Bheinn. It hadn't taken him long to catch up with them, for the king and his men had not pushed their mounts to their limits over the steep hills and muddy terrain as Colin had. He was angry and he wanted answers. If he had to ride all the way back to England to get them, he would. He was aware of the king's soldiers moving to surround him, quick to protect their liege lord. Colin gave them only half his attention. If they wanted a fight, he would give them one, but first he would have his say. "Ye gave me yer word."

James raised his hand, signaling his men to back down. "And I have kept it. Your family remains unharmed."

"Unharmed?" Colin seethed, glaring at the man he had begun to like, even respect. "Ye might as well have cut oot my brother's heart!"

A sound, like a soft moan, drew his attention to Davina, saddled on a spotted gelding a few feet away. When he met her bloodshot gaze, he looked away. He should have known she loved Rob. He should have recognized it in the tender way she looked at his brother while they traveled back to Skye. The way she rested against his chest, a trace of pure contentment curling her mouth. Hell, what had he done?

"I have no control over your brother's heart, Colin."

"Aye, ye do," Colin argued. "Ye are the law, are ye no'? Ye didna' have to take her away. What should it matter if a Royal loves a commoner?"

The king offered him a rueful smile. "You are young, and have much to learn."

"Aboot love?" Colin asked and then nodded, "Aye. Mayhap, I do. I brought ye here because I was foolish and believed that ye loved yer daughter. But what kind of faither could ignore his bairn's tears? Can ye no' see that she loves him? Nae, ye canna' see it because ye dinna' know her, and as long as yer laws come before her, ye never will."

"I've given you too much leave to speak to me as you will, Colin MacGregor. I . . ."

Colin wasn't listening. Someone moved slowly on his mount to Colin's right, and when he saw who it was, his eyes blazed like fiery jewels beneath the afternoon sun. "Och, hell, what is he doin' here?"

"Captain Asher belongs in England with—"

"He belongs on a noose! Ye rip yer daughter from the arms of the man who would have given his life to protect her and coddle the man who told Gilles where to find her at the Abbey?"

"What are you saying?" The king's face went taut with anger, and he turned toward Asher. "Is this true?"

"Aye, 'tis," Colin said before the captain could. "He admitted it to her. Everyone in Camlochlin knows it."

"I'll have you flayed alive."

"Father, no!" Davina kicked her horse forward, coming to Asher's defense.

"Silence!" the king commanded without looking at her, and it seemed even the birds in the air obeyed.

In that moment of startling stillness, another sound could be heard in the distance, and everyone, save for Colin and Davina's captain, turned to the group of riders approaching from Camlochlin's deep vale.

Because Colin and Asher were the only two looking at Davina, they alone saw the blinding flash of sunlight coming from beyond a rocky crest to her right. Colin scowled, not knowing right away what had caused his momentary blindness, or why Asher took off like a cannonball headed straight for Rob's wife.

A shot rang out, echoing through the braes, just as the captain leaped from his saddle and crashed into Davina, knocking them both to the ground.

Everywhere around Colin, men were shouting and

taking cover. Davina was screaming, trying to free herself of the dead weight on top of her. They were under attack, and she was the target.

Scraping his sword from its scabbard, Colin moved to go to her but Rob flew past him on his stallion, bounded from his saddle, and hauled Asher's body off her.

"Get her behind the braes!" Colin heard his brother shout to Will as a small horde of more men appeared from where they had lain in wait for the king's troupe to pass. Some of them brandished pistols and made a quick end to four of the king's soldiers before the battle even began.

Colin hated pistols. Even more, he hated men who used them to try to kill bonnie lasses who would likely plead for their souls before God after they slew her.

Thanks to that first flash of light, he knew where the bastard who fired at Davina had been hiding. He'd watched as the coward left his cover to fight alongside his comrades, and with a smile as cold and merciless as a Highland winter night, Colin slipped from his saddle and ran straight for him. He did not stop or slow his pace but twirled his deadly blade in his hand, making it dance at his command. Spotting him, his enemy hurried to empty more powder and another ball into his weapon, but he fumbled, growing more frantic as Colin sprinted closer.

"I feel 'tis only fair to tell ye," Colin warned, about to fall upon him. "I'm no' opposed to killin' unarmed men."

The man looked up from his impotent pistol and then closed his eyes an instant before Colin separated him from his head.

After that, Colin turned his bloodstained face toward the next shooter and smiled.

* * *

Rob watched Will disappear on his horse with Davina beyond the shadow of Bla Bheinn. When he was certain they were safe, he ripped his sword free of its long scabbard and turned to enter the combat coming to life around him. He looked down in time to see Asher's eyes open. The captain had received a fatal wound and was about to die, but the terror widening his gaze was not for himself.

With shots ringing out around them, Rob dragged the captain over a small incline and hunkered down beside him. Whatever sins Edward Asher had committed in the past, he loved Davina now and had given his life to save her. Rob owed him much. "She's safe, Captain," he told him. "Ye saved her life yet again."

Edward genuinely smiled at him for the first time and a trickle of blood seeped from between his lips. "Gilles," he rasped.

"Aye, I know," Rob said, growing serious. "I promise 'twill be my blade that kills him, but ye must describe him to me."

Drawing his last breath, Edward told him. "Dark hair...cold eyes."

Rob rose to his feet when there was nothing else he could do for Davina's friend. He was ready to find Gilles and kill as many of these Dutch bastards as he could on the way.

"Formation!" He heard a man's frenzied command behind him. "Get the king back to the castle!"

Rob turned to see seven English soldiers surrounding the king, ready to flee. "Nae!" he shouted, his voice overriding the others. "'Tis too open. Ye'll all be shot doun before ye reach safety." He moved forward, and though he was on foot and the soldier on horseback, the soldier moved back. "Go there"—his steady gaze met the king's—"beyond that hill. 'Tis deeper than this one and they canna' fire aroond it." The king nodded. "Wait there until we stop their pistols."

"Then you best hurry," King James told him, angling his head around Rob's shoulder. "Your brother is attempting to stop them all without any aid."

Rob turned, and together with the king, watched his youngest brother hack his way through three more shooters and emerge unscathed. Hell, he was reckless and— Rob noted with pride—terrifying.

"Go!" He wheeled on the king's men. "Remember to wait."

From a carefully guarded position behind one of the many rocky hillsides that dotted the open terrain, King James watched Robert MacGregor with something akin to stunned disbelief marking his features. The Highlander had gone from a tactical commander to a savage warrior with the first arc of his blade. He'd gained his horse and rode straight into the fray, slashing torsos and severing limbs with speed, power, and precision, ensuring that one swipe served its purpose—to get him to the next man quicker. James wanted Rob in his army, and his brother with him. But he wanted something else even more, something for her.

He looked toward Bla Bheinn, knowing where his daughter was safely hidden, and knowing whom to thank for it. He knew also that Gilles—may God have no mercy on the blackheart's soul—was behind this attack. James wanted him alive for the Wheel, but where in blazes was he?

*   *   *

Rob knew the fight had tipped in their favor. Even without the English at their sides, the MacGregors would not lose this day to their enemies. Most of Gilles's men lay strewn on the ground, a good number of them, by his blade. The only shooting being done was from the English and the king was on his way back to the castle. The battle was almost at an end and Rob still had not found Gilles. None of the men he had killed fit Asher's description. Their eyes were terror stricken, not cold. Where the hell was the bastard? Could he be dead already? Rob hoped not. He whirled his horse around to find his next opponent and came face to face with one.

"Wait!" the man shouted out as Rob lifted his blade. "There is something I must tell you before you slay me!"

"Ye dinna' have much time," Rob promised, circling him, his blade outstretched and ready.

"I am the Admiral's captain, Maarten Hendrickson. You must go to the castle now. Go to the king and his daughter."

Rob glanced into the vale leading to Camlochlin and to the king's small troupe in the distance. He knew Davina wasn't with them. Will would not have moved her until the battle was over.

"Gilles is among them," Captain Hendrickson told him, stilling Rob's heart. "He took a coat from the body of an English and joined the king's party at the rear when they..."

A shot rang out close to Rob's ear. So close, in fact, that he went momentarily deaf. A few feet away from him, Gilles's captain slipped from his horse, blood and smoke issuing from a hole in his chest. Rob turned as the

Dutchman fell to the ground, and looked up the hillside at his brother waving a cloud of smoke out of his face. Colin smiled at him through the fog, lifted the smoking barrel of a pistol to his lips, and blew. Rob was gone before his brother shoved his new weapon into his belt.

Chapter Thirty-six

❦

*Y*our daughter is a hard bitch to kill, James."

The king sat alone on his horse. Around him, the seven men who had accompanied him into the deep vale lay dead. They were close to the castle when his first soldier fell. After that, everything happened so quickly. The king's men barely had time to react before they were cut down by one of their own, his blade flashing red beneath the sun, swift and unexpected. But this assassin did not belong to James's regiment and as the king met his unholy snarl, he almost admired the man's craftiness and determination.

"You have ruined all my carefully laid-out plans. You, and that bastard MacGregor."

James looked around for aid, but the remainder of his men were too far away, fighting and winning, with the aid of the MacGregors. He reached for his sword, but the man inching his steed closer only laughed.

"Gilles," James spat as the tip of the Admiral's blade poked his chest. "I'll see you crushed beneath the Wheel."

"Will you?" the Admiral laughed again, bounding from his horse and directing the king to do the same. "I think it will be you whose life will end this day." He shoved James off the path and ducked behind a hilly slope dotted with sheep. "I intend to cut out your heart to make way for the true king. It is not how my lord planned it, but I have no choice now, you see. I could shoot you and make it quick, but even at the risk of my own peril, I want to look in your eyes while you die. As for your daughter, if I don't kill her, someone else will be sent after you are gone. She will never be safe as long as she is on this earth."

"No one will get past her guardian." James smiled just as victoriously, remembering the skill and power of Robert MacGregor.

"We shall see about that. Well, you won't, but I might." Gilles flashed a grin and slid his blade almost lovingly across James's throat, drawing no blood. He was playing with him, enjoying the king's last moments. "Now that I've seen her"—he leaned in so that his breath fell on James's face—"I'm a bit more inclined to make her scream beneath me before I kill her."

James closed his eyes, sickened at the thought. "You will never touch her." He prayed it would be so. He pleaded with God to protect his daughter from this devil. When he opened his eyes again, Gilles had taken a step back. A movement along the hillside captured the king's eye. Someone was coming, moving silently against the wind. The king's breath stalled when he saw that it was Robert MacGregor.

Standing beneath the towering madman in the solar would have rattled any man's nerves, but seeing him creeping forward, his bloody claymore gripped in his hand and the promise of death in his eyes, was terrifying. The king wondered if this man who clearly loved his daughter was coming after Gilles, or him?

Gilles caught the direction of James's gaze over his shoulder and began to turn around.

With less time than it took for the Admiral to change the direction of his rapier, the Highlander lunged forward and brought his blade down in a chopping blow over Gilles's wrist.

Blood splattered across James's chest and the king looked down in horror and satisfaction at Gilles's sword lying on the ground with his hand still attached to it.

"That's fer bringin' yer men to my land," MacGregor growled while Gilles gaped at his bloody stump. "And this"—he moved like a rush of wind, and wasting no time on idle words or threats, rammed his sword deep into the Admiral's belly—"is fer tryin' to kill my wife."

King James stared mutely at MacGregor's hard profile fixed on the life fading from Gilles's eyes. His...wife? Davina's father barely had time to take in what he had just heard, or thought he'd heard, when the efficient killer yanked his weapon free and moved toward him next.

"Are ye injured?"

James shook his head. "No, I.... What did you say to him just then?" He probably should not have asked that particular question just yet, for the Highlander suddenly looked at him with the same unyielding hatred he'd just shown to the dead man behind him. Hatred, and something else.

"Ye heard right. Davina is my wife and I canna' let ye take her from me."

In that instant, James was certain MacGregor was going to kill him. But Rob did not lift his blade, and the anger in his gaze faded into a contemptible plea. "Have ye never loved a woman more than yer own life? A woman ye would have sacrificed everything fer?"

James blinked at him and felt a wave of sorrow wash over him he hadn't felt since the night of his first wife's death. Even the assumed death of his daughter hadn't surpassed the anguish of losing his dear Anne. "Yes, I must confess I have loved a woman that much. I sacrificed a future crown when I married her and followed her faith."

It was not the answer MacGregor had expected, and for a moment, he simply stared at James in surprise. Then, "Then ye should know how serious I am. My wife is no' returnin' back to England with ye."

"Son," the king began, "let us speak of this later. I have—Behind you!" he shouted, eyes wide, and snatched MacGregor's shoulders to push him out of the way.

For an instant, Peter Gilles stood motionless, one useless arm pressed to his bloody belly, the other poised above his shoulder, ready to bring down his sword. The arrow jutting out of his neck stopped him. As he sank to the ground, his lifeblood spilling into the grass, James set his gaze toward the braes of Bla Bheinn. His daughter stood against a backdrop of impenetrable rock, her long pale tresses snapping behind her as she dropped a bow to her feet and started running.

"Rob!" her sweet, unfamiliar voice carried across the moors, turning her father's gaze to the man beside him. Quietly, he watched her fly into the Highlander's arms, where after a tearful kiss, she examined him for injuries. "And you, father?" She turned to James. "Were you harmed?"

The king shook his head no. At least, not visibly. But what right did he have to expect that this warrior should not come before him? James had given his daughter too little. He'd stayed away too long and he'd lost her. She'd told him she did not love Robert MacGregor, but it was clear that she did. Could he take even more from her?

He almost cringed at the swarm of Highlanders riding over the hills, their bloody swords raised high over their heads. Dear God, they were a ferocious-looking lot. Among them, the remainder of his men appeared worn and lifeless.

"What happened?" the MacGregor chief demanded as he leaped from his saddle upon reaching them. "Is that Gilles?"

Robert told him all that had taken place, and after the chief was assured that none of them were injured, he brought them home.

Chapter Thirty-seven

The king sat in Camlochlin Castle's Great Hall sipping a lethal concoction of what the MacGregors had affectionately called "the best poison in the Highlands." He had to admit, the brew was exceptional, if not a bit scorching on the way down. After burying the dead, they drank to a good fight and to the king's fallen—thirteen soldiers that a young man called Finn promised to honor in a song later.

James's daughter was not among those at the table. She was off somewhere instead in the company of the chief's wife and his sister. According to Finn, Maggie MacGregor loved Davina as her own daughter, and if the king tried to fetch her before the celebration ended, Katie MacGregor would give him a tongue-lashing he would not soon forget, king or not.

As James listened to the men's laughter around him, he thought of days long past, when he fought in Spain and France, beside men who had become his brothers.

That same camaraderie and respect existed here. These men knew that whatever came, they would fight together to protect their home. Not because they had to, but because they wanted to. Such loyalty was difficult to find in England, and James couldn't blame Davina for not wanting to leave. After seeing the MacGregors fight, he knew that Colin had been truthful when he said there was no safer place on earth for Davina than at Camlochlin. How could he take her away from this and bring her to a place where every smile was false and any hand could be working against him? How wise was it for him, being on the throne for so short a time, to expose his most precious secret to the world? But he wanted to know her, to hear of her life and learn what made her laugh or cry. He wanted to finally take her home, but there was more for his daughter here than just security and trust.

There was *him*. James looked across the heavy table at Robert MacGregor staring into his cup like he'd just lost both legs in the battle. He had no doubts that the man loved Davina, or that he would kill or die for her. He knew it was more than his other two daughters' husbands would do for their wives, and no less than he would have done for Anne Hyde. His Anne, his beloved. What would she have to say about all this? They'd given up Davina to protect her, to ensure a Catholic monarchy in the future. But did it have to be Davina? She had not been raised to be a queen. It was clear to see in her eyes that she lacked the ruthless desire to rule, unlike his second-eldest daughter. His wife Mary was young and eager in his bed. If she gave him an heir...

"M' lord, ye and yer men are welcomed to stay in Camlochlin fer as long as ye like."

James turned to Callum MacGregor and smiled. "As much as I would enjoy that, I'm afraid I must return to England with haste. We left without a word and I shudder to think what my sons-in-law are scheming in my absence."

Callum nodded and settled his mournful gaze on his son.

"You taught your sons to fight well, MacGregor. Their skill surpasses that of some of my captains. There is a question I would put to you, but first, one I would ask Robert."

Callum nodded and looked at his son together with the king.

"Back there," James said, motioning his chin northward, "when my men were about to bring me here and you stopped them, did you not realize that if I was shot and killed, she would have been free? No one knows she is here save for us—and Gilles, who is no longer a threat. Why did you protect me?"

For a moment, Robert simply looked at him as if he genuinely did not know how to answer the question. James hoped he would confess his fealty to his king. The question he wanted to ask Callum next depended on it.

"I simply did what is in my nature to do."

The lad's first instinct was to protect. The king could not fault such a reply, though it was not the one he'd hoped for. Nevertheless, he downed his brew, giving himself an extra moment or two to decide how best to propose his next question, then turned to the chief. He didn't need permission to draft anyone into his army, but he wanted to keep the MacGregors on his side. Any king would be foolish not to.

"I have grown quite fond of Colin. He is courageous, boldly honest, and quite deadly with a sword. He already knows much about the politics of the land and despises the Covenanters as much as I do. Robert, I do not yet know, but his skill on the field today impressed me. I would like to bring your sons back to England with me and enlist them in my army. Colin is your youngest, I know, but with—"

"I've nae interest in England," Rob cut him off without hesitation. "My place is here and I'll no' leave it."

"But son," the king implored. "You and Davina can—"

"—spend each day wonderin' which hand conceals the next dagger planned fer her back?" Rob finished for him. "Is that the life ye want fer her? Hell, she deserves more than that. I can give it to her, but no' in yer courts. Even I canna' guard her from hundreds of unknown enemies."

James sat back in his chair, unable to argue the truth. He was barely on the throne a month and his enemies had already tried to kill him. How long would Davina last if the next attempt succeeded? "She is my child," he said in a low voice.

"And she is likely carryin' mine."

Every Highlander around the table seemed to groan at the same time. The chief looked about to be seriously ill. Stunned by both Robert's courage and his arrogance to blurt out such a thing, the king began to rise to his feet. "Do you understand what I can do to you for this?"

"Aye, I do," Robert answered, holding up his palm to stop his father from speaking in his defense. "But what kind of faither would I be no' to do everything I can to protect my bairn? How different am I from ye?"

The king fell back into his chair and closed his eyes. Every choice he'd ever made involving Davina came rushing back to his mind. He'd done all to protect her, even at the cost of his brother, the king's, objection.

"I will go."

James opened his eyes and looked, along with everyone else, at Colin.

"Nae," the chief answered quickly. "Yer place is here with yer kin."

"Faither, I dinna' want to spend my life fighting the MacPhersons over cattle. Rob is to be chief someday. There is naught here fer me. I want to fight fer something I believe in."

"I will need a man with his intelligence and skill to protect my son," the king interjected, "should I be fortunate enough to have one in the future."

"So ye believe in England's causes now?" Colin's father asked his son skeptically.

"I believe in him." Colin shifted his gaze to the king. A hint of a smile hovered about his lips and then his expression hardened. "I will go, yer Majesty. But I ask ye to spare my brother in return."

James spread his cool gaze over Colin and then onto his eldest brother. "Ask something else of me. I have already decided to forgive my daughter's champion. As for her future, I will let her decide."

Surprisingly, James noted the sickened look on Rob's face. Did he doubt Davina would choose him? Why would he when it was so clear that she loved him? "Bring her to me, will you, Robert? I trust your mother and your aunt will not take offense to giving her over to you."

Robert rose from his chair and gave the stairs and what lay beyond a determined scowl, much like the one he wore on the battlefield. Watching him leave the hall, the king knew that whatever life his daughter chose, Robert MacGregor would not give her up without a fight.

"Colin," his father said, dragging the king's thoughts back to the table. "Are ye certain aboot this?" His concern for his youngest still marred his brow.

"Aye, faither. Someone's got to keep the Protestants at bay, and better me than Mairi."

His father didn't laugh. In fact, James noticed that he'd gone even paler than before.

"Is your daughter as loyal to Scotland as your sons, then?" the king asked.

"Worse."

James chuckled, but he envied the mighty chief for his fine family. It wasn't until he saw Rob leading his beautiful daughter down the stairs that he felt God's favor in his life as well. He loved his daughters, Mary and Anne, but they had grown hard from their lives at this court and that, and from their arranged marriages to men they did not love. Everything about Davina was delicate and graceful, like a pale swan gliding toward him. Her gait lacked the air of self-righteousness that her sisters possessed. The tilt of Davina's chin was wrought with inner strength, not conceit. Watching her, he thought of his first wife. Anne had never cared about becoming queen. Being his was enough and she'd filled his halls and his days with her laughter. She would want the same life for her firstborn.

When they reached him, Davina's defiant gaze followed James as he rose to his feet, but she said nothing and clung to her husband's hand.

James folded his hands together behind his back to keep himself from dragging her into them and rejoicing that she lived. "You wed without my knowledge or consent, daughter."

"You were not here to give it," she replied evenly.

"No, I wasn't. An unforgivable error I intend to remedy."

He almost smiled when her eyes softened on him.

All hope was not lost. "Clearly you were not forced into becoming his wife."

Her mouth relaxed into an unbidden smile when she looked up at the man at her side. "I was ecstatic."

"Then I am prepared," James announced, pulling their attention off each other and back to him, "to allow you to remain here with him if you choose to."

"If I choose . . . ?" Her voice trailed off as her large eyes opened wider and filled with tears. "I choose to remain here with him."

James smiled, finally able to grant his daughter something she wished. He had no idea that he had just become her bright star in the sky. "Then accept the first of many gifts I will be giving you, and take my blessing."

The men around him cheered and someone even pounded him on the back, but King James saw no one, heard no one save the girl before him, and then she was in his arms and he finally felt forgiven.

"You and I have much to learn about each other, daughter," he whispered close to her ear. "I will be visiting often."

"I would like that, Father. Very much."

Rob pulled his tunic over his head and climbed into bed. The candlelight brushed his face in broad strokes of light and dark. Beneath the sexy stray curl falling over his forehead, his eyes glittered with the hunger consuming him. Davina reached out her arms to gather him to her sooner.

"When was the day you knew you loved me?" she asked as his mouth fell gently on hers. "I want to thank God for it every day and night."

"'Twas the verra first day I met ye," Rob told her, biting

her lip. "Ye had just lost everything, and I wanted to give it all back to ye."

"You succeeded and gave me even more." She curled her lips and closed her eyes at the feel of him hot and thick against her entrance.

"I never doubted I would." He entered her with a smile as intoxicating as every other inch of him.

"Do you fail at nothing then?"

"I'm a MacGregor," he groaned against her chin, sending a wave of pleasure through her body. "There's verra little we dinna' do right."

"Is that so?" She lifted a provocative brow at him and rolled him over on his back. Straddling him, she gazed down at his broad chest and his flat, fit belly and smiled rather wickedly as she buried him deep inside her. "Lucky for you then. I'm a MacGregor now, too."

"Aye, and ye're mine."

She was his, and it was more than enough to keep his halls forever filled with her laughter.

More stunning Scottish romance
from Paula Quinn!

Please turn this page
for a preview of

Seduced by a Highlander

Chapter One

———⊢————

"*A*rrogant imbecile!" Isobel Fergusson pushed through the heavy wooden doors and entered Whitehall Palace's enormous privy garden with a dozen venomous oaths spilling from her lips. Her brother Alex was going to get them all killed. Oh, why had they come to England? And damnation, if they had to attend the Duke of York's coronation, it should be Patrick, her eldest brother and heir to their father, the late Fergusson chieftain, here with her and not Alex. They were only supposed to stay for a se'nnight or two, but when the future king invited all his guests to remain at Whitehall for another month, Alex had accepted. She kicked a small rock out of her path and swore again. How could she have raised such an imprudent, thoughtless bratling?

'Twasn't that Isobel was impervious to the lure of Whitehall's luxurious feathered mattresses, its grand galleries with vaulted ceilings where even the softest whispers, uttered by elegant lords and ladies powdered to look like living, breathing statues, echoed. 'Twas all quite... unusual and beguiling in a queer sort of way. But Alex had accepted knowing the MacGregors were here!

"Dear God," she beseeched, stopping at a large, stone

sundial in the center of the garden, "give me strength and my witless brother wisdom before he starts another war!"

A movement to her right drew her attention to a row of tall bronze statues gleaming in the sun. When one of them moved, Isobel startled back and bumped her hip against the sundial.

"Careful, lass."

He wasn't a statue at all, but a man—though his face could have been crafted by the same artist who had created the masterpieces lining the garden. Isobel took in every inch of him as he stepped out from behind the golden likeness of an archangel, wings paused forever in flight as it landed on its pedestal. He wore the garb of an Englishman, but without all the finery...or the wig. His hair hung loose to his shoulders in shades of rich chestnut and sun-streaked gold. The ruffled collar of his cream-colored shirt hung open at his throat, giving him a more roguish appearance than a noble one. He was tall and lithe, with long, muscular legs encased in snug-fitting breeches and dull black boots. His steps were light but deliberate as he moved toward her.

"I didna' mean to startle ye." The musical pitch of his voice branded him Scottish, mayhap even a Highlander. "I thought ye were my sister."

His smile was utterly guileless, save for the flash of a playful dimple in one cheek, and as warm and inviting as the heavenly body perched behind him. For a moment that went completely out of her control, Isobel could not move as she took in the full measure of his striking countenance. Save for the slight bend at the bridge, his nose was classically cut, residing above a mouth fashioned to strip a woman of all her defenses, including reasonable thought. The way his eyes changed from brown to simmering gold, like a hawk's that spotted its prey, hinted of something far more primitive beyond the boyish smile.

"I am infinitely grateful that I was mistaken."

Isobel took a step around the sundial, instinctively keeping her distance from a force that befuddled her logic and tightened her breath.

Damnation, she had to say something before he thought her exactly what she was—exactly what any other woman with two working eyes in her head was when they saw him—a doddering fool. With a tilt of her chin that suggested she was a fool for no man, she flicked her deep auburn braid over her shoulder and said, "Yer sister thinks ye are an arrogant imbecile, also?"

"Aye," he answered with a grin that was all innocence and innately seductive at the same time. "That, and much worse."

As if to prove his statement true, a movement beyond the statue caught Isobel's attention. She looked in time to spy a glimpse of sapphire blue skirts and flaxen curls rushing back toward the palace.

"My guess," Isobel muttered, peering around his back to watch the lady's departure, "is that yer sister is likely correct."

"She most certainly is," he agreed, not bothering to look behind him. The cadence of his voice deepened with his smile. "But I'm no' completely irredeemable."

Rather than argue the point with such an obvious rogue when she should be thinking of a way to convince Alex to leave with her and Cam, Isobel quirked a dubious brow at him and turned to leave. "As difficult as that is to believe, I will have to take ye at yer word. Good day."

Her breath quickened an instant later when the stranger appeared at her side and leaned down toward her ear.

"Or ye could spend the afternoon with me and find oot fer yerself."

His nearness permeated the air around her with heat and the familiar scent of heather. He was definitely a Highlander, mayhap a Gordon or of the Donaldson clan, though he wore no plaid. She thought to ask his name, but decided against it. He might consider her interest in him an acceptance of his offer. She could not afford to allow her senses to be addled by a whole afternoon spent with him when her family's safety was at stake.

"Thank ye, m'lord, but I've matters to think on." She quickened her pace but he would not be so easily dismissed.

"Do these matters have to do with the witless brother ye were prayin' fer?"

"Why?" Isobel asked, trying to sound unaffected by his boldness to follow her. "Are ye worried he might have usurped yer title?"

She was completely unprepared for his laughter, or for the way it rang through her veins, coarse and carefree. A dozen other men would have scowled at her accusation, though she meant it only to show her disinterest, but this charismatic stranger found it humorous. She liked that he had enough confidence to laugh, even at himself.

"His name is Alex," she conceded with a smile and began to walk with him. "And truly, if there is a title of witless brother, he has already taken it." She felt a tad bit guilty about speaking so of her brother with a man she didn't even know, but perhaps not knowing him made it easier. She needed someone to talk to about her dilemma. Someone to just listen and perhaps point her on the right path to take in order to get her brothers the hell out of Whitehall the quickest way possible. This man seemed clever enough. Besides, he made her smile, and she hadn't done the like all morning.

Beside her, he bent to pick up a rock and threw it into a small pond a few feet ahead of them. "And what has Alex done that is so terrible?"

"He refuses to leave Whitehall and go home."

"Ah, unfergivable."

Isobel cut him a sidelong glance and found him smiling back at her. "Ye don't understand."

He raised a dark brow and waited for her to continue.

She looked around before she spoke again. "Our most hated enemies have recently arrived to pay homage to the king. Alex is cocky and prideful. If we remain here, he is likely to insult them and bring the barbarians down on our heads once again."

He nodded, leading her around the pool. "Now I see yer point more clearly. But why is it yer strait to ponder?" he asked, turning to her. "Where is yer faither that his son should make decisions which put his kin in jeopardy?"

"He's dead," Isobel told him, her eyes going hard on the Palace doors and the beasts that strolled somewhere within. "Killed by these same enemies. I swear if I could get just one of them alone, I would slice open his throat and sing him back to the devil who spawned him."

She was a bit surprised to find both sympathy and amusement softening the man's features when she looked at him.

"It sounds to me like yer enemies have more to fear from ye, than ye do from them, lass."

Isobel shook her head. "I am not foolhardy like Alex.

I know that killing one of them would rekindle the feud. It has been ten years since they murdered my father. They have left us alone, and I wish it to stay that way."

"Wise," he said, and Isobel was glad she'd told him. He agreed that she was correct in wanting to leave. Perhaps he would be willing to talk some sense into Alex's ear.

"Alex thinks he is not afraid of them, but Oliver Cromwell himself shyt in his breeches at the mention of their name."

The handsome stranger paused in his steps for a moment, his smile fading as if something unpleasant had just crossed his thoughts. "Who are these unholy miscreants ye speak of?"

"The MacGregors," Isobel told him quietly, hating to even have to utter their names. "Do ye know them, then?" she asked when his eyes narrowed slightly on her.

As effortlessly as it had appeared the first time, his light smile returned. "I know of them."

"Aye," she sighed, looking forward along their path, "everyone does. They are the infamous and imperishable scourges of Scotland."

He did not laugh this time, but seemed to grow uncomfortable in his own clothes. Isobel guessed that he was afraid of the MacGregors too.

"Ye didna' tell me why they killed yer father."

Isobel didn't want to talk about it, or even think on it anymore, but if she could persuade this kind gentleman to dissuade her brother... "They believed my father killed the Earl of Argyll during a raid. The Earl was their kin, the Devil MacGregor's brother-in-law, I was told. Without proof that the Fergussons were even responsible, they murdered my father. The MacGregors are ruthless and cruel. If the Earl was anything like his relatives, he deserved his death."

She stopped walking when she realized her stranger had stopped a few paces behind her. She turned and for an instant, wasn't certain if he was the same man. He stared at her, but not like before. Now, she thought she saw anger slash across the deep amber of his eyes. All traces of anything charming had vanished from his face, leaving his jaw hard, his shapely mouth taut.

"Is something the matter?" Isobel asked him, not knowing what it could possibly be.

"Nae, 'tis nothin'. I just recalled that I promised my sister I would show her the king's theater and she'll never let me ferget it if I dinna' keep my word." His smile flashed and was gone an instant before he was.

Isobel stood in the garden a bit taken back by the abruptness of his departure. But as she watched him disappear into the Palace, she thought it rather thoughtful of him to care so much about keeping his word to his sister. She smiled. He wasn't anywhere near gaining the title.

THE DISH

Where authors give you the inside scoop!

♥ ♥ ♥ ♥ ♥ ♥ ♥ ♥ ♥ ♥ ♥ ♥ ♥ ♥ ♥

From the desk of Paula Quinn

Dear Reader,

While doing research for LAIRD OF THE MIST, I fell in love with Clan MacGregor. Their staunch resolve to overcome trials and countless tribulations during a three-hundred-year proscription earned them a very special place in my heart. So when I was given the chance to write a brand-new series featuring Callum and Kate MacGregor's grown children, I was ecstatic.

The first of my new four-book series, RAVISHED BY A HIGHLANDER (available now), stars Robert MacGregor, whom you met briefly in A HIGHLANDER NEVER SURRENDERS. He was a babe then, and things haven't changed. He's still a babe, but in an entirely different way!

My favorite type of hero is a rogue who can sweep a lady off her feet with a slant of his lips. Or a cool, unsmiling brute with a soft spot no one sees but his woman. Rob was neither of those men when I began writing his story. He was more. I didn't think I could love a character I created as much as I loved his father, but I was wrong, and I'm not ashamed to say it.

Rob isn't careless with women's hearts. His smile isn't reckless but a bit awkward. It's about the only thing he *hasn't* practiced every day of his life. Born to fill his father's boots as chief and protector of his clan, Rob takes life and the duties that come with his birthright seriously. He's uncompromising in his loyalty to his kin and unrelenting in his beliefs. He's a warrior who is confident in the skill of his arm, but not rash in drawing his sword. However, once it's out, someone's head is going to roll. Yes, he's tall and handsome, with dark curls and eyes the color of sunset against a summer-blue loch, but his beauty can best be seen in his devotion to those he loves.

He is . . . exactly what a lady needs in her life if an entire Dutch fleet is on her tail.

I'll tell you a little about Davina Montgomery, the lass who not only softens Rob's staunch heart, but comes to claim it in her delicate fingers. But I won't tell you too much, because I don't want to reveal the secret that has taken everyone she's ever loved away from her. She came to me filled with sorrow, chained by duty, and in need of things so very basic, yet always beyond her reach: safety, and the love of someone who would never betray her or abandon her to danger.

I saw Rob through Davina's eyes the moment he plucked her from the flames of her burning abbey. A hero: capable, courageous, and hot as hell.

We both knew Rob was perfect for her, and for the first time, I saw hope in Davina's eyes—and her beauty can best be seen when she looks at him.

Travel back to the Scottish Highlands with Rob and Davina and discover what happens when duty and desire collide. And I love to hear from readers, so please visit me at www.paulaquinn.com.

Enjoy!

Paula Quinn

♥ ♥ ♥ ♥ ♥ ♥ ♥ ♥ ♥ ♥ ♥ ♥ ♥ ♥ ♥

From the desk of R. C. Ryan

Dear Reader,

Are you as intrigued by family dynamics as I am? I know that, having written a number of family sagas, I've been forced to confront a lot of family drama. But fiction mirrors real life. And in the real world, there's nothing more complicated or more dramatic than our individual relationships with the different members of our families.

We read a lot about mother–daughter and father–son relationships, not to mention sibling rivalry. Psychologists tell us life paths are often determined by birth order. And yet there are always exceptions to the rule— the child of poverty who builds a financial empire. The man with a learning disability who lifts himself to the ranks of genius. The girl who loses a leg and goes on to run marathons.

And so, while I'm fascinated with family dynamics, and our so-called place in the universe, I'm even more intrigued by those who refuse to fit into any mold. Instead, by the sheer force of their determination, they rise above society's rules to become something rare and wonderful. Whether they climb Mount Everest or never leave the neighborhood where they were born, they live each day to the fullest. And whether they change the world or just change one life, they defy the experts and prove wrong those who believe a life's course is predetermined.

In MONTANA DESTINY, the second book in my Fool's Gold series, Wyatt McCord returns to the Lost Nugget Ranch after years of living life on the edge, only to lose his heart to the fiercely independent Marilee Trainor, a loner who has broken a few rules of her own. These two, who searched the world over for a place to belong, will laugh, love, and fight often, while being forced to dig deep within themselves to survive.

I hope you enjoy watching Wyatt and Marilee take charge of their lives and forge their own destinies.

R. C. Ryan

www.ryanlangan.com

♥ ♥ ♥ ♥ ♥ ♥ ♥ ♥ ♥ ♥ ♥ ♥ ♥ ♥

From the desk of Robin Wells

Dear Reader,

"So, Robin—what's your latest book about?"

I get that question a lot, and I always find it difficult to answer. I usually start off by describing the plot in varying degrees of detail. Here's the short version:

STILL THE ONE is the story of Katie Charmaine, a hairdresser in Chartreuse, Louisiana—the same colorful small town where my previous book, BETWEEN THE SHEETS, took place. Katie lost her husband in Iraq, and she thinks she'll never love again. But when her first love, Zack Ferguson, returns, she feels the same irresistible attraction that stole her heart at seventeen. To Katie's shock, he's accompanied by the teenage daughter Katie gave up for adoption at birth. The daughter, Gracie, has a major attitude, a smart mouth—and is now pregnant herself.

The medium-length version adds: Gracie's adoptive parents were killed in a car accident, and when she discovers her birth parents' identities, she locates Zack first. She wants him to declare her an emancipated minor and give her a nice wad of cash. Instead, Zack takes Gracie to Chartreuse, where he and Katie share custody until Gracie turns eighteen.

The long version gives still more detail: Zack and Katie experience the ups and downs of parenting a difficult teenager, while rediscovering the love that initially drew them together. Can they forgive each other for their past mistakes? Can Zack overcome his commitment-phobic ways? Can Katie get beyond her feelings of disloyalty to her late husband and her fear of opening her heart again? Can Gracie let go of her anger and open her heart to Katie?

The long version still doesn't fully cover everything that happens, but then, a book is much more than a plot. So I also answer the "what's your book about?" question by citing the following themes present in STILL THE ONE:

Romance. There's nothing like the heady feeling of falling in love, and nothing worse than believing you're falling alone.

Family. This book is about some of the ways that families shape us, for better and for worse.

Grief. Love doesn't die, even though people do. How do we get past the feeling that loving someone else is disloyal to the deceased? How do we ever find the courage to care that deeply again, knowing how much it hurts to lose someone you love?

Mistakes. Teenagers aren't known for making wise choices, but adults don't always make the best decisions, either. Regardless of age, we all can get lost in the moment, make incorrect assumptions, repeat a destructive pattern, or neglect to say something that needs to be said.

Blessings. Sometimes mistakes that have haunted us for years can turn out to be life's biggest blessings.

Forgiveness. How do we let go of hurts—especially big, bad ones? Once we've been hurt by someone, can we ever fully trust that person again?

And last but not least, **Love.** If I had to give a single answer to what my book is about, this would be it. I believe that love has the power to heal and redeem and transform anyone and any situation, no matter how hopeless it may seem, and that's the major underlying theme of this novel—and all my novels, come to think of it. I hope you'll drop by my website, www.robinwells.com, to see a short video about the book, read an excerpt from my next novel, and/or let me know your thoughts. I love to hear from readers, and I can be reached at my website or at P.O. Box 303, Mandeville, LA 70470.

Here's hoping your life will be filled with love, laughter, and lots of good books!

Robin Wells